ENTER PREHISTORIC

SECOND IN THE WEST OF PREHISTORIC SERIES.

ERIK 'TRACER' TESTERMAN

SEVERED PRESS
HOBART TASMANIA

ENTER PREHISTORIC

WWW.SEVEREDPRESS.COM

ISBN: 978-1-922551-86-3

For my kids - Dream big, and never give up.

ENTER PREHISTORIC

August 1885
Four miles north of Granite Falls, Wyoming.

The summer sun beat down on me as I watched the massive dinosaur feasting on Jason Harper's corpse.

Hunched over on all four legs, the top of the dinosaur's back was eight feet high and from blood covered snout to the tip of tail was easily sixteen feet in length. A scarlet fin rose between its eyes, increasing in height over a sloping skull before running down the neck and fading away between the beast's shoulder blades. The rest of its body, corded with thick muscle and sinew, was a light green, with smudges of brown for added camouflage.

It was the biggest dinosaur we'd found yet on this side of the tunnel. So, of course, it had to be a predator and not one of those cute plant eaters with the long necks.

The beast raised the mangled remains with both front claws and crunched the man's skull between blood-stained teeth. Even from this distance, the sound was sickening. The dinosaur shook the corpse and a severed arm fell. The torn limb landed amongst scattered remains of Harper's ill-fated herd of sheep that he'd apparently died trying to protect.

Carbine stomped his hooves impatiently. He was anxious to be away, but I knew the soldiers needed more time to prepare, so I watched and waited as the dinosaur feasted.

Wrapping my fingers on the black Allosaurus claw that dangled from its leather cord around my neck, I leaned forward on the saddle pommel and thought about the events of the past couple of months.

Battle of the Apes.

That's what newspapers across America called it.

At the time, we just called it survival. And the only reason I was there at all was because I was hiding from my vengeful outlaw past. I was just trying to make a fresh start. Then a dinosaur killed one of my horses and tried to eat me. I barely survived by filling it full of lead and finishing the beast off with a crate of dynamite. Then I ate it, and now I wear its claw as a memento of the occasion.

After that, some prehistoric, Triceratops riding, giant apes visited my ranch and tried to kill me. I backtracked them to their home where I saw their leader ritualistically rip a man's heart out of his chest. That ticked me off, so I killed a bunch of them in return, possibly sparking a war in

1

the process. But the apes didn't seem fans of peaceful coexistence anyways. Then, as we prepared our town's defenses against an army of invading apes, I crossed paths with the Union raider that'd whipped me near to death as a child. The same man I'd spent my entire outlaw life searching for, was now the owner of the East-West Railroad. He's still alive, and I still owe him a great deal of pain and misery. That's coming soon. You can bet your bottom dollar on that. The thick strips of scar tissue across my back are a constant reminder that some debts can only be repaid in blood.

Then came the attack on the little town of Granite Falls. We were outnumbered, a paltry four to one. I thought for sure we were all going to die. Which was a shame, because I'd just met the love of my life, Skyla, a paleontologist from the Smithsonian Institute. Did I mention she's beautiful? In the rarest of ways, because she's beautiful inside and out. But she doesn't know who I really am or the terrible things I've done for mostly good reasons. That's a problem for another day that will hopefully never come.

When the battle joined, things got real bad, real quick when waves of hairy, savage monkeys swarmed our town. We slayed them by the dozens but they just kept coming. They quickly overwhelmed our defenses, slaughtering us with spears, clubs, and arrows while their tamed raptors bounded amongst us, shredding men apart with tooth and claw.

But with the help of the local Shaynee Indian tribe, willing to bury the hatchet between white and red men to kill a mutual enemy, and timely reinforcements arriving by railroad brought by my mortal enemy, we managed to turn the tide of battle and soundly defeat them.

We still lost over eighty percent of the men and women defending the town that day, including a good friend of mine and his two nephews.

Sighing, I arched my back to work out a kink.

I must have moved too quickly, because the finned beast whipped its fearsome head in our direction and snorted loudly as if trying to get my scent.

Carbine tensed beneath me, and I took in a sharp breath, realizing my mistake.

Apparently still hungry, the dinosaur growled and charged.

Dropping onto all fours, the clawed feet sent tufts of prairie grass into the air as it raced towards us. It moved faster than I'd have thought possible for an animal of its size.

Whipping Carbine around, I kicked my heels to his flanks and he surged forward into a dead sprint towards where we'd left the soldiers.

My current name is Jedidiah Huckleberry Smith.

And this is my story.

***

My dun mustang stretched his legs out, black mane and tail waving in the wind as we raced across the rolling plains.

"Good boy," I told him fondly while resting a hand on the grip of one of my twin Colt Peacemakers. Twisting about in the saddle, I considered trying to put a .45 caliber slug into the dinosaur chasing us. At this distance, the chance of hitting was slim, but just running and not shooting seemed foreign to me and I'd have felt better if I could wound it a little.

Because it was gaining on us.

The large reptilian head opened its mouth wide, exposing jagged teeth and let loose an ear-piercing roar as it closed the distance between us in large bounds.

Carbine responded by stretching his neck out and giving his all as he charged up a grassy hill toward a pair of Gatling guns waiting on the crest. Groups of soldiers stood by the weapons under the watchful eye of Lieutenant Carson. The young officer stood tall between them, sword raised, waiting to give the order for the multi-barreled guns to open fire once I was clear.

The dinosaur was dangerous enough, but worrying about a man getting fearful and firing before I reached safety certainly didn't help my nerves any. I crouched lower over Carbine's back and urged him on with a yell.

With less than a hundred yards left between us and the angry dinosaur, I raced between the Gatlings.

It was close.

Too close.

Sunlight glinted off the Lieutenant's blade as he swept it down and screamed, "FIRE!"

Immediately, the gun on the left fired on the rampaging monster.

A steady pop-pop-pop-pop erupted from the rotating barrels as the gunner cranked the handle, sending bullet after bullet towards the red crested beast.

The first few bullets hit the dinosaur, the heavy slugs causing the snarling creature to stumble to the side and the other rounds to miss. Swearing, the soldier fought the traversing mechanism to line the gun up on the rapidly approaching predator as the rest of his team dumped more cartridges into the gun's hopper to keep it firing.

The monster roared in pain and anger, circling away from the loud contraption. The gunner twisted the weapon after the dinosaur, struggling to catch up to the moving beast.

The other Gatling remained silent. A soldier jerked the handle back and forth, but it appeared jammed. He shouted for help in frustration.

Without that second weapon, we were in for a world of hurt.

I pulled my *Eighty-Six* from its tooled leather scabbard. Racking the lever, I sent a large .45-70 cartridge into the chamber of the custom prototype 1886 Winchester rifle.

Dinosaurs never go down easy.

Ever.

"Get that gun operational!" Carson shouted as he rushed over to the crew served weapon. Soldiers manning the gun worked feverishly to fix it. The officer shoved a man aside and slid underneath the wheeled carriage, jamming his hands inside the gun from below. His young face contorted painfully as he worked to free the gun.

The beast slowed, hesitating, and a jagged row of bullets stitched into the beast's chest and hind quarters as the Gatling gunner found his mark. The monster roared fearsomely and rushed further to our right side, circling around our position to flank us. Blood trickled from puckered wounds, but the beast seemed unfazed.

Tucking the polished wood rifle stock into my shoulder, I fired into the creature's chest at twenty yards away. The bullet hit, sending a splash of blood across the green pebbled hide. The finned dinosaur didn't seem to notice and charged directly towards us.

"Oh hell," I muttered as I worked the lever, slamming the action open and close, and sending an empty brass shell spinning to the ground.

Soldiers working on the malfunctioning gun grabbed stacked rifles and began to open fire with their small arms.

Two more large strides and the monster was upon us.

With a swing of its red-finned head, the working Gatling was knocked aside and the soldier operating the weapon snatched up in the creature's teeth. With a savage twist of its sloping head, the shrieking man was bitten in half. His legs flopped beside another soldier who scrambled away and ran for the picketed horses fifty yards behind us.

Another followed, throwing down his weapon to flee the monster among us. The rest, braver, and perhaps more foolish, stood their ground and fought. They circled around the beast, firing rifles upwards into its large body as it twisted and thrashed, ripping men apart with tooth and claw.

The young Lieutenant crawled out from under the malfunctioning gun and was immediately flung a dozen feet into the tall grass with a slap of the dinosaur's tail as it twisted about on the small grassy crest.

Claws swiped across the front of another soldier to my right. Blood sprayed in an arc and splattered Carbine. My horse jerked his head and fought the bit to get away as I hammered the beast with large rounds from my rifle. Bullets cracked past me as soldiers missed from the other side of the dinosaur. I swore and ducked involuntarily before firing again.

Behind us, the pair of fleeing soldiers leapt onto horses, whipping them frantically with reins as they rode away.

Kicking my heels against Carbine, I put him into a trot, moving in a circle to maintain distance away from the beast as I concentrated on putting as many bullets from my expensive rifle into the dinosaur's finned head as possible. It was difficult with the thrashing, roaring, biting dinosaur rampaging amongst the remaining soldiers. Only a couple of shots connected, tearing hide away and glancing off the thick bone of its skull. The beast seemed to be weakening and slowing, but it still contained enough life in it to kill us all.

The dinosaur's tail smashed into the other Gatling, sending it tumbling over a pair of disfigured corpses. It rolled, crushing mutilated bodies under the iron clad wheels before bumping down the hill and toppling over.

Rifle empty, I thrust it into the scabbard and drew my matching Colt Peacemakers. Not the stoutest of fire power against such a large beast but they were faster than a reload and this dinosaur needed to go down fast as soldiers were dying quickly.

Carson burst from the tall grass, armed with only his sword. Bleeding and limping, the young Lieutenant raced towards the beast, slashing and hacking at its back legs and tail. The blade did little damage, but the temporary distraction allowed the two remaining soldiers time to flee to the horses and mount.

"Run!" I yelled at the officer and kicked Carbine's flanks, sending him rushing towards the dinosaur and wounded Lieutenant. Firing both pistols, I screamed a rebel yell at the beast to distract it from the officer standing before it with bloodied sword raised high in defiance.

Ignoring me, the dinosaur raised a clawed foot and stomped down.

Thick talons sliced through Carson's face, chest, and stomach. Loops of severed intestines fell as the officer grabbed at his mortally wounded body and collapsed.

The beast viciously bit the officer's face and savaged his body with front claws.

Screaming in rage, I let Carbine race us away from the gruesome scene.

The dinosaur didn't seem interested in pursuing us, and we stopped on the next ridge by the remaining staged horses of the now dead soldiers.

From where we'd set our ambush, there was nothing but broken Gatling guns and mangled corpses. Dismounting cautiously, with an eye on the dinosaur, I dropped to my feet and kicked a rock in frustration. All those men, dead, because one of our two guns malfunctioned. And Lieutenant Carson had been a good man. Smart, funny, filled with the youthful enthusiasm that I barely remembered having... now also dead.

Raising its blood-covered face towards the sky, the wounded beast roared dominance over mankind then took two steps and fell. It struggled to rise, pulling its legs beneath its large body, but only managing to raise its head off the ground.

Drawing my rifle from its scabbard, I began reloading the *Eighty-Six* as I looked after the other soldiers who'd escaped. Trails of dust showed they were riding towards town with no intent to come back. Cowardly, but I couldn't blame them. Only four of them survived and their commanding officer was dead.

The remaining horses were uneasy. They could smell the scent of blood and death in the air. I pulled up their stakes and gave them a gentle slap on the rump to send them on their way. They'd wander back to town in a day or two. Unless something ate them, or they were caught by the Indians. After the battle, the local Shaynee tribe had so much U.S. Government marked equipment that another dozen horses wouldn't be noticed. The Indians got away with a lot now, because without their sacrifice, we wouldn't have survived until the railroad reinforcements arrived. Also, they were no longer our main concern. Apes and dinosaurs were. For the moment, we were at peace with the Indians.

Picking a spot that looked relatively comfortable, I crawled into the prone position with the *Eighty-Six*. Lying on my belly in the tall grass and cradling the gun in my hands, I flipped the peep sight upright and squinted at the ivory bladed front sight. The lone Gatling and soldier's bullets had done their job, the beast was dying. But until it stopped breathing, it was dangerous.

I waited for a clean shot. The Lieutenant and his men were going to be avenged by my bullet. Skyla wouldn't like it. She'd want the head as unmutilated as possible. But we'd already shot the creature to rags and it still didn't quit.

The dinosaur struggled again, thrashing its tail against the ground. This time it managed to stand. Blood oozed from puckered wounds along its chest and side. It took one careful step and halted, swaying slightly. The finned head swung towards me and glared. A long gash from a bullet ran along the side of its head from snout to jaw line, revealing a row of jagged teeth and the white of bone beneath the flap of torn hide.

I squeezed the trigger, letting the break of the hammer be a surprise and sending the large 200 grain bullet into the dinosaur's skull. The beast staggered, the large toothed head dipping as the creature wobbled. It clawed a front leg at its face, then toppled over. The beast spasmed, legs and claws tearing up chunks of prairie dirt in death throes.

Racking the lever, I waited, much longer than was probably necessary, to make sure the beast was dead. The skull was thick, probably a inch or more, and I wanted to be certain that I punctured it instead of just knocking the dinosaur out. The risk of being eaten wasn't worth the time saved by impatience.

After fifteen minutes had passed, I put another bullet into the dinosaur's chest. This time it didn't so much as twitch. Ejecting the shell casing, I stood and rested the rifle over a shoulder.

All manner of dinosaurs had made it through the tunnel before Fort York was built to block off the entrance to our side. Most of the things that passed through were relatively harmless. But some, like this strange red-finned predator, were menaces that needed to be put down.

And put them down we did.

***

My ranch was on the way back to town, so I stopped by to check on the place.

Looking back on when I first came to Granite Falls, I realize I didn't have a plan. I just wanted to stop outlawing and settle down somewhere. That I accomplished. But I never truly planned for the rest of my future. I never thought about getting married, having kids, or doing whatever it is that normal folks do. I just wanted to disappear from my past, and for two solid years, I did.

And except for the recent appearances of apes and dinosaurs, I couldn't have found a more ideal place to lay low.

With a large field in the front with a flowing creek, and surrounded by forest on the other three sides, my ranch was a pretty place. And a steal, because I'd bought it with stolen loot from the final heist I was involved with.

But it'd seen better days, namely before an Allosaurus attacked. During that small battle, the barn caught on fire and I blew it apart with the dinosaur inside with a crate of dynamite. It'd been a near thing. I'd almost been eaten.

Before I discovered the tunnel to the lost world, I was already reaching the end of my rope for taking care of the place alone. Afterwards, between helping Skyla and being paid by the government to help track down and dispose of dinosaurs, I had more money and less time than I needed to be a cattle rancher. After asking around town, I settled on a pair of men well-known for being honest and hardworking. Both were veterans of the ape battle. Currently, the two of them were nailing rafters into place for the new barn when I rode down the wagon trail and into the open fields around my house.

I was halfway across the field before the youngest one noticed me and shouted a greeting with a wave of his hat that I returned.

The pair climbed down from the partially constructed barn and waited for me.

Bo was an older fellow, a little shorter than my six feet and with shoulders as broad as the barn he was working on. With short white hair and a deeply tanned face cragged with wrinkles from a life in the sun, he was a wealth of hard-earned wisdom. Jim was younger, more of a hot head, but a good solid kid and more of a man every day he was under the influence of Bo. His black hair was long and hung around his shoulders.

"You know, if we did a barn raisin', this could've been built within two days," Bo wryly said as I approached on horseback.

"Then you two would be out of a job." Slowing Carbine to a stop, I laughed the suggestion off. A barn raising was a big to do out here. A big social gathering with lots of good food, music, and dancing. There was also the benefit of free labor. But being a wanted man had its dilemmas. For instance, I had to skirt around having a barn raising. It'd be fun, but since the battle, I was already entirely too well known around these parts to be comfortable with everyone whooping it up on my ranch.

Jim's face was sour. "But... Jed... there'd be girls..."

The opportunity to mingle with womenfolk was a rare treat, and for a young man, it was just about the only way to meet a nice girl unless you bumped into her in town.

"You're too young for ladies." Bo shoved him playfully.

"Am not! I just turned sixteen!" he protested weakly and swept the dangling hair from his eyes.

"That does makes you a man," I agreed and eyed the pile of dwindling lumber stacked to the side of the partially constructed barn beside a pair of saw horses. "It looks like you'll be taking the wagon into town soon anyways. I'm sure some farmer's daughter will be hoping to catch your eye."

The young kid grinned at the compliment and shoved Bo back. The big man barely budged.

They'd been taking care of the place in my continued absences. First thing they did was build a bunkhouse across the yard from the house to live in, then they started rebuilding the barn for me while keeping an eye on the critters.

"How are our little dinos?" I asked, trying to distract the two men from their jokes while walking Carbine towards the fenced pasture beside the barn. In addition to my small herd of cattle, I managed to add almost two dozen heads of something no one else in the world owned.

Protoceratops, or Protos as we called them, milled around the fenced pasture, munching on thin prairie grass and playfully butting heads. The size of a large sheep, they looked like small, colorful Triceratops. Their bodies were white with large red spots. Blue dabs dotted the frill that extended behind their skull, and their heads were adorned with a single small raised horn bump between their nostrils, and a hawk-like beak used for ripping up plants from the ground. A mane of thick brown hairs rose vertically from their thick tails. On their sides was my new brand, a circle with a Triceratops outlined in the center.

I owned the only Protos this side of the tunnel. Before the battle, my group crossed paths with the small herd, and once I'd hired the help, we found and herded the peaceful dinosaurs back to my ranch for safe keeping.

"They're doing well. Seem content enough also," Bo said as he leaned on the split rail fence. "They haven't tried escaping or digging under the fence."

A pair of braver Protos walked to the edge of the fence, twisting their heads to the side to stick beaked snouts through the corral bars. Jim stooped over and gave one a scratch. "They're getting pretty friendly, boss."

I tugged my saddle bags off then opened the gate to the small horse corral where Bo and Jim's horses stood side by side, flipping their tails in each other's faces to chase off flies. Carbine stepped through, nipping playfully at my hat as he passed. I swatted him on the rump with the battered Stetson and shut the gate behind him. Eventually I'd need another horse to give him the occasional break, but he seemed to enjoy having all my attention as he tormented me with his tricks and mischievousness.

"I'm not looking forward to finding out if they are good eating," Jim said sadly. The second brave Proto butted the side of the other, pushing it out of the way to get a rub. The young man chuckled and scratched both their heads.

"Me neither," I admitted. "But right now, they're too rare to do anything with but breed. I believe we'll make a fortune off these little critters," I glanced at the men out of the corner of my eyes. "Assuming we get the barn done before winter."

Bo looked insulted at my skepticism of their progress on the building. "She'll be done in time. Although the Protos don't seem to be bothered by the cool nights as it is, they may handle winter just fine."

"We can't bank on it and we can't afford to lose any of them either. With luck, we'll get more in the spring... or whenever they lay eggs and they hatch."

Skyla had spent a good amount of time with the little beasts. She suspected they'd lay eggs, since the Triceratops did, and they were of the same scientific family. But we had no idea when, or what they might require to lay.

Jim pointed at a large one. "She's been spending time over in the corner of the corral, by the tall bushes. Kind of twisting grass and hay around. It's odd seeing something like her making a giant bird nest."

I looked in the direction he pointed. Sure enough, there was the beginnings of a large nest.

"That's a good sign, maybe she'll lay soon," I said hopefully.

I'd seen Triceratops nests before, and the one she was making looked similar but on a smaller scale. Compared to the difficulties of calving cattle, I hoped dinosaurs laying and hatching eggs would be like chickens; you just provided food, water, and shelter with ample protection and they did the rest. It was amazing how many cattle you could lose during birthing.

"Question, boss. You don't think the gov'ment is going to take them like they did your land?" Bo spat on the ground and kicked at the spot with the toe of his boot. He was talking about the tunnel; after discovering it, I'd staked the land and filed claim. But once the battle was over, my land was taken under the premise of eminent domain as soon as the Wyoming Territory was granted statehood a couple of days afterwards.

"I think they'd be harder to lay claim to than an entrance to a lost world." The thought had crossed my mind before; it wasn't one I liked to dwell on. "But in the meantime, keep your mouths shut about them, or dinosaur rustlers will be a new problem." I put my hands on my hips and looked around. "Where's Sara?"

The two men grinned at each other. "Watch this, boss," Bo said. He stuck his fingers in his mouth and whistled loudly. From behind the house came a thumping sound as Sara burst around the corner at a full run.

She'd grown.

The little triceratops rushed towards me, kicking up small clods of dirt and dust as she ran. I leapt out of the way as she skidded to a stop in front of us and wagged her thick tail.

Laughing, I reached down and scratched her jaw line beside her beak. "Good girl. Is Bo teaching you tricks?"

"There's more," Jim raised a hand, palm up. "Sit, girl!" he commanded.

Sara dropped her rump in the ground and tilted her sloped head at him questioningly as if expecting a reward. At three feet long, she'd grown significantly since I'd found her in the apes' abandoned canyon. Her budding horns were already four inches long and the sloped shield at the base of her skull protecting her neck was beginning to get small protrusions of bone. With a tan and yellow streaked body, and dark nubs and beak, she was as cute as a button.

I'd found her, but she'd taken to Skyla more than me. Whenever they were together, they were inseparable. She was like a dog, we had to lock her in the house when Skyla left, or else Sara would chase after her. Even then she'd bellow pitifully from inside.

I patted her pebbled back and stood. "I just swung by to check on things before heading back to town."

"Did you get that big dinosaur?" Jim asked.

Nodding my head, I sighed. "We got it. But not before it killed Jason Harper and was munching on him and his sheep by the time we located it. Then it played hell on the soldiers, killed almost all of them and that fresh Lieutenant from back East."

Bo whistled under his breath. "Tough break. Harper was a good man and it's a shame about those soldiers. Glad you made it out okay though."

"I bet you are, I'm the one that pays you!" I teased, trying to make light of all the death and mayhem that'd just occurred a couple of hours ago. Sometimes you've got to laugh to keep from letting it get to you.

Jim shook his head and patted Sara. She nuzzled him with her bone shield and her tail swung back and forth.

Bo shifted the hammer in his tool belt. "Well, things are going good here. We're staying busy."

I tossed the saddle bags over a shoulder and started walking towards my house. Sara followed. "Don't let me get in your way then," I called over my shoulder.

"Yes, sir," Jim nodded to Bo who grabbed a board off the saw horses and the pair crossed the yard towards the ladders leaning against the barn frame.

Stepping onto the porch, I ran a fingertip along the broken ape spear shaft sticking out from the wall. That one had almost gotten me. Opening the door, I let Sara in, then looked around the one room house. Nothing appeared disturbed since my last stay a few days ago. Closing the door behind me, I crossed the room and pulled down a Wyatt Earp dime novel from the book shelf. Flipping it open revealed a hollowed-out space inside with a small brass key.

Tossing a pair of blankets off a large banded trunk at the foot of the bed, I used the key and opened the lid. Reaching inside, I pulled out several boxes of .45-70 for the *Eighty-Six* and tossed them into the saddle bags. I'd gone through a lot of ammunition over the past few months and was almost out of my stash. When I made it to town I'd need to order more.

As I pulled out one of the last boxes, a rough sketched face stared back at me from where it rested on the bottom of the trunk.

My wanted poster.

It was an old one from when I'd been in my teens. We'd always been careful to stay beneath the notice of the law, but I'd made a mistake one night and had been seen. Thus, the poorly sketched drawing on a wanted poster for a trivial amount of reward.

I don't know why I kept it. Once upon a time I'd been proud to have been wanted for doing what I thought was the right thing. In my youth I wanted to feel like I was accomplishing something, and being a wanted man meant that I was.

Growling, I slammed the trunk lid shut with a bang. The poster needed to be burned. Sometimes a man needed to recall where he came from to see how far he'd come, but I'd bad memories and dreams enough to tide me over. And I couldn't afford to have anyone find it.

I twisted the key out of the brass lock then slipped it back into its hiding place. Sara watched me lazily from where she'd curled up on top of the blankets that I'd pulled off the trunk.

It was time to get going.

***

The sun was getting low when I crossed paths with a hunting party of natives on the open plains. They were unusually close to town, but their game seemed intent on leading them straight towards it.

Slowing Carbine, I watched the group of Shaynee braves chasing after a large trike along the heavily rutted wagon trail. The green and yellow streaked beast was bellowing in pain as the Indians loosened arrows from decorated bows into the dinosaur at close range from the backs of racing ponies. Tattered remains of leather ape tack were still wrapped around its bone shield from an ape rider long dead.

The horned mount stumbled, regained its footing, and ran for another dozen yards as several more arrows thumped into its side and flanks. With the last arrow, the dinosaur dropped, horns and bone shield digging into the ground as it slid. The creature's sides heaved heavily as it gasped for breath and kicked feebly.

A brave slid off his unsaddled mount and stalked to the trike. With knife in hand, he rested a hand on the bone shield and leaned down to cut its large throat.

The beast twisted its head around, slamming a black upper horn into the Indian's chest and sending him sprawling. Braves circled the pair on their ponies, laughing as the humiliated man scrambled back to his feet. Tucking the knife into its sheath, he snatched a spear held out by a familiar Indian with an ugly scarring across his chest.

Stalking forward, carefully this time, the humiliated brave lined the spear up on the beast's head then stabbed forward with all his weight behind it. The tip entered the trike's eye, skewering into the brain. In its death throes, the dinosaur kicked and twitched, and the Indian danced aside from thrashing limbs.

The heavily scarred Indian saw me and spoke to the others. They stopped laughing and stared as he turned his pony and rode towards me alone.

I rested a hand on one of my Colt's grips, the other held the reins loosely, ready to whip Carbine into a run. When dealing with Indians, you never knew what you'd get. Especially with an Indian who once wanted your scalp.

Slowing his paint pony, Otto stopped beside us and gave me a frown. "Huck Berry," he said simply, using my middle name. The Shaynee's chest was an ugly mass of scar tissue from shoulder to hip where a grizzly had tried to rip him apart for having the unfortunate luck of stepping between her and her cubs. I'd found him after and saved his life, sparking a feud that lasted over a year between us until he saved my life from an ape about to run me through with a spear. That act restored the honor he'd lost by being saved by an inferior white man.

I tipped my hat slightly with the hand that held the reins. "Otto."

It was the first time I'd seen him since the Battle of the Apes when the men of his tribe rode down the valley to attack the ape army from behind. It was a magnificent charge, directly into the face of the ape's mounted trike cavalry. Spear on spear, horse versus trike, uncouth Indian against savage prehistoric ape. From what I gathered, there was much mourning that night in the Indians' village for the dead, followed by days of dancing and celebrating for the victory and honor won. Otto himself had taken many ape scalps.

"I see hairy men no kill you yet," he spoke in broken English.

"Not yet." My eyes dropped to the tomahawk stuffed into his beaded belt. A neat hole was punched through the center. Ashley James, a friend of mine, had shot that very weapon out of his hand when he threatened to kill me with it once.

Good times.

He grunted, "Good. You eat hairy men chief's heart. They come for you now. Eat yours and take your power." I'd killed the ape's leader by blowing his legs off with a shotgun, cutting his heart out, and then taking a bite out of it during the battle. Otto had witnessed that and approved of the act.

"They can try," I grinned at him warily.

Otto smirked, no doubt recalling that not too long ago he'd wanted me dead. "Maybe I try."

My thumb shifted to the hammer on the Colt and my grip tightened as my smile faded. "Be my guest." I wasn't looking forward to having him as my enemy again, but if we were about to resort back to our previous animosity before he saved my life, I'd just as soon kill him now than worry about him later.

Grinning mischievously, he spun the paint pony and raced back to the Indians beginning to butcher the trike.

I clucked my tongue and flicked the reins, leaving the Indians to their kill and making my way on to town. I hoped Otto was joking, but I wasn't so sure.

***

Two months ago, Granite Falls had been the home to almost five hundred people.

Now it held several thousand.

The place was booming.

Even now, as gas lamps were lit in small bursts of flame and light, probably over a hundred folks walked and rode along Main Street. But in a couple more hours, once the more reputable citizens were home, the streets would be empty except for whatever drunk or broke riffraff was trying to find a place to sleep it off.

I'd never been a fan of coming to town before. Now I really disliked it. More people meant a greater possibility that someone from my past might recognize me. More people also meant less room to move about in and I had a general distrust of strangers anyways.

A group of Chinese workers stood arguing loudly with a white man in a dark suit as we rode past the northern entrance to town. With the expansion of the East-West railroad in the area, Asian workers had been brought in large numbers to speed the rail through the tunnel and to the other side. There were a lot of blacks as well, many still bearing scars of slavery and seeking the freedom they'd been denied not so long ago. And in the mix, were a few handfuls of hard scrabble Irish, tired of grubbing potatoes out of barren rock fields back home I supposed. Like everyone else, they were looking for a better life and the railroad paid cash every week.

The Bucket O' Blood saloon was packed. Laughter, smoke, and piano music drifted through the batwing doors and open windows as I rode past. The bar seemed to have trouble daily. Last time I was here, there'd been a knifing over a working woman. If the trouble continued, it might just earn the joke of a name that'd been given to it by its owner.

The original tent city that'd been built between town and the stockyards and rail station had begun turning into a regular bunch of stick framed buildings. The town was no longer made up of just a single main street running through the center; there were several back streets and intersections as the town expanded inside the large valley. Almost two dozen wooden buildings had been erected in the past couple of months. Small houses had begun to spring up as well around the outskirts of town, especially along the river that flowed to the west.

It never ceased to impress me how people overcame hardships.

This town had burned during the battle. Dozens died in the buildings, along the boardwalks, on the roofs. Yet you couldn't tell now looking at it. The bodies had been buried and the blood scrubbed away. All that remained were the occasional discolored spot and some scorch marks from the flames.

Humanity certainly didn't give up easily.

Clicking my tongue, I urged Carbine between a pair of parked wagons being loaded with sacks from the General Store. I knew staying here was a risk and if it hadn't been for Skyla, I'd have been long gone.

The foolish things we do for love.

***

After letting Carbine drink his fill and hitching him to a post, I stepped onto the boardwalk and paused, looking sadly at the closed door to the Sheriff's Office.

Sheriff Dan had been a good man, a good friend, and an even better lawman. His nephews, on the other hand, I hadn't been a fan of. But as deputies they'd shown great potential in the days leading up to the Battle of the Apes, where they died courageously in a trike charge trying to save their uncle.

Sighing, I walked to the next building. It'd been the Mayor's Office once, but the job hadn't been filled yet after the former Mayor's untimely demise. Elections were still a few weeks away. In the meantime, the military was using the office for their temporary local headquarters as their small fort and barracks buildings were being built near the tunnel entrance to the other side.

Loud voices came through the open door.

Removing my hat, I stepped into the room and found myself looking at the backs of a half dozen men standing before Captain Brandthorn. They were all heavily armed, each with a rifle, some with a shotgun, and all of them wore at least one pistol if not two. They reminded me of bandits… and a little of my old gang.

A man in the front, with a bandoleer of rifle cartridges slung over a shoulder, spoke earnestly, "You should have seen it, sir. The bullet just hit that monkey right along the scalp and knocked him out. A real fluke. Then Jimmy wanted to hang the big ape. Hang him! So, we tied his hairy hands together, threw a pair of ropes over a tree and it took two horses to raise the big savage into the air. Stupid ape woke up, kicked and struggled for half an hour before going limp. We dropped it, thinking it was dead. Once it hit the ground, Jimmy went to get his rope back. Damn ape jumped up and beat him to death with his fists before we could kill it. You just can't hang these things, their necks are too thick. I tried telling him!"

A bald black man in the back of the group spoke up, "Jimmy always liked a hanging. He'd ride a hundred miles to watch one. He was a little off like that."

Captain Brandthorn sat on his desk, legs crossed and looking out the dust smeared glass window at the darkening street. Short with a barrel chest and an Irish accent, he spoke in an almost detached, uncaring manner, "I've told you. Mr. Simon. Find them and shoot them. Do not try to etch out some small manner of justice. There's none to be had when it comes to the apes." Sighing, he turned to face them and noticed me leaning against the wall. He gave a slight nod to acknowledge my presence.

Simon shrugged, and the bandoleer almost slid from his shoulder. With a hand, he pushed the strap of leather and bullets back into place. "I know, sir. It just gets boring. We track apes for days with no entertainment. Some of the lads, like Jimmy, was just wanting to have some fun."

Brandthorn looked down and flicked a speck of dust off his uniform. "And is he having fun now?" he said softly.

The man scratched the inside of an ear with a finger. "Well… no. On account of him being dead and all."

"Then let that be a lesson to the rest of you," the officer's voice hardened. "If you want entertainment, the bar is across the street. Ladies, drinking and gambling... but no hangings." The Captain looked at them, his eyes hard and showing that he was in no mood for an argument.

"Yes, sir. Understood, sir."

The short officer stood and smoothed out the wrinkles in his uniform coat. "Do you have the proof for bounty?"

One of the men pushed through the group, a dirt and stained flour sack clutched in hand. Dried blood caked the edge of the bag. Unceremoniously, he dropped it onto the table where it thumped and fell over. A large black severed thumb slid out.

The Captain opened the bag and I watched his lips move as he counted silently. Seemingly satisfied, he bent over and wrote a script that was handed to the bounty hunter's leader. "The United States Army, and newly formed State of Wyoming, thank you for your service. Happy hunting."

"Sir-" Simon looked at the paper and hesitated.

Brandthorn scowled, and the small white scar that cut through an eyebrow shifted. "Is there a problem? The fee has not changed."

"Not that, sir. It's them Indians. They been watching us."

Several men whispered to each other, moving uneasily.

"If they attack you, kill them. Otherwise, do not bother them. At all. Don't even approach them. Do you understand? And if you see a big one with a nasty scar across his chest, steer clear. He's an angry Injun."

"Yes, sir." Smith turned and pushed back through the crowd, glancing at me as he stepped out the door. "Let's get paid!" he shouted happily as he waved the paper overhead.

With a chorus of boisterous shouts, the bounty hunters followed.

I waited until the last one left before dropping into a chair in front of the desk. "Funny you should mention Otto, I ran into him on the way here."

"You kill him?"

"Nope, but he seemed like he was interested in killing me again."

Brandthorn pointed a scolding finger at me. "Didn't you hear me with those ape hunters just now? Don't stir up the Indians! We're on delicate enough footing with the Shaynee as it is."

I raised my hands in mock protest. "It's not like I want to keep looking over my shoulder for a scarred Indian with a rusty scalping knife."

"Uh-huh," he grunted and sat heavily in the chair opposite me. "So, killing that monster of a dinosaur went badly, I hear. Any more survivors, other than those three who raced back here a couple of hours ago?"

"Three?" I cut my eyes at him suspiciously. "Four got away."

"The fourth deserted. Told the others he didn't sign up to fight dinosaurs and that he had a sister to think of down in Texas. I reckon that's where we'll find him. The fool. He was a good man too, but this decision will haunt him now," Brandthorn swore colorfully, revealing his

Irish background and temperament. "And you... they said you stayed behind. Why?"

"Perks of being a civilian I reckon. I can do almost anything I want." I ran a hand through my mop of black hair. "The dinosaur was about dead, so I finished it off. I gotta tell you, Lieutenant Carson was a brave one. He charged the beast with just his sword, so the others could escape."

Brandthorn shook his head. "Brave but stupid," he said sadly. Reaching under his desk he opened a drawer and pulled out a brown bottle and a pair of glasses. Twisting off the top, he poured while speaking softly. "Close the door, Jed."

Standing, I crossed the room and shut it.

"You know I've lost more men in the past three months than my entire career combined." He passed me a glass with a small measure of amber liquid, then downed his immediately.

I didn't know what to say, so I mimicked him. The whiskey burned down my throat and warmed me from the inside.

He held the empty glass up, turning it between his fingers. "You served. You fought the Nez Perce with Sheriff Dan. Why?"

That question had an answer that was hard to explain. The truth was I enlisted to try to get away from outlawing. I enjoyed the military at times, the comradery was something I cherished, but I hated the lack of freedom and the chaffing restrictions. Soon I found myself turning in my blue uniform to rob a bank owned by a Yankee in Kansas who'd robbed, threatened, and beaten his way through the war ravaged South to financial success.

I slid the empty glass back across the desk and decided to be truthful but vague with the officer, "Seemed like a good idea at the time. We ended up chasing the Nez across several territories... Lost some good men, and I'm sure we killed plenty of good Indians as well as the bad." I watched his reaction carefully at that last bit.

He shrugged simply, uncaring that I was expressing an unpopular opinion. "Well, that's changing now. After the Shaynee helped save us, public opinion has turned in favor of them. Now there's less talk of moving them off their land. Which ought to mean less conflict and fighting."

"Good. It's theirs. Let them have it," I guided our conversation back to more comfortable grounds. "That dinosaur, it's the biggest I've seen on this side. I appreciate the job and the very good pay... But wire Fredrick in. He's famous for killing things, and he'd be eager and willing."

Brandthorn laughed mirthlessly. "Fredrick von Holsak? I couldn't get a hold of him; he was somewhere in the mountains tracking a critter down. Besides, he can't hit the broad side of the barn. That's why he's always armed to the teeth. For the life of me, I'll never figure out what made such a terrible shot as him so popular."

"I suppose it's the books he keeps writing about his exploits. From what I gather, he's writing one on the big battle."

"That'll be an interesting read. I hope he paints me in a good light," Brandthorn mused.

"You and me both!" I chuckled, but I had concern for how he may describe me. That's the problem with your friends not knowing you're a wanted outlaw, they don't know when to keep their mouths shut. Luckily, I was a pretty bland looking fellow so any description of me shouldn't give me away.

Brandthorn laughed along with me then got serious. "I think I'd rather have someone accurate to dispatch these things from long distance. What about Wade and Ashley?"

"Last I heard they were still in Cheyenne, busy with show preparations." Wolverine Wade Mackin and Ashley James were business partners and more. They'd both fought with us. Wolverine Wade killed the scar-faced ape leader's trike before it gored me, and Ashley James was a sharpshooter who saved many of our lives from her position in the church steeple. She was the best shot I'd ever seen with a rifle.

He shrugged apologetically. "That's it then. I don't have anyone accurate enough that I'd trust right now. So, we're back to using Gatlings," he sighed. "Welcome to the New West."

New West was a term that'd been bandied about by the papers. The Old West, that is the former Wild West frontier, had all but died under the onslaught of iron horses riding steel rails across the plains and connecting the nation together. The New West was the Second Age of Dinosaurs. Since my discovery of a tunnel to a lost world, things had changed for the west, significantly.

A knock sounded a moment before Skyla opened the door and stepped through. "Hey, Captain!" Before I could move, she'd crossed the small room, hugged me about the neck, and kissed my stubbled face. "Jed, I hear you got another one. Something new this time?" She bounced from one foot to the other excitedly.

I nodded and couldn't help myself but grin at the raven-haired paleontologist. "You know I could have been eaten, right?"

"Oh hush, of course I do. I'm glad you're okay. Now, when do I get to see it?"

"At first light, we'll take an escort and go see what you think of it," Brandthorn told her.

She grimaced, her face contorting in a cute pout. "Do we need an escort?"

The Captain chuckled and smoothed the front of his uniform with his hands. "It's okay for these… locals," he grinned at me, "to go running around foolishly. But there are still apes out there and who knows what else. Besides, no lady should go unescorted with such a ruffian as Jed here."

I laughed with them. If only they knew.

"I know, but I hate tying up dozens of soldiers to watch an examination and butchering of a dinosaur." Skyla tried to justify her point.

"Too bad-" I started.

"It's their job," Brandthorn finished for me.

She cut her eyes at us in mock indignation.

"When do your parents arrive?" I asked Skyla, changing the topic. I wasn't looking forward to meeting them. Neither sounded like the sort to approve of me or my courting of their daughter.

"Tomorrow, and it's only my mother. Father had to stay behind, his work as Regent of the Smithsonian keeps him busy." She smiled at me. "Worried, Jed?"

"A little," I admitted. I figured of the two, her father would be the hardest to deal with. A father's love for his daughter is often hard on any suitors. But a mother can be a real stickler also, and Skyla had warned me before that her mother was fairly uptight about how a lady should act, behave, and who she should court. Which meant she was just not going to be pleased with her daughter being around me. I was also hoping to make our courtship official with her father's blessing, although I expected that'd be hard to come by. I didn't know if you could even call us courting. We did. But we were a very non-typical couple in the regards that Skyla was a scientist in a male dominated field and I was essentially a retired gunman, bank robber, and vigilante rolled into a rancher.

Skyla intertwined her arm in mine and leaned against me. "Oh, Jed. Just try not to be so… violent. She's an easterner, remember?" She teased me with a playful wink. Skyla had been an easterner when she came west a couple of months ago, but now she was a certified gun totin' westerner like the rest of us. Except she was entirely too polite to ever really fit in.

The Captain struck a match and lit the wick on a lantern hanging on the wall. "On to more pressing matters. I'm traveling through the Shimmer day after tomorrow, taking a bunch of supply wagons and troop reinforcements to Fort Jipson. I reckon you two are anxious to get back, so you might as well come along if you want."

We'd only been to the other side twice since I'd led Brandthorn and his men through the tunnel and to the ape canyon after the battle. Since then, the canyon had been renamed, in honor of Andrew Jipson, a soldier who died at his post, firing our lone cannon one final time, instead of defending himself against the apes overwhelming his position. His body was barely recognizable after the attack. Having your head caved in by a stone club does that to a man.

"The Shimmer?" I repeated and winced. "That's a terribly simple name for a magical, science-defying tunnel."

"I think it's a nice name, and of course we're ready! All my notes have been written in detail and sent with sketches back to the Smithsonian," Skyla radiated happiness at the thought of returning to the lost world. She loved the other side, and the only reason we'd come back last week was on account of her parents' arrival. They hadn't been too happy on her insistence on staying during the battle and not returning home afterwards either. I suspected she'd catch an earful from her mother about that... and about me.

"Good, and I'm with you, Jed. The name is terrible." Brandthorn shifted a stack of papers to the other side of his desk. "But since no one knows what it is, and since the air shimmers as you walk through it to the other side, the name has stuck," he sighed. "Personally, I call it a pain in my backside. I miss the good old days of worrying about Indians, outlaws, and the occasional rustler."

I stayed silent since I was one of the outlaws he would prefer to hunt down and hang. I was deep in the lion's den these days.

"We will be ready, Captain!" Skyla said with a pretty grin and a mock salute.

"I'm sure you will, Miss Skyla," he wagged his bushy eyebrows at her and leaned forward and whispered, "but will you be ready for the expedition?"

I groaned loudly while Skyla beamed from ear to ear. Brandthorn and her both had been discussing taking a week-long expedition to survey the area around Fort Jipson. "Is it safe enough?" I asked, knowing full well that Brandthorn would never agree to this unless he thought so. But I still wanted to hear it from the officer's mouth.

"We've patrols riding along the canyon edge. Other than the occasional ape track, it appears they've abandoned the area." He shrugged. "We can't wait forever. We need to know what's around us. Lone scouts can only bring back so much information and at great risk to themselves. A full two dozen man expedition should be able to get around with minimal risk."

"That's fine. But there's no need to risk Skyla's life." My voice hardened with my disdain at the notion of a female scientist riding with dozens of soldiers for a week in a prehistoric lost world full of dangerous creatures that we didn't even have names for yet.

"Hey-" she started.

Brandthorn cut her off. "Jed, we've discussed this to death. I've my orders. And Skyla works as much for the government now as she does the Smithsonian. Unless you'd prefer Oscar come with us and get all the glory..."

Oscar Ellis was Skyla's major rival now. A former boss of hers, he'd left the Smithsonian to work for Reydan White, my mortal enemy and the railroad tycoon, whose track was being laid to the cliff side where the tunnel was located.

"No. Absolutely not." There was no way I was going to let Oscar take Skyla's place. I looked at her. She glared back at me and I sighed. "Fine. Since I'm never going to win this argument, I may as well go along." I looked back to the Captain. "Can you make that happen?"

Brandthorn shared a conspiring smile with Skyla. "Oh, we always planned on you going."

I shook my head, exasperated with the two of them. "Of course."

"We know you all too well, Jed," Skyla told me with a grin, and the words cut me to the bone as I thought of how little she truly knew me.

***

Next morning there was a tapping at the hotel door. A thin stream of light blazed between the thick canvas curtains covering the glass windows, and the sound of crowing roosters could be heard faintly. I'd already been awake for about ten minutes, just enjoying the comforts of sleeping in a bed instead of on the hard ground like I had the past couple of nights. But the tapping noise urged me out of bed and into my clothes.

Skyla stood outside the door, beautiful as always, but instead of having her gun belt strapped on, she carried it rolled up. She handed it to me with an apologetic look. "I don't want to overwhelm my mother with too much at once. Besides," she batted her eyelashes, "the hero of Granite Falls will be with us today. He'll protect little, defenseless me."

I gave her a kiss and pointed at my battered brown hat on the table beside the door. "Nope. No hero here. See? I wear a brown hat."

"One day I'm going to throw that out and buy you a white one."

"And on that day, you'll find out just how hard I can spank a lady."

She blushed and laughed mockingly. "Such a gentleman."

I grabbed her small hands, pulled her close and grinned. "I've a surprise for you."

She looked up at me suspiciously. "What is it?"

Letting her go, I quickly shoved her gun belt into my worn leather saddle bags, slung them over a shoulder, and motioned for her to follow me out of the room. "Come find out."

The streets were busy and noisy. It was all but impossible to walk side by side without knocking shoulders with others. After ignoring or dodging pushy vendors, and stepping around wagons, manure piles, and groups of workers and families, we finally managed to reach the stable.

The corral that'd been removed to open a field of fire for our only cannon during the battle had been rebuilt, but the stable still showed signs of war. Broken arrow shafts puckered the siding, patches of new boards had been worked into the old where trikes had slammed into it. Smears and splashes of blood still stained parts of it. All the defenders who'd taken refuge there had died. But they'd fought valiantly. After the fight, the area had been surrounded by a ring of ape and trike corpses. I paused for a moment as I always did when I passed this area, paying my respects and thanking our heavenly Father for the bravery and tenacity of such men as Andrew Jipson. Without them, the town would have fallen.

Carbine came prancing over to the edge of the corral when he saw us. Skyla stopped to give the dun-colored mustang a scratch on his neck. He tossed his black mane and tail in pleasure.

"Stay here, I'll be back in a minute," I told her.

At her puzzled face, I gave her a roguish grin, and entered the darkened interior of the stables.

Minutes later, I emerged leading a dapple-gray mare by the reins. A tooled leather saddle rested on her back, polished to a deep, glistening brown.

Her smile lit my world as she laid a hand on the pale gray muzzle of the horse. "She's beautiful!"

"A pretty girl needs a pretty horse," I told her honestly as I held the reins out.

"You got me a horse?" Her brown eyes lit with excitement. She practically squealed and repeated herself. "You got me a horse!"

"Yes, ma'am. Can't have you borrowing Carbine all the time or being stuck riding in wagons."

Skyla grabbed me in a tight hug before turning back to run her hands along the mare's gray ringed coat. I'd paid the stable boy well to keep her groomed while I waited for the proper moment to unveil Skyla's surprise. Now the horse's eyes were bright and her hair clean and smooth. She was the prettiest horse I'd ever laid eyes on, and that included mine.

"What's her name?"

"Smoke."

"Smoke and Carbine. What great western horse names!"

I laughed. "The name suits her color, and she can go from standing to running so quick she'll leave her rider behind if they aren't careful."

"Is that the sort of horse I need?" She flashed me a smile.

"Considering what I killed yesterday, it's exactly what you need," I said sincerely as I scratched the mare's neck. "She's also got a disposition that's almost as sweet as yours."

"She must have cost a fortune!"

"She wasn't cheap," I admitted. "But good horses never are." Between buying Smoke, the saddle and tack, and ordering more lumber for my barn, it'd been an expensive week. Luckily, government contracts for helping them with dinosaurs were keeping me flush with cash for the time being. And there was still plenty of buried stolen loot, I just had to ride across half a state to get it.

Skyla grabbed the pommel and slid onto Smoke's back. The horse shifted, side stepping to adjust for the weight. She ran her hands through the horse's almost white mane. "I'm going to have to show her to mother."

I worked on adjusting the stirrups for her height. "When does she arrive?"

"Her train should be here in about an hour."

"Why don't I saddle Carbine, and we ride down to meet her?"

"Jed..." she hesitated. "I think it would be best if I met her alone. She doesn't know about you yet."

I faked a shocked face. "You didn't write to your parents about me? How insidious of you." I wasn't insulted. We'd been busy the last few months, and I knew her parents hated her involvement in the battle as well as the events leading up to and after it. I knew she intentionally didn't write her father much except to send reports and sketches of the dinosaurs we discovered.

"You can show off your education and big words to my mother later. That may take some of the sting out of her daughter courting a gunman," she pointed at my pistols.

"Ouch." I stuck my thumbs behind my belt buckle and looked down at my matching Colts. "I guess I don't pass for a rancher anymore?"

"Not really, especially with your new reputation around town as an ape slayer. Go have breakfast and meet me at the hotel in a couple of hours. It'll take that long to get mother's things unloaded."

"Alright. Just make sure you tell her good things about me."

"Don't worry. I'll lie," she teased. Clucking her tongue, she turned Smoke's head and rode away. Skyla had gotten good riding western style, although she still instinctively sat stiff as though she couldn't break free of her proper English rider upbringing.

Turning, I reached into a pocket and flipped a coin at the boy standing just inside the stable door. "Thanks, kid." He caught it with both hands and a toothy grin. I'd learned long ago that if you cared for your horses, you tipped the stable hands well. Sometimes it made the difference between getting out of a place alive or hanging from a post.

***

Empty eye sockets in a giant trike skull stared at me from between the bar counter and the door. One of the top twin horns was broken and an almost perfect hole had been punched between them from where Wolverine Wade killed the beast moments before it would have gored me to death.

I raised my cup of coffee in mock salute to the dead ape leader's mount then raised my fork and attacked the pile of steaming eggs and beef hungrily as a slow melody trickled from the piano in the corner. The player seemed to be practicing a new tune, because it was terrible, and he kept repeating portions of the song.

On my third bite, the batwing doors to the bar opened. Three men stepped inside.

Forkful of eggs halfway raised, I froze for a moment before recovering and stuffing the food into my open mouth.

One of the men was older; he had a muscular build with a thick gray beard and a pistol slung low on his left side, butt turned forward for a cross draw. The others were younger, but tall and lean with faces that reflected a predatory nature. One of them cradled a shotgun in his arms.

Their eyes settled on me.

The young men's faces hardened while the older simply squinted as he took me in, then he walked to the bar and the other two followed. "Coffee," the old man demanded quietly. His voice cut through the quiet of the bar and the few working girls that lounged in the room perked up at the possibility of some early morning customers.

Another man entered. This one was clean cut, tall and lanky, with a dark brown leather vest and stayed close to the door beside the trike skull. Smiling, he waved at the bartender for a drink and ran a hand over the beast's black horns in admiration with a low whistle. I noticed his black boots were polished to a heavy shine and had silver spurs on them. He was a fancy man.

Out of sight of the men, I slowly eased a revolver from its holster with my left hand. When Left Arm O'Malley thumped a cup of coffee onto the counter with his one good hand, I used the opportunity to mask the sound of my gun's hammer being cocked back.

"You gents looking for a good time?" A pair of working girls separated from the others and eased up to the trio of men, batting eyelashes and pouring on the charm. From the slur of their words, they were still moving under the influence of last night's whiskey.

"No," the old man said firmly. He grabbed the cup and crossed the room to my table, flanked by the two younger men. Dismayed, the girls moved to the smiling man by the trike skull who appeared happy to have their affections. My eyes flicked back and forth between him and the group in front of me. The timing of his arrival was suspicious.

Without asking for permission, the bearded man pulled a chair out and sat across from me. Tilting his head slightly, his intense blue eyes studied me curiously.

The other men flanked him, one standing on each side, looking intimidating. The one with the shotgun leaned the barrel against a shoulder and crossed his arms over the stock. The other, a red head, smirked. He carried an ivory gripped pistol tucked into a holster. Behind them the girls chatted with the tall, well-dressed man. A mellow, pleasant tune came from the piano player as he began practicing something he could actually play.

I jabbed my fork into the eggs with my right hand. "What do you want?" I growled.

"Jedidiah Huckleberry Smith," he spoke the name slowly, as though rolling it around in his mouth to get a taste for it. "Seems you've been busy." He took a sip of coffee from the steaming cup. "We thought we would swing by and see how you were doing." His voice had a clear southern aristocratic drawl. It wasn't the sort you'd expect to hear from a man who kept company with the gunmen standing behind him.

I stared at him. "I'm doing just dandy. Nice talking to you. There's the door."

"Show some respect, asshole," said the red headed man on the left, his hand moving to the butt of his pistol. He was tense, like a wild dog, ready to be unleashed to commit violence. I shifted my gun slightly under the table to cover him.

The bearded man raised a hand in warning, "Quiet, Kid." He stared at me for a moment before laughing. It was a harsh sound and without humor. "Still angry, huh? Don't be," he waved his hand dismissively. "Innocent people die all the time."

"Not by my hand… Father," I spat the word at him.

He leaned forward over the table, jaw flexing in anger. "You're right, son. They don't die by yours. They die by Franklins. And where is he now? Oh, that's right. You shot his friends and beat him to death with a chunk of firewood," he spat onto the floor and leaned back. "All over an accident."

"They shouldn't have laughed about it afterwards. But they weren't the only ones responsible. You had a part in it as well. You allowed a bunch of cutthroat murderers to join us," I snarled, feeling heat rising into my face as I remembered the gunshot and screams of the bystanders, followed by the shocked look on the dying kid's face. We were just there to rob a bank, taking back money stolen by Union thugs who'd gotten rich spilling Southern blood. No one was supposed to have been hurt.

"Murderers? Son, we're all murderers, killers, cutthroats and thieves. How many folks have you killed? I bet you've lost count." He showed me his hands, they were calloused and worn. "Yours have as much blood on them as mine. If not more."

"Not all spilled blood is equal. You and your..." I glanced at the men he'd brought in disgust, "friends... kill people who get in your way. Good, bad, doesn't matter to you. But it matters to me."

The man by the trike skull waved the ladies away with a laugh. He shifted his holster on his belt slightly and took a drink from his bottle as he glanced around the room. For a moment, his eyes seemed to linger on our table. Turning away, he set the bottle down and tapped his fingers to the piano player's tune.

Father sat back in his chair and took another sip of coffee. "You know we put out a reward for your location. Offered a good price as well, with the stipulation that you were left alive and unaware that we wanted to find you. We chased a few leads, but you seem to have just... disappeared," he peered at me over the rim of his cup. "Until now."

"I heard." Wesley Gardner had been in town when the battle commenced. A notorious gunman, he'd warned me that my old gang wanted me something bad. I hadn't seen him since he'd fled after the battle with a full saddle bag from robbing the very bar I sat in now.

He rubbed a hand along his beard thoughtfully. "I figured you'd have gone south, maybe back home to South Carolina. Didn't expect you this far west."

"It's got a lovely climate and best of all, none of my past."

"I take it you're not interested in coming back then?"

"No," I said with all the disgust and bitterness I could summon. Which was a considerable amount.

He frowned, then spoke, with a sense of sadness, "Then there is the matter of atonement."

"Bring it on," I snarled back as I gently laid down the fork with specks of eggs still impaled on the tines. I figured that's what this was about from the moment I saw the three of them walk in the door. Sometimes you must pay for your past, no matter how in the right you were.

"Very well." Father set his cup down gently, stood, and didn't bother to push the chair back under the table. "I had high hopes for you, son; it's a damn shame you didn't turn out more like me."

"No, it's not."

He nodded, frowning again slightly. My words hurt him. I knew they would, but he'd changed since my childhood. He was a good man back then, honest and fair. I wanted to be just like him. But over time, I reckoned all the killing got to him, twisted him up inside. It was a shame.

"Well, Jedidiah, I like your new name. It's got a nice ring to it." He turned, head held high as he walked away.

I looked at the gunman still staring at me. "Kid, huh?" I asked.

"That's right," he smirked. "Blue Ridge Kid."

"Never heard of you."

"I'm well known."

"Most public nuisances are."

His smirk slipped, the corners of his lips turning down as he tapped a finger against the ivory plated pistol butt impatiently. The other man with the shotgun shifted his feet, moving further to the right and away from his partner.

I was lying through my teeth. I knew who the Blue Ridge Kid was. Before I beat Franklin to death, he used to tell us tales of how good his little brother was with a gun. But I had nothing to gain by playing to the Kid's ego, and possibly something to gain by twisting him up with faked nonchalance. From his shifting posture, it was working; he was irritated.

Reaching the batwing doors, my old man spoke without looking back, "Make it quick."

He stepped out of the building as the Blue Ridge Kid drew his pistol.

He was fast. Faster than I'd ever be. And cocky. The smirk came back as his gun cleared leather in a blur. He knew I couldn't outdraw him.

My bullet burst through the table in a spray of splinters, hitting him above the belt buckle.

A twisted grimace of pain and disbelief crossed his face as he folded in half and collapsed. His fancy pistol fell, spinning away across the stained wood floor.

Surprise. Old age and treachery beats youth and skill every time.

My gun blast shocked the room quiet. The girls and piano player stopped and stared with mouths open.

In the quiet, I thumbed the hammer back with an audible click.

The other man swung the shotgun down from his shoulder and I stood quickly, flipping the table towards him. Coffee splattered on the floor and eggs flew as the flimsy boards slammed into him, knocking the gunman off balance. The shotgun discharged harmlessly to the side and the girls screamed fearfully. I fired through the top of the table, blasting another hole through the rough boards and missing, sending the bullet slamming into the bar across the room.

The crack of a bullet zipping past my skull made me drop to a crouch behind the overturned table.

The clean-cut man by the trike skull fired from the hip again, the muzzle blossoming fire and smoke as his bullet clipped the table top and deflected, pelting me with only splinters.

If I stayed where I was, I was dead.

Drawing my second Colt, I ran across the room as he fired again. Weaving between tables and chairs, I fired both guns towards him without aiming before diving over the top of the polished bar.

Slamming to the stained wood floor, I huddled against the underside of the bar as bullets shattered the large picture mirror and bottles on shelves above me. Sprays of glass shards and whiskey rained down. I flinched as a mostly intact bottle fell on my head, thumping my skull hard enough to send stars dancing across my vision. Left Arm was crawling along the length of the bar on all threes, I suspected going for the pistol the bartender kept under the cash drawer.

Peeking over the top of the polished counter, I found the gunmen. The one by the trike skull was still standing there, frantically reloading cartridges into his pistol. I fired both guns and at least one shot connected. He twitched then stumbled, running out the door as I held my fire for fear of sending bullets winging out into the open street beyond him.

Buckshot hit the bar beside me with an explosion of splintered wood shrapnel. Swearing, I twisted about and fired both guns again. The shooter took one of the bullets through the shoulder. Dropping the shotgun, he fell, crying out in pain and clutching his wound.

In moments, one man was dead, another wounded, and the third missing. No sign of my father.

Pistols still in hand, I cautiously stood and walked around the damaged bar. Broken glass crunched under my boots. O'Malley crept around the far side, gun in hand as he looked around the damaged room of his saloon.

A woman's cry came from by the piano, and I saw the first shotgun blast hadn't been harmless. Blood was oozing through a girl's hands as she pressed at the gaping wound in the piano player's stomach. His face was deathly white, and one of the girls was mumbling a prayer.

The loud roar of a gun blast from behind made me spin.

Both the batwing doors were swinging. Below them lay a pair of black boots with silver spurs twitching in death spasms.

It was the third outlaw who didn't look like an outlaw. My old man would never be caught dead in such gaudy boots.

Left Arm O'Malley waved a massive smoking Colt Dragoon pistol and shouted at me angrily, "What have ya done, Jed? Damn ye!"

"Get the Doc!" I shouted back, but he was already moving. At a run, he leapt over the corpse and into the street, heavy pistol still swinging in his hand.

Walking to the last surviving gunman, I glared down at him. His shirt was soaked with blood, but he looked like he'd live. "Get me out of here," he said through teeth clenched in pain. "Or I'll tell them who you are."

I looked at the girls. They were all focused on the dying piano player. No one else was in the room and nobody was looking in from outside. Everyone was still too fearful of more bullets being fired to come close enough to investigate what happened.

With the toe of my boot, I slid the fallen shotgun across the floor to him.

Grabbing the stock with a bloodied hand, he looked up in surprise as though not expecting that I'd help him. "Thanks," he said with the beginnings of a painful smile.

The gun bucked in my hand as I shot him through the heart.

At the gun blast, the girls startled and twisted around fearfully again, only to see a dead man with a shotgun in hand and myself standing over him with a smoking pistol.

It looked like self-defense.

It wasn't.

But it wasn't quite murder either. If he ran with my father's pack, he deserved it.

Besides, I couldn't let him talk.

Doc barged in, leather bag in hand, followed closely by O'Malley. Doc rushed to the wounded piano player and pushed the girl's blood-covered hands aside to see the wound. I could tell from where I stood it'd be a miracle if the man survived. His head lolled around on his shoulders lifelessly as Doc began cutting away the shredded fabric of his vest and shirt.

Left Arm looked at the bodies strewn about the bar. His face contorted in anger. "What the hell was all this about, Jed? You've got Jimmy hurt and me bar shot up!" His hand holding the pistol twitched at his side. It did that when he was getting agitated.

"They thought I was someone else." It was the best lie I could come up with on the fly, and it was true enough. I wasn't who I used to be.

I watched as Doc stopped, shook his head and closed Jimmy's eyes with his fingers. One of the girls grabbed the pianist's bloodied vest and sobbed. Her body wracked with cries of grief.

"Where's the old man that was with them?" I growled.

"Gone," Left Arm grunted. "He was riding out of town, cool as could be, when I grabbed Doc."

I gritted my teeth.

In a way, I was responsible for this. The outlaws were after me.

But if you take on the burden of other's actions as your own, the weight will crush you.

No. This was my father's fault for bringing death to my town.

***

Sheriff Beauford Johnson stepped over the well-dressed corpse disdainfully and through the bullet holed batwing doors. His angry mustached scowl focused on me as he stomped across the floor, his dusty black slicker billowing around him like a villain from a dime novel.

"You," he growled, then stopped and looked down at the dead outlaw. The shotgun was still held in the dead man's grip amidst a growing pool of blood.

"Me," I replied equally bluntly as I kept working on reloading the twin Peacemakers. There was something dark and dangerous about our new Sheriff. And I doubted the stories of men crossing him, then disappearing weren't based on nothing.

The lawman spat a stream of tobacco juice into the pool of thickening blood and grunted, "Death just follows you everywhere, don't it?"

"Seems so." I watched Doc and Left Arm pick up the dead pianist and carry him past us, followed by the same girl who'd cried over his body. Her painted face was streaked with tears, and she gave me a despairing glance that cut deeper than anger would have.

I couldn't fault her; someone needed to be blamed, and I was still alive.

The Sheriff stared at me with hard eyes. "Why did three men try to kill you?"

"Mistaken identity," I replied.

Beauford grunted. "Uh-huh." He looked at the shattered mirror and bullet holes in the table and bar. The remaining working girls were at the far end of the polished counter, passing around a bottle. "Three men just walked in here and shot the place up... all because they thought you were someone else?"

"I must have one of those faces."

The Sheriff's right eye twitched. "Left Arm says an older man talked to you then left before the gun fire."

"He did. He thought I was someone else. I tried to tell him otherwise." I doubted anyone overheard our conversation.

"Who'd he think you were?"

"Johnson Brown," I lied easily with the only name that came to mind. When I was picking out my new one for a fresh start in this town, I went over several before settling on Jedidiah. Johnson Brown was a tempting one, but a bit too bland for my tastes.

Beauford spat more tobacco, this time at a dull brass spittoon. He missed, and the brown liquid splashed against the underside of the bar. The man didn't seem to care. "Johnson Brown, huh? And did he give his name?"

"He neglected to do so."

The Sheriff stood still for several long moments, locking eyes with me as he no doubt pondered my responses. I could tell he didn't figure my story added up. "Don't leave town," he finally said, before starting to walk towards the girls in the corner. No doubt to compare our stories.

"I will be," I said after him.

He stopped abruptly and turned back slowly, face pinched in anger.

I shrugged. "Government business. Going to Fort Jipson in two days. If you don't like it, arrest me. You can explain it to Captain Brandthorn."

Grunting, the lawman turned away wordlessly, no doubt hoping a dinosaur would eat me on my travels. I lucked out though; apparently, he'd rather let me go instead of locking me up until the judge came to town. That'd probably have taken a week or more.

Walking out of the room, I took one last glance at the outlaw bodies scattered on the floor.

I always assumed my past would catch up to me one day, but the world-wide publicity of the Battle of the Apes had made that a much higher possibility. I desperately wanted to find another small town to relocate to. But with Skyla here, I was torn between being with her and the danger I was in by being here. Not that it was a choice I could make… we males do stupid things for females.

Now I wondered what my father's next move would be. I had no intention of killing him, but it was hard to ignore the fact that he'd just let his men try to kill me. I wondered if he'd allowed it, or if his hold on the gang was slipping and he hadn't a choice but let Franklin's little brother and friends have at me. A lot can change in two years. But an assault like this wasn't his style. We'd always worked quietly, spreading out over multiple states and playing it smart and safe with as little violence as possible. That's why we managed to work for almost two decades without being caught or catching any notoriety.

I peeked out the door before I stepped through, looking for any more gunmen trying to kill me. No obvious ones were in sight, just the busy traffic of folks moving around, so I stepped onto the boardwalk and looked down at my clothes. They were soaked with whiskey and small glass shards reflecting with the rising sun.

Things weren't going to plan this morning.

***

When the Reverend stepped in front of me and raised his bible to slow me down, I sighed. I didn't have time to talk to the man, but he always gave pearls of wisdom whether I wanted them or not it seemed.

"Hello, Jedidiah," he said in greeting, his face stern and serious. "I heard you were involved in the shooting at the saloon."

I nodded an affirmative.

The man of cloth looked at me peculiarly. "They were looking for you, weren't they?" He knew of my past and had the decency to ignore my hiding out around these parts so long as I stayed on the right side of moral and immoral. I'd done a mostly good job so far, but I'd always tended to stick to the gray areas between right and wrong. Personally, I thought I was always right, regardless of what the law said.

"What makes you think that?" I asked, curious but avoiding the question.

He shrugged. "Three men tried to kill you. That's not your typical bar fight." He clasped me on the shoulder. "As I keep telling you, you aren't the only one with a sordid past." For the first time, I noticed how scarred his knuckles were.

"You're right. They were for me," I admitted.

"Your father sent them?"

For a moment I stared at him, confused how he knew. But then I recalled that the Reverend knew about Wesley's warning to me before the Battle of the Apes, that my father was looking for my location. "He was with them. Hell, he turned 'em loose on me, but didn't seem too anxious to watch me die."

Reverend shook his bible at me. "Sometimes it's not the prodigal son we have to worry about. Parents can be just as bad."

"I don't think he's going to turn to the good side. There's too much darkness in him these days," I said bitterly.

"Nonsense," he scoffed. "Everyone is redeemable."

The scar tissue across my back suddenly itched and I rolled my shoulders to stretch it. I hoped that Reydan White wasn't redeemed. I wanted him to suffer for eternity. But I was vindictive when it came to stuff like me being near whipped to death as a kid. "Redeemable by the good Lord maybe, but not by me," I snapped, angry at the dark thoughts that were boiling to the surface in my mind.

He chuckled. "Endless grace covers all sins, regardless of those it affects. If we were forgiven only by each other, we'd all be hell bound." He nodded at a dark suited man crossing the street with a large drooping mustache and a flat brimmed hat. "Take that gentleman. He had some choice words to say earlier when I found myself in his way at the General Store. I've forgiven him of course, but it wasn't easy."

I watched the man swagger across the street and step onto the boardwalk. There was a flash of a badge on his hip. "Oh no, he's a Pinkerton." Now I was really in it.

"Yes. They were brought in to protect the railroad's interests." Clasping the bible with both hands, Reverend turned to watch the man enter the bar I'd just left.

"Protection?" I snorted. "They're thugs with badges. A private military that pretends to be detectives when they aren't killing workers on strike or intimidating families who won't sell their land to the railroad with firebombs."

"They aren't particularly polite either."

"That line of work doesn't draw polite folks to it. But if he knew you kept a shotgun under the pulpit, he might think twice before trying to push you around."

"What makes you think I still have it?" He met my eyes and winked. The man had revealed the scripture engraved weapon to me just before the Battle, where he used it to good effect to protect his church from attacking apes.

I searched myself for an answer, "Because you know the evil that lurks in men's hearts. And just because an obvious threat is gone, doesn't mean there aren't others out there."

He patted me on the shoulder. "And your understanding of good and evil is what will keep you alive. The Lord has plans for you, Jedidiah. I don't know what they are," he gestured towards my twin pistols strapped around my waist, "but I reckon they got something to do with them."

"Since when does God need a remorseful gunman?"

"He needs all sorts." Smiling, he turned away whistling Amazing Grace and walked towards the first of the corpses being carried outside on a wooden shutter. It was the red headed Blue Ridge Kid by the looks of it. I pitied the dead piano player and the working girl who cared for him, but not the Kid or the other two. They'd made their choices, just like I had. But I'd learned from mine and moved on, while they'd lingered and paid the price.

Grace is a funny thing. You never know when it may be too late to take it.

I quickly walked to the hotel next door and practically ran up the stairs to my room to get cleaned up before meeting Skyla's mother.

***

By the time I rinsed off and changed, I was cutting the timing close. I rushed down the stairs to the lobby to see Skyla shaking her head at a lady who could only be her mother. The woman wore a red dress, and was equally as beautiful as her daughter, but with wisps of gray hair showing from beneath her feathered hat. She was as pale as Skyla had been when she'd first arrived, before the long hours outside during the past two months had turned the paleontologist's skin a light bronze.

A man was with them, lounging casually against the bar. Tan and fit, with gray hair neatly combed to the side. He was clean shaven, and his dark brown suit looked as though it had been custom tailored as it lacked the creases of a store-bought outfit. From the bulge under his coat, I was certain the man was packing. He said something to the others that I couldn't make out.

"Charles, darling. We must wait on Skyla's friend," I overheard Skyla's mother reply.

My hackles bristled at being called 'friend'.

"Here he is, mother." Skyla stepped past her and crossed the room. She grabbed me by the arm before stopping abruptly and looking at me suspiciously. "Have you been drinking?" The smell was from my gun belt and boots that'd been splashed. Try as I might to clean the whiskey out of the leather, the stench would stay until it wore off in a few days I suspected.

"Bar fight. Not my fault, I promise," I whispered to her. I'd fill her in on the details later, except for the part about my father being a gang leader and why they were looking for me.

"Jed!" she exclaimed as she looked me over for any obvious wounds.

"I know, I know. I'm fine. I'll tell you more later," I told her honestly. I felt far worse about letting Skyla down than I did killing three men. That's just how much she meant to me. Also, how little the dead men meant to me.

Skyla's mother stiffened as we approached. Her nose rose into the air as she took me in, then it wrinkled as I stopped before her.

I stretched my hand out towards her mother. "Ma'am, I'm Jedidiah Huckleberry Smith."

She looked at my extended hand disdainfully for a moment before reluctantly shaking it. "Elizabeth Stratten." She pulled her hand back almost immediately. "Are you drunk, sir?"

I forced a chuckle. "No, ma'am. Just an unfriendly fight next door at the bar during breakfast. A little whiskey was sloshed on me."

"Unfriendly fight? I heard they carried three bodies out." The well-dressed man spoke, his voice carrying a British accent. He thrust a hand through his gray hair, sweeping it to the side. "Seems it was a shootout more than a bar fight."

Skyla looked at me accusingly. "A shooting? Jed, are you sure you're okay?" She looked me up and down for wounds again.

"I'm peachy. It was just a misunderstanding that got out of hand." I tried to be as vague as possible. This was not the impression I wanted to give the mother of my girl. And this was certainly not the time or place where I was going to tell Skyla about it.

Elizabeth harrumphed with disdain. "A misunderstanding does not get three people killed, sir." She sniffed. "Speaking of death, I understand you are the reason my daughter has been risking her life in this horrid, forsaken town." Her brown eyes bored into me. They reminded me of her daughter's, but there was significantly less warmth in them.

"Mother, I chose to-" Skyla started to explain.

"No. I want to hear what your gunman friend has to say." Her mother cut her off viciously.

"Well, ma'am-" I started.

"You'll not silence me, Mother," Skyla's voice was sharp and cutting. "I'll speak for myself."

Her mother's eyebrows rose in surprise and she turned to her daughter. I looked back and forth between them, unsure of what to say or do. It seemed the best thing was to remain silent.

Skyla continued, not giving Elizabeth a chance to speak. "I stayed behind for the battle because I wanted to. That was my choice, not yours or father's, nor Jed's. In fact, he tried to get me to leave, several times. But I wanted to be here. I wanted to help."

"Be that as it may, young lady, I've come to fetch you home. We can discuss your future back east," she held a handkerchief to her nose, "far away from such a foul place as this and where there are more suitable suitors."

I felt my jaw clench in a burst of anger.

"Mother, I've about had-" Skyla started as she stepped forward angrily.

"Excuse me, ladies." The unknown man must have decided to put a stop to the arguing, because he chose that moment to slide between the women and extended a hand towards me. "Jedidiah, is it? I'm Charles Arthur." He smiled politely, his teeth straight and even.

I took him in at a glance. He reeked of an aristocrat background but had the bearing of a military man. No doubt an officer of some sort.

Skyla stopped arguing with her mother, her face flushed with anger. She gritted her teeth and introduced us, "Jed, Charles is my father's personal assistant."

He smiled easily. "I take care of his problems."

From the twinkle in his eyes, I reckoned that meant me. Giving him a nod, I shook his hand. He applied pressure to his grip, trying to crush my hand to establish dominance. My fingers began to flare in pain.

Staring into his pale blue eyes, I matched his grip, then squeezed harder, grinding his knuckles together beneath my calloused hand.

He jerked his hand from mine in barely concealed shock.

Surprise, asshole. No weakling could survive what I've been through.

Flexing his fingers discretely, his eyes narrowed as if re-examining my self-worth.

Skyla's mother wasn't finished with me. "You…" she pointed at me with a shaking finger. "You are the cause of this corruption of my daughter."

"I don't know about that," I raised my hands defensively, trying to calm her. This was not at all going how I expected.

"Please. You're standing here, sir, directly after a bar shooting in which several men died, reeking of alcohol, and telling me that you have not corrupted my daughter? Surely you do not believe me so gullible?"

I tried my best to look innocent as I pushed back against her claims about my personage. "Welcome to the West, Mrs. Stratten. Things ain't so black and white out here. As for your daughter's corruption, she's turned into a formidable woman in her own right. You should be proud of her, not belittling." Skyla grabbed my arm tightly and held her head high.

Elizabeth Stratten took a half step closer, her eyes burning into mine. "Your opinion is unwelcomed, cowboy."

I shifted my feet slightly, uncomfortable with the closeness of a strange woman into my personal space. It was tempting to take a step back. "Cowboy isn't a derogatory word out here."

"It is where I come from," she sneered. "And how do you know what derogatory means?"

I smirked, "I can spell my name too."

Skyla had had enough. "Stop it! Both of you!" She shot me a warning look before turning back to her mother. "You don't know how things are out here. You just got off the train. And you're about to see what sort of New West this is when we go fetch the dinosaur that Jed killed. The butchers and our escort are waiting for us. Let's go." Spinning, Skyla stalked away with me in tow.

***

Elizabeth and Charles rode in a rented carriage with two Pinkertons riding on top as Skyla and I walked Smoke down the street to the stable to fetch Carbine and meet the soldiers.

I glanced back at the coach as it rumbled along slowly behind us. "Your mother is a real peach; did she at least like your new horse?"

Skyla sighed and shrugged. "No, and mother's always been harsh and cold. Don't take it personal, she's pushed me around my entire life... but not anymore."

I leaned over and whispered in her ear, "I'm glad you're sticking up for yourself."

She flashed me a warm smile. "Me too."

"I'm a bit mystified that she didn't like Smoke though."

Skyla snorted. "She's a poor judge of horses and men, she thinks pedigree is everything."

I laughed and shook my head. "What an easterner."

In addition to Brandthorn's soldiers waiting at the stables, there was a young officer with insignia signifying that he was a fresh Lieutenant. There were also five wagons to recover the soldiers' bodies, the damaged Gatlings, and bring back the dinosaur remains.

With the wagons were four butchers, who were just that. They were employed by the Smithsonian, under Skyla's direction, and would break the dinosaur down into large components to be shipped in specialized cargo cars back east for detailed study. Nice fellows, all of them. Big, amicable, and good with knives. They'd showed me a few things with using my Bowie that I hadn't thought of before and taught me the basics of throwing knives. I'd never admit it to anyone, but I'd started practicing throwing my knife almost as much as I practiced drawing and shooting my guns. Weapons are tools, and the man who is master of his tools, is the master of his surroundings. And you never knew when you might have to kill someone or something with your tools.

While everyone watched, I struggled to harness and saddle Carbine.

The obnoxious mustang kept grabbing the blanket I placed on his back and pulling it off. I don't know where he'd picked that up from. It was a new nuisance for my horse to annoy me with. It took Skyla's distracting him with an apple to finally get him ready.

Skyla's mother watched in amusement from her carriage, a tight-lipped smirk on her face as she watched my horse embarrass me. My first impressions with her were going quite poorly.

As I was finishing getting ready, the stable hand brought out a beautiful chestnut colored Arabian already saddled and handed the reins to Charles. The horse stood at least a hand taller than Carbine. The Arabian looked perfect, immaculately brushed, no doubt meticulously cared for and exercised, and probably didn't even get poop on his tail. Captain Brandthorn and the young Lieutenant complimented the man on his horse.

"Gelding?" Brandthorn asked, wondering if the horse had been neutered.

"Nonsense, I only ride stallions. I wouldn't trust a half horse any more than I would a half man."

Rolling my eyes, I grabbed the pommel of my saddle and pulled myself up. Carbine may not be an expensive thoroughbred, and an immense pain in the ass, but he's still the mustang I'd prefer over such finery. Price doesn't always equal value, and I'd rather have mine than his.

The Arabian stepped forward and nuzzled Smoke's neck. Skyla clucked her teeth and pulled her mare away from the stallion. "Easy there, Sir Lancelot, Carbine might get jealous." She leaned over and gave my horse a scratch on his head.

"Sir Lancelot, huh?" I looked from the Arabian to his owner in mock shock. "You'd name your horse after an adulterous betrayer?"

Charles removed his coat and folded it carefully, exposing a pistol with pearl inlaid grips tucked into a fancy tooled holster. "And you'd name your horse after a weapon?" he challenged me back.

I shrugged and leaned forward to pat Carbine's neck. "Least mine is faithful and unpretentious. Lancelot was neither."

The Brit snorted while tying the folded coat behind his saddle. "It is a regal name for a regal beast."

Shaking my head, I reached down and made sure my rifle was loose in its scabbard and prepared to be drawn if needed. Heading out onto the prairie these days meant more danger than ever before.

"Shall we?" Brandthorn spoke from the head of the column, moving his horse forward without waiting for a response from his men.

The row of troops followed him. Charles, Skyla and myself rode after. Behind us, the cracks of reins being snapped over the backs of horses and mules were followed by wheels rumbling and wagons creaking and groaning as they rolled forward.

***

Our group raised a trail of dust that could be seen for miles across the clear sky. I hoped it wouldn't draw any unhappy attention to us, although we should have plenty of people who could fight off an ape attack. We hadn't seen a large gathering of apes since the battle. They appeared to have scattered to the winds, regrouping only in small numbers to attack homesteads and loners, and stealing livestock to eat. They'd become more of a pest rather than a real threat. But we didn't know how many were still out there. Dozens likely survived the battle, perhaps even fifty or sixty, and many still had their trikes they'd ridden to attack us with. If they banded back together, they'd be a formidable force. So far, we hadn't seen any sign that any raptors had survived the battle, but heaven help us if those vicious feathered little bastards were still around.

I glanced back at the sour faced men on top of Elizabeth's coach. The Pinkertons' presence bothered me. Charles rode beside the carriage, conversing with Skyla's mother as the armed detectives drove from above. I glanced over at Skyla, "Your family usually use Pinkertons when they come west?"

She shrugged. "My parents never come west. But father uses them occasionally for his protection detail, mother does more often. The owners of the company are close family friends. Whenever they are in D.C. for work, they're always over for dinner."

Great. I was just surrounding myself with future troubles. "Your father needs a protective detail?"

"People take their science and reputation very serious. The Smithsonian can ruin a man as easily as make one. Father's been challenged to duels several times, but it has never come to that. Although if it did, he'd simply have Charles duel in his stead. He's an expert pistol shot."

I rolled my eyes. Of course he was. "I thought dueling was outlawed."

"It is. But so long as it's discrete and no one dies, no one seems to mind."

I supposed I shouldn't be surprised that dueling still occurred. Upper society had their own sets of rules and ways to live by. Just like we on the outskirts had as well.

Skyla looked behind us, then to me, checking to see if we were alone enough to talk. "Okay, Jed. What was this bar shootout about?"

"Mistaken identity. They thought I was someone who owed them something," I partially lied.

"But you weren't?"

"No. I didn't owe them a thing." I felt terrible about not telling her the entire truth. She needed to know, especially now that my father was in the area. But the time needed to be right and when we were alone. I didn't know how long it might take her to come to terms with the fact that I was a former outlaw. Or if she ever would for that matter. It was a glum thought.

"I don't know how anyone could mistake you for someone else."

"Thanks... I guess."

She smiled slightly. "I'm glad you're okay. But I can't believe you had a shootout with three men over a simple mistake. Couldn't you explain it to them?"

"They didn't give me much of a chance before they started blasting," I lied again smoothly.

Sir Lancelot trotted beside us and Charles stretched in the saddle, the grips of his pistol flashing in the sun. "Much further, Jedidiah?"

I was glad for the interruption, but I also got the impression he liked saying my full name because it made him feel superior. Funny thing is, if he'd known my real name, he'd have really felt superior.

I pointed with a finger, "Over that ridge ahead, about a mile to go." I looked around the area again. Even with the escort, I didn't want to get caught unaware. But so far, except for a lone pterodactyl flying high overhead, we hadn't seen hide nor hair of any dinosaurs or apes.

"Outstanding, Elizabeth grows weary of the bumping of the prairie."

"Poor pampered thing," I muttered under my breath. Skyla heard me and shot me a dirty look.

Charles seemed oblivious to my response as he asked, "I understand you killed the beast?"

"I finished it off."

"You seem to have a knack for killing things," he said, seemingly impressed at my ability to put bullets into living objects.

"I've managed to stay alive so far," I glanced at him and then away again. "So, you're something like a butler?"

"No. As Skyla said, I'm a personal assistant," he clarified as he leaned forward and patted Sir Lancelot's neck. "I help the family out with anything they need."

"But I take it you were military once?" I asked, voicing my guess from earlier.

He frowned. "Yes, I served in the British East Indian Company for a while."

Knowing something of history, I tried to do the math in my head as to when he may have been in. "Did you serve during the Indian Mutiny?" I wasn't up to date on British history, but I had read about the failed rebellion against the Crown. It'd been an awful, bloody mess filled with atrocities on both sides. Afterwards, the East Indian Company had been disbanded.

Charles twisted in the saddle to study me intently. "You are far more knowledgeable and educated than I initially assumed. You have my apologies for that."

I rolled my eyes. "I'm glad I could impress you."

He nodded and turned away, his face darkening as he looked in the direction we traveled. I gathered that our conversation was over and my assumption about his service was correct. He couldn't have known it but regret for our past was something we had in common.

"I'm going to go meet our new officer," I told Skyla before tapping Carbine's flanks and riding to the front of the column.

The young officer turned to me as I rode up. Brandthorn made the introductions. "Jed, this is Lieutenant Daniels. Daniels, this is Jedidiah Huckleberry Smith."

Leaning over in our saddles, we shook hands.

"Sir, your reputation precedes you. I've already heard several stories of your exploits. But I'm curious, are you always introduced with all three names?" Daniels asked.

"Reckon people just like the sound my middle name makes when it rolls off the tongue," I grinned. It was a made-up name, but as my old man said earlier, it had a particular ring to it. And it was much better than the name I was born into. I might not be able to change the blood in my veins, or my past, but at least I could change my birth name and fake a fresh start.

The Lieutenant had brown hair neatly combed over beneath his field cap, his blue uniform was freshly pressed, and his rank insignia glistened on his collar. In addition to a pistol carried in a flap holster, he also wore an officer's sword and rifle in scabbard.

I looked at the stock of the rifle sticking out and leaned forward for a better view. "So, our government has finally seen fit to issue you repeaters? About time."

Brandthorn laughed sarcastically and without humor. "Yes, but only to those of us who are either stationed at Fort York or Fort Jipson... Imagine how the battle would have turned out if my men had repeating Winchesters instead of single shot Springfields," he grimaced. "More of them would still be alive."

Prior to the Battle, his platoon had arrived in Granite Falls with a full platoon of forty men. Within the first twenty-four hours he'd lost a dozen on a failed rescue mission. And after the vicious battle with the apes, he was down to six soldiers and himself.

"Still carrying your sword, I see," I told the Captain. He'd been out of ammunition, wounded, and slashing about with the bladed weapon when the reinforcements arrived to save us from being wiped out.

He patted the brass handle of the sword sheathed at his waist. "This thing saved my life, seemed a shame to get rid of it because it got a little bent."

I nodded. A good weapon was worth holding onto. It's hard not to get nostalgic for something your life has depended on time and time again.

"Daniels, is this your first tour?" Since we were traveling together, I figured I may as well get to know the new Lieutenant. An outlaw never knows when he might need an ally in a position that can keep him from getting hung if he's ever caught.

"Yes, sir." He dipped his head in an affirmative. "Arrived last week with Lieutenant Carson."

"Shame about him. He was a good man… brave to the very end," I told him.

"He was certainly that," Daniels said sincerely. "We got to know each other on the train ride west and were looking forward to serving together."

"So, you've spent one week in the New West. Sounds like you've been broken in the hard way to life out here," I told him.

He sighed and gestured at Brandthorn. "On my second day, the Captain here sent me with a squad to track down apes that'd been spotted past the old Clayton ranch. They ambushed us, killed two of my men and wounded three others before we beat them back. And now I'm going to recover soldiers' bodies along with a big dinosaur corpse," he shook his head in disbelief. "I can tell you it's been much different than I expected back in the academy."

Brandthorn shrugged with one shoulder. "Everything's changed. We used to worry about the Indians, now we worry about seven-foot-tall apes ripping our hearts out and eating them. And who knows what sort of prehistoric lizards coming out of the tunnel to eat ranchers and livestock."

His Lieutenant tilted his head at me. "Is it true?"

"What's that?" There was no telling what he'd heard. Half the rumors going around town were ridiculous bullshit spun up to make the storyteller sound important, like he'd witnessed or been part of something important. Everyone also claimed to have been a survivor of the battle, but there hadn't been that many of us.

"That you ate the ape leader's heart."

I sighed. "I didn't eat it. I just took a bite and spat it out."

Brandthorn laughed and shifted in his saddle. "I suggested you for being the new Sheriff, but that single act made everyone uncomfortable with you being in charge."

If I'd pinned a lawman's star to my chest, it'd have probably burst into flames and me with it. "It was in the heat of battle. Seemed fitting. A poetic justice of sorts. The Shaynee loved it."

"That's because it's the sort of thing a bunch of Indians would respect," the Captain snickered.

Shaking my head, I turned in the saddle and looked behind us. Skyla was laughing at something Charles was telling her. As I watched, the older man gestured wildly with his hands and she had to grab the pommel on her saddle to keep from falling off. Then behind them, I saw Elizabeth leaning slightly out of the carriage, staring at me. That woman really didn't seem to like me.

***

The red-finned monstrosity lay in pure, shot to pieces form amongst ripped apart soldiers and demolished Gatling guns. Just as I'd left it. No wolves, buzzards, pterodactyls, or the small green whip-tailed scavenger dinosaurs had begun to feast on its remains. Even the Indians hadn't stolen the equipment off the dead soldiers yet.

Elizabeth peeked out the window of the carriage as it bumped to a stop. Her face turned a subtle shade of green before she ducked back inside with a handkerchief held against her nose. Personally, I thought the smell wasn't as bad as I'd have expected by now. Up top, the Pinkertons sat watching the surrounding landscape with suspicious expressions on their faces and rifles in hand. No doubt they'd rather be off kicking crutches out from under children or plucking wings from butterflies than pulling guard duty.

Skyla slid off Smoke and tied her to the coach. One of the Pinkertons passed down a couple of small leather bags to her. Before I could dismount, Charles was off his Arabian horse and taking the bags from her to carry. The man really was a butler of sorts.

I walked my horse closer to Brandthorn. "Well-"

A gunshot made Carbine jump and buck beneath me.

"Got him! You see that! Yeehaw!" a Pinkerton hooted as he waved his rifle in the air. His partner craned his neck in the seat, looking in the distance, his rifle at the ready but with the barrel still pointed at the ground. Below them, Elizabeth hunkered down behind the door of the carriage, the top of her face peeking over the edge, her eyes wide and fearful.

"What the hell did you just shoot?" I shouted at the detective as I jerked the *Eighty-Six* from its scabbard.

The mustached detective pointed at a small ridge about a hundred yards away. "Injun!"

"Don't let them get me!" Mrs. Stratten squealed loudly as she huddled inside the coach.

"Oh no…" I kicked my heels against Carbine and raced him in the direction the trigger-happy guard had pointed. If he'd just wounded or killed one of the Shaynee, there would be hell to pay in this territory. Possibly an all-out war, depending on who it was.

Behind me, I heard Brandthorn swear at the man. "I told you! No shooting at anything other than apes or attacking dinosaurs! We're at peace with the Indians!"

"Ain't no peace with Indians! They'd scalp us as soon as look at us!" the Pinkerton shouted back. "They're cold-blooded savages and…"

The shouting faded away as I reached the ridge crest. Rifle at the ready, I stopped Carbine and peered off the bank into the gulley over the iron sights.

A large rock, close to the size of a man's head had been knocked off the edge, with a cratered splash of white from the bullet impact.

Glancing back, I saw the soldiers had all dismounted with their rifles at the ready, looking for attackers while Brandthorn gestured angrily with the two Pinkertons. Skyla knelt beside the dinosaur, watching me with Charles looming protectively over her. The butchers waited behind her, their cloth aprons hanging from their necks and large knives and saws rolled up in oiled leather.

I waved my hat to get the Captain's attention. "Just a rock!" I bellowed at him. Brandthorn threw his hands up and waved dismissively back.

The Pinkertons were going to be trouble. They were the sort of men who shot first and asked questions later. They'd brought a new level of danger and hazard to an area already filled to the brim with it. I took one last look at the rock; it'd been a good shot for a man shooting offhand with a rifle at a head-sized target. Thank goodness it hadn't been anyone we were on friendly terms with.

Turning Carbine, I rode back to the others as soldiers began loading the torn and savaged remains of their brothers in arms into the back of one of the wagons.

It was a grisly affair. Several of them had been ripped to pieces and required putting limbs together with torsos. One of the Privates threw up into the blood-stained prairie grass and a couple others had to take breaks from loading the bodies to gather their wits. I hadn't seen carnage like it since the Battle of the Apes.

While Skyla studied the red-finned dinosaur with Charles and Lt. Daniels, I took Captain Brandthorn and the corpse wagon to the remaining pieces of the sheep rancher. There wasn't much left of Jason Harper, just a headless torso with one leg barely attached by a few thin strands of gristle. A lone scavenger stood amongst the remains, worrying a chunk of flesh out of a discarded and ripped boot.

Dismounting, Brandthorn walked over to the tiny dinosaur. Gnawing on a severed toe, it looked at the Captain fearlessly as the man drew his foot back. With a swift kick, the small green dinosaur flipped end over end, long tail curling around its body as it bounced through the grass. Leaping back upright, it shrieked angrily at the officer and rushed away, leaving only moving grass in its wake.

Captain Brandthorn squinted after the foul little creature, as if wondering if he should shoot after it. "Hate those things. They're worse than buzzards."

A pair of soldiers picked up the torso and loaded it reverently into the back of the wagon. The bloated body squished sickeningly as it rested on top of the other corpses. I felt bile rise in the back of my throat at the sound and sight of so many bodies and parts piled together.

Brandthorn shook his head. "Three months ago, if you'd told me I'd be out here cleaning up after extinct animals invaded our world, I'd have sent you to the nut house. Now look at us," he grimaced and looked behind him in the direction of Elizabeth's carriage. "And we've got to worry about whatever messes the damned Pinkertons are going to leave us with." He spat. "They're almost as bad as the apes for stirring up trouble."

By the time we made it back, Lieutenant Daniels and his men had the broken Gatling disassembled and the pieces piled into the back of a wagon. The other weapon was being turned over by several soldiers and appeared to be in working condition, except for the jam that caused our hunt to go so badly prior. They backed up the wagon and attached the tongue on the Gatling chassis for hauling.

The coach with Elizabeth had moved upwind of the corpses, and through the window I could see her waving a paper fan back and forth in front of her face. No doubt fanning herself from the heat and stench of the dead. Above her the two Pinkertons talked while the trigger happy one with the mustache practiced twirling his pistol around a finger.

I walked Carbine over to Skyla and Charles. My horse hesitated at the size and scent of the bloody beast, but seemed content knowing that it was dead. Skyla had shoulder length butcher gloves on, and a set of knives and saws unrolled on a sheet of treated leather beside her. Several of the tools already had blood and bits of flesh on the blades from her initial incisions.

Tilting my hat to block the sun from my eyes, I asked, "Any idea what this monster is?"

Skyla made a small incision along the base of the red fin along the skull with a scalpel and poked a finger inside. "Cartilage."

"Come again?"

"The fin on its head and neck is made of cartilage. Cartilage doesn't typically fossilize, so growths like this," she wobbled the thick scarlet fin running along the creature's head back and forth, "rarely show when we find fossil remains. Take a human skull, you never find them with noses. You just find a large gap and assume that something must have been there. Or you may find an imprint in rock of where a shape had been. That's how we know the Allosaurus, like the one you killed, has the double row of ridges above its eyes. Well… that and the protrusions on its skull." She ran a hand along the blood smeared snout. "But off the top of my head, I've no idea what this is. I'd have to dig through the Smithsonian files and compare the bone structure to see if we've ever found anything like it. Chances are it's something new and undiscovered. For right now though, I'm just doing some basic, preliminary studies and sketches. I'll let my father and the Smithsonian figure out what it is."

I nodded as I listened. Skyla always had a knack for teaching while working. She'd have made a fantastic schoolteacher. Around her the butcher team worked quietly, cutting the corpse carefully into pieces and loading the heavy meat pieces into the wagons. Already a clawed leg and arm were lying in the blood-splattered wagon. The attached four oxen team waited impatiently, flicking tails as flies buzzed around them and their gory load of dinosaur parts.

Charles knelt beside her and ran a finger along the dinosaur's teeth. Bits of human flesh were still crammed between them. He poked the pink tongue that lolled out of the mouth and in the grass. "Remind me to not get eaten while I'm out here."

"Same here," Skyla muttered as she removed a glove and jotted notes in her journal.

Standing, Charles put hands on hips and looked around. He pointed a finger at a large green and red tinged fern nearby. "That plant doesn't look like it belongs here."

"It's from the other side. We've seen them starting to sprout all over the place. We're guessing they are carried over in seed form in animal dung or carried by birds and pterodactyls. Life finds a way," Skyla told him without looking up.

"Shouldn't we cut them down or something? Before they spread?" Charles asked.

"We're pretty confident they won't survive the winter. It takes a hardy animal or plant to make it out here when the temperature drops a dozen degrees below freezing. If they're still here come spring, we'll start getting worried," she replied, taking a sharpened pencil and carefully sketching the head of the dinosaur in her notepad. I looked over her shoulder. Her sketches were impressive. I wished I could draw, instead the best I could do was stick figures.

"Mr. Smith?" I heard my name called faintly behind me.

Grimacing, I looked over a shoulder. Elizabeth Stratten waved at me with her fan, beckoning me to come over.

Skyla glanced at me sympathetically. "Jed. Please be careful with what you say," she warned. "Don't get angry. When you get angry you tend to say stupid things."

"Yes, ma'am. Say no stupid things. Shall do." She really did know me well.

I walked past the blood-soaked wagons of dinosaur parts, the mangled remains of soldiers, and to her mother's coach.

She glanced at me then away in disgust. "I understand you mean to take my daughter into Prehistoria."

I blinked, confused. "Where?"

"Prehistoria. That's what the papers back east have taken to calling the other side," she said matter of factly. "Now please, answer me, are you taking her across this Shimmer thing?"

"Fancy name for a lost world... No, ma'am. I'm not taking, just accompanying. She has a mind of her own, I just try to keep up and keep her alive."

Elizabeth scoffed. "She has always had a mind of her own, to her own detriment. Who are you then, to my daughter?"

"Well," I scuffed a boot toe against the ground, "I reckon I'm just the man courting her. Which means I support her, love her, help her, guide her, protect her, and she does the same for me. We're in this chaos together, for as long as she sees fit to let me walk beside her, I will."

"And you would let her cross into a lost world full of hairy man beasts and dangerous creatures such as that," she waved her fan at the dismembered dead dinosaur and the butchers carefully cutting it apart.

"Dinosaurs are her passion," I shrugged a shoulder. "So, yes, I'd let her. Do I want her to? No. Do I think it's dangerous? Yes."

"And silly, if you ask me. That's why I brought Charles with me. After I leave, he will stay behind and protect her as long as she is here." She looked at me pointedly. "Especially from you, sir."

I glanced at Charles; he was kneeling beside Skyla as they looked at something in her journal. So that's why he was here. The Stratten family butler was to keep an eye on their daughter and to keep me at bay.

"Well, ma'am, he's going to have his work cut out for him," I replied coldly and turned my back on her to return to Skyla and the dead monster. I'd had enough of this conversation, and my desire to be on friendly terms with Skyla's mother was decreasing with every word spoken between us.

And now I had Charles to contend with, the Pinkertons, my father's gang, and always in the background was Reydan White.

Things were getting complicated.

***

It was evening by the time we returned to town.

The broken Gatlings were carted off to the small armory beside the makeshift officer's barracks. A telegram was sent to the Smithsonian by Skyla about the dinosaur, and a squad of soldiers dispatched to protect the beast from gawkers as the creature's parts were loaded into specialty cargo cars on the train.

After Skyla finished sending the telegram, we put our horses away in the stable and walked to the diner to meet Charles and Elizabeth. I wasn't looking forward to the evening, my boots and gun belt still reeked of stale whiskey and alcohol, and from what I'd learned and experienced during the day, I wasn't pleased with either Skyla's mother or her fancy British butler.

On the way I realized there were noticeably more Pinkertons around. At least half a dozen stood outside the bar, smoking and jawing between themselves. They must have just started trickling into town earlier. Now the itch to get to Fort Jipson was stronger than ever. This place was becoming more threatening than the other side that was full of apes and dinosaurs and who knows what else that just might kill or eat you.

Glancing at the Sheriff's Office, I saw Beauford's face staring at me through the bar-covered windows. His mustached face shifted as he worked the large wad of tobacco between his jaws. Sighing to myself, I turned and entered the diner. I couldn't get out of this town fast enough.

The diner was about half full of patrons eating and socializing. Elizabeth and Charles were sitting at a small table towards the back of the building. I noted the Brit was sitting with his back to the wall and his front towards the door. The man was no fool, I'd give him that. I faked a smile as we crossed the room. Pulling a chair back for Skyla, I waited for her to sit before sliding it towards the table.

"I didn't expect to see such manners out west," Elizabeth said coldly as she watched.

"I come from an old family and I was raised right," I explained as I sat, shifting my twin holsters so the pistols wouldn't dig into my thighs.

"An old family you say. The Smiths? A rather common name. Doesn't sound particularly blue blooded... Where are you from? Somewhere southern with that accent of yours, no doubt," Elizabeth said with a skeptical look and a raised eyebrow.

"Mother, that's not considered a polite question to ask out here," Skyla warned. She'd learned quickly that many of us who've come west were either running towards something or running from something and asking about someone's background was a big no-no.

I was proud that she'd adapted so quickly to life on the old frontier but having trapped myself into revealing my true heritage or waving it away, I chose the better option of valor. "My family hails from the Deep South. Not a blue blood lineage by any means, but we do bleed a lovely shade of red," I smiled patronizingly.

Charles laughed. He had an easy laugh, one that could easily pass as genuine and sincere. But his eyes didn't twinkle, making it a scornful laugh at my expense.

"There's no such thing as blue blood," Skyla shot her mother a warning look that I doubted she would obey. "But if there was, it'd be the perfect color for snobbery."

The waiter came over and took our order. I ordered a steak and a whiskey. Skyla's mother already thought the worst about me, and I wanted to rip my teeth into something meaty and bloody and have something sharp to drown it with.

Charles leaned forward, his perfect teeth flashing as he spoke. "I've spent some time in the South, what part?"

Before I could deflect the question, Skyla answered for me, "South Carolina, near Charleston."

He looked from her to me. "Charleston is beautiful, I've spent a lot of time there. Especially around the old plantations." His look changed to one of suspicion. "Were your family slave owners?"

I dabbed the corners of my mouth with a napkin to hide the clenching of my jaw. This was not the first sort of conversation I'd had along these lines over the years. Everyone assumes you must have owned slaves to be in the South. "No, they were not. We did have freed blacks working for us though."

"Disgusting practice. The notion that people could own others," Elizabeth raised her nose at me. "Your people did such disgraceful things."

"I find it a disgusting practice as well, but what do you mean, your people?"

"Southerners..." she waved her hand. "Confederates. Those who killed hundreds of thousands, so they could torture, abuse, and *own* others."

I felt the thick mass of scar tissue I carried across my back itch and resisted the urge to roll my shoulders to ease the tension that suddenly developed. Skyla's hand gripped my arm tightly and she glanced from her mother to me, then back again. She shot me a warning look that I was treading into dangerous ground, but I couldn't stop, my hackles were raised.

"Not everyone from the South was a devil, just like not everyone in the north was a saint. There were a lot of atrocities committed on both sides of the war." Thinking of the abuse I received at the hands of Union raiders after the end of the war made my hand start to tremble, and I ground my teeth together as I scowled at my drink.

Charles noticed and pressed the issue.

"Whose side did your family fight for?"

"Both," I snapped.

Charles sniffed and raised his glass. "Well, here's to your ancestors who chose wisely."

Skyla glared at him, not raising her glass of water even as her mother did. "I'll not drink to that. The war is long over. Leave it in the past where it belongs."

I'd had enough of this talk. I lifted my glass mockingly with a sarcastic smile playing across my lips. "No, I'll drink. Here's to the one that killed all the damned northern invaders." It felt odd toasting people like my father after he just tried to kill me, but I didn't care. I wanted to verbally slap the pair of obnoxious easterners across their smug faces.

Elizabeth gasped, and Charles' face froze as his eyes flashed in anger. Skyla's grip almost cut the blood flow off to my arm. The waiter began to set our plates down on the table. Mine smelled delicious.

I knocked back the rest of my drink and dropped the glass to the covered table with a muffled thump.

"I'm done for the day. Have a good evening." Gently shaking Skyla's hand from my arm, I stood and dropped a couple bills beside my plate, then walked away from my lovely, rare steak. It was tempting to snatch it off the plate and eat it by hand as I left, but manners dictated that I leave somewhat graciously after such an insult.

I didn't look back. But I could feel their eyes on me. And it was only Skyla's that gave me a moment of pause before I jerked the door open and stepped out onto the street.

***

The Bucket O' Blood might not give me a warm welcome anytime soon, on account of the shooting, but the hotel had a nice, if small, bar. The only problem was that Skyla's mother and assistant were staying there as well. Running into them after they finished their meal was a risk that I was willing to take for a stiff drink alone.

But moments later, when Skyla entered, face flushed with anger, I knew I was in for it.

"What was that?" she demanded as she grabbed a nearby chair and dragged it across the floor loudly.

"Your mother is a..." I struggled for acceptable words to use, "well, she's an unpleasant person."

"She lost friends she'd known since childhood in the war, one of whom she thought she'd marry." Stopping beside me, she sat angrily in the seat.

"We've all lost someone because of that war. Her losses don't give her the right to take all southerners and lump them all together with the worst we had. I'm no damned slave owner, neither was my family. You know that."

She slapped her hand on the bar and leaned towards me. "Actually, I don't know much about you at all. You know a lot about me and my family, but you're still a mystery."

"It's... complicated." I rolled my glass between my fingers, looking at the amber liquid inside, hesitant to say anything else.

"Uh-huh. Look Jed, I know you aren't pro-slavery and I know your family isn't the worst of the South. You're a good man. A regular white hat. You're just too stubborn to realize it. But that was wrong of you to let those two get under your skin and storm out of there."

She was right, I could have handled it better. I told her as much, then added, "She's not coming with us to the other side, is she?"

Skyla waved at the bartender for a glass. "Certainly not. As mother would put it, 'It's no place for a lady'." The glass was slid in front of her, and she took my bottle and poured a drink.

"Then I'm glad you're not up to her horrible standards of being a lady." I swirled my drink before downing it and enjoying the harsh burn. "I'm not sure how I feel about us going on this expedition tomorrow into the unknowns of..." I searched for the name of the lost world that Elizabeth used, "Prehistoria. I wish you weren't going."

"So, you heard that name too? Prehistoria. It's rather catchy, I think. But either I go, or Oscar goes. And I have an obligation to the Smithsonian, my father, and to science. I go where the discoveries are. Unless you'd rather have that nasty little man get all the credit..."

I nodded my head, knowing that even before she said it. That's just who she was. And Oscar wasn't a possibility. He worked for the Smithsonian previously as Skyla's boss, but now he worked for Reydan White, no doubt searching for riches on the other side that could be exploited for the evil railroad tycoon's gain. A fat, pompous little man, who cared nothing for me and me nothing for him.

Skyla lifted her glass before continuing, "My mother may not be coming, but Charles is."

I groaned, "That's what I figured. Maybe he'll get eaten."

She frowned. "He's not so bad once you get to know him."

"Sure, he is," I muttered wryly as I watched her knock the glass back and down the amber liquid in one solid gulp. I wondered how much of a pain in the butt the personal assistant to her father would be once out of sight of Elizabeth.

Probably a lot.

***

The sun was cresting the valley edge as we said our goodbyes to Mrs. Elizabeth Stratten the following morning at the train station. Behind her, the locomotive blew coal dust out of the top of its stack and whistled loudly, signaling to everyone that it was about to leave the station. The same two Pinkerton Detectives that had driven her coach lounged nearby, smoking and jawing as they gave us some semblance of privacy.

"Charles, do look after my wayward daughter. Don't let her get into any trouble that you can't get her out of."

"Yes, Mrs. Stratten," he promised as he shifted the pistol at his waist to a better position.

"And Skyla. For the last time, I do not approve and wish you would return with me back home."

Skyla straightened her back and looked her mother in the eye. "I've a job to do and an opportunity of a lifetime. I'm staying. Jed will be with me."

Elizabeth sniffed and looked down her nose at me before turning away. "Very well. I'll return to your father and let him deal with you both later."

"Travel safe, mother." Skyla was curt. They stood apart from each other and didn't embrace. With one last disgusted look at me, her mother boarded the train with her two Pinkerton bodyguards.

I took solace in the fact that I was heavily armed with two pistols, the *Eighty-Six*, a sawed-off shotgun tucked into my bedroll, and all the Stratten family butler had was a pistol. If anyone was going to be protecting my girl or keeping her out of trouble, it'd be me.

With her mother gone, we saddled up and rode out the eastern entrance of town with the army detachment. The railroad had been extended to the east, circling around north and towards the Granite Mountains where the tunnel was located. A wagon trail had been cut alongside the rail and would allow us quicker access to the cliff face and budding Fort York near the Shimmer than if we had cut cross country over the rolling prairie and through the small forests that dotted the landscape.

Captain Brandthorn led the way with Lieutenant Daniels beside him, six soldiers on horseback, then myself, Skyla, and Charles, as well as five wagons. Four were loaded with food and supplies and driven by soldiers. Each wagon had two soldiers riding on the bench. Six beef cows were tied to the backs of the wagons, fresh meat to supplement the wagons full of potatoes, flour, sugar, and beans. Military food is never anything worth writing home about. The fifth wagon was driven by two Pinkertons, the crated cargo in the back covered under a heavy tan canvas sheet. Something for the railroad I suspected as they were just tagging along for part of the trip and not crossing over to the other side.

The stench of Asian food wafted over us as we passed the newly formed tent city aptly called China Town that grew outwards into the eastern side of the valley. Even with my hearty breakfast, my stomach growled at the rich smells. The new influx of Chinamen helping build the railroad had added a lot of diversity to the area, especially in food. But it wasn't without its problems.

A handful of angry white men were protesting on the outskirts of the tents, their makeshift signs proclaiming that the Chinese were taking their jobs. That was a lie, the railroad was still hiring like mad. The Chinese just worked cheap, which made it hard for anyone else to make a decent wage.

"How's she doing?" I asked Skyla about her horse as we rode past the outskirts of the rapidly expanding town and into the large open valley.

She patted the gray spotted coat of Smoke's neck. "I love her. She's so gentle and sweet."

"Well, she's no Carbine, that's for sure."

"You say that like it's a bad thing," Skyla scoffed. She'd grown close with my horse over our adventures and seemed to forever be standing up for his shenanigans that he tormented me with.

"It is." I grinned as Carbine snorted. If a horse's ears could burn, I bet his were right now.

We passed the cemetery at the top of the valley. Before the battle, there'd only been about two dozen graves. Now there were over a hundred, including our former Sheriff and his two deputies. The neatly lined headstones were a sad reminder of how our western world had changed.

Here also a monument to the soldiers and defenders had been built, the money quickly raised by donations and placed at the edge of the cemetery, overlooking the town below. Their names were etched into large brass plaques embedded into a towering chunk of granite. It would be there for some time and rightfully so.

Reaching the edge of the valley, the wagon trail turned with the railroad tracks north towards the small mountain range at the end of the prairie and scattered forests. Our wagons bumped and groaned as their steel-clad wheels struggled to turn inside the deep ruts of the road.

I had to give the railroad credit. It connected the entire US together over long lengths of steel. Now a man could ride from New York to San Francisco in less than four days. In comparison, it took Lewis and Clark over two years to go from Illinois to the Pacific Coast. But with the railroads came government, bureaucrats, swindlers, hustlers, and tycoons, and all their villainy with them. Such is the history of the world; great blessings bring with them great challenges. Rise to the occasion or be left behind in the mud.

***

After a couple of hours of riding, Captain Brandthorn suddenly raised a hand and slowed his horse to a stop while pulling his Winchester out of its scabbard. Behind us the rumble of wagon wheels ceased, followed by the stamping of impatient hooves as horses stood idle and the creak of leather as soldiers shifted in their saddles to draw rifles as well.

I slid the *Eighty-Six* from its tooled leather scabbard. The heavy gun and its eight cartridges in the tubular magazine below the barrel gave me comfort.

We'd been approaching a watering station. It wasn't much, just a small house, quickly thrown together, with a corral beside it and a pole shed. Fifty yards away stood a large circular metal water tank raised off the ground on thick crisscrossed metal beams to feed a steam engine. Nearby a stream fed into a small pond, with hoses and pipes from a pump leading to the tank. This had been the site of a train town, where workers and crew had pitched tents and lived while working on the expanding track line. Temporary rail tracks had been laid in a circle here for the train to turn around, with the station providing water for locomotives as they waited and unloaded equipment before returning to Cheyenne. After the rail moved on, the 'town' had been razed and the rails pulled up for the next one further along the newly placed track.

Now, the corralled fence was knocked down and the remains of a butchered horse lay between us and the house.

Reaching into one of the saddle bags behind me, I pulled out Skyla's holstered pistol, knife, and rolled gun belt. Charles looked shocked as I passed them to her. She deftly slung it about her waist and cinched the buckle tight. Grimly, I tapped my heels and walked Carbine towards the head of the column as the soldiers warily watched the rolling hills for any attackers. The two Pinkertons already had their rifles nestled in the nook of their shoulders as they waited. I hoped these two would make sure of their targets before firing, unlike the last set I traveled with.

Brandthorn dropped the lever slightly on his rifle, checking the chamber to make sure it was loaded. "Lieutenant, stay with the men," he glanced at me as he snicked the lever back into place. "Shall we?"

I looked at the group of soldiers strung out behind us. "Me?" Certainly, he had enough men to ride with him to investigate.

"You've a knack for staying alive. And I'd like to stay that way as well."

I sighed. "Lucky me, I reckon." I gently kicked my heels against Carbine's flanks, and with a snort he walked cautiously towards the building.

The entire town setup had been quickly thrown together and quickly pulled apart. Trampled fields nearby showed dead grass killed by temporary tents and stacks of material. Piles of gravel and cracked rail ties lay discarded in large swaths of dried dirt. Everything was open and flat for the most part, that was why this area had been selected, but beyond it there were dips and hills nearby that could be hiding any number of enemies.

And just because apes were a bigger threat these days than the Indians, didn't mean they couldn't get stirred up as well. After the battle, Indians took as many rifles with them as they could carry. Now they would have been a much more formidable force than before, had they not lost so many braves. The Shaynee risked a lot for us and paid dearly for it, but if they hadn't, they'd have lost everything once the apes turned their attention on them.

We made it a dozen steps before Charles raced his horse to catch up to us. The Captain and I both gave him a disdainful look. The man was oblivious to our disapproval as he stood in the saddle and looked around. He carried a nickel-plated Schofield revolver in his right hand, trigger cocked back and held vertically with barrel upright, as though he were about to engage in a duel.

I rolled my eyes and we kept moving forward with the Brit shadowing us on his beautiful Arabian steed.

Our horses became skittish around the butchered carcass, and we gave the body a wide berth. The corpse looked like it had been dead for hours. Flies were already crawling over the exposed flesh and bones. The stench was strong. I pulled my red bandana up over my mouth and nose. It barely helped.

As we got closer, we saw the door to the house had been bashed off and thick three-foot-long yellow and green feathered arrows were sticking in the bodies of two men crumpled in the front yard. Beside one of them lay a fishing pole. Rounding the corner of the corral, we discovered another man had been tied to the side of the building. His shirt was ripped open, the buttons torn off. He hung limp from braided cords, rivets of dried blood running down his belt buckle and pants from the gaping wound in the center of his chest. Insects buzzed and crawled over the slash that ran from rib cage to belly button.

"Damned apes," Brandthorn muttered angrily.

Charles appeared unbothered by the sight of the dead and mutilated bodies, and his pistol stayed high and his finger straight along the trigger. "Ugly way to go," he said simply as he continued to twist about in his saddle, looking for threats.

"Yes, it is. Cover me," I told them. Dismounting, I raised the barrel of my rifle and walked forward to peek inside the building. The open shutters gave enough light inside to see there weren't any more bodies, but the place had been riffled through. Odds and ends were thrown aside, chairs and a table overturned. A small scattering of brass shells showed where at least one man had put up a token resistance briefly. But the smear of blood across the floor showed that he'd eventually been wounded, then dragged outside and gutted in offering to a dark ape god.

"Empty," I called back to Brandthorn.

"I reckon they aren't suckering us into an ambush then." The Captain waved at Daniels to bring everyone else forward. The column started moving again, this time with Skyla protected in the center. The soldiers' heads were on swivels, watching the rises and dips of the ground for any hiding attackers. Twenty-one of us should be enough to ward off an attack, but you never know.

"Do you know how many men were stationed here?" I asked Brandthorn.

"Three," he said simply as he stood in his stirrups to get a better look around us.

"No survivors then," I said grimly.

Dismounting, Charles walked over to one of the nearby bodies, grasped an arrow and jerked it out of the corpse. He curiously looked at the bloodied black tip as Skyla approached on Smoke. Around us the soldiers began directing the wagons to move into a rough circle, as an extra precaution against an attack.

"Obsidian. They use it on most of their spears and arrows tips, but only some of their larger weapons," Skyla said as she pulled an obsidian bladed knife with worn trike horn handle from the sheath on her belt.

Tossing the arrow back on top of the bloated body, Charles held his hand out and accepted the large knife. Touching the tip of his finger gently to the black blade, he watched a drop of blood well up from the tiny cut.

"Beautiful and impressive," he admitted.

"It's from Jed. The leader of the ape army that he killed carried it," she told him as he flipped the knife in his hand to look at the carved trike horn handle.

"Let me get this straight." He turned to me and raised an eyebrow. "You killed the ape, cut his heart out, ate it, then looted his corpse?"

I sighed. I was getting tired of that story. "I didn't eat the whole thing. But I'm a firm believer in the spoils of war going to the victors, and Skyla needed a good knife. Besides, if I hadn't taken it, one of the Indians would have."

Skyla took the knife back and carefully slipped it into the leather sheath. An obsidian bladed knife with trike horn hilt suited the paleontologist perfectly. And it balanced out the long barreled Merwin-Hulbert Pocket pistol on the other side of her belt well.

The circle of wagons rumbled to a halt as the officers approached us. "Must have been attacked right after the train passed by this morning," Brandthorn said as he gestured at the pair of bodies lying before us with the fishing pole. "These two never saw the attack coming. From the blood splatter around the door, the man inside managed to wing at least one of the monkeys before they grabbed him and cut his heart out." Kneeling, he traced a finger around a trike hoof print. "No telling why they did it. Either just to kill people, or to get the horse meat. I don't know."

Charles looked at the sacrificed body tied to the building. "I'd heard about the apes' savagery, but it's something else to see in person."

Skyla shook her head sadly. "You never get used to it."

Brandthorn called out to the soldiers cutting down the sacrificed man. "Place the bodies inside the building. We will send a wire back to town once we reach the end of the track. The rail company can come clear the area with their Pinkertons and bury their own dead."

Charles stepped back as a pair of soldiers grabbed one of the corpses in front of us by the feet and dragged the first body into the building. The dead man's arms dangled limply as his head and torso slid through the dirt and splotches of grass.

The Captain turned to his Lieutenant. "Make sure to send word to Smith and his bounty hunters as well. Let them know there's a group of apes in the area."

The young officer nodded, "Yes, sir."

Within minutes, the bodies were cleared away and teams of horses were being led to the manmade pond for water. A half hour later and all our horses were watered, except the Pinkerton's team who made no effort to unhook their mules from their mysterious cargo.

I asked Brandthorn what he thought they were hauling.

He shifted in his saddle to look back at the wagon in question. "Some sort of new weapon that Mr. White ordered."

That piqued my curiosity. "So, the rail tycoon ordered a gun?"

"Seems like. Only reason I know that is because I heard them talking about it back in town. White ordered it straight from Europe. Something British."

I studied the misshapen lump under the canvas. If it was a gun, it was a pretty big one. "I reckon he won't let me try it out, will he?"

"Doubtful, since you want each other dead." He slid his Winchester rifle into its scabbard. "Saddle up!" he shouted to his men. "We move in five minutes."

As they prepared themselves to move, I took one long look around the site before dodging Carbine's nip at my hat and climbing into the saddle. This place would be manned again before nightfall, and bounty hunters tracking down the attackers to collect their hairy thumbs. The wheel of life keeps turning, even after you're dead.

***

A couple of hours later, we reached the end of the tracks.

It appeared to be barely contained chaos.

Large, sweaty, dirty men hauled heavy rails between them, maneuvering the stretches of forged steel carefully into place on top of rail ties laid on beds of gravel. There, other men waited with sledgehammers to pound home thick iron spikes through the rails and into the wooden ties to hold them in place. Around them Chinamen scurried back and forth, carting loads of gravel and dirt, rail ties in wagons, and buckets of water to keep men hydrated and working. Supervisors rode horses amongst them, shouting coarsely at workers who were slowing, and rhythmic songs reached our ears from men distracting themselves from the misery of hard labor.

In the distance, crews cut trees and pulled stumps out of the way with teams of oxen, while dozens of men dug cuts into the gradual hills, leveling out a path for the gravel bed and cross ties. Other crews filled low spots and packed the dirt firm, so it wouldn't settle later and break the steel rails apart at their joints under the thousands of pounds of weight of a steam engine. Occasionally, a gout of rock and dirt would fly into the air as a rock ledge was blasted into submission by dynamite.

And along the edges of the groups of workers, rode pairs of Pinkertons, armed and willing to shoot anything that looked suspicious and out of place.

In its bid to reach the other side, the East-West Railroad was pushing their crews at a feverish pace. Trains were running along the completed portion of the track twice a day, bringing tons of timber, steel rail, gravel, and coal to the workers.

I noted the disgusted looks from the workers towards Charles. Anyone nicely dressed around them was considered to be of a different class, the sort that hard workers scorned as having soft hands. The Brit seemed oblivious to the attention as he looked around the rail site. Or maybe he simply didn't care.

Skyla rode beside me, and while Charles was receiving disapproving looks, she had all the approving and lustful looks that a rare beauty will have in a place full of lonely men. My hand inched closer to my pistol as I guided Carbine with the other. If anyone pawed at her, they were going to take a bullet for their sin.

As we watched, a black man wielding a shovel collapsed in one of the cuts, and his friends quickly pulled him out of the way and into the shade of a stopped wagon. They made sure he took several sips of water before quickly rushing back to work as their supervisor shouted at them.

"The workers are being pushed to the point of exhaustion. The railroad has declared no expense would be spared in building this section of track. They want it through to the other side and they want it now," Brandthorn was telling the young Lieutenant.

"And they'll get it. From what I hear, they're paying bonuses based off miles laid. I've half a mind to turn in my commission and pick up a shovel," Daniels said.

"And miss out on all this soldierly fun and a paycheck too?" The Captain laughed darkly.

Across the beaten dirt field, a steam locomotive huffed as its line of supply cars were unloaded. I did a double take as I noticed the passenger car at the end.

It appeared to be made of sheets of metal riveted together with small cross shaped slots for firing ports. An armored passenger car of sorts. Even the wheels had protective plates over the upper half of them. I bet the entire thing weighed an incredible amount. The coal needed for a locomotive to burn to move such a creation would be immense.

The single wagon driven by the Pinkertons left our column without a word and rode across the field. Stopping beside the steel car, the driver pulled the brake and the other hopped down and stretched. One of the heavy railcar doors opened and a black man with two tied down holsters stepped onto the small balcony attached to the back of the car.

Cato.

The gunman shut the door and leaned forward on the wrought iron balcony rails. As usual, he was dressed in all black clothing, with a flat brimmed hat pushed back on his face so he could keep an eye on the surroundings. The butts of his twin pistols exposed on his fancy tooled leather gun belt rested beneath his elbows. Inlaid silver in the holsters flashed in the sun with his movements.

"Jed-" Skyla warned as she stared.

"I see him," I scowled.

As the railroad tycoon's personal hired killer, Cato and I had a complicated past. He'd once pointed a pistol at Skyla because I was about to turn his employer's head into a canoe. It's hard to get over things like that, even though we were once childhood friends before I was whipped to the brink of death and he was taken and raised by the man who did it.

The door opened again and Reydan White, the East-West owner and former Union raider, stepped onto the small porch to survey the continued building of his empire. His face was seared into my memory. Even though his bright red beard had mostly faded to gray, it was a face I'd never forget.

My knuckles went white on Carbine's reins.

As if on cue, Cato's head swiveled toward me and he straightened. At this distance I couldn't see his dark, empty eyes. But I knew they were watching me like a hawk. One of the Pinkertons approached and spoke to Reydan, gesturing at the canvas-covered back of the wagon.

"You're not going to do anything, are you?" Skyla asked quietly.

I mulled it over. I hadn't seen either of them since I'd punched Reydan in the face after the Battle of the Apes. "That man still owes me a large debt." I rolled my shoulders as the old scar tissue across my back suddenly felt tight and restricting. Then, with a shock, I realized that when I'd run into my father in the saloon, it'd been such a surprise that I hadn't had the thought to mention that his adopted son was still alive and working for the man who burned our home two decades ago. He'd have been very interested in that tidbit of information.

"I know. And one day he'll pay for his crimes. But right now, I need you." She waved a hand around the area. "We all need you. You're the hero of Granite Falls and we've an expedition to go on in the name of discovery and science. The first of its kind in Prehistoria. Are you about to throw all of that away to gun down such a sorry excuse of a man?"

Honestly, yes. I'd risk everything for my revenge but her. She was the only reason I hadn't already cut that man's head off and put it on a spike.

But that didn't mean I had to be happy about it. If I could find a way to discretely murder the man, I'd do it. A knife through his back would be just as appealing as a bullet through his forehead. Maybe even more so if he thrashed a good bit before dying.

I forced a smile and tried to ignore my murderous thoughts. "No, I'm not. But I would like to talk to Cato," I paused, thinking of our past meetings. "If he can even speak. You know… we've never heard him say a word."

"I know. He just uses those guns to speak for him." She still held animosity towards both men as well.

The silent gunman touched the rail tycoon's arm and pointed. Turning towards us, Reydan's face twisted into an angry grimace.

Skyla didn't understand. Reydan White would try to kill me first or kill us both just out of spite from the shriveled black worm of a heart the man held inside. He knew who I was, and I was a witness to his raiding of the South after the War Between the States. Every day I lived was a threat to him. Not even counting the fact that I almost killed him a split second after we saw each other the first time. Then there was the whole punching thing… But eventually, he would have me killed before my story spread to far. And I wondered if he'd send Cato to try and do it.

Brandthorn looked back and saw Reydan and myself glaring at each other and stopped his horse, letting soldiers pass him as he waited for me to catch up.

"You're not going to do anything, are you Jed?" His heels tapped his horse's flanks, urging him back into a walk to keep pace with Skyla and myself.

"That's what Skyla asked. But no, I reckon not."

"Good. Because Cato's fast. Real fast. He killed three workers who tried to rob Reydan a week ago. They say the gunshots were like rolling thunder, one after the other, close enough that it didn't sound like he'd even had time to pull the trigger. And that's from people I know who don't exaggerate." He cut his eyes towards me. "I've seen you in action, and he's faster. My men have taken to calling him 'The Black Plague'. Not a very creative name, but effective. Most people avoid him now."

"I know. Face to face, I'd never stand a chance," I muttered. Good thing I didn't believe in a fair fight. I was more than willing to shoot a man in the back if the need arose.

The Captain leaned over in the saddle and slapped me on the back gently. "Good. I've buried enough friends as it is."

The Black Plague, ever so subtly, tilted his hat towards me with a pair of fingers as we rode out of view behind rows of dirty canvas-topped tents.

***

Passing through the temporary train town and end of the rail, we kept moving ahead and skirting around the advance crews working in the cuts to ease the grade on the iron tracks to make the engine move faster and pull more efficiently. Coal cost money, human labor is cheap.

Riding around several small forests and stands of trees, we made good time crossing the open plains and reached Fort York and the tunnel by noon.

Here the prairie ended abruptly against the Granite Mountain range. The cliff face, a good sixty feet tall, stretched a quarter mile along this section of mountain. The cliff was full of craggy rocks with small shrubs and trees attempting to make a go of it in the narrow crevasses and cracks. Piles of rocks had fallen over time and created a gentle slope of rubble at the bottom.

In front of the cliff were several long, low buildings with a waist high fence that served as Fort York. A dozen large tents were pitched nearby in neat orderly rows, giving shade and shelter to the men stationed here guarding the gate to the Shimmer and those waiting to pass through. Several dozen horses were kept in a large split rail corral built around a small stream and a pair of soldiers were forking hay to them. Others were brushing their horses, and a small forge was set up behind the corral where a man was hammering steel into shape. From somewhere in the tents came the faint musical sound of a harmonica and laughter.

When I first discovered the tunnel, I had tried to blow it shut with dynamite and collapse the mountain on top of it. Afterwards, the apes dug through and crossed their army onto our side. Since then, the top of the cliff face had been reinforced against collapsing, making the tunnel appear much like a giant mine entrance with thick wooden beams on the side and heavy timbers stretching across the top.

The opening was a touch over twenty feet tall and the base almost forty feet wide. The bottom now had an eight-foot-tall palisade built across it of thick tree trunks, with a large set of double gates that required two men on each side to open. They were taking no chances in letting more dinosaurs come through to our side, or another army of apes for that matter. If either tried, a pair of Gatlings had been placed on raised berms behind the palisade.

"You know that Jed laid claim on this land after he discovered the tunnel?" Skyla was talking to Charles. "The government took the property afterward, citing public use."

"Yes, and then they barred the public from going through to the other side without the Army's permission," I added wryly.

"Eminent Domain, huh? Rough deal, Jedidiah," Charles replied with a shake of his head.

"You could say that again. Forfeiture without compensation. They didn't even return the claim fee I paid."

Brandthorn stopped our column and dismounted to talk to one of the soldiers guarding the gate. The soldier motioned several others over and conferred with them before dispatching them into one of the buildings of the fort. Daniels rode his horse over to a small building with wires running out the roof and back in the direction we came on tall poles. No doubt to send the telegram that Brandthorn had ordered.

"What now?" Charles asked, as we sat on the horses in the hot sun.

"We wait for our escort," Skyla said simply.

Charles stood in his saddle and looked at the column of men and wagons behind us. "How big of an escort do we need?"

"Trust me, the bigger the better," I told him.

A spectacled man in a fringed leather jacket and leggings strolled out from one of the log buildings. His large mustache flared as he spied us and grinned widely.

"Jed! Skyla!" he boomed happily.

"Fredrick!" Skyla shouted back excitedly as he stormed across the yard to us.

We dismounted, and I took Smoke's reins as Skyla hugged him around the neck tightly.

The mustached hunter shook my hand firmly and his eyes twinkled behind thick glasses. "What are you two doing here?"

Skyla grinned. "It's finally time for our expedition. Just waiting to cross over. How are the hunts? I heard you were chasing a dinosaur around these parts?" The Smithsonian Institute had jumped at the opportunity to pay Fredrick to hunt dinosaurs and send their corpses back to be stuffed and put on display. He'd cleared out several beasts on this side of the tunnel so far. The only reason he hadn't hunted our red-finned fiend from the other day was because Brandthorn preferred to use the military. There was an agreement between the two parties; any beasts discovered and brought to the Captain's attention was hunted by his men. Any that Fredrick discovered on his own, he was welcome to harvest for the Smithsonian. Either way, the museum got them. According to Skyla, her father and the rest of the Board of Regents were already planning an entire new wing to be built to house the mounted dinosaurs. And it was going to be huge.

"No luck. That Shaynee squaw said she saw something little with a row of large, flat spikes along its back, but I looked all over. No sign, no track, no nothing. Whatever it is, I couldn't find it."

"I reckon the cute, defenseless, lost world creature gets to live another day," I quipped.

He glared. "I doubt it's defenseless, she said it had spikes on its tail… but it may be cute."

"What about you, Fredrick, why are you here?" Skyla patted Smoke's side.

The spectacled man adjusted his glasses. "Crossing over. I've finally gotten permission from Brandthorn to prepare a hunting expedition into the other side. But this trip I'll just be scouting a bit around the area and Fort Jipson, next time I'll bring an entourage."

Charles interrupted us. "Fredrick? Fredrick von Holsak?"

The famed hunter nodded. "Yes sir, and you are?"

"Charles Arthur, at your service." He leaned down from his saddle and stuck his hand out. "I work for Skyla's father."

After shaking hands, Fredrick twirled the end of his mustache between his fingers. "Nice to meet you, Charles."

"And you as well," Charles pursed his lips. "Did I overhear that you plan on going on a hunt? I'd very much like to go with you on a jaunt. I'm an excellent fox hunter."

"Trust me, hunting dinosaurs is a good deal different than any sort of other hunting. Foxes can't eat you. Are you going on the expedition with these two?" He gestured towards Skyla and me.

The Brit gave a curt nod. "I intend on going everywhere Skyla goes. Her mother requested I keep an eye on her."

"Really?" Fredrick shot a puzzled look at me and I shrugged with one shoulder. I would explain the situation later to him in private. The hunter turned back to our Brit. "Well Charles, it should be quite the adventure!"

Brandthorn exited the building. "Twenty minutes!" he shouted in warning and his thickly accented Irish voice reverberated against the cliff wall. A dozen soldiers, the addition to our escort I supposed, exited the building behind him and walked to the corral to ready their horses. That would bump our column up to over thirty men and one woman.

"Will you be coming with us, Fredrick?" Skyla asked.

"Why not? I was going to wait until tomorrow and ride with the reinforcements, but I'd enjoy all of your company much better." He patted the stock of the rifle slung over his back. "Besides, you never know what you might collect until you go into the woods. I'll go get my things." He waved and bounded away, full of energy.

"Fredrick von Holsak, master hunter, author, and shooter. I've seen his contributions to the Smithsonian and read of his exploits for years," Charles said admirably.

I chuckled. "Well, I don't know about master shooter. He's not the most accurate of folks."

"What?" Charles looked as though I was pulling his leg.

Skyla nodded with a slight smile. "There's a reason Wolverine Wade taught me to shoot rifles and not Fredrick. He shoots a lot, but hits little."

The British butler looked crestfallen. "Still... he's famous."

"Yes... yes, he is," I admitted.

***

The brightest brains couldn't explain the tunnel or the Shimmer inside it.

They'd studied it fanatically though over the last couple of months. But still, no one knew how it worked or why it existed. It defied reality. I'd been questioned over and over about my initial discovery, and if anything had changed since. It hadn't, the thing just was. Which created questions such as, why did it appear? How long would it stay? What or who created it? Are there more of them? Will it disappear? Too many questions, no answers. We just hoped for the best that anyone going through would be able to come back later.

Going through the tunnel was old news to Skyla and myself as well as most of our escort who'd crossed over before. Charles had read articles and reports on the Shimmer but had obviously never actually seen it. He was mighty excited to though.

As we lined up in a long column with our new escort, pairs of soldiers leaned into the heavy, reinforced gates and pushed them open into the tunnel to allow us entrance. The thick timbers creaked and shook as the men turned the doors on large steel forged hinges.

Above us, on the palisade, men stood by the Gatling guns, ready to unleash a barrage of bullets should something suddenly try to break through to our side as we entered.

Brandthorn and Daniels led the way as we rode past the gate and entered the tunnel.

Where the Shimmer was, rock walls and ceiling exposed a sudden change between sides. Granite from our side suddenly turned to limestone. Even natural cracks in the rock stopped abruptly and transformed into solid stone of the other type. A straight line ran through the center of the tunnel, crossing beneath the crushed gravel we rode over, along each side and arcing over us. A perfectly straight line, abruptly joining two worlds together.

You could see through one side to the other. Everything appeared normal at first, until you crossed through the circular visible line in the surrounding rock.

The column of soldiers went first, leaving us civilians more protected in the rear as we entered the Shimmer and large open valley on the other side. Once through, they'd post up, and keep an eye out as the rest of us followed.

When it was my turn, I walked Carbine through the Shimmer. The air rippled faintly outwards, starting with his nose first and widening outwards as he leapt through quickly, still uncomfortable with the slight tingle that came with the ripple. Smoke was more difficult, hesitating at first, but with Skyla's gentle coaching, her horse pushed her muzzle in then quickly stepped through, followed by a shake from tip to tail.

Charles' horse walked right through, and if the tingle bothered the pedigreed beast, he didn't show any sign. The Brit himself was impressed with the ripple and grinned as he passed through, before turning in his saddle to watch Fredrick ride in after him. The famed hunter whooped, and the edges of his mustache lifted with his big grin as the shimmering air radiated outwards from him then vanished.

Behind him the first of the wagons pulled through, the attached beef cattle bellowing pitifully and fighting against their ropes as they were practically dragged through the shimmer. Even a cow knew there was something unnatural about all this.

Once out of the tunnel, we rode along a rise overlooking a large valley below us with a wide river running lazily along the bottom. To our right, the open grassy hills gave way to a forest of giant trees arching hundreds of feet into the air. Green and red-tinged ferns dotted the landscape mixed amongst knee-high, thick bladed grasses and small stands of trees. On the gentle breeze blowing from the west came the faint scent of salt water.

This valley was popular with the dinosaurs, but for now only a single herd of a dozen crested dinosaurs were in view. The yellow and tan beasts, with strange colorful elongated protrusions on the backs of their heads, ripped plants from the edge of the river and warily kept an eye on their surroundings. The odd-looking dinosaurs walked on four legs, but several young, protected near the center of the group, walked on their rear legs with their front arms dangling low. From the mountains above us the screech of small pterodactyls reverberated, reminding us that even the skies here weren't safe from attack.

Charles stood in his saddle to get a better view of the valley below us. "Incredible," he exclaimed.

"Yes, it is." Even after seeing it several times, the view still gave me pause. It was another world over here. Something older, more savage and dangerous. But also, beautiful in its own way.

"Skyla, what are those magnificent beasts?" the Brit asked as he stared at the herd of dinosaurs with the odd shaped heads.

"Hadrosaurs of some type. The soldiers have taken to calling them 'Cresteds' after that long thin cranial crest that juts out behind their heads. It's a species we haven't discovered on our side yet... Or maybe never will. But they are pretty peaceful creatures and show no fear of man."

"Could be because they are almost twice as tall as one of us," I said wryly.

The column kept moving, and I noted that most of the soldiers appeared to have done this so often as to have become routine. But I was pleased to see the men pull rifles from scabbards and rest them across saddle pommels. We were in dangerous territory now, with all manner of creatures that would kill and eat us if they could. From here until Fort Jipson, there would be little relaxing.

As we rode the winding trail through the forest, the heat and humidity became stifling, and I poured some water from my canteen onto my red checkered bandana and unbuttoned a couple of buttons on my shirt to cool off.

Charles saw the large black claw hanging from a braided cord around my neck. "What's that from?"

Skyla leaned forward to see what he was pointing at and smiled. I rubbed the claw between my fingers. "It's from an Allosaurus that tried to eat me."

He squinted against the sunlight. "Must have been a small one."

I chuckled without humor. Smartass. "It was a juvenile, but killing it was no easy task."

"I should say it wasn't. I've killed a few things not nearly so big, and it's been hard to do," Fredrick added as he removed his spectacles and mopped sweat off his face with his shirt sleeve.

"I made that for him," Skyla said. "It was the smallest claw the dinosaur had. Jed would look rather silly with a nine-inch dinosaur claw hanging from his neck."

"It's basically a pinky toe," Fredrick said with a grin.

"And I promised to never take it off." For as long as I lived, I would never forget the terror, rage, or choking smoke from the flames as I helplessly emptied my guns into the beast. It had soaked up everything I had and kept coming. If it hadn't been for a box of left-over dynamite, I'd have been dinosaur food.

Charles turned away rebuked, finished with our conversation and preferring to watch the small pterodactyls in the giant trees as we rode the wagon trail through the towering forest. The trail was well established now, a pair of deep ruts that meandered through the forest and around the massive trees. Some work had been done, smaller shrubs, ferns, and trees cut out of the way. But it was still slow going.

We made it another half a mile before passing a carriage coach thrown onto its side.

The door had been ripped off; the edges pulled away. Large tooth and claw marks showed where it had been shredded apart like a tin can. Dried blood was splattered on the side. The leather seat inside had been chewed away, and something skittered around inside. We slowed as we rode past.

A Private near me leaned over in his saddle to speak. "A senator. Came from back east to see this lost world place," he spat to the side. "I was with them." He pointed to our right. "A giant beast came out of the woods. It soaked up dozens of bullets as it ripped the coach apart. Yanked the man out and carried him off, screaming."

"I read about that in the papers. What'd the dinosaur look like?"

"Big. Yellow and green. Long snout full of teeth and sharp claws," the soldier shrugged. "About like most things on this side. All ugly."

"Private Hendricks! Close your mouth and pay attention!" A gruff looking black Sergeant at the front of the column glared back at us over a shoulder.

The soldier rolled his eyes then looked away from me and back into the woods around us. Feeling a bit abashed at getting him in trouble, I let Carbine plod along and Hendricks pass me.

"I don't like you being here, Skyla," I overheard Charles say faintly behind me.

"I'm sorry. But this is where I belong," she replied.

"You belong in the museum... studying, learning. Teaching, even! But not in the field," he protested. "This is no place for a woman."

"I've been in the field since I've arrived," she sounded exasperated.

"You've been at risk since you've arrived," he tried to correct her.

"Is this what my mother has you up to? Convincing me to return?"

"Of course. But in the meantime, I'm to help protect you, including from Jedidiah."

I grinned and pulled back on the reins to slow Carbine down. He snorted and tossed his head but obeyed, and a few moments later I was between the pair.

"How's it going?" I asked innocently.

Charles grunted and tapped Sir Lancelot's flanks, riding into my spot in the column ahead and giving Skyla and myself a tiny bit of privacy as we rode along.

"He's not happy I'm here," she said with a toss of her black hair.

"Well, I'm not happy you're here either." At the withering look she gave me, I smiled. "But I do support you. You were born for this. And you're the best person here for it." I gave her my most roguish grin. "Honest Injun."

She laughed. "Thanks, Jed."

***

When I first visited the ape canyon, the big monkeys had moved large boulders into the opening and shallow river that flowed from the entrance to slow down any beasts or attackers that might want into the canyon. Which made me wonder just who the apes had been worried about being attacked by when there were several hundred of them in the canyon. But once our army took it over and turned it into Fort Jipson, the rocks had been dragged aside. We humans preferred large open spaces, so we could put a lot of bullets into anything coming at us. And the boulders pulled aside helped make a nice funnel to drive attackers directly into our fire.

Fort Jipson was a tentative hold on this lost world, but we intended to keep it.

"After the Battle of the Apes, I can't believe you wouldn't pick the high ground," I told Brandthorn, referring to the valley that Granite Falls was in and how that gave the attackers an advantage.

He grimaced. "It wasn't my choice, like usual. We were ordered to secure the apes' base of operations for research purposes. None of which I care about. Being here puts us at a severe tactical disadvantage; if apes lined the walls, they could fire arrows over almost the entire canyon. But it makes it easier to keep dinosaurs out, which I assume is why my superiors chose it as well."

"Any dinosaurs try to come in?"

"A few trikes have wandered back. The guards have been told to let them through. The scientists can't seem to get enough of them. Some of them are docile enough that we can pet them, but no one has dared to try and ride one yet."

"What about raptors?" The apes used them like feathered attack dogs and the vicious little beasts were quick to gut a man with their talons and teeth. I figured like a dog; they would be likely to return to their master's camp if lost.

"Just one. It didn't get far before the guards cut her down."

I was silent as we rode along the slow flowing river that twisted out of the canyon entrance. At the narrowest part of the canyon entrance was a manmade wall made of boulders, piled earth, and logs. There weren't many trees nearby that were small enough for us to use, but we were able to cut down some inside the canyon that were manageable. Dirty white canvas tarps were stretched overhead to give shade to the men manning the opening and the four Gatlings that stood ready to unleash death at a moment's notice.

Captain Brandthorn stopped to talk to the men guarding the entrance as we rode in with Lieutenant Daniels.

Once past the makeshift palisade, the column fell apart at Daniels' dismissal. Soldiers split off to water and care for their horses, while the cattle were led to a separate corral closer to the caves where the butchering and cooking was done. We'd lucked out; dinosaurs could eat the plants on our side it seemed, and our cattle and horses could eat theirs on this side as well. But from what I'd heard, they'd brought a small herd of sheep over, and they got sick within several days and had to be put out of their misery. The discussion of what caused that was still going on.

A small fort may have been established here, but there were still no framed buildings, making it more of an encampment than a hardened outpost. It was hard enough to bring men, cattle, and supplies into the canyon as it was, much less heavy loads of lumber. Once the railroad was built through the tunnel, giving the fort faster reinforcements from Fort York and the rough wagon trail more protection, the canyon would have log buildings soon enough.

As for troops, there was about a hundred of them stationed here. Half of them rotated in and out at one-month intervals. This caused a lot of problems in town. After a month away from women and drink, they tended to get wild when they returned to civilization. Sheriff Beauford kept busy arresting them for the night, or longer, which gave Captain Brandthorn no end of a headache I was certain. Both from his own troublesome men and dealing with an ornery Sheriff.

The thirty extra soldiers that escorted us in would stay the night and return tomorrow with the emptied wagons once the usual reinforcements arrived and swapped out with the men already here. It would be crowded tonight, with lots of men sleeping under the open sky. There were the caves that folks could have slept in, but they all stunk from the apes living in them. It smelled like a mixture of wet dog, skunk, and smoke. I doubted that they would ever air out.

In addition to the troops, there were probably a dozen scientists from around the country here as well, going over the caves and left over tools from the apes plus whatever dinosaurs they might spy on short trips outside the canyon. The tamed trikes that came back also kept them busy. They were corralled in the back of the canyon with a thick log and boulder fence. It didn't seem strong enough to hold them, but it worked so far. They seemed content to simply eat inside their containment and be observed by the scientists.

The ritual stone was still present, its obsidian altar giving a dark looming presence inside the canyon. A solemn reminder of the brutality and savagery of the apes.

"Jed, Skyla, Fredrick!" Daniels called to us from where he sat on the back of his horse, watching his men turn to their designated tasks.

We rode our horses over to where he waited. "Captain said to meet him in the big tent in thirty minutes and we'll go over the expedition plans. In the meantime, I'm to show you your lodgings. If you'll follow me, we'll put the horses to pasture and see what we can scrounge up for a place to sleep." He turned to Fredrick, "By the way, Captain also said no shooting anything, unless we're under attack or he gives you permission."

The famous hunter laughed. "Well, I certainly hope that doesn't happen. I'm simply here as a visitor for now." He pointed at the waterfall at the back of the canyon, cascading over a hundred feet over the cliffs and into a large pool at its base from which the river flowed through the fort. "I am tempted to try some fishing though. No one said I couldn't fish!"

Daniels curled his lip in disgust. "Good luck, I hear they've caught some hideous critters out of that pool."

"Perfect for the Smithsonian," Fredrick's mustache flared as he grinned toothily. "The uglier, the better."

***

Our lodgings consisted of a scattered collection of tents amongst the scientists' area. I would be sharing a tent with Fredrick, while Charles was sharing with a scientist from California and Skyla had a tent all to herself nearby.

Thirty minutes later, we'd unpacked what few belongings we'd brought, and entered the large command tent only to find ourselves with Daniels, Brandthorn and a tall, thin Captain named Hawney who rotated command of the fort with Brandthorn every other month. We were all standing around a poorly filled out map lying across a makeshift table in the center of the room. A pair of lanterns hung from pegs on the tent posts, but with the front and back tent flaps thrown open, there was plenty of sunlight to see by and a slight breeze that cooled us off and ruffled the papers on the table.

Since Fredrick wasn't coming with us on the expedition, he was busy lurking around the scientists, trying to get a feel for any new dinosaurs they may have seen, as well as telling of his adventurous exploits to anyone who would listen. I expected after this trip to Fort Jipson, he'd come back with a posse full of hunters, trappers, and butchers to start collecting anything that breathed on this side. Idly, I wondered if it bothered the Smithsonian with how many bullet holes were in the hides they mounted.

"One more and we'll all be here," Daniels mused as he walked over and looked out the tent entrance. "Ah, here we go."

The Lieutenant stepped aside as a large man entered the canvas draped room, dressed in a rumpled suit with glasses perched on the end of a bulbous nose. He was so tall that he had to duck his head to stand inside the tent. Sweat poured from his face and soaked into the collar of his shirt. It was entirely too hot to be wearing a dress coat, but this man was.

"Skyla, Jed. This is Beau Gable," Captain Hawney made the introduction. "He's a paleontologist dispatched from the Museum of Natural Science in Chicago and will be foraying with you on your expedition."

Gable half bowed, then pressed his spectacles back on his nose with a finger. "Nice to make your acquaintances," he said breathlessly.

I smiled politely and nodded in greeting as Hawney introduced each of us in turn, but inwardly cringed. The scientist didn't seem fit enough to survive this trip. He was breathing heavily just after the exertion of walking to the command tent. And this was the sort of dangerous expedition you read about where the majority of its participants don't make it back.

"Nice to meet you, Beau," Skyla gushed. "I've read several of your journals. Your article on the Ankylosaurs was especially well written. And from the ones we saw on our last visit to this side, you were correct on many accounts."

"Yes, ah... thank you," he took a deep wheezing breath. "However, having observed several Ankylosaurus grazing along the riverbank by the tunnel, I can tell you that my article was wrong in some regards. I thought the clubbed tail was purely defensive, but I saw it being used to communicate by occasionally thumping on the ground in warning. It's..." he raised his hands in mock resignation, "rather fascinating to see your life's work in front of you being proved right and wrong at the same time."

She nodded. "I understand completely. We've hypothesized for years and now we are seeing the truth of the matter firsthand."

Captain Hawney coughed politely to get our attention. "Since I'll be leaving the fort in Captain Brandthorn's hands tomorrow, I'll let him take over the briefing from here. Ms. Stratten, gentlemen..." He gave us a nod with a slight smile then turned and exited the tent.

Brandthorn wasted no time and pointed at the map. The only portion sketched in any detail was the nearby areas around the fort and the trail that led to the tunnel back to the other side.

"This is what little information our scouts have given us. The river that flows through our fort we've taken to calling 'Trike River' and eventually meets with 'Ape River' that runs through the valley below the tunnel, before ending at what we assume is an ocean since it's salt water. But it could very well be a massive salt lake like the one the Mormons live near in Utah." He shrugged. "Either way, our scouts haven't strayed far because we keep losing them. Some have simply disappeared, others killed and eaten by beasts. Their mangled remains found later by others…" He raised his head, looking at us pointedly. "Be careful out there. I can't stress that enough. You'll have twenty soldiers armed with repeaters, plus Lieutenant Daniels and yourselves. You should be able to fend off any dinosaurs or apes you come across. But as the red-finned beast that Jed killed on our side proves, they don't have any fear of gunfire. To them it's just another loud noise and some pain. Over here, that's nothing compared to these beasts roaring and trying to eat each other."

He pointed at the large, sweating scientist who was busy wiping his brow with a soaked handkerchief. "Beau, you're new to this group. Jedidiah has the most experience of anyone with apes and dinosaurs. Skyla was at the Battle of the Apes, and Charles, you seem to carry yourself well and you are armed. That's good, stay that way. Beau, you just stay safe."

The scientist nodded rapidly then looked at the rest of us almost apologetically. He raised his hands, palms up. "I'm a pacifist. So, there'll be no help from me if a fight occurs."

"Make no mistake, Gable," I spoke up from across the table, "there'll be fighting. You have studied these creatures; you know their size and ferocity. They'll try to kill and eat us, and then there's the apes to worry about. I'd feel better if you were armed."

"No… ah, no sir. I don't believe in guns."

I rolled my eyes and ground my teeth in disgust. Skyla looked at me and grimaced. She'd come a long way from the girl who reluctantly shot an ape to save her friends to a full-fledged, pistol toting westerner in a short amount of time. It didn't take much to convince her that out here, life expectancy increases depending on the level to which you are armed and capable of fighting back.

"That's noble of you," Charles interjected. "I'll do my very best to look out for you."

"Thank you, sir," Beau replied.

"So will the soldiers. That's why they are with you. You should be well protected," Brandthorn motioned to his second in command. "Before I pass the rest of the briefing over to Lieutenant Daniels, you should know that there will be two more men arriving with the reinforcements tomorrow. Mr. Parsons, a journalist for the New York Times, who will be coming with us on the expedition, and his photographer, a Mr. Webley, who will be staying here. So, prepare to be bombarded with their questions and be ready to pose for photographs." He grinned at me. "Jed, you might want to do something about that mop of hair of yours."

Skyla patted my back. "I'll cut it tonight. Got to make sure my man is presentable."

I groaned. The last thing I wanted was photos of me plastered in one of the most popular newspapers in America. I'd have to avoid both men like leprosy.

Chuckling, the Captain took a step back. "Lieutenant Daniels, if you will, please."

The young officer stepped closer to the table and began to move a finger along the map. "This is us, Fort Jipson. From here, we'll follow Trike River north until it hits Ape River. From there, we'll turn east, circling out," he shifted his finger in a wide circular arc, "all through this area the best we can, and back to the Trike River that feeds into our little canyon base at the waterfall. Essentially, we'll be covering a loop to the north and east around Fort Jipson."

He took a rock from a small pile beside the map and carefully placed one near the center of the blank area we were going to travel through. "Our scouts have seen a large mountain in the distance. It looks like a dormant volcano. We expect that this is where the altar rock outside came from, as well as most of the apes' obsidian tips for their weapons. Which means there may be some apes in the area. We don't know. Regardless, we're going to play it safe and give the mountain a wide berth."

Brandthorn spoke up from where he stood behind his Lieutenant. "As discussed before, this is a scientific expedition. There is to only be defensive engagement with any apes you may cross paths with. Any information you find that shows us where their civilization is located will be useful, but under no circumstances are you to follow or backtrack any apes you discover. Stick to studying dinosaurs and vegetation. Science is the purpose of this foray, not battle. Any questions?"

"Any signs of people?" Skyla asked. When I first discovered the canyon, I'd witnessed a human having his heart ripped out. We later found out that he was not of our side, and we'd also found several strange artifacts that could have only come from our world hidden in the depths of the ape caves. Also, according to their own history, the Shaynee Indians were descendants of whoever lived here. This was more proof that in previous times our two worlds had collided before through the Shimmer or one like it.

The Captain nodded. "Yes. Some footprints around the fort edge. But our patrols haven't seen anyone. We hope they'll try to reach out to us soon. Keep an eye out for any natives or any sign of where they are coming from. They seem harmless so far, but you can never tell. Anything else?"

I shifted my rifle to my other shoulder and looked at Brandthorn. "Have you seen the Tyrannosaur around here? Or any other dinosaurs that will pose a threat to us?"

When I first crossed over, Carbine and I had witnessed a monstrous dinosaur chasing a flock of flightless birds as I backtracked the apes that attacked me at my house. The beast was terrifying to behold, and the ground shook as it raced after its prey. Its roar was so loud that my ears rang afterwards. And there were times I'd woken in a cold sweat after dreaming about the Tyrannosaur chasing me. It was the most fearsome creature I'd ever seen.

Captain Brandthorn stepped forward to the table, "No tracks or sign of any kind. But, as Skyla has informed me, there's no telling how large of an area a single Tyrannosaur may roam. As for any other large beasts, well, just about all of them are big." He grinned crookedly, then grew serious. "We have seen raptor tracks though, and we suspect they've killed at least one of our scouts before we stopped sending men out by themselves. If you come across any, kill them. We've a shoot on sight order for them."

I nodded, and Skyla nervously shifted closer to me. The raptors were vicious little feathered creatures, and she'd had her own close run in with them before the Battle of the Apes. It'd been a near thing.

There were no other questions, but Beau Gable looked like he'd eaten something that disagreed with him. I worried about his presence on the expedition.

"Okay, folks. This is it. Tomorrow the men will arrive, and the morning after you will set off on the first expedition of the lost world of Prehistoria." Brandthorn looked at each of us. "This is history in the making. I've the utmost faith that you will be successful. Take it easy and get some rest. Life is going to get hard once you leave."

Gable gulped loudly.

***

We spent the remainder of the day going through the caves gouged and carved out of the canyon's side. Charles was fascinated, and since Gable had studied them extensively over the past week, he acted as our guide.

There was only a single cave that was off limits. A door had been built on the entrance into that room and padlocked. Gable grumbled about not knowing what was in there, but the military was holding that close to the chest. Rumors abounded about what was on the other side, the most popular seemed to be a vein of gold that ran deep into the canyon side. Those of us who'd originally entered, Skyla, me, and Fredrick, had been sworn to secrecy by Brandthorn.

I supposed, rightfully so, that both Captain Brandthorn and Haywood were worried the cave paintings on the walls were real and not mythological or religious.

Personally, I figured it was real. Because why not? Anything was possible on this side, and it worried me.

Gable wheezed and pointed at a large finger-painting mural of stick figure apes around a central figure painted in red dye. "As you can see here, the apes have been sacrificing for some time. I'd love to witness one. Out of a morbid curiosity of sorts." He laughed. It was a high-pitched tittering sound that reverberated off the rock walls.

Shaking my head in disgust, I told him, "I've seen them. They ain't that great."

He reached out and grasped my arm. For such a weak looking man, he had an equally weak grip. "You've actually witnessed a sacrifice? Tell me more! I hear they remove the heart while it still beats!"

I pulled my arm away, disgusted at the paleontologist's eagerness. "They chant, beat their fists against their chests, then one of them guts a man alive." I narrowed my eyes at him. "You do understand a man dies, right? Painfully."

"Astounding. And of course I do. Very sad. What sort of knife do they use?"

Charles pointed at Skyla's belt where the obsidian bladed knife was sheathed. "With something like that."

Skyla glared at the British butler as though he'd given away something she wanted to keep secret, then drew the blade with a sigh. "Careful, it's sharp."

Gable grabbed it from her hand and spun it over in the lantern light. The caves had numerous holes carved in the rock for torches, but with good old fashioned American ingenuity, we just hammered steel spikes into the rock and hung lanterns instead.

"It's magnificent." He rubbed his hand along the trike horn handle. "And this... this is intriguing. We've found several artifacts made with trike horn, but this is by far the nicest piece. I'd very much like to have it for our collection. What would you take for it?"

Skyla gently pried the chipped blade knife from his fingers and slid it back into the sheath. "It's not for sale."

He looked saddened by the news. "Well, if you change your mind. I'll pay handsomely."

"What sort of gods do these apes worship, Gable?" Charles asked him, changing the subject.

"We don't know. Strangely, we haven't found anything that seems to deify any godlike beings. They do have all sorts of dinosaurs painted, but they certainly aren't worshipping them." He thumbed in the direction of the locked door. "I want to know what's in there. I don't care if it's a gold vein the size of my leg, I want to see what's on the walls."

So, Gable believed the gold rumor. I'd started that one and was pleased to see it was catching. But the two Captains and the Army couldn't keep the truth locked away forever. At some point we'd have to deal with the possibility of dragons existing. It was almost as if the government didn't know how to combat such a possibility, so they decided to not prepare anyone for such a thing.

But then, maybe it was just some evil mythological god that the apes worshiped that never existed.

***

The sun was lowering itself over the valley's edge as we made our way out of the caves. A scientist stood in our way, with his black suit tightly fitted around his ample waist and a black top hat rested firmly on his head. A pair of Pinkertons flanked him, armed with rifles slung and pistols tucked into holsters.

"Oscar," I growled.

When we'd first met, the fat little scientist had come with Skyla to Granite Falls to see my dead Allosaurus, then fled the town before the battle, only to end up in Reydan White's employ. I'd once pointed a pistol barrel between his eyes for calling me an imbecile, so there was a little bad blood between us still.

He rolled his eyes and grasped his lapel between his fingers. "Of course, you are here... Decapitate anything lately?"

"Day ain't over yet," I smirked back at him. He'd taken issue with how I killed attacking dinosaurs and apes, which was namely by any method possible. But I did cut the head off my Allosaurus so that Sheriff Dan could haul it into town as a warning for everyone. Oscar took great offense at me damaging the first living dinosaur discovered in such a grotesque fashion.

"How have you been, Oscar?" Skyla asked her old boss.

Oscar looked at her in obvious surprise as though noticing her for the first time. He blinked. "Why are you here?"

Charles stepped beside her and fixed Oscar with a glare.

"Oh, and look, you brought your father's lap dog, the royal British butler," Oscar chortled.

Charles smirked and took a half step forward towards the paleontologist. Both Pinkertons rested their hands on their holstered pistols in warning. "You always were a slimy little man." He turned to Skyla, "If you need me, I'll be checking on our horses." The Brit gave a disgusted look at Oscar, then quickly walked away towards the corrals.

"I never could stand him," the short former paleontologist said, apparently amused with his ability to get under Charles' skin so easily.

Skyla answered his earlier question, "I'm here for the same reason as you, Oscar, research and science. But without the exploitation-"

"Don't be so naïve," he cut her off. "If we don't exploit our discoveries, we'll never be able to fund more of them. Come to our side, Skyla. Working for a bunch of stuffy old suits who think they are scientific nobility is beneath you. If you hadn't been here already, they'd never have let you become involved with such a discovery as all of this."

He was speaking the truth. Skyla's father was one of the head regents of the Smithsonian, and it'd taken her years to convince him to let her travel west to the dig sites, which led to her meeting me and my dead Allosaurus.

"That's not who I am, Oscar. You know that. I'm here for the knowledge and the thrill of discovery."

"Yes, I suppose so," he shrugged indifferently, as though he had never cared what she chose in the first place. "There's plenty of that around here. Although did I hear that you're going on an expedition?"

"We are. We leave tomorrow once our escort arrives."

"It's a shame that I wasn't asked to come along." He peered around me towards the command tent where I assumed Hawney, Brandthorn, and Lieutenant Daniels were still working. "After all, I know more than you do. At any rate, good luck." Oscar nodded to us stiffly, then waddled past me towards the cave entrance with his protective detail in tow. Both of the Pinkertons snatched a pair of lanterns from a table beside the entrance and quickly lit them before leading the former paleontologist inside.

Skyla and I watched them go.

"I'm glad Oscar's not coming, but I wish Fredrick were. The more guns the merrier," I told her.

She put her arm around my waist and rested her head against my shoulder. "It really bothers you that Beau Gable isn't carrying, doesn't it?"

"The notion of being disarmed baffles me; it's unbecoming of a man."

Thumping a fist against my chest, she looked up at me. "That's probably because you're paranoid."

I grinned. "Well, yes. There is that. But it keeps a fella alive."

***

Once the sun went down, the temperature dropped to a more tolerable degree. My little group gathered around a fire, not to stay warm, but for companionship. Fredrick cleaned one of his rifles while the rest of us made small talk.

"Charles, what do you think of this side?" Skyla asked as she snipped off a lock of my hair. Where she'd found scissors, I didn't know, but I didn't appreciate whoever loaned them to her.

"It's incredible. I had read reports and news articles of course but seeing it in person is different. I never would have thought such a place could exist."

"It's something else, that's for sure." I looked around at the darkened cliff walls rising around us. Beyond them was incredible discoveries waiting to be found, along with untold dangers. And in one more day, I was about to go with Skyla in search of them both.

Fredrick looked up at me as he ran a cleaning patch through the barrel of his rifle. "You were the first man to cross through the Shimmer, and the first to lay eyes on this canyon. What do you think now, seeing us here?"

Charles glanced over the flames at me, his eyebrows rising and obviously unknowing of my part in initially finding this place.

"I backtracked some apes that attacked me at my ranch, and found this place," I explained to him before pointing up at a section of the rock edge. "Right over there, I lay and watched their leader gut a man and rip out his heart."

"A terrible thing to see." Fredrick pulled the cleaning rod from his rifle and checked the patch on the end. It was light brown. The humidity on this side was hell on blued metal.

"It was. And I can still pick out spots where I shot the apes afterwards. Heck, I can show you where I missed their leader and blasted a chunk of obsidian out of their altar. But I never thought that we'd be here, taking over their place and making it our own fort."

"Who was the man they sacrificed?" Charles asked. "A rancher? Or just some unlucky bloke?"

"He was certainly unlucky. But I don't know. I thought he was one of the Shaynee at first but found out later he was from this side. But so far, no one has seen hide nor hair of any other men here. And then there's the old flintlock pistol and armored breastplate we found in the caves." I looked up at Skyla standing behind me and shrugged. "No one seems to know how they ended up over here."

She ran a comb through my hair before making another snip of the scissors. "One of the great mysteries of this side. We've no idea. Best guess is another tunnel opened long ago and some items found their way over. But both the gun and armor were certainly European in origin."

"Where are they now?" Fredrick asked.

"Smithsonian, being studied," she replied.

It was quiet except for the crackle of flames, the distant murmur of voices from an encampment preparing itself for night, and Fredrick working the small cleaning brush inside his rifle's chamber. I made a mental note to clean the *Eighty-Six* and my Peacemakers tomorrow morning before we stepped off. I'd cleaned them before we left Granite Falls, but it was a habit of mine to clean my weapons before doing anything dangerous. Skyla was right; I was paranoid about more than a few things when it came to weapons.

"The apes almost make the Indians look tame," Charles said suddenly.

I thought about it for a moment before responding, "Indians are noble in their own way. They have a sense of honor. They also scalp folks which is utterly barbaric. But then we believe in owning land, and they think we are daft in the head for that. They also think we are horrible for giving them small pox infested blankets and wiping out the buffalo herds to starve them out."

"So, you side with the heathens? That white men should leave their land and them alone?" Charles asked flatly.

"No. We white men are conquerors and settlers. We move into new areas and the natives can either join or die. Cultures clash. Always. It's the way of the world. Might ain't always right, but the mighty will prevail most often," I argued.

"Interesting thought. Being a historian of sorts, I've concluded that the natives are doomed. Technologically and culturally, they cannot compete. Either they assimilate, or they will end up pushed to the most miserable patches of land our government can find. Somewhere out of the way of progress," Charles shook his head. "But keep in mind there is a ninety-nine percent failure rate for civilizations. The Indians may outlast us all."

"They did survive long before us," Fredrick offered. "With far less than what we have."

"I've found them rather romantic," Skyla added with a smile as she dusted clippings of black hair off my shoulders. "Except for Otto, they seem nice."

I laughed. "You've only seen them at their best. Giving us shelter after being attacked by apes, fixing up Ashley and Oscar, and coming to our aid during battle." I shook my head. "You haven't seen them murder, rape, pillage and torture. They can be utter savages as well."

"But so can we whites," Charles stated sarcastically.

"Yes, sir." I looked at the moon-illuminated valley around us. "We men are wretched things."

"I recognize that. Shakespeare?"

"No. Homer from the Iliad."

He looked at me in surprise. "You've read the Iliad?"

"And the Odyssey. As I told you and Skyla's mother, I've something of an education. I also spent a lot of my free time reading." I sighed. There were long periods where my father's gang did nothing. Times where we had no leads or targets to go after. Those days were spent working odd jobs and father made sure I continued my studies. As a learned man himself, he was a wealth of information and knowledge that he passed on to me.

"A wise man," the Brit suggested.

I didn't say anything. If only they knew the truth. I glanced at Skyla as she tossed the last clippings of my hair into the flames. If only she knew...

"All done, Jed. What do the rest of you think?" she asked the others.

"He looks respectable," Fredrick said.

Charles nodded. "He could almost pass as civilized now."

I ran a hand over my shortened hair. It felt odd, I usually cut it myself with a knife, so it was something else to be trimmed to shape by a woman. "Thanks, Skyla," I said honestly, even though I hoped I didn't look like some sort of a dandy now.

Leaning down, she kissed me on the cheek. "You're welcome."

"I believe I'll turn in," Fredrick said abruptly, yawning as he put away his cleaning gear into an oiled leather pouch. "In this place, you never know what dawn may bring."

"Same here. Goodnight, Skyla, Jed." Charles stood and dusted the seat of his pants before walking towards his tent.

That left just Skyla and myself. She shifted over into the spot that Fredrick left and leaned against me. "It's good to see Fredrick again. But what do you think of Charles?"

I thought about the Stratten family butler. "He cares for you very much and doesn't trust my intentions. And I don't blame him one bit." I brushed my lips against hers and smiled, her face inches away from mine. "Do you think he's watching right now?" I asked, my words soft so they wouldn't carry.

She laughed as a loud cough came from behind us.

Surprised, I turned and saw Brandthorn looking at the two of us nestled together, the corners of his mouth turned upward in a slight smile. "Am I interrupting?"

"Yes-" I started to say.

"No," Skyla said at the same time. "I was just about to retire for the evening." She kissed me again and patted my back before standing and walking to her tent. I watched her open the flap, smile at me, then disappear inside as Brandthorn sat across the fire. Searching around my spot, I found a thin twig to poke the fire with as the Captain got settled.

"Just wanted to share some last minute news with you." He met my eyes above the flickering flames. "Mr. White will be here when you get back. He's also bringing with him a small army of Pinkerton Detectives."

I flicked the twig into the fire and ground my teeth. "And here I was hoping to escape his presence on this side. Why's he coming here?"

"He's adamant that he has a front row seat for the construction of the railroad through the tunnel and wants to visit the fort. I didn't have a choice; I was ordered to allow him passage. Our government has a stake in his trains running through to Prehistoria." He raised a hand. "Jed, I know there's bad blood between you two, but I need you to keep the peace. No fighting, shooting, or anything else. You need to promise me when you come back from the expedition, you'll play nice."

I chewed on the inside of my lips for a moment before slowly nodding. Most likely, this wouldn't be the time or place to kill him. But it might offer me a chance if I was lucky. "I promise," I lied easily.

Captain Brandthorn stood. "Thank you, Jed."

"Hey, Captain?" I spoke softly.

"Yes?"

I looked up at him. "Gable was asking about that locked door in the caves. Seems a lot of scientists are getting really intrigued about what might be on the other side. Eventually you'll have to do something about that."

He nodded thoughtfully as he glanced around to see if we were along. "Those damned cave paintings of apes worshipping fire breathing dragons. We should have just scraped them off the wall... What's the chances that dragons are real?"

"On this side? What's the chances that they aren't real?" I scoffed. "Anything seems possible over here. Hell, there are pterodactyls everywhere. Why shouldn't there be another giant flying lizard that happens to breathe fire?"

"What does Skyla think?"

I scuffed my toe in the dirt surrounding the fire pit. "She thinks it's possible. She said there are some sort of Bombardier beetles on our side that can mix chemicals in their body to shoot out flaming acid from their butts. So why not something larger with wings on this side?"

He rubbed his chin. "Could you imagine? How could we defend against something like that?"

"We need to consider the possibility. But off the top of my head, lots and lots of gunfire."

"Keep your eyes open on this expedition. If the apes have dragons, heaven help us."

I nodded, more to myself than him as he walked back towards his command tent, leaving me alone with the small crackling fire and the small sounds of soldiers and scientists in the darkened encampment around me. Occasionally, something roared fiercely in the distance.

Stooping forward, I pushed the small stack of extra firewood further away from the ringed fire. It would burn out in a few hours. I stood and stretched, looking around. There were probably a dozen small fires such as mine, plus a couple of larger ones that ringed the outside edge of the tents where the guards stood post. The canyon was empty, but that didn't mean something couldn't crawl or slither down the cliff face and into our camp while we slept. As long as I was staying here, it'd be restless sleep and constant watchfulness. This place was full of threats.

Ducking into my canvased tent, I quietly pulled my boots off and left them on the floor nearby. My rifle and gun belt lay beside me. I tended to sleep on my side, which made the guns really dig into me and made sleeping uncomfortable. My double-barreled shotgun rested near my head, removed from the bedroll where I normally kept it.

I also slept fully clothed. This side was so full of surprises that I didn't feel comfortable unless I was ready for battle in a moment's notice. Gripping the black claw hanging from my neck, I rubbed its worn surface, closed my eyes, and fell asleep to the sound of Fredrick's soft snoring.

***

The rustle of grass woke me.

I lay still, and the sound came again.

Pushing the blanket off, I quietly reached for the sawed-off shotgun. The noise wasn't the sound of boots, but the steps were heavy. The faint glow of fading firelight reflected moving shadows outside the canvas. Feeling a sense of dread, I cocked one of the hammers back with my free hand, muffling the faint click with the other.

Whatever was outside was moving quietly, as if it didn't want to be heard.

Reaching over, I shoved Fredrick and his snoring stopped abruptly. In the dimly lit darkness, I saw his eyes blink once, twice, and then his face turn towards me, puzzled. I gestured outside of the tent with the twin barrels.

One of the shadows stopped.

The flap opening to the tent shifted, and a large, hairy hand reached through.

It wasn't human.

That was enough for me.

Jerking the shotgun up, I fired past the hand and through the canvas at the large shadow outside. The burst of flame from the barrel was blinding as an ape roared in pain and anger.

At my booming shot, the camp suddenly woke with startled shouts of surprised men and immediately followed with the powerful roars of apes on the attack.

Quickly cocking the second hammer, I fired again through the cloth, lower this time, and the shadow fell and thrashed.

Ripping a pistol from my gun belt beside me, I dove through the tent flap, landing on top of the wounded ape. The bloodied and buckshot mangled seven-foot-tall hairy savage bared his yellowed canines and weakly grasped for me. I knocked his hands aside, shoved the pistol barrel under his chin and pulled the trigger.

The broad, ugly black face went slack as brains and goo splattered me from the bullet bursting through his skull.

He was a big fellow. Black hair covered his body except for his face and muscular chest that'd been painted with red and white swirls and patterns. The hide cloth wrapped around his waist had a small knife tucked into it, and beside him lay a large, decorated spear with an obsidian tip.

Around our encampment, tents burst into fire as apes flung burning logs and sticks from the dying fires onto the dry canvas tops. Bright flames shot up into the night sky, adding to the chaos and confusion.

Screams came from the nearby tents as the unarmed and helpless scientists were being attacked. Shifting shadows showed heavy clubs being swung and thick spears being thrown or jabbed through men as they struggled to arm themselves or escape the deadly confines of their tents.

Fredrick burst from the tent after me, and without hesitation, raised his rifle and fired at an ape tugging a spear out of a motionless man at its feet. The beast twisted around and roared, flinging the spear in our direction.

It passed harmlessly overhead, and the famed hunter fired again. The ape toppled over on top of its victim and twitched in death throes.

Stooping over, I quickly tugged the *Eighty-Six* out from inside the tent. Shoving the Colt pistol into my pants, I rushed to Skyla's tent which was mercifully still standing with no apes nearby.

Jerking the flap back, I froze and stared down the dark barrel of her pistol. Her eyes were wide and fearful. Realizing it was me, she let out a deep breath. "Jed!"

"C'mon!" I reached inside and grabbed her by the arm, pulling her out. She had her gun belt in hand and quickly slung it around her waist. Spinning around, I tried to take stock of our situation. A group had formed around the command tent, and I could make out Brandthorn and Hawney amongst them, firing rifles at the attackers. Otherwise, the encampment was violent pandemonium and chaos.

Fredrick whipped his rifle up and shot an ape charging us with a stone axe raised overhead. Dropping to a knee, the painted hairy savage bared canines in a throaty roar of anger as Skyla finished him off with a pair of shots from her pistol.

"Fredrick!" I shouted to be heard over the sound of battle. He looked at me and I pointed at the Captain's group. "Take Skyla!"

Slinging his rifle over a shoulder, he grabbed Skyla by the arm.

"Jed!" she cried out.

"Go! Go!" I urged them on.

Half pulling, half running with her, Fredrick drew and fired his pistol one handed at a pair of apes bludgeoning a soldier to death with stone clubs. One of the savages dropped their weapon and roared as a bullet connected.

Trusting Skyla to safely reach the Captain's defensive position, I racked a round into the rifle's chamber and ran towards the closest human scream. Leaping over a dead soldier with an arrow through his chest, I slammed into an ape rushing between the tents with a burning log in hairy hand.

The flaming brand swung for my skull, and narrowly missed as I tripped over a tent rope and fell.

Laying on my back, I jerked the rifle barrel up and fired without aiming.

The bullet burst through the ape's arm, hitting the elbow. Bone shattered and flesh shredded. Blood splattered me as he staggered back, roaring in fury with a dangling arm partially severed. With the burning log in his good hand, he lunged forward, swinging downwards at my face. I twisted the rifle sideways, raising it to block the assault, but knowing I didn't have the strength to stop the blow.

Fire blossomed from a muzzle above me, and the hairy beast fell beside me on top of the burning log he'd been using as a weapon. Flesh sizzled, and the scent of singed hair stung my nostrils. The ape lay still as smoke wafted from underneath its body.

I rolled to my feet and looked for my savior.

Charles stood between the tents, head held high, arm extended with pistol in hand. Closing one eye, he calmly fired as an ape chased a scientist running past us in their underwear. The bullet hit, and the ape dropped.

Mumbling thanks, I crawled into a kneeling position and fired at an ape drawing back his bow. The arrow loosened a moment before my shot pierced his back, zinging off into the darkness towards the consolidating soldiers by the command tent.

A spear thrust towards me from the left, and I jerked aside as the razor-sharp chipped obsidian tip ripped through my shirt.

Pulling away, the gray ape swung the weapon sideways at me. With a twist of my rifle, I managed to parry the swing with my rifle's barrel. The jarring impact stung my hands and knocked the weapon from my grasp. Jerking the pistol out of my pants with numb hands, I fired it into his body. He fell, and I gave him a coupe de grace as he reached a trembling hairy hand for me.

On the other side of the campfire, a man feebly lifted his hands to protect himself and was smashed down with the swing of a stone axe. Bones in his arm shattered as the flesh split, and the axe battered through the raised limbs and buried itself into the man's skull. With a kick, the she-ape punted the man's corpse into the fire where his clothing began to smolder and burn.

I fired with the pistol and missed.

The hairy savage hurled her blood drenched axe at me.

I dropped to the ground and the chipped stone weapon whiffed past, narrowly missing. I fired again and hit. Thrashing, the ape toppled backwards, falling into the burning canvas and tangling herself in a tent top. She roared and writhed amongst the rising flames.

An arrow zipped through the air, ripping through the canvas tent behind me and thunking into someone hiding inside with a meaty thud followed by a high-pitched scream. I looked for the archer but couldn't make out who it was in the billowing smoke and firelit darkness.

An ape ran between the tents and a partially dressed scientist laid it out with a hard swing of a chunk of firewood. Once it dropped, he began smashing its skull in, screaming in anger and fear. Droplets of blood splattered onto his face.

Turning away, I stumbled over something and fell to a knee.

The something was someone. It was Gable, with a gaping hole in his chest where a spear had been rammed through him. His eyes were open, but unseeing, and his face locked in a look of terror and pain.

A massive weight tackled me from the side.

Falling to the ground, I struggled against the hairy force pinning me down.

Twisting around, I managed to free an arm and laid the barrel of my pistol over the ape's head with an audible crack. Roaring, it reared back, clutching its gashed open head. Blood dribbled down its painted brow.

With an open-handed slap, the ape smacked me across the face, and I saw stars.

A split-second later the stars faded, and I saw red as anger burst through me. I began beating the monkey with my pistol barrel until the ape lay limp beside me, its exposed brain a gooey gray mush in the dancing firelight.

From where I lay, I could see Fredrick laying heavy fire into our attackers with Skyla and Brandthorn. Beside the three of them, in the swirling smoke and eerie light of the burning tents, Charles stood doggedly, carefully reloading his single pistol as an arrow zipped past his head. The Brit had steel, I'd give him that.

I shot an ape in the thigh and it fell. Before it could crawl away, a scientist raised a heavy ape spear overhead and rammed it down through the monkey's back, pinning it to the ground. The ape thrashed, side to side, trying to grab the shaft jutting from its back but the scientist leaned onto the long-handled weapon, and the ape stopped moving.

The tide was beginning to turn now that the surprise attack was losing its momentum. The remaining men were getting their act together and beginning to fight back. Several of the unarmed scientists picked up burning sticks and smashed them across the faces and chests of their attackers. It was desperate but helped. The surviving apes began to disappear into the night.

Gunfire was sporadic now, and only the screams and moans of the wounded filled the air as the noises of battle died away.

Staggering to my feet, I made my way to Skyla, stepping over corpses on the way.

***

We'd been hit hard.

Over three dozen people had been killed, including at least five scientists and the unfortunate paleontologist Beau Gable. Many of them died in their tents. In return, we killed only fourteen apes, and from the blood trails, wounded several others.

The gate had been attacked by a small band of apes after the soldiers left their post to support the camp. With no one to defend the position, the apes managed to smash apart the Gatling guns with stone clubs. With their barrels bent, and small parts broken, they weren't fixable here. Heck, most of their parts weren't even salvageable. Brass is an easy metal to bend under the weight of a chunk of granite being slammed against it repeatedly.

Apparently, some of these apes survived the battle in Granite Falls and brought some knowledge of our tactics back with them. They targeted our heavy weapons, and we were just lucky there hadn't been a larger ape force held in reserve to attack or we'd have all died.

Amid the battle, one poor scientist had been overpowered and sacrificed on the altar, his beating heart ripped from his chest as the rest of us fought for our own survival a mere hundred feet away.

We were shorthanded now until the replacement forces and expeditionary group arrived later today. A pair of riders were detached, with orders to ride like hell, don't get eaten, and bring back more men and weapons as soon as possible. Then our two Captains had the unpleasant task of manning the gate, the tent encampment, and searching out any apes who may still be lurking inside the large canyon with what men they had left.

In the end, myself and Fredrick were tasked with finding out where the attackers came from while Lieutenant Daniels' men searched out any surviving apes that may be hiding in our canyon still. Skyla wanted to come but gave in to my wishes and stayed behind to help protect and rebuild the camp. She'd been in danger once already today, and that was enough for me. And regardless of how far she'd come since she arrived in the west, she wasn't a warrior. She was just an adaptable survivor. Killing didn't come easy to her like it did some of the rest of us.

While Fredrick fetched the horses, I sought out Charles. I found the Brit kicking dirt over the smoldering remains of a collapsed tent.

"Charles," I said in greeting.

He looked up at me and squinted in the early morning light. "Jedidiah. What can I do for you?"

"I just wanted to say thanks," I said briskly. "For saving my life last night. If it hadn't been for you, that ape would have killed me."

"Ah, yes. That. You are welcome." He peered at me for a moment before drawing his pistol out and flipping it around, exposing the pearl inlaid butt of the nickel-plated gun towards me. "You seem like a man who cares about his weapons. Have a look."

Curious, I accepted the pistol. It was a Smith and Wesson Russian Number 3, also known as a Schofield revolver. I'd lusted after one of these for years. A top-break revolver, you could snap it open, and all six cartridges would be dumped out at once. Reloads were much faster than individually removing cartridges and reloading one at a time like my Colt Peacemakers. Turning the gun in my hand, I ran a finger over the grips.

Carved into them were Charles' initials, CA. "It's a beautiful piece," I told him sincerely as I handed the pistol back.

"Thank you."

Fredrick shouted my name from the corral, and I waved at him. He'd saddled both our horses. It was time to track the attackers.

"You know you could have let me die." I watched his face for a reaction. "That would have solved several Stratten family problems."

He shrugged and looked down at the pistol in his hand before holstering it into his waistband. "Not my style. And just because Elizabeth doesn't approve of you, doesn't mean I don't as well."

"Well, I reckon I appreciate that." I made to leave, then stopped and turned back. "You know I love her, right?"

He smiled at me, his perfectly even teeth flashing. "I suppose you do."

Shaking my head, I quickly walked to Carbine and grabbed the reins. He snorted and tried to step away, but I held them fast. "Don't be an ass," I told him as I grabbed the pommel and pulled myself up.

Daniels' men had already begun searching in pairs, and he'd placed their best shooters in higher locations on the small rises to watch for any moving apes. There were several blood trails near the camp, all ending with a dead ape. But a few petered out, which meant there were wounded somewhere nearby. A shot suddenly rang out followed by a shouted, "One less!" that echoed distantly through the canyon. Several nearby soldiers cheered then went back to wading through the waist high grass with rifles at the ready.

As they searched for any remaining apes, Fredrick and I backtracked the attacking apes to find where they'd come from. We started by riding along the outskirts of the tents. The apes had split up before their surprise attack, taking out a couple of sentries by the large outlying fires with arrows, but before that they'd crossed the canyon in the dark of night as one large group. And a group as big as theirs left a trail that was easy to follow.

We followed the tracks, past the trike corral, through the stream, twice, to the back of the valley by the waterfall. This was the deepest part of the canyon, with the water from Trike River falling over two hundred feet over the cliff edge. Here it was cool and wet. The spray and fine mist in the air was refreshing compared to the rising heat from the morning sun.

The tracks led directly behind the waterfall, along a narrow strip of rock in the cliff face. The trail was large enough a horse could make it, but it'd have to be led. And the narrow rock path rose over a dozen feet above the large pool of clear blue water that fed the river running through the canyon. It wasn't so strange the trail had gone undetected, it blended in easily with cliff.

Tying off our horses, we stalked forward on foot with guns at the ready. Behind the mist and falling water, we found a cave hidden amongst the cliff face. The entrance was well concealed from anyone who didn't know the existence of the narrow trail. From here, nothing could be seen until you moved along the rock outcropping far enough to see around the thick sheet of falling water that roared before us. And it did roar. Standing between the cliff and water the sound was deafening. Fredrick and I had to shout to be heard.

It didn't seem like a good idea for us to enter alone, so we returned to our horses and rode to the nearest group of soldiers. Lieutenant Daniels happened to be with them. They'd tracked one of the blood trails and found it ended with a bullet-riddled corpse. After filling them in, Daniels sent his men to the waterfall to secure the entrance and rode back with us to the smoldering encampment.

The stench of battle was still thick in the air as we approached.

Ape corpses had been dragged far away from the makeshift fort and piled high on a small patch of grass beside an assortment of large ferns. Here they'd be burned eventually, far enough away that the stench of burning flesh and hair wouldn't chase us out of the canyon. As we rode past, large flies buzzed over the mound of corpses.

Daniels pointed across the river where several soldiers worked with shovels and picks, digging graves for our fallen. Rows of dead men were stretched out beside them. "Our little graveyard is growing rapidly," he said solemnly.

"They certainly won't be the last," I told him. "We'll get our revenge, just give it time."

"We got stomped though." Fredrick twisted one of the ends of his mustache. He'd been strangely silent during most of the search, but now he spoke bitterly. "This fort is a damned death trap. We need to find somewhere else to set up." He looked at me. "If you find someplace on your little jaunt that we could use, we need to push hard to move camp."

Shifting in the saddle, Daniels slid his rifle back into its scabbard, apparently unworried about any more apes this close to the encampment. "In Captain Brandthorn's defense, his hands are tied. He's been ordered to hold this place as it has great relevance to the enemy and it's a treasure trove of their artifacts. Plus, it's close to the Shimmer. If we had telegram wires, we could have reinforcements within a couple of hours." He shrugged with one shoulder. "Except every beast around here would tear the wires down within hours of us raising them probably."

"Being here is still a mistake," Fredrick said flatly.

I couldn't agree more. We were in a bowl; apes could hurl arrows at us from all around. They could rush us through the front and climb down the cliffs around us. If a large enough force hit us, we'd be up the proverbial creek with nowhere to go. We'd be surrounded and cut off.

Skyla and Charles were keeping watch over the encampment for more apes from the small knoll where I'd found Sara in an abandoned trike nest, and I slowed Carbine as we approached.

"I didn't hear any more shots," she said optimistically.

The Lieutenant shook his head. "No, ma'am. The canyon appears to be clear." As if to make certain, he stood in his stirrups and looked around. From this spot you could see almost the entire canyon except for the low parts around the river. Teams of soldiers were making their way back towards the encampment.

"We did find the cave they snuck in through. It was hidden behind the waterfall," I told her.

She shaded her eyes with a hand and looked at the back of the canyon. "They came in right behind us... after we'd been here long enough to relax our guard."

"Clever ain't it?"

Charles was holding the remnants of a broken egg shell between his hands, and tossed it back onto the remains of a trike nest. "Good thing their numbers were small, or they'd have wiped us out."

I took my hat off and wiped the sweat off the hat band. "We're all in agreement about that. Let's just hope those were the last of the apes in the area and we'll have some peace long enough to move somewhere else or build some decent defenses."

With a little smile and wink directed at Skyla, I touched Carbine's flanks and we rode to the command tent. It was singed in a few places, but they'd managed to douse it with water after the fight before it fully caught fire. Dismounting, we tied off our horses. Running a hand along the feathers of an ape arrow embedded into one of the tent posts, I entered the large tent behind the Lieutenant and Fredrick.

Patches of sunlight shined through the burnt holes in the thick canvas. Both Captains were in the tent. Several sawn stumps that'd been used as chairs had been kicked over, and I was certain it was from Brandthorn. When he stopped pacing and faced us, his face was twisted in fury.

"Well?" he demanded.

"Best we can tell, there are no more apes," I told him. "But your men are still searching."

"Over thirty dead, and at least two more wounded men who may not make it. Where'd the damn things come from?"

"Cave behind the waterfall, sir. My men have secured it," Daniels told him.

"A damn cave." He spun around and glared at Captain Hawney. "How did we miss that?" Brandthorn asked rhetorically. He kicked an overturned stump and it rolled against the staked tent edge and stopped.

"We thought we were safe," Hawney said quietly. Dark circles had formed under the Captain's eyes from lack of sleep and dried blood was smeared across the front of his uniform. "We were wrong."

Fredrick shifted his rifle from one hand to the other. "We'll need to scour the entire cliff face. There could be more caves hidden in them. And we'll need to search through them. Either the apes have been hiding here the entire time, watching us, or the caves lead outside the valley and that's where they entered." He glanced at me. "Care to play with some dynamite again and seal this one?"

Brandthorn stopped pacing and fixed us with a glare. "No," he said firmly. "I want to know where that cave leads. If it's a back entrance to this canyon, it might be of value one day. You never know when you may need another exit. And we still don't know what we are up against. Or who sent these apes, or if they did it on their own in retaliation for taking their valley." He swore and looked up through a burnt hole in the canvas at the cliff face a hundred yards away. "This damnable low spot leaves us so open to observation it should be a sin." He looked at Daniels. "I want the cave well-guarded for now. But no one enters it until we can spare the manpower to go through it properly. The rest of your men are to start searching the cliff walls in pairs. If there are any more caves in this valley, I want them found by nightfall."

"Yes, sir." The Lieutenant snapped to attention, spun about and left the tent.

I glanced at the map on the table. It hadn't escaped the battle unscathed, an arrow had zipped through the tent and embedded itself into the boards.

Captain Hawney stepped forward and rubbed his chin thoughtfully. "Gable's dead. We're a paleontologist short now for the expedition."

"Aye, we'll find another," Brandthorn replied before turning to me. "From what I gather, it was you who fired the first shot last night."

I shifted the *Eighty-Six* on my shoulder. "One of the apes made the mistake of sticking his hand into the wrong tent."

Fredrick chuckled. "I'll say so. I don't think there's another man in existence who has killed as many apes as you."

Hawney ran his hands down his uniform, picking flakes of dried blood off the material. "Jed, you saved a lot of lives. Thank you."

Unsure of how to reply, I simply nodded before turning to leave. "If you need us, we'll be searching for cliffs with the others."

Fredrick followed me out.

***

By noon, the replacements and our reinforcements had arrived for the expedition. With them they brought two Gatling guns, on loan from Fort York for the time being, with promises of more as soon as they could be acquired. We were really burning through the crew served weapons, but luckily there were plenty of the older models still around from the War Between the States that could be found quickly in military warehouses around the states and shipped to the New West. It was our best defense against the apes and dinosaurs.

Also with the reinforcements came the journalist, Mr. Parsons, and the photographer, Mr. Webley. I was adamant to stay out of their way as much as possible, although Skyla was excited at the notion of getting our picture taken together. I didn't have the heart to tell her no.

A soldier fetched me as I rode Carbine with Skyla and Charles along the canyon cliff bottom's edge. We'd found one small cave that went about a dozen feet before dead ending. It was a wet and miserable location near the waterfall. There was nearly two inches of stagnant water on the floor and no sign that any apes had ever inhabited it.

"Sir, Captain Brandthorn requests your presence in an hour," he told me as he slowed his horse beside ours.

I glanced at the rank on the sleeves of his uniform. "Alright, Private, I'll be there."

"Actually, he'd like to see all three of you. It's about the expedition leaving tomorrow."

I looked at Skyla then Charles. "I figured he'd have at least delayed it."

The soldier shrugged and gestured back towards the camp. "I guess there's more than enough troops here now that we won't be missed."

"I'm glad we're going," Skyla said. "I don't feel safe here anymore."

"Safer here than out there," I muttered to myself. Charles must have overheard because he glanced at me and nodded slightly.

The soldier coughed politely to get our attention again. "Except for the expedition forces, the Captains are keeping everyone here another few days to get everything cleaned up and make sure we aren't hit again. They've requested to Headquarters that we double our forces and firepower from here on out."

"Sounds like a good plan," I told him, as if my opinion mattered.

The Private nodded and raced his horse away, skirting past the fenced trike pasture and towards the far end of the canyon by the new tents being erected.

I watched the trikes lift their horned heads and watch the soldier ride past. There were five of them now, another one had wandered back that morning. It had several old bullet wounds. "You know, if they'd stampeded those beasts into us, it'd been something terrible."

"They'd have caused so much destruction. Thankfully, the apes don't think like us," Skyla said.

"Thankfully," Charles repeated. "They seem to have some understanding of tactics, but like all foes, the learning curve is steep. This time they knew to hit us from behind instead of advancing into the Gatling guns like what happened during your battle at Granite Falls. Then they knew to destroy the guns while they had the opportunity. That's smart. It shows learning."

"Just what we need, a smart enemy," I groused.

The British butler looked from Skyla to me. "The officers would be wise to not underestimate them."

I clucked my tongue and tapped heels to Carbine's sides. "Captain Hawney might, but I doubt Brandthorn would."

***

"Everyone listen up."

The rows of soldiers abruptly grew quiet as they stopped talking and moved to stand at attention.

Brandthorn pointed at the thick chested black soldier standing next to him. I recognized him from snapping at the Private who was telling me of the Senator that'd been eaten on the trail here. "You all know Sergeant Gibbons. He'll be reporting directly to Lieutenant Daniels. You've twenty men, plus civilians, who are Skyla, Jed, Charles, Oscar, and John," he pointed to us each in turn.

I tipped my hat with a pair of fingers when my name was said then looked at the journalist who'd just joined our little outing.

John Parsons, the journalist for the New York Times, was dressed in a dark suit, with a small black bowler's hat perched on his head. A small pair of spectacles rested on his nose, and he looked about like what you'd expect an eastern reporter would. When his name was called, he grinned and lifted his hat up into the air before setting it back down on his sand-colored hair.

We stood in the open area where a dozen smoldering remains of tents had been cleared away. The entire expedition team had been assembled, minus the horses and pack mules that wouldn't be needed until we stepped off. We weren't taking any wagons due to the terrain, and the number of people we were taking was carefully considered and planned. Enough men were required to be able to kill or turn away any aggressive dinosaurs, but also not enough to bog us down on supplies. It was a delicate balance, and unspoken was that we expected to lose people on the way.

As Brandthorn talked, I glanced at Oscar.

He stood a bit further away from the rest of us. I wasn't happy with his coming, but with the death of Beau Gable, we were one scientist short. Oscar was more than pleased to step up. After the assault last night, he was also the only scientist to accept the offer. We'd basically traded an unarmed pacifist for an unarmed asshole. The other scientists were more than willing to simply risk their lives in a death bowl, researching the ape's civilization and whatever dinosaurs they happened to run across or have killed nearby without wandering away into the forest for a week.

As for Oscar, Reydan hired him to lead his future expeditions, but the man had no field experience on his own. He wasn't an outdoorsy type, but he had book knowledge and he was smart. He was also an obnoxious and pompous coward, so I wasn't past letting him die if the occasion arose. Skyla's safety was my only concern for this trip, I couldn't care less what we discovered, unless it was something lethal. And unfortunately, I suspected almost everything we encountered would be.

Brandthorn seemed to be wrapping up his speech, and I paid attention. "This is the first expedition through Prehistoria. It's history. And the success of this little jaunt will determine future expeditions. You're well-armed and you'll be well supplied. Your objective is not to kill dinosaurs unless necessary, but to provide protection for the civilians who will be observing and chronicling your trip. Play it safe but shoot fast and accurate if need be."

He looked around the group one more time. "That's all. Direct any questions to Sergeant Gibbons and you leave in the morning."

Behind him, there was a bright flash of burnt powder as the New York Times photographer, Mr. Webley, took a picture.

When I turned to Skyla, she was beaming from ear to ear. Her excitement appeared to be infectious as both Charles and Oscar seemed in good spirits as well. John Parsons seemed positively thrilled as he clutched his notebook and chased after Captain Brandthorn. But not me.

I knew people were going to die.

***

John stopped me later that evening as I walked between the tents looking for mine. The reporter popped into view like a carnival magician, seemingly coming out of nowhere.

"Ah, the Hero of Granite Falls. I was hoping for a moment of your time," he said with a friendly, easy smile.

"Don't call me that," I said briskly as I stepped to go around him.

He moved faster, putting himself firmly in my way.

I choked back the urge to push him aside.

"But you are. After all, you're the one who brought the soldiers to the town, fended off the apes from attacking the train with a Gatling gun, then killed their leader in single combat. These are the feats of legends."

I shrugged. "I had a lot of help. Skyla, Fredrick, Wolverine Wade, Ashley James... You should talk to them."

"Oh." He looked confused. "I will. But I'd like to hear your story first."

"Well," I dragged the word out, thinking of how to get rid of the reporter. "Maybe some other time; right now I've some weapons to clean."

"Oh, outstanding." He peered down at the brace of guns I wore on my hips. "What would a Wild West hero be without his guns?"

I groaned inwardly. "Look, they're just a couple of pistols and a rifle. Nothing fancy to see."

He raised a single finger to stop me. "On the contrary, I hear you carry a very special rifle. A prototype of John Moses Browning himself."

"Uh huh," I glared at him, hoping to frighten the man into leaving me alone.

Instead, John just gave me a patient grin and waited for me to explain. I reckoned the hair cut Skyla gave me was ruining my intimidatingly good looks.

"Jed, may I call you Jed?"

Sighing, I nodded. The man had stones, I'd give him that.

"This is my tent," he gestured at the one to his right. "I've managed to... wrangle, as you westerners would say, a couple of makeshift chairs." He chuckled to himself. "Would you mind sitting down and answering some questions?"

Turning my head, I looked for someone to save me. But there was no one nearby and I couldn't think of any good excuses. Resigning myself, I moved over and picked the cleanest of the two chairs. The small piece of canvas was spread out over a wooden tripod beneath, and settling down, I got comfortable.

"Excellent. So, Jed. Let's talk about your past. Where are you from?"

Oh, this was going to be fun. At least my father's gang already knew where I was, so I didn't have to worry about them finding me anymore. But I still had a checkered past I'd rather keep to myself for now. I'd have to be careful what I told this man.

"First off, out here a man's past is his own business. Nothing shows you are more of a green horn than going around asking about someone's business that doesn't concern you."

John looked perplexed. "But I'm a reporter. Asking questions is what I do." He picked up a thin journal from inside the tent and opened it. A nub of pencil was tucked inside.

"That's fine and all, but don't go expecting to get answers to questions like that."

He tapped the nub against his leg thoughtfully. "Why? Unless they've something to hide?"

There it was. What I was afraid of. The inevitable thought that comes to people not used to the privacy and fresh start that the west gives everyone.

I gave him an easy and confident smile that I didn't quite feel. "No, I was just giving you a word of advice."

He stopped tapping the pencil. "Thank you." Then he gave that patient grin again. "Why don't you start the story where you want?"

I decided to start the story where it mattered. Beginning with the night I was attacked by an Allosaurus…

***

That night the guard was doubled, and extra soldiers were used to reinforce the gate since we only had two functioning Gatling guns. A few other caves had been found, none of any merit, and the one past the waterfall was temporarily boarded up as strongly as possible with plenty of men guarding it. Until we knew where it went, we had to treat it as though there was an army of apes on the other side, because for all we knew, there was.

I was hoping for the opportunity to speak with Skyla, to finally tell her about my past, and the ramifications of my father and the shooting back in Granite Falls. But with the extra men moving about through the night there was nowhere we could have a private conversation, and I didn't want to cross paths with John Parsons again. The reporter made me uncomfortable. I managed to deflect most of his questions about my past, but he was a smart one and I was afraid he might go digging.

As for me and Skyla having a private moment alone, it didn't help that we were all also confined to the immediate fort area and the tents within it. There was no privacy to be had. Charles, Fredrick, and myself shared a slightly battle damaged tent now. It was tight quarters. Most of the soldiers were sleeping outside as we had almost three times the number of troops in the encampment that it could comfortably contain. Until the expedition left, and more tents were brought, there'd be a lot of starry nights for most of the soldiers.

Bitter that I couldn't speak alone with Skyla, I quickly cleaned my guns, then settled in for the night, and hoped for a solid last night's sleep without interruption. Once we stepped off the next morning, there wouldn't be another restful night's sleep until we returned. And even then, after the surprise attack, I doubted anyone would have a restful sleep inside of Fort Jipson anytime soon.

Fredrick snorted and rolled onto his side.

We'd already said goodbye to the hunter. He would continue scouting nearby, riding with patrols and getting a feel for what sort of creatures were nearby. I suspected anything small and potable would be brought back. He did have a job to do after all. I'd also wished him luck with locating a Tyrannosaurus. He'd been obsessed with being the first to kill one. But until the train ran through the Shimmer and onto this side, it would be nigh impossible to butcher and haul the giant pieces away for the Smithsonian to mount.

Resting on my back, I looked over at Charles. The nickel-plated butt of his pistol gleaned beneath the folded coat that he used for a pillow. He seemed capable enough. And I knew I could count on him to protect Skyla. But ultimately, the man was something of an enigma. He was here to steal Skyla back to the East if possible, but he didn't appear to be in any hurry. Perhaps he'd learned his lesson before when trying to talk her out of coming here.

I sighed into the partial darkness and closed my eyes.

Like everything else, he was another problem for another day.

***

The morning sun rose over the canyon on a tired group of soldiers rising from bed and preparing themselves for the expedition. Lieutenant Daniels and Sergeant Gibbons were the only ones who looked refreshed, and they had pulled extra security shifts as well. They just hid it better for the sake of their men. I was tired as well, but not from pulling a shift. That was one of the perks of being a civilian inside the Fort. Instead, I was tired from Fredrick's incessant snoring and being sandwiched between him and Charles in the pitched tent. I was tempted to climb into Skyla's for more room but knew the movement would probably wake the two other men. And with the Stratten family butler sleeping with his hand on the butt of his Schofield pistol, I didn't want to test his reaction to being suddenly woken.

Fredrick was off exploring the pool by the waterfall. Last night he'd proclaimed that the strange, colorful fish the men were catching would work just as well in a water exhibit of Prehistoria as would dinosaurs in a land exhibit. And it gave the famed hunter something to do, fish. Which he admitted he did poorly and planned on borrowing several soldiers to help him build water traps.

Skyla and I skipped breakfast to get our picture taken together in front of the trike corral. Webley turned out to be a nice fellow, even with his thick Yankee accent. He had been taking a lot of pictures in the same place, with groups and individuals near the command tent, but was so smitten by Skyla that he agreed to her request to get rather close to the trikes for our picture.

We stood together, side by side, loaded for bear. Or dinosaur. She wore her prettiest outfit that she'd brought, tan pants and white buttoned shirt with black riding boots, and I wore my usual red shirt and jeans. The pictures were black and white, so I figured color wouldn't matter anyways. I rested the *Eighty-Six* front and center on its butt plate and held the barrel with my free hand. Behind us, the biggest trike, the one with the bullet scars, stood and watched us from beneath his black horns curiously.

It was quite the picture.

Then we grabbed our horses and headed towards the entrance. Just in time to get into formation before we stepped off.

Daniels and Gibbons led the column as we rode through the dirt and rock makeshift palisade of the canyon fort's entrance. Captain Brandthorn was there, standing on the berm with a salute raised. The soldiers around us saluted him in return as they passed. There was an air of excitement to the new expedition. Even with my doubts about this trip, I couldn't help but feel excited as well at being involved. As the first man from our side to cross through the Shimmer, I'd been amazed at this world and its monstrous inhabitants. But that was before I realized the dangers that lurked everywhere around us. As I thought of that, my excitement began to fade, only to be replaced with an uneasy feeling that we'd be lucky to survive this little jaunt of ours.

I rode Carbine beside Skyla and Smoke, while Charles rode Sir Lancelot behind us. John and Oscar rode their horses near the back, preferring to be towards the rear of the column where they no doubt felt they would be more protected. That was fine by me; the more distance between us, the safer Skyla's former boss would be from me. And John had turned out to be a persistent talker. Even now, the two of them were deep in discussion. No doubt with Oscar glorifying himself to the reporter about his time on this side.

In total we had twenty-six men and Skyla, plus horses for everyone, and six pack mules. The soldiers were all heavily armed with a Winchester repeater, a Colt pistol, a filled bandoleer of cartridges slung across their chest and another in their saddle bags. Ammunition was one thing we did not want to run out of. We'd be leaving one hell of an easy-to-follow trail for any apes that wanted to pick a fight. Or for any curious beasts that wanted to see what our strange scents led to. With any luck, we wiped out the remaining apes the other night and would be free and clear of them for a while. But I didn't want to get my hopes up. We defeated an army of apes a couple months ago and an army must be supported by a civilization somewhere.

Regardless of what might happen over the next week, I knew my only reason for being here was to keep Skyla safe. I couldn't give a damn about any discoveries of beasts or resources; they weren't my concern. Only us staying alive.

The ride down the Trike River was uneventful. Most of the dinosaurs that were nearby had been seen often enough to have already been well studied from a distance. And a few had already been killed to provide fresh dissections to the scientists. We rode past them without much fanfare. Nothing new to see. Just some more Hadrosaurs, or Cresteds, as the soldiers had taken to calling them. The big herbivores were so docile that we could ride within twenty feet of them as the yellow and green beasts fed along the river's edge and they would only look at us with bored interest. Later, we came across a flock of the brown feathered flightless birds that I'd discovered on my first trip over here; they seemed to be a favorite snack for both the local dinosaurs, apes, and occasionally for the fort as well. And as such, they were skittish around us and kept far away from our little caravan.

Our first night we set up camp near the junction of the Trike River flowing from Fort Jipson and Ape River that went through the valley by the Shimmer and on to the sea. Several men fished for fresh meat and caught strange fish with sharp pointed teeth and thick scales that resembled armor. They were terribly unappealing creatures and were promptly thrown back into the water.

We were all living in close quarters, three of us men sharing a tent again and Skyla having her own. Daniels made sure that hers was pitched beside me, near the center of our small encampment. Any rocks or logs nearby were moved and shifted about to create something of a small defensive perimeter around our position. With the river to our backs, we could primarily focus our manpower in all the other directions. Every man slept with their rifle and took turns at watch, even we civilians. Skyla demanded that she be allowed to keep watch as well, and at her insistence, Daniels relented on the condition that she shared it with Charles and not me. We also used several large fires along the outskirts of our group to keep curious beasts at bay and to illuminate the darkness around us. But even with the fires, we were still plagued with the small brown furry rodents that inhabited this side. The rat-like creatures scurried in the darkness between the fires, snagging bits of food that soldiers tossed away or left sitting for a few moments. After a few insufferable hours, Sergeant Gibbons dispatched several with his sword and scattered their corpses nearby in the brush. That seemed to deter the others to stay away.

The next morning, we woke to the thundering splashes of a herd of long neck dinosaurs crossing through the water beside us. The giant hundred-foot-tall beasts plodded through the murky brown water, sending up great waves, as they lifted their feet and plunged them down into the depths. Several young ones struggled in the center of the herd, occasionally touching bottom then swimming awkwardly as they kept up with the adults.

"Good heavens!" Charles exclaimed as he scrambled out of the tent.

"Impressive, aren't they?" I said as we watched the brownish gray beasts send waves of water three feet tall splashing against the shore by our encampment.

"Terribly," he said, with his hand resting on the butt of his Schofield pistol. "I do hope they don't get angry with us camping on their river."

I laughed. "If they do, that pistol of yours ain't gonna do much for us."

He nodded in agreement but kept his hand on the gun.

The entire expedition was awake now and staring in awe as the creatures stepped up the river's edge, sending tremors through the ground with their steps. For a moment it appeared that they'd walk right through our encampment, but the lead one, a massive bull that had to have been over a hundred feet long from head to tip of giant tail, sniffed the smoke from our fires that lingered over the water and turned away, leading the others downstream.

"Such graceful creatures." Skyla stepped beside us. Her dark hair was pulled back into a ponytail beneath her floppy brimmed hat. She was dressed for the expedition in tan pants with a tucked in white shirt, looking every bit like an African explorer. "It's a shame that eventually Fredrick will need to kill one to dissect and take to the Smithsonian."

"Yes, it is," I agreed.

We watched until they moved out of sight behind the trees before beginning to pack our belongings and saddle the horses.

Daniels led us as we followed Ape River upstream. The river's edge provided us a place to ride, and through the thick bladed grass and waist high ferns we rode.

We'd been riding for two hours in the sweltering sun and heat when the beastly reptile struck.

It hit us halfway down the column, letting the first half of us ride right past it while it laid in wait.

The giant creature charged forward, silently bursting from between the tall ferns and brush that lined the edge of the forest.

At a hoarse shout I turned in the saddle, but all I saw was a flash of yellow and green streaked with red as the beast attacked.

A horse bucked, throwing its rider to the ground. The soldier managed to roll over just in time for the monster to chomp down on his head and shoulder.

Muffled screams came from inside the dinosaur's maw as it shook the man's body like a rag doll. Nearby horses fought their riders, trying to flee after the riderless horse that raced away through the forest. Men cursed and swore as they fought their horses to bring rifles to bear on the creature.

The entire column broke into chaos. Shouts arose as everyone tried to respond at once.

Twirling Carbine around, I jerked out the *Eighty-Six* and watched for other threats while the soldiers began unloading rifles into the hideous creature's body.

The monster soaked up their bullets.

Blood sprayed, and the beast thrashed as soldiers' bullets found their mark amongst its scaly green and yellow hide.

With an awful crunch, the dinosaur bit the soldier's head and shoulder off, then slammed a clawed foot across the lower half of the corpse, spilling guts and intestines into the lush trampled green river grass. The wide bodied, ugly, reptilian thing swallowed, then shook its head back and forth, snapping and gnashing at men and horse alike.

Charles jerked Sir Lancelot around and raced back down the column, pistol in hand. Leaping the magnificent Arabian horse over the beast, he fired the Schofield downwards into its skull.

The dinosaur let out an ear-piercing shriek and shuddered as Lancelot landed gracefully on all fours and rushed past, dodging between the mounted soldiers waving rifles around. Charles twirled his mount around again, but the beast shivered violently and stopped moving.

Within seconds, one man was dead, another lightly wounded from a ricocheting bullet, and a horse was lost.

***

Once everything calmed down and order restored, Skyla and Oscar examined the beast as the wounded soldier was tended to and the rest of us formed a perimeter around the area.

Charles stood guard over our two paleontologists. He seemed pleased with himself, but I thought what he'd done, racing in front of a dozen rifle muzzles, to place a well shot bullet into the skull of the beast, was both ballsy and foolish. It wasn't the kill shot that bothered me, it was needlessly placing himself in harm's way. The only surgeon we had was back at Fort Jipson, a solid day's ride away. And contrary to Charles' purpose of taking Skyla back East, we'd begun to have a grudging respect for each other over the past few days. It would be a shame for the butler to die now that our friendship was just beginning to blossom.

The creature reminded me of a lizard by the way it had moved, thrusting one side of its body forward at a time, then the other with a side to side motion. The long fin on its back, beginning at the base of its neck, rising three feet high before dropping back to the base of the creature's tail, had blended in perfectly with the tall grasses and red tinged ferns along the river grass. And it'd waited, with reptilian patience, as we rode past before finally giving into its craving and snatching one of the soldiers.

Dismounting, I tied Carbine's reins to a branch and found a thick stick to jam between the beast's jaws. Prying the mouth open revealed two large canine-like teeth at the front of its mouth, followed by rows of smaller jagged teeth that ran back towards its jaw. Bits of shredded human flesh dangled from them.

Skyla leaned forward to get a better look. "Oscar, look. Its teeth are serrated." She pulled out her journal and flipped to a fresh page.

Her former boss moved from studying the fin on the beast's back and crouched beside her. "You're right. That's how it removed the man's head so easily. It ground its teeth forward and back while flinging his body side to side." He pulled out his own journal, and as he flipped through the pages, I saw that his sketches weren't nearly as good as Skyla's.

"What do you think this creature would have a giant fin for?" Charles asked as he looked at the murky water behind us. "Swimming?"

"Maybe, but..." Skyla grinned and pointed at the sun. "I think it's to help warm its body. Just like a reptile, I think this sail type fin lets the creature keep its body hidden for hunting, but still soak up the warmth of the sun."

Oscar looked at the beast, then at the depression of where the dinosaur had hidden. From the sign around the spot, the creature had backed into the brush, and its sail would certainly have been exposed enough to catch sunlight from the east.

He shook his head. "Preposterous. Most likely it's just camouflage."

Skyla shrugged and continued taking notes. "We'll just have to observe a living one to see, I suppose. Eventually we'll know who is right and who is wrong."

Oscar harrumphed and grabbed the stick I was still holding. Leaning his ample weight against it, the jaws stretched further apart. He leaned down to get a better look inside the creature's mouth.

"Charles," I nodded in Daniels' direction, "I'm going to go talk to the Lieutenant. Keep an eye out please?"

"Certainly." He propped a foot on the creature and rested his pistol across his knee and turned towards the tree line behind Skyla and Oscar.

The dead soldier's rifle was lying on the ground still, and scooping it up, I held it out towards him. "You may want to learn to use one of these."

He was silent for a moment as he stared at the rifle, then holstered his pistol and took it. With a deft flick of his hand, he worked the lever on the Winchester to see if a cartridge had been loaded into the chamber. Satisfied, he flicked the lever back into place. With a knowing grin, he gave me a curt nod and spoke sarcastically, "Thanks, chap."

Rolling my eyes, I turned away as John Parsons rode his horse closer and dug a notebook out of his saddlebag.

As I walked on towards the commanding officer of this little party, I heard the reporter beginning to question Charles about what he was thinking as he heroically charged the reptilian dinosaur.

Sighing, I stepped around a swath of blood splattered grass and worked my way towards the front of the column.

Daniels was deep in discussion with Sergeant Gibbons when I approached.

"Second day and we lose Private Timmons and a horse. And now we've got a wounded soldier, from a ricochet of all things," Daniels said angrily as he snapped a stick between his hands.

The big Sergeant sighed. "We knew it would be this way, sir. There's no reward without risk. Most likely we're going to lose a few more before we return to the fort. But there ain't nothing we can do about it, except bury Timmons and move forward."

"Jed," Daniels spotted me. "What do our scientists think about this beast?"

"They're studying it, but I think we need to be a helluva lot more careful if any of us are going to survive. We let our guard down since yesterday was an easy day. But we're in strange country now, there's no telling what we'll run across. Plus, we got the apes to worry about."

"Yes. Yes, we do." Daniels flung the two pieces of stick into the water. Pulling a small map from a pocket, he unfolded it. It was identical to the one we'd looked at two days ago at the Fort.

"Other than this attack, we're making good time along the river. A few more days and we'll take a turn south and skirt the dormant volcano."

I looked up. The hundred plus foot tall trees made it difficult to see much of the sky, but I could just barely make out the shattered rock edges of the mountain. It was tall and jagged, covered with trees and vegetation along the steep sides. If that's where the apes were from, we were risking a lot getting so close to them.

"Let's play it safe until we get back," I told them.

***

For two more days we did just that. We didn't lose a single man or horse, except we did have a mule break a leg. A well-placed shot put the beast of burden out of its misery. We ate well that night. The meat was a little tough, but better than the jerky we'd been eating for the past few days. No one wanted to eat the finned dinosaur that swallowed the head of a soldier.

We were halfway through our trip, making good time and about to turn away from the river to make our move around the mountain. We were getting lots of observations and sketches of new species. Oscar had a mule loaded down with plants and leaves to study later while Skyla had already filled several journals with notes that she kept on Smoke. We discovered several new small dinosaurs and found another finned beast like the one that killed Private Timmons. But even after several hours of observation, our two paleontologists still couldn't agree on what the reptilian creature's fin was used for. In the end, they were both even more adamant about their theories. I tended to side with Skyla, but that was probably because I was in love with her and detested Oscar.

But these days, we were playing it safe. Moving slowly and cautiously. Approaching everything as though it may be lethal. Because it most likely was.

At one point we found several giant plants that would snap shut when we tossed a pebble into their red center. The spindly light green outer portion, beautiful until seen in action, had long black 'claws' that folded shut together and trapped whatever landed on it inside. One of the soldiers caught a brown rodent and tossed it onto one. The little creature struggled for twenty minutes after the plant snapped shut, finally dying as it was squeezed to death while trying to frantically claw its way out.

We left them alone after that.

But things were going well.

Too well.

By dawn of day four, we were moving along the lush grassy edge of a wide field. To our right were towering trees that hung over us, giving shade with their thick mesh of leaves, and to our left about fifty yards away was the muddy, slow moving water of the river. The humidity was so thick I felt like I could swim through it.

Riding beside Oscar, I wiped sweat from my brow and looked up the column of soldiers towards the front where Skyla and Charles were with Lieutenant Daniels and Parsons. The journalist appeared to be deep in conversation with the young officer.

Carbine's ears flicked forward, and he turned his head towards the forest.

"Oscar..." I started, as I stared into the underbrush among the thick tree trunks. Something wasn't right. A large fern along the edge of the forest rustled slightly. Then another.

Then it hit me.

There was no wind.

"What?" the paleontologist looked at me peevishly, beads of sweat rolling down his chubby face.

A three-foot-long arrow with green and yellow fletching pierced through a soldier's side in front of us. Grabbing the shaft, he let out a hoarse scream that turned to a gurgle and fell from his mount.

"AMBUSH!" I roared and lifted the *Eighty-Six* from where it rested across my pommel.

Around us came a chorus of confusion as arrows flew from the brush and among our column.

Horses reared and screamed as the ape arrows penetrated their bodies. Soldiers toppled from mounts, flailing their arms as obsidian arrow tips whistled into them.

Twisting the reins, I spun Carbine around, searching for targets. I couldn't see anything to shoot at, there was only the darkened interior of the forest, so I began unloading my rifle into places where I thought I saw movement. I was happy to hear roars of animalistic pain as several apes took bullets of mine through the thick brush and ferns.

Then came horrifying shrieks as raptors rushed from the brush between the trees and attacked.

The six-foot-long beasts only stood several feet tall, but they were pure lethality. Men recognized the little creatures immediately and began shouting in warning as they swung their rifles to bear on the new threat.

Leaping with claws outstretched, the dinosaurs bit and slashed at anything within reach. More horses and men fell, screaming in agony as bellies were sliced open and faces ripped off under the feathered beast's fangs and claws. One of the raptors locked its claws on Oscar's horse, and the scientist fell with his mount as the creature ripped out his horse's throat in a bright spray of arterial blood.

An ape slammed to the ground in front of me with a heavy thud and soft patter of falling leaves. His spear jabbed upwards at my head, the obsidian point sending a sliver of pain across my cheek as I jerked aside. Jamming my rifle into his chest, I pulled the trigger, blowing a large hole through him. Glancing upwards, I saw more of them hanging from branches and thick vines above us with weapons in hand.

"They're in the trees!" I screamed in warning as they dropped amongst us and the apes in the underbrush charged forwards. In a moment, our already panicked column was swarming with the painted, hairy savages. Men and horses raced away from the trees and into the open field between the river and forest, attempting to get distance between themselves and the enemy.

At the front of the column, I saw Skyla thrown from Smoke and the Lieutenant's horse take a spear through the chest. They both fell, and I lost sight of them for all the chaos between us.

Thick fingers grabbed my leg with an iron grip and jerked me off Carbine. Tumbling over, I fell as my horse bolted away into the forest. The *Eighty-Six* dropped from my grasp as I hit the ground with a painful thud.

The ape that grabbed me reared back with a stone axe held in both large hands, roaring as it began to bring the weapon down on me.

A soldier butt stroked the ape with his rifle from behind.

The ape dropped to the ground and the man battered the monkey's head apart with repeated blows, sending an eyeball flying. An ape tumbled into him, already bleeding from several bullet holes. The same soldier, a Corporal by his rank, shoved the hairy savage away before firing his Winchester into the monkey's back and finishing him off.

I lurched to my feet.

Dropping my hands down, I drew.

The Colt Peacemakers rose from their holsters with bursts of flame flaring from the muzzles.

Apes near me died as I began pumping them full of heavy .45 slugs as fast as I could pull the triggers.

A feathered arrow slammed into the Corporal who had saved me, and he staggered backwards, hands grasping at the shaft jutting from his chest. His scream was cut short as a raptor pounced onto him and ripped his throat and face apart.

We were all going to die.

And if I was going to die, it'd be beside Skyla.

I ran.

Rushing between soldiers grappling with apes and dying as their bodies were beaten and split open by the heavy swings of stone axes and clubs, I fired round after round into the hairy beasts along the way. Several times the apes were so busy killing that I jammed the pistol barrel against their heads or bodies and pulled the trigger before they knew what was happening.

A raptor, red feathers along its head and neck waving, raced through the open grass and tackled a soldier off his horse. He shrieked in terror as the small vicious dinosaur began ripping and tearing at him.

Without stopping I put a bullet through its body and ran on as it fell thrashing and the soldier gurgled from a series of hideous gashes ripping him from throat to groin.

Now the twin pistols were out of ammunition.

I flung them, one after the other at the nearest ape.

It roared and swatted at them with a free hand, while the other hand struggled to jerk a spear from a dead horse.

Fear and fury gripped me, and I snatched a discarded rifle from the ground. Swinging it like a bat, I cracked the wooden stock across the back of an ape that was ripping a gore-stained stone axe from the chest of a dead soldier. The monkey toppled forward and died as someone else put a bullet through the beast's red and green painted face.

Charles had already reached Skyla. He'd lost his rifle and horse but stood firing with his pistol at arm's length as she knelt beside him, struggling to reload her rifle. Several dead apes were piled before them. Parsons, face pale in fear, had picked up a revolver, and was cocking and firing it two handed at anything that came near them.

A dozen yards away, the Lieutenant stood back-to-back with his black Sergeant, both down to their swords. Gibbons batted a spear thrust aside with the flat of his blade, stepped forward and sent the point of his sword through the ape's throat. With a twist he jerked the blade free, sending a stream of blood squirting from a severed artery. An arrow zipped past the black Sergeant, slicing his arm open, and he dropped to a knee, swearing fluently in pain.

Dodging the swing of a club, I tripped and went spinning into a blood-covered raptor. Tumbling, I managed to dodge the talons and fire into its body with the broken rifle. Shrieking, the small dinosaur raced away, bleeding heavily and leaving small red feathers behind as it disappeared into the brush.

Rolling over, I slammed into a pair of hairy legs. Looking up at the hide clothed female ape, I watched helplessly as her heavy stone club swung down towards my skull.

This was the end.

My eyes flicked towards Skyla as she screamed my name in horror.

Without warning, the ape jerked away as large leathery wings beat heavy air down on me.

A giant pterodactyl lifted the struggling she-ape into the air. Her club fell beside me, nearly crushing my head as it thudded into the soft ground.

Two dozen yards away, a second ape was lifted away, clenched in the tight claws of another pterodactyl and a raptor was scooped up inside the long sharp toothed jaws of a third winged dinosaur. From the backs of the leather winged creatures rode men dressed in bits of metal armor and hide, clutching tightly to the birds with what looked like swords strapped to their sides.

I lay frozen, staring in shock at men who flew through the air on the backs of the giant pterodactyls.

My shock ended with loud explosions of gunfire and gouts of white smoke that billowed from between the trees and ferns. Around us apes fell in a cascade. Others took notice and began to run.

Never one to leave an enemy alive, I rolled onto my chest, tucked the soldier's broken rifle into my shoulder and began to gun them down as they fled. Each time I fired; the shattered stock was driven painfully into my shoulder. Two more dropped from my bullets in their backs before the rest disappeared amongst thick leaves of the forest undergrowth. Sharp whistles blasted through the air and the remaining two raptors bounded away after them.

Then an ape fell screaming from the sky, and thudded to the ground beside me, the sound of smashing meat and breaking bone a sickening noise. I glanced up in time to see the raptor released from hundreds of feet in the air, twisting and shrieking as it fell to its death in the open field.

It was then that a dozen men, armed with crudely shaped muskets slung over their backs and medieval swords in hand, stepped from the trees. Like the pterodactyl riders, they wore bits of darkened metal armor around their torsos with leather pants and shirts. Their shoes and leggings appeared to be of a hardened leather, boiled to stiffness and stitched together. Necklaces of gold and pieces of bone hung from their necks, bouncing against their armor.

Stranger still, was that they were a mixture of white men and Indian. Some had blonde hair with blue eyes while others skin was a deep bronze with dark almond shaped eyes. But they were all dressed and armed equally.

A couple of the bizarrely dressed and armed men quickly began to administer aid to the wounded soldiers, while others began jabbing the points of their swords through the chests of any wounded or dead apes. A gravely wounded raptor was cornered between three of them and with their swords they hemmed it in, before another chopped down with the large blade and severed its head from its body.

With obvious disgust, they left the raptor corpse twitching on the ground.

Skyla rushed to me, grabbed me about the waist, and gave me a hug, ignoring the splatters of blood across my shirt. I hugged her back then dropped the broken rifle and took in the death around us. It was horrific. Bodies of soldiers, apes, and horses lay strewn about the field.

"Looks like we survived another one," I whispered to her as I looked over the field of death for my guns.

"Yes, but at what cost?" she replied, with tears welling and trickling down her cheeks.

Almost all the men we'd gotten to know over the past few days were dead. Only pierced, crushed, and mangled bodies remained. Most of the horses had been killed as well. Carbine was missing, but Smoke had already been gathered with Lancelot. Skyla touched my cheek, and I realized the burning sensation I felt was the cut from the spear. Touching my fingers to the wound, I pulled them away with bloodied tips.

"It's not bad, just a deep scratch," she assured me.

"Just another scar," I muttered as I let her go and looked around for my Colts. Finding them beside a pair of ape and soldier corpses, I picked them up and began cleaning them off with the tail end of my shirt. Bits of grass and debris were stuck to them, and small droplets of blood.

We heard a startled shout from one of the strange men who was stabbing the dead apes. Two of them sprang to his side and pointed their swords as an ape corpse shifted and rolled over. From beneath crawled Oscar, covered in blood, and sputtering angrily. Seeing me staring, he unloaded his anger.

"Right here!" He gestured at the ape corpse angrily. "I was right here the entire time! I was screaming for help and no one came!" He suddenly noticed the strange appearance of his saviors. "Oh. Hello... gentlemen."

The strangers looked at each other and shrugged before stabbing both their sword points into the ape body that Oscar had crawled out from under. They were all business in making sure every single ape was finished off.

A loud screech sounded from above and Skyla and I ducked as a pair of the massive pterodactyls swooped overhead and landed a dozen yards away.

The birds were huge, their wingspan easily stretching well over forty feet, and their leathery bodies stood ten feet tall before ending in a yellow head with a large red fin on the back of the skull. Their coloring was yellow above, and a mixed green beneath, with a pale whiteness along their bare feet and dark claws. A leather harness with a saddle of sorts rested on the creature's backs, intertwined amongst the wings, and complete with stirrups.

The other men seemed indifferent to the two riders as they went about stabbing the rest of the ape corpses.

Oscar quickly made his way to our sides as a pair of men untied themselves from their strange mounts and dismounted. Their clothing was of hide shirt, pants, and moccasins, and they too were armed with swords and crude firearms. At one of their waists was tucked an old flintlock pistol like the one we'd found in the ape cave.

"Skyla...the pistol..."

"I see it," she whispered back.

High above us, the third pterodactyl screeched as it circled the battlefield.

The man with the pistol stepped forward. He was small and lithe, with dark tan skin and a mop of blonde hair pulled back into a ponytail with bits of feathers braided into the locks. A necklace of fangs and gold beads decorated his chest. He extended a hand as his dark eyes darted from person to person, taking in our weapons and what was surely considered strange dress to him. "Well met fair lady and gentlemen, who are thou?"

"Oh, what the hell," Sergeant Gibbons muttered as he staggered to us while tying off a bandage around his arm. Blood seeped through the cloth as he struggled to pull it tight with one hand.

I looked at the strange newcomer in shock. He spoke English, and an old form of English at that.

Daniels stepped forward, surprise evident across his sweat dripping face. "I'm Lieutenant Daniels of the United States Army. We owe you and your men thanks for our rescue." He reached out and shook the strange speaking man's hand.

"I am Thenory, Chief of Shayana and the hairy men are enemies of us all."

Parsons pushed past us. "You... ah, thee... speaketh our language?" the reporter blurted, looking as puzzled as we all must have felt.

He nodded at him as though he were simple, then walked to the soldier holding the reins of one of our horses. He ran a hand along Smoke's shoulder thoughtfully. "Beautiful beasts... Our stories tell of such animals, but we have never seen them."

Charles looked at me, and I shrugged. Hell if I knew what was going on. Skyla shook her head in bewilderment.

Oscar rushed forward, knocking into me in his hurry. "Who are you? How did you come to be here? Where are you from?" His questions were hurried, stumbling over one another in his excitement to ask them all.

Thenory held up a hand to silence the scientist then pointed at the mountain in the distance. The dormant volcano. "Let us gather thou wounded, and we shall take thee to our village for recovery." He gazed on the battlefield as his men finished giving final coupe de graces with a thrust and twist of their bloodied swords. "Tis not safe out here."

***

By the time I recovered the irreplaceable *Eighty-Six* and reloaded my weapons, the survivors of our expedition managed to find enough horses for all of us, plus a couple spares. The pack mules were long gone, and I doubted they'd survive long on their own or have the sense to find their way back to the Fort.

I'd already mounted an unclaimed US branded horse with blood splattered on its saddle when Carbine gamely stepped from between the trees and pranced alongside our column. As usual, his head and black tail were held high, as though proud to have come back on his own. I quickly swapped horses for my own troublesome mount.

From twenty-six people, we were down to twelve. Our protective detail had been successful I supposed, Skyla and Oscar were still alive, as was our reporter. But it was hard to stomach the loss of so many men.

Having given his large pterodactyl over to another of his men to fly overhead, Thenory led the way on foot. Once we entered the forest, the large birds were only occasionally glimpsed gliding overhead through the leaves of the hundred-foot-tall trees.

The Shayana and their leader moved quickly on foot and took us through a difficult trail that only they seemed to know. With our horses we could keep up, but on foot it'd have been a real challenge to maintain the same pace as the strange mix of English and Indian men whom we followed. Still, numerous times we had to dismount and lead the horses by hand as the path through low hanging branches and brush wasn't tall enough for riders.

"How is it you speak English?" Daniels asked the Shayana leader.

"Our forefathers came from the old world to settle in the new Americas." He shrugged and waved a hand around him. "Instead, they found this."

Skyla gasped, and the implications raced through my mind. Daniels looked back at us and shook his head, warning us to silence. He turned back to Thenory. "How'd they end up here?"

"There was a great blizzard, and they took refuge in a cave. They found a tunnel and went through it only to end up here," he raised his hands to show our surroundings. "But then they were set upon by hairy men who chased them far away from the cave. For weeks they walked, trying to find peaceful lands, but this place was full of violence and strange beasts. Then they found the other people of this strange land and lived with them. But they still looked for a home, and finally found one to make their own." He looked back at us, then at the Lieutenant. "Where does thee hail from?"

Daniels ducked a low branch and spoke loudly enough for us all to hear. "A canyon, from many days away." It seemed the Lieutenant wanted to keep our world's location a secret for now; I couldn't blame him. The ramifications of finding a civilization of something other than barbaric natives were unexpected. Never did any of our wildest discussions of what we might find on this side involve white men living with Indians who'd come from another place and time in our country.

Skyla leaned over on Smoke to get closer to me. "This is greater than anything we ever expected."

"It's one for the books, that's for sure," Charles whispered from behind, just loud enough for us to hear.

John grinned happily. "I thought this expedition would make my career. Now I know it will."

"Yeah, assuming we survive," I muttered. I didn't trust these new people yet. Not that they'd given me a reason, but I just didn't trust folks I didn't know. And we were outnumbered, following strangers to their home, and their pterodactyls would give them a distinct advantage in a fight. Hell, for all I knew, they were cannibals, and I didn't like the way they kept eyeballing our weapons.

As if reading my mind, one of the Shayanas on foot shifted his black powder rifle in his arms and offered me a piece of what looked like dried meat pulled from a leather pouch strapped around his waist. At my skeptical face he put his hand against his forehead with the index and pinky finger sticking out. "Three horns," he said as he pretended to pull his nose into the shape of a third horn.

Nodding, I reached over and took the meat. Apparently, they weren't cannibals after all. The meat had a spiced flavor to it and was rather pleasing. Chewing on the meat, I looked over at Skyla and shrugged. They might kill us and take our weapons, but at least they wouldn't eat us.

Our trail continued, and through the trees I saw we were approaching the large mountain rising above the forest floor.

***

The top of the lone mountain was broken off. Blown off was probably the correct phrase, and the jagged edges jutted into the sky menacingly. John had tried questioning the natives as we moved along the slightly widening trail about everything from their origin in this strange place to what their women looked like, but they seemed content to simply shrug him off or ignore him completely. The journalist was getting increasingly annoyed at their deflections and finally settled into a sullen fit of quiet. Only the Shayana Chief seemed to have answers, and those were reserved for the Lieutenant.

Sweat poured off us as we approached through the dense forest that ringed the base of the mountain. The humidity was awful. Skyla mopped sweat off her face with a bandana, and she slipped her hat back, hanging it on the band. Her black hair was plastered flat across her scalp. I followed suit and splashed some water from my canteen onto my bandana to cool off with.

Thenory noticed the black curved dinosaur claw hanging from its leather thong around my neck and nodded towards it. "Did thou kill the beast from which the claw came?" he asked.

"I did."

"From what did it come?"

"We call it an Allosaurus. A big beast that walks on back legs, with small ridges above the eyes, almost like little horns."

The Chief of the Shayana grimaced. "I know of what thee speak. They are great and terrible. But it appears as though thou killed a young one."

I held back a sigh. "It was half-grown, yes."

He grinned crookedly at me. "Still a great feat of strength to defeat such an animal."

"Thank you."

We carefully rode around small cracks in the ground where heat rose in gasps of stinking fumes that reeked of rotten eggs. The sulfuric scent of the volcanic activity beneath us was nauseating.

Moving along the edge of the forest, we came across wooden stakes jutting upright from the ground. On their sharpened points rested severed ape heads. They were in various forms of decay, most appeared ancient and bleached by the sun. But some still had rotting flesh hanging off, as though our rescuers had refreshed their yard decorations recently.

Brandthorn turned to me suddenly and several of the Shayana nearby twitched with their weapons. They may have saved us, but that didn't mean they trusted us yet. The Lieutenant noticed as well and finished the movement slowly. "Seems we aren't the only enemies that apes have around here. These gentlemen appear to have devised a new manner for keeping them at bay. Maybe we should surround the fort with ape skulls?"

"That's an idea," Charles agreed.

"That's barbaric," Skyla said, gagging as we rode past a fresher specimen. A bright green snake slithered from the open mouth, curling around the spear and darting its forked pink tongue out at us. She shuddered and moved Smoke closer to me, giving the reptile a wide berth.

"It is. But it is hard to argue with results," I admitted.

"I don't see any scalps hanging from their belts though," Charles whispered, as if to keep the locals from hearing him.

Skyla chewed her lower lip. "That is interesting. Makes me think that the Shaynee must have picked it up from other neighboring tribes like the Sioux or Cheyenne. And, well, these aren't the same Shaynee we know. Not only is their name different, Shayana, but they've an obvious European influence. And they've outdated armor and weapons that the Indians on our side don't. But where do they get the gunpowder?"

Daniels spoke up. "Not gunpowder, but black powder," he gestured at the mountain towering over the trees in front of us. "Perfect place for it too. So long as they have a dormant volcano for a home they can come up with the basic ingredients for black powder. I'd be curious to see what sort of smithy set up they have for making the weapons and equipment. It's an old volcano! The possibilities are almost endless. Imagine the forges they could have!"

"Black powder can be made in volcanoes?" Skyla asked.

"Sort of." The Lieutenant scratched the stubble on his chin. "There's basically three main ingredients to black powder. Sulfur, which should be easy to come by in a volcano. Charcoal, which can be made anywhere, and nitrate, or salt peter. As for that," he pointed above us as a pterodactyl screeched out of sight, "I'm willing to bet wherever they keep those giant birds has plenty of dung that could be used for salt peter. After all, the Confederates mined bat guano from caves during the War Between the States to make black powder for their weapons."

"I never knew that," she admitted.

"Probably because no one wants to brag about how they spent the war shoveling bat poop for the southern cause," I chuckled. Even coming from the war-ravaged South, I'd never known that either.

A shriek came from above, loud and unnerving, and instinctively I ducked. A pair of pterodactyls and their riders swooped overhead, skimming the tops of the trees close enough that leaves dislodged and fell around us.

"I thought I was impressed with the mounted trikes, but those..." Daniels whistled. "Those are something else."

Gibbons spoke from behind us where he rode beside Charles. "Could you imagine? Flying? It's preposterous. People aren't made to be in the air. That's why all those loco inventions folks come up with keep failing. I watched a fellow with makeshift wings try to fly off a barn once at a fair. He'd covered these sticks with feathers, strapped them to arms and legs. Took a running leap off the top of the roof. Magnificent. For a moment he looked like he was going to fly away," the big Sergeant chuckled. "Then he dropped like a rock. Snapped his leg right in two. Screamed like a little girl until we got some whiskey in him." He shook his head. "Never thought I'd ever see someone actually pulling it off and flying through the air. Especially on the back of such a giant leathery beast as that."

"It is incredible," I told him.

"I'd like to give it a try," Charles said admirably.

I glanced over at Skyla. She smiled at me gamely.

"How are you holding up?" I asked.

"Oh, I'm alright, but I'm mighty tired of riding."

I patted Carbine's neck. "I bet they're tired of being ridden." I nodded towards the lithe, strange men around us. "They don't seem tired though. But I reckon you've got to be a hearty person to survive around here."

"What do you think of their armor?" she asked.

"Pretty similar to that piece we found in the ape canyon. Looks heavy and hot, but I suppose it's an advantage on the apes. A glancing hit with an arrow might sheer off without penetrating, but I'm willing to bet a direct hit will puncture right through it. The armor also gives them some protection against teeth and claws, and well, this place is full of dinosaurs with those." I thought of our men killed by raptors, it would certainly have helped them.

"I'd bet most of the critters on this side would crunch them like a tin can though," Gibbons said as he hacked and spat off to the side. One of the Shayana glared at him with disgust. The black Sergeant didn't so much as flinch but met the glare with a stare of his own as if daring the man to say something. After several moments, the Shayana looked away.

"Do try not to offend them, Sergeant," Daniels said as he looked back in the saddle.

"Yes, sir," the big Sergeant replied. "I'll do my best."

The small trail we rode eventually merged with others and gave way to a beaten path as we began climbing around the dormant volcano. The sides of the mountain were steep, thick with chunks of volcanic rock jutting out and dense green vegetation growing between them. The mountain looked like a fortress with a winding path, at times only a scant six feet wide, that circled around the base of the volcano, rising higher and higher. An approaching army would be under fire almost the entire way up the mountain, and any advantage in numbers would be greatly diminished by the narrowness of the path that led to the top. I doubted that my side, even with our superior weaponry, would be able to take this mountain with conventional means. It'd be suicide.

After what seemed like an hour, we reached the top where the mountain path walked through a large cavern of black stone that was thirty feet deep before revealing an interior to the mountaintop. Crossing through the volcanic tunnel of stone and rock, we reached the inside where a green paradise awaited us.

***

It took several days to get used to the safety inside the protected mountain as well as figure out the Shayana's society and culture. A lot had to be said for Parsons. After their initial reluctance to talk to the man, they began opening up and he took many pages of notes in his slim journals.

Their village contained about two hundred people in total, an obvious mixture of white English descendants and an Indian people who appeared to be descendants of the same people that the Shaynee on our side came from as well. It was as if two cultures had merged together generations ago, neither fully assimilating the other, but both learning a peaceful cohabitation of sorts. But while they worked in harmony, it was easy to see that the English culture was dominant in language, technology, society, and governing.

The Shayana lived in houses, or huts really, made of a mixture of wood and volcanic rock gleamed from the ground and surrounding mountainside. Between the houses lay hardened paths of rocks lined with neatly trimmed grass and small, delicate yellow and pink flowers. They'd set several houses aside for us to stay in, and I slept in one with Skyla and the other civilians. It was roomier than the tents we'd been sharing, but we all made sure to give Skyla all the privacy she needed.

The people here used English tools as well, wheelbarrows, small single-man pulled wagons, metal axes and hoes in addition to the metal armor that some of the men wore. The village had a lovely smithy set up using a volcanic fissure to help create and temper the metal. We were told the iron ore required to make the steel came from a mine that was worked by another village to the west. The ore was hard to get, and anything made of metal was treated with great reverence and respect. They also grew crops, and the soil was rich and dark. We were told there was once a thick forest growing on top of the entire mountain, and over time it was worked away, and the slash burned to help fertilize the soil.

The village seemed peaceful, well protected by terrain, and their rudimentary black powder weapons appeared capable of keeping the apes away. Plus, they had the advantage of the flying beasts that could carry them in and out of battle, swooping down on any attackers.

The pterodactyls themselves were called breehas, after the terrible screeching noises they made at each other. The Shayana had dozens of them that were tamed, with great big nests on one side of the broken rim far away from the small village. The creatures made a great racket when they were stirred up, and their nests and cliffs were covered in unmeasurable amounts of poop, feathers, and bits of bone and debris from their meals. Large eggs, bigger than my head, lay in their nests, and the squawking of their young was ear piercing and unnerving.

But humans and the breehas weren't the only thing that lived at the top of the mountain.

There were slaves as well.

Ape slaves.

They lived in shabby, squalid looking huts, working the fields and harvesting guano from breehas and sulfur and metals from mines that were carved deep inside the passages within the mountain. They all appeared young, none of them as large or vicious looking like the ones we'd been fighting. And they all bore scars of whip lashes across their backs and shoulders, the sight of which made my skin crawl.

It was a strange but thriving culture and it appeared as though we'd found an ally.

***

I walked hand in hand with Skyla through rows of young corn stalks. After three days of being here, we were finally feeling somewhat safe and secure for the first time in Prehistoria. The sun was shining high overhead, fluffy white clouds drifted across the sky, and everything, for the moment, seemed right in the world.

But we were still heavily armed because we weren't idiots, and occasionally something fierce and terrifying roared in the distance.

Standing several feet high, the field of green shoots were being hoed by some young apes. Nearby stood a Shayana overseer with a bullwhip on his waist and a black powder rifle slung across his shoulder. The man looked bored as he watched the apes carefully hoe around the young stalks. Occasionally, he'd bark a command in the apes' own language to spur them onwards if they appeared to be slacking in their work.

Large fields were scattered over the mountaintop. The terrain rolled inside the broken rim, but the area was massive. At least several miles wide and a half dozen long and included a large forest on one side. The rest was a big open area with the occasional patch of trees to give shade.

It was peaceful and scenic.

The sudden screech of a breeha split the peaceful morning air as a pterodactyl swept down through the clouds and swooped up the largest of the apes hoeing the field. The claws of the dinosaur pierced through the ape's hairy hide about the shoulders and back, and he roared out in pain.

Shocked, we watched as the Shayana-mounted pterodactyl carried the struggling ape high into the air.

Other slaves ran after the dangling ape, shouting in gibberish as he was carried away. Fighting against the large bird, the ape hammered his fists helplessly against the leathery pterodactyl's legs over and over. The Shayana overseer stood and watched, uncaring as one of his charges was carried away and the others chased after him.

"Where are they taking-" Skyla started then stopped abruptly as the ape was carried past the edge of the mountain rim and released.

Skyla gasped and grabbed my arm as he tumbled out of view.

"Holy..." I stared, shocked.

The Shayana overseer shouted something at the surviving apes in their own guttural, rough language while he pulled the whip off his side and cracked it overhead. Meekly, the young apes returned to their work.

"Good for them," the deep voice came from behind us.

Turning, we saw Sergeant Gibbons approaching. The big black man shrugged as he watched the mounted pterodactyl winging back towards the nests. "Parsons mentioned that he found out they kill off the apes before they get large enough to fight back. Not a bad plan if you ask me."

"It's cruel," Skyla told him.

He dismissed the concept with a swipe of his good arm. "They're apes, ma'am. Who cares? It ain't like they're people."

"Slavery doesn't bother you?" she challenged back.

He smiled slightly, "No, ma'am. Not of apes it don't." Turning, he ran a hand across the leaves of the corn stalks as he walked away. The

Shayana had sewn his cut shut, smeared a poultice made of the small flowers outside their houses on it, and wrapped the wound in a clean bandage. The man still favored the arm, and I suspected it'd be several weeks before he would be able to regain full mobility.

Skyla looked at me. Her eyes were large. "This is terrible."

"Yes, it is," I agreed.

We turned back toward the village; our peaceful moment shattered by the sudden violent demise of the young ape.

Later that evening, as our small group gathered to eat, we saw an ape whipped after overturning a wagon carrying large yellow and orange gourds. The Shayana overseer had peeled the whip off his belt so fast that it cracked against the ape's back before she could even bend over to pick up the fallen food. A half dozen lashes later, the wagon was righted, and the ape was once again pulling the load. Fresh crimson dripped from the new cuts across her hairy back.

I winced with every crack and the tendrils of scar tissue stretching across my back burned with every lash. Skyla looked like she was going to be sick, and I noticed Lieutenant Daniels watching with what I was certain was a carefully crafted blank look on his face. Afterwards, Oscar walked over to the Shayana and questioned him about the making of his whip. I watched as the former paleontologist unrolled it and gave several practice cracks before jotting notes down in one of his journals.

Skyla walked away in disgust, her food left behind uneaten, and I followed.

We made it twenty yards before I heard someone jogging up behind us.

Hand on a pistol, I spun around to confront the runner.

John Parsons slowed to a stop and held his hands up. "Whoa there, Jed. Just thought I might have a word with you two."

"What is it, John?" Skyla asked while I released the butt of my pistol and tucked my thumbs behind my belt buckle instead.

"I'm writing an article on Jed and-"

"Oh no you're not," I growled.

Skyla quickly grabbed my arm with a broad smile. "That's wonderful news."

"Yes, thank you, Skyla." John looked from her to me. "Jed, the world needs to hear of your actions. You're a hero. You saved a town."

"A lot of us saved Granite Falls… And a lot of us died doing it. Write about them."

"I will… I will. And honestly, I'm writing about a lot. About this expedition, about these Shayana and their ape workers. All fascinating things. I think it will be a large series of articles, but I must start at the beginning. And the beginning begins with you." He grinned. "But now I've come to ask a few more questions about the days leading up to the Battle of the Apes, would you and Skyla be so gracious as to help me with the answers?"

"Of course, John!" Skyla answered while I gritted my teeth and tried to find a way out of this.

"Why don't you ask Skyla, I need to go exercise Carbine. I bet he's getting antsy to go for a ride," I lied.

"Nonsense, your valiant steed can wait." The reporter grabbed both our arms and steered us towards a pair of rough sawn wooden benches in front of our huts. I grumbled about how Carbine was far from being valiant as I was led along, but neither Skyla nor John seemed to be listening.

***

The Shayana buried our dead.

That's what they told us when a dozen men appeared one afternoon carrying the weapons and equipment of our fallen soldiers. They also managed to find and bring back several horses and the mule carrying Oscar's vegetation specimens which they placed in our makeshift corral.

In return, Chief Thenory asked for the weapons and training in how to use them.

Daniels allowed them to keep the weapons, ammunition, and equipment, but any personalized gear we were to bring back with us for surviving relatives. The Lieutenant also had one of the Winchesters disassembled and its inner mechanisms explained to the natives, so they could grasp how to care for the weapons that were now the most prized and valuable commodity in Prehistoria.

I didn't care for that, and when I caught the Lieutenant alone by the horses, I brought up my concerns.

"I know the enemy of our enemy is our friend, but how well do you trust them?"

The young officer put his hands on his hips and watched a pair of small apes struggle with a heavy load of what looked like potatoes in a wheeled cart. "They saved us from the ape ambush and gave us shelter. We owe them a certain amount of courtesy in return. If you're worried about the rifles and pistols, they don't have the mechanical or metallurgical ability to remake our repeaters, and certainly not the ammunition. And the dozen they have shouldn't turn a battle against us. But we could use allies on this side, and so far, they seem to be willing to work with us."

Carbine saw me and trotted over from where he was chasing Smoke. I ran my hands through his mane. He was due for a good brushing.

"It bothers you that they use ape labor." It was a statement from the Lieutenant, not a question.

I looked him in the eye. "Let's call them what they are... slaves."

Daniels rolled his eyes and shrugged. "They aren't humans, Jed. They're just a bunch of hairy barbarians that would kill us if given the chance to grow up. And we may have fought a war over slavery two decades ago, but things on this side are different. You can't expect them to know better... yet. Do apes have rights? Not right now. Now they're just the uncivilized, barbaric enemy that have killed over a dozen of my men."

"And I don't mind killing them," I snapped back. "But I ain't killing baby apes by dropping them from hundreds of feet in the air."

"They aren't ape babies, Jed!" He fixed me with a glare. "They're half grown, and they're property. What do you want from me? To start a damn war over how our enemy is treated by an ally? You think that will help or hinder us?"

I ground my teeth. He was right. It would cause a lot of bad blood if we caused a scene over it. I changed the subject, "When are we leaving?"

He glanced from me to Carbine. "Anxious to be away?"

"Yes. And partly because if they wanted to kill us and take all our rifles, there'd be jack shit we could do about it. They outnumber us dozens to one. No one would ever know what happened to us. You can trust them all you want, but I question their motives still."

"We've got to trust them. We don't have any other choice. But another day here won't hurt, and it seems like Skyla and Oscar are enjoying themselves." He gestured across the fields. Thenory had landed his bird and the two paleontologists were touching the leathery winged beast and talking amongst themselves. Charles stood near my favored paleontologist, his arms crossed as he watched the giant bird carefully. The large pterodactyl raised its yellow head into the air and opened its beaked mouth wide, making the loud call that the creature was named for.

I had to admit, the breehas were fascinating. The ability for a human being to fly was incredulous. I was tempted to try and trade one of my Colt Peacemakers for one of the young birds but trading away the tools your life will most likely depend upon is never a good idea. And I still had my little trike back home. I was going to go out on a limb and guess that raising Sara without any experience would be difficult enough without adding a giant prehistoric bird to the mix.

Carbine snapped at my hat and I jerked away from his grasp and swatted him across the neck with it. "Do you think we'll end up arming the rest of them?"

"I expect if they keep being our friends and help fend off the apes then we'll send them a few more crates of rifles and ammunition. Maybe even a Gatling gun, that's all it'd take to defend their entrance with that winding trail up the mountain."

"Speaking of the apes, they say where the others are located?"

Daniels tapped his pocket. "Yes. I've updated the map. There's a couple of small villages of apes around us, but their civilization is further away to the north east." He frowned. "There is one village that's not far from the fort. I suspect that's where our attackers came from. We'll have to hit them after we return. They're too close for comfort."

"There's talk of other Shayana settlements. Did Chief Thenory point them out as well?"

The Lieutenant shook his head slightly. "No. But you can't blame them for keeping their cards close to their chests. They don't know the truth about where we come from either."

We stopped talking as Parsons and one of the natives approached us. He was a big, strapping fellow named Henon. Tan skinned with black hair and dark eyes; he looked every bit like a Shaynee from our side. He'd been one of the men who'd helped rescue us during the ambush.

"John, Henon," Daniels said with a nod, acknowledging the pair.

"Lieutenant." The Shayana butchered the pronunciation of the title. But that was to be expected since it was one of many new words they were beginning to learn from us. They'd adapted well to our extra lingo, but it was still awkward. And it took Daniels some time to get them to believe that he was not the Chief of our people, but just a lowly military leader. They didn't get the nuances of rank very well; it'd been lost to time for them.

"I was just interviewing Henon about his people and Prehistoria. It's fascinating," the reporter told us. "For example, did you know that there is a tribe of what the Shayana call 'axe men' to the far east by the sea?"

"Axe men?" I glanced at the Lieutenant. This was interesting news. "Are they friend or foe?"

Parsons leaned against the makeshift corral and shook his head slightly. "I get the impression they aren't exactly either one. The Shayana and these axe men tend to avoid each other but do on occasion trade."

"How far away are they?" Daniels asked the native as he pulled out the folded map from his breast pocket.

Henon shrugged. "Four or five days on foot. One day on breehas."

"Can you show me on this map?"

The big Shayana circled an area with his finger by the ocean's edge. "Here. But easier to show thou."

Daniels marked the spot. "We will take you up on that offer one day."

This seemed like a good opportunity to get some information of my own, so I began asking questions to the Shayana.

"I killed an ape a while back. Big... ugly... scarred face." I ran a finger from eye to jaw to show the location of the hideous scar on the ape leader I'd killed in Granite Falls. "Ever seen him before?"

Henon nodded. "We knew of him well. Our raids on his villages yielded many slaves and he sought us out with his army. We were preparing defenses to fight him when he left the canyon and fought thou instead."

I nodded, wondering how much they knew about where he'd gone. Surely, they could have tracked them and found the tunnel to our side. But no one, not even Thenory, had made mention of it, so we'd followed the Lieutenant's lead and kept our mouths shut about where we came from.

"I saw them sacrifice a man on their altar. Was he one of yours?"

The Shayana grunted. "Tis likely. We lost several scouts watching their army and never saw them again."

It seemed my shooting up their ritual sacrifice ruined their plans to attack the Shayana and they went after us instead. That meant everyone who died on our side was my fault for trying to assassinate the ape leader after I saw him rip out the Shayana scout's heart.

Damn.

I looked around the village; there were a lot of little kids running around and dozens of women in view. Maybe I did some good after all. But it meant that Sheriff Dan and his nephew's blood, and that of nearly a hundred others, was on my hands.

Daniels saw the look on my face and turned towards me. He'd been well briefed in the events leading up to and through the battle. "Not your fault, Jed. They attacked your ranch first, remember?"

I kicked a small volcanic rock with the toe of my boot under the makeshift corral fence, thinking about the ramifications of my actions. It hurt to think of the course I'd set myself and others on. But there was no changing it; what was done was done.

Henon looked back and forth between us, puzzled. "Thou did the right thing. The apes are wretched creatures, foul things from hell. Large ones are royalty. They lead armies and rule over villages. Killing him was of benefit to all."

"Royalty, huh?" John Parsons looked at me with admiration and I knew he'd be putting that in his stupid article about me.

"That's pretty neat," I admitted. Strangely enough, killing a royal ape made me feel better about all of it.

The big Shayana nodded vigorously while reaching out to run a hand on Carbine's side. My horse side stepped away from him. For some reason he didn't seem to care for any of the natives.

Across the field, I saw Thenory point at the obsidian blade sheathed on Skyla's hip. Bidding Carbine and the men goodbye, I walked to where Skyla stood, careful to not step on any of the plants growing in their neat rows.

The big pterodactyl turned its head sideways at me as I approached, and inwardly I shuddered. The beady black eyes appeared intelligent, but there was something strange and different that lurked in their depths. I got the impression that such prehistoric beasts and mankind were never meant to exist together.

Skyla had passed the sacrificial knife over and Chief Thenory was running his fingers over the flat of the chipped black obsidian blade.

"This knife has killed dozens, maybe hundreds, of our kind," he said with a mixture of reverence and disgust. He flipped it around in his hand and rubbed a thumb along the trike horn handle. I'd always suspected that the handle had been made from the ape leader's trike with its one horn snapped off.

He passed the sacrificial blade back to Skyla who carefully slipped it into its sheath.

I pointed at the flintlock pistol tucked into Thenory's waistband. "I bet that gun has some stories to tell as well."

He drew it, turned it sideways, and looked down on the gun. The polished wood grip and dark metal of the barrel gleamed in the sun. The Shayana took meticulous care of their weapons, no doubt because of how difficult they were to make. And I was willing to bet my *Eighty-Six* that they didn't have the ability to make more pistols. "'Twas my father's, and his before him, and before him. It has killed many apes."

"No doubt," I admitted in reverence. Gotta love an heirloom gun.

Thenory's pterodactyl ducked its head down and pushed its beak against its master. He placed the gun back into his waistband and patted the bird's head as it let out a piercing call.

"How did your people come to fly the breehas?" I asked curiously.

"Slowly," he said with a sideways grin. "When the Shayana first came to this place, the breehas were here already. But there were only a few left, under attack by others." He pointed at the long red feathers braided into his hair. "The Shayana fought to protect them and saved their eggs and young. In return, the breehas let them soar on their backs. Once our

English fathers arrived, they were taught as well, once they proved themselves and earned the right."

"Okay," I said, confused. One of the problems with the Shayana is that you never knew if you were going to get an English explanation, or something that was more along the lines of an Indian one. I was just glad that English had become the predominate language amongst these people.

Oscar looked up from his sketching. "Is it possible for me to fly with you?"

The Chief frowned and shook his head. His fanged and beaded necklace shimmered in the sunlight. "By custom, only members of the Shayana tribe can soar. The advantage the breehas give in battle is great and cannot be taught to outsiders."

The portly paleontologist looked dismayed as the Chief reached into a satchel slung over a shoulder and pulled out a dead brown rodent. "Would thou liken a chance to feed her?"

Oscar's frown turned into a boyish grin as he took the small rat-like corpse eagerly and threw it upwards. In a darting snap the breeha's beak snatched it from the air, and with a toss of the creature's head, gulped the morsel down.

"Incredible," he whispered to Skyla as the lump slid down inside the pterodactyl's wobbly neck and into its large, sleek body.

Charles held out a hand towards the breehas. "May I?" he asked.

At a nod from Thenory, the Brit carefully placed his hand against one folded wing and caressed it. "A magnificent animal, Chief."

"It is." Placing his foot in the stirrups, he climbed into the saddle and grasped the braided leather reins with both hands. We all stepped back from the bird, moving far enough away to not be hit by its wings when stretched out. Clucking his tongue, Thenory snapped the reins against the creatures' back and the wings beat us with air as the beast lifted into the sky. With another snap of the Chief's wrist, the bird flew towards the nests at the far side of the shattered mountaintop.

I whistled. "That is something else."

Skyla grabbed my arm and leaned against me. "Wouldn't it be something to fly?"

"Not for me, I'd rather stay on the ground or on Carbine."

"My sentiments exactly," Charles stated firmly as he watched the Chief's breeha descend into the nests. A terrible racket echoed over to us as the pterodactyls shifted and hopped from rock outcropping to outcropping to make room for the landing bird.

In the distance, standing near a small group of apes and their Shayana overseer, Sergeant Gibbons stood with his arms folded over his massive chest. He'd been tasked with learning the apes' language by Daniels. He hadn't been pleased with the task as he considered the big monkey children to be inferior beings but, as I watched, he pointed to various objects and was no doubt repeating the rough language of the young apes as they named them.

I chewed my lower lip and stared.

"Penny for your thoughts?" Skyla asked.

"I was just thinking about how little we know of the apes. And I was thinking about our future together, us and them, that is. If we'll ever come to peaceful terms or always be at each other's throats."

"I figured you hated them."

"Part of me does," I admitted. "The part of me that hates bullies, aggressors, and cowards. But we once viewed the Indians as inferior and almost wiped them out, and then they came to our aid in Granite Falls. If it hadn't been for them, we certainly would have all been killed before the reinforcements arrived. But the apes…" I patted the butts of my pistols, "most likely we'll have to beat them into submission before they are willing to accept the notion of peace. I got the feeling they view us as the lesser race, and that ain't acceptable in my book."

She patted my arm. "Things will work out the way they're supposed to."

Oscar had been quiet until now and turned towards the three of us. "We'll kill them all. I've no doubt of that. It's inevitable. Like the Indians, they've something we want. Vast resources and land. They can either give them to us, or we'll take them. And I believe it will require us wiping them out to do so."

"Is that what Reydan White has you doing, Oscar? Hunting resources?"

He grinned wolfishly beneath his spectacles and smudged top hat. From his pocket he brought out a gold nugget several inches long and held it up between his thumb and forefinger. In its rough form it still had impurities in it, but it was the sort of gold that folks would kill each other for back home. "Oh, the Shayana have already found them for us." With a knowing smile he tucked the nugget away and waddled off.

I took off my hat and raked to the side my sweaty black hair. "Well, we've been talking about the apes. But maybe it's the Shayana that should be worried."

"Yes," Skyla agreed with a concerned look across her face.

We stood silent for a moment, just taking in the peace and quiet of the mountaintop. Reaching down, I checked the looseness of my Colts in their holsters, making sure they were ready to draw at a moment's notice. It was a paranoid tick I seemed to have picked up lately.

Thinking, I turned to Skyla. "Have you heard about these 'axe men' that live to the far east?" I asked.

"No, nothing." She frowned in puzzlement. "Another civilization?"

"Seems so."

"I guess we know where our next expedition will take us."

"Yes, ma'am," I grimaced. "Let's hope it goes better than this one."

***

I spent the rest of the day watching the Shayana practice with the new rifles. They had enough help from the remaining soldiers that I didn't bother to assist. Ammunition was limited, so there was a lot of dry firing and working the levers and pulling the triggers without a cartridge in the chamber for the first few hours. After that and drilling them endlessly with firearms safety, they were given several loaded cartridges each and most managed to passably hit a decent-sized target at close range. Daniels and Chief Thenory were pleased with their progression through the day.

During that time, I made my mind up.

It was time to tell Skyla about me.

I dreaded telling her the truth, but I'd put it off long enough. If she took it badly, she'd have time to decide what to do about the information I shared before we returned to the fort. Hopefully, it wouldn't end up with me in chains. I didn't think it would. She loved me, and love covers a multitude of sins.

I found Charles and Skyla sitting on a large outcropping of rock, with the paleontologist sketching the view of the forest below. Fifty yards behind them came the pleasant sounds of the village ending their day and the faint scent of roasted dinosaur meat and vegetables drifting on the gentle breeze. Earlier that afternoon, several Shayana had returned with great slabs of meat, hopefully taken from a fresh kill and not something they came across already dead in the jungle.

Coughing gently, the pair turned to me.

The way the setting sun's light lit Skyla's face was beautiful. It was moments like this I wished I had some artistic ability. Sadly, I could barely draw little more than stick figures in the dirt.

"Charles? May I have a moment alone with Skyla?" I asked the Brit.

Charles looked at Skyla and she nodded. "Certainly, Jedidiah." Shifting his gun belt, he stood and picked up the deceased Private Timmons' rifle. "I'll be with the horses if you need me."

"Thanks." I sat in the place he vacated.

"What is it, Jed?" She looked at me with innocent brown eyes and I swallowed hard.

"There have been some things I've been meaning to tell you about myself..." I hesitated, building up the courage to go on as she burrowed her forehead and squinted at me in the light of the setting sun. "There's a lot you don't know about me. And-"

"No," she interrupted me. "I don't know, and I don't need to. I don't care about your past. Just who you are now. That's all that matters."

I looked away over the rim and watched a flock of small pterodactyls take flight from one of the trees below. The blue and green leathery birds flapped their wings and soared on the breeze. "I appreciate that. But you need to know..."

"Does this have something to do with the shootout at the bar?"

"Yes." I hung my head, dreading telling her the truth of the matter. Taking a deep breath, I pressed on. "I already told you part of my story. About when I was ten, how Reydan White and his men took Cato, burned my home, and whipped me near to death."

She nodded slowly. "Those men you killed in the bar, they were the same ones who whipped you?"

If only it'd been so simple. I shook my head. "No. My father came back from the war soon after, and we went looking for Cato and the men who'd taken him. They'd burned a swath across a dozen countries, torturing, killing, and looting. We never found Cato, but we found the man that whipped me," I grimaced. He'd been my first kill. Executed in the same outhouse we found him in, after we got some of the information we needed. "Anyways, their leader, who we know is Reydan now, had left the group with Cato and the raiders had split up. So... we began tracking them down, one by one."

"Did you..." She hesitated, as if afraid to ask a question that she already knew the answer to.

I dipped my head in an affirmative to the unasked question. "We killed them all. But we could never find Reydan because they never had a name for him, just his title 'Captain'. Eventually we found more men like us... men with deep grudges against carpet baggers, thieves, and scum who were milking the South dry and taking farms and ruining lives. We began to fight back. Stealing, robbing... killing sometimes. It's what we did. But we also were on the lookout for Cato or the man who took him."

"And you were ten when this started?" she asked quietly.

"I'd just turned eleven when I killed my first man. Our little group began to take on bigger and more evil folks. We traveled around the country, doing what we needed to do. Sometimes we'd take law abiding work between jobs, that's how I learned to ranch and work cattle. I was also a banker once. But that was for an inside job..."

She sat in stunned silence, and after a moment, I continued.

"Anyways, I stopped a couple of years ago and came to Wyoming to hide out and get away from it all. But before I left the gang, I was sent on a job." I sighed and rubbed my temple as dark thoughts surfaced. "It went bad. A kid was killed. Afterwards, we were supposed to link up with my father and deliver the money. Except the man who killed the kid drank too much and started laughing about it. He was a killer, and crazy to boot. He and the other men were drinking, just letting off some steam after a job, then they started talking about the things they'd done... the people they'd hurt or killed."

I looked away, feeling the shame burning deep within me. "I'd been on the fence about quitting the gang for years. I'd even left them once to fight the Nez Perce with Sheriff Dan. But I came back because of my old man. But that night, I was sick of it all. Sick of what we were doing, feeling like it wasn't right, wishing I had a normal life, no longer wanting to be part of any of it. And when they went to bragging about what wretched men they were, I killed them. Then I took the loot, buried some of it, and started working my way west. I bought my ranch and met you," I smiled at her sadly. "Problem is that my past won't stay gone. Those men I shot... they were from my father's gang. He brought them there to kill me."

She gasped. "Your father?!"

"Yep. So, they know where I am. Which means they probably know who you are. And I've got to do something about them. But I'm not sure what, short of killing them all."

"Why would he want you dead?"

"I probably made him look bad. Gang leader's son killing three of his men, taking the money, and disappearing. Or maybe he's grown weak and can't keep the men in line anymore. Last I'd heard, they were nothing more than a bunch of killers and thieves now. They aren't out to make things right over the South, those days are long gone. Now they're in it for themselves."

She was quiet as we watched the sun slowly setting on the lost world. After several minutes she wrapped her arm in mine. "So... you're an outlaw." It wasn't a question, but a statement of fact.

"Yes."

"And your father wants you dead."

"Seems like it."

"Do we need to run?"

I looked at her and chuckled. Her dark hair glistened in the sun, and her brown eyes looked at me fearlessly. "No. I can't have you run from your dream of studying all this." I waved my hand at the world around us as something roared in the forest below. "I've just got to make my way.

But there will be problems. If Reydan doesn't know who I am, he might figure it out. But it'd be hard for him to act without revealing his part in who I am. Then there is also Sheriff Beauford. He's a mean one, and sly. He knows there is something about me that's off, and if he's a decent bloodhound he'll figure it out. Dropping bodies in the town bar really didn't help with him, because now he's motivated to figure me out. And I'm confident he didn't believe me when I told him I didn't know them."

"What about John?" she asked of the reporter.

"Him. Yeah... I've been vague with my answers regarding my past. Since my old gang knows where I am, I don't think it will matter too much. Unless there is someone out there tracking me down for my misdeeds of the past, I don't think anything he'll write about me will give me away."

"So, we're staying put, and handling whatever happens together... right?" she asked as she rested her head on my shoulder.

I pressed the side of my face against the top of her head. "Together. No matter what." For a moment we were quiet, then I grinned slightly. "Unless I get hanged. That I'll do alone."

She slapped my chest, hard. "Don't say that."

"Yes, ma'am."

We sat quietly for a moment, taking in the beauty of the lost world before she spoke again, "I take it Jedidiah isn't your real name?"

I cringed. "No... it's Orville... Orville Eugene Landry."

She laughed. "Orville? I'm not calling you that. You're a Jed to me."

"For that, I'm grateful!"

***

Chief Thenory found me gazing over the mountaintop after Skyla had gone back to our hut to sleep. I noted he now carried a dead soldier's Colt pistol, flapped holster, and belt slung around his waist. The recovered guns had become status symbols, handed out to the Chief's most prized fighters. Henon had a set as well. The Shayana with them strutted like peacocks around the village, while the men with their archaic black powder weapons looked on in jealousy.

"Thou does not trust us," he said softly.

I glanced at him then looked up at the moon peeking from behind the soft fluffy clouds that floated overhead. "What makes you say that?"

"The way thou looks at us. The way thou hand stays near thine weapons."

"Don't take it personal. That's just a habit... a manner of my being."

He nodded. "I know the word, habit. I pledge to thee, we mean no harm to any but the hairy men."

"Yeah," I looked at the fields the young apes had been hoeing earlier in the hot sun, "the hairy men."

He noticed. "Ye do not approve of our keeping the young?"

"We had a great war over the enslavement of man. Many lives were lost."

"Ah, but our slaves are not men, they are hairy men. Apes, as thine calls them."

"Yes," I admitted.

He sat beside me. "Would ye rather we kill young apes as we raid villages? Or take them, care for them, raise them, and use them as we see fit?" he argued.

"I don't reckon I'd kill them."

"I do not know this word... reckon."

I shook my head. "Doesn't matter. I wouldn't kill them. And you kill them anyways, once they get too big."

He shrugged. "Does thou see the problem? Kill them then, or use them and kill them later. Tis a choice we make. Ye understand this?"

I grimaced. He was right, there was no good answer. "I understand," I said.

He clapped me on the back, harder than I thought necessary. "Good."

"Chief," I turned and looked him in the eye. There'd been something on my mind ever since we met the natives and I wanted to get to the bottom of it. I asked him point blank, "Are there dragons here? Do you know what I speak of?"

Taking a deep breath, the Shayana leader looked up at the dark sky and nodded. "Yes. Dragons from the stories of old... The apes have great beasts that can breathe fire and consume everything. They are few. In all my years, I've only seen them two times. Leaders of the apes sometimes ride them into battle. My father fell fighting one from the back of his breehas."

I gulped; so the cave paintings hidden back at the fort were real. "How do you defeat such a beast?"

Thenory pointed across the mountaintop, to where the breehas rested. "We swarm them. At great cost to us. Many die to kill one."

"Do the apes have one now?"

He shrugged. "It has been many years since we've seen one. But they have not attacked us in large numbers since the days of my father."

"What do they look like?" I asked.

"Large wings, much bigger than breehas. More beast than bird. Large mouth, horns, sharp teeth, long tail. Very different."

That tied in with the cave paintings I saw in the locked cave back at Fort Jipson. "And they breathe fire?"

"Yes." He stood, and I could tell our conversation was over.

As he turned away to leave, I spoke his name softly and he looked back at me. The dark fanged necklace with its gold beads glittered in the moonlight.

"Thank you for rescuing us and taking us in."

He dipped his head in acknowledgement. "Thou art welcome. Goodnight... Jed."

I sat alone for a moment, listening to the Chief walk away and thinking of the possibilities. An ape army, led by a leader mounted on a stinking dragon. That'd be a hellacious fight. And we needed to figure out a defense against such a creature.

***

I woke Skyla with a gentle shake. Lieutenant Daniels and Sergeant Gibbons had already entered our hut, and everyone was present, including Oscar. That was Daniels' call to bring him in to the conversation we were about to have, he hoped he might have some insight. But we couldn't find John; he was no doubt off bugging someone for more information.

She stirred up from her bedding, brushing hair off her face as she looked around the room. "What? What is it?" she asked sleepily.

"Dragons," I said simply.

She sat upright, grabbed me by the shoulders, and looked into my eyes. "The cave paintings? They're real?" Her voice grew louder with concern.

I nodded slowly.

"There aren't any cave paintings of dragons..." Oscar started before he caught himself. "Wait. The locked room... is that what's in there? Why would you not show it to us?" he huffed in anger.

"Because the Captains didn't want to start a panic," Daniels confessed with some measure of embarrassment. "Which we're going to have now."

"Oh, bloody hell. Dragons aren't real!" Charles scoffed.

"Almost every culture has legends of dragons. Even the Bible references them several times," Skyla said. "Although, in the Bible they were dragons of the sea. But I suppose dragons of the land are possible as well."

I spoke up, "Not just possible. Real. Chief Thenory told me the ape leaders of their armies sometimes ride, or rather, fly them into battle. But they are rare. He's only seen one a couple of times and it's been a long time since he saw one last."

"Rare, well that's something at least," the Brit replied. "Maybe they're all gone now?"

"We can hope for that as long as we prepare for the worst," I said.

"Well, what were the paintings of?" Oscar interrupted as he leaned forward with interest.

Skyla pulled out one of her journals and flipped through it. "Here," she said as she spun the leather-bound book around for us to see. "I made a copy."

The sketch was of a giant pyramid. On top sat a horned winged lizard beast breathing yellow flames, and below it was men and other beasts being sacrificed by apes. Rivers of what could only be blood ran down the pyramid steps and below the apes. It was pretty dark and twisted for a cave painting.

"Holy hells," Gibbons muttered as he snuck a glance at his Lieutenant. "No wonder they kept the door locked."

"Seemed like a good idea at the time," Daniels admitted. "But now that we know dragons exist, we've got to let the Captains know so they can prepare defenses against such a threat. But how?"

"Bullets. Lots and lots of bullets," I muttered darkly.

The hut was silent as we all speculated on the future of our hold on Prehistoria.

***

We were attacked at the first light of dawn.

It was a scream that woke us. A woman's, high pitched and filled with terror, that ended abruptly with a heavy thud.

Immediately, a loud chorus of squawks and screams came from the breehas' nests on the other side of the mountaintop.

Charles grabbed his rifle and charged outside of the hut, and I rushed out after him with the *Eighty-Six* in hand.

We burst from our hut looking for attacking apes.

Instead, we witnessed a fifteen-foot-tall, red feathered bird flapping large wings, beating grass down, and taking off with a limp young woman pinned between its toothed beak.

Significantly larger than the breehas, the giant bird bounced, thrusting upwards with its thick muscular back legs, fighting to overcome the weight in its mouth.

"Mother of…" Charles stood still, frozen in place at the sight.

Pulling the *Eighty-Six* against my shoulder, I fired and rode the recoil of the gun blast.

The bird dropped the woman and shrieked as the bullet missed its large body but punctured through both wings, knocking small tufts of feathers off. Still flapping, it turned its pink feather-crested head towards me, screeched loudly, and began to rise into the air. Racking the lever, I shot again and put a large bullet into its body this time.

Charles recovered from his surprise and jerked his rifle up, firing wildly after the feathered beast.

Sergeant Gibbons raced out of one of the huts, wearing only his pants with pistol held in good hand. Taking careful aim, he began firing. Several black powder rifles boomed around us, sending white tufts of smoke into the cool morning air as the Shayana began to react as well.

Henon, yelling a war cry, chased after the bird, waving his sword and struggling against the great gusts of wind forced down on him by the bird. Unable to reach the beast, he dropped the sword and drew the government issue Colt pistol from its flapped holster. He awkwardly fired the gun, missing repeatedly, as the giant pterodactyl rose into the air.

Loud thuds surrounded us as four more of the large birds slammed into the ground on hind legs and folded wings. Twisting and turning, they moved to grab defenders. The neat, tidy fields were stomped flat, and ape slaves that'd been already at work in the fields took off running, drawing the attention of the new pterodactyls.

The pterodactyl I'd already shot swooped from the sky, screeching as it soared towards the running slaves. The same small ape child I saw being whipped earlier wasn't fast enough to dodge out of the way. She was snapped up in its tooth beak and carried away.

Only seconds had passed, and already the sharp crack of Winchesters from the soldiers and armed Shayanas split the morning dawn as they opened fire amongst the loud booms of the black powder guns.

One of the birds hopped onto the roof of one of the huts, the beams and thatched roof snapping and partially collapsing under its weight. A uniformed soldier ran out of the building, only to have a large beak burst through his chest then opened, ripping the man apart in a gory spray of blood. Snapping sharp teeth onto an arm, the bird stepped down onto his corpse and ripped the limb off.

Tossing its head back, the bird gulped the body part down as several plumes of white smoke blasted from nearby Shayanas.

Shrieking, the bird picked up the lower half of the man and, unfolding its massive wings, began to flap away.

Chief Thenory popped up from behind a stone wall adjacent to the ruined hut and fired his Colt pistol empty after the bird. He'd managed to put his metal breastplate on, but not a leather shirt. Shoving the gun back into its holster, he grabbed up his new Winchester and raced down the pathway towards the fields with the other birds. His archaic pistol was still jammed down the front of his trousers.

The bird closest to us lashed out towards Skyla.

Charles shoved her out of the way and fell on top of her.

Hitting the ground with his body over Skyla's, he fired his Schofield at point blank range into the feathered dinosaur's face. Screeching, it jerked away and snapped its toothed beak angrily. A clawed foot stomped down perilously close to my girl. Opening its beak, the bird reared its head back to bite.

Firing from a dozen yards away, I worked the action on the *Eighty-Six* like their lives depended on it.

The remaining three rounds I pumped into its long body as the creature jerked away. Once the hammer dropped on empty, I slung the rifle, drew my Colts and stalked towards the bird, firing them one after the other.

With each muzzle blast, bullets punctured red feathered hide and flesh. The bird twisted about frantically, nipping at the wounds and thrashing as it tried to move away. Charles joined in, emptying his revolver in seconds before rolling away from Skyla as she opened up with her pistol from where she lay prone on the ground.

Between the three of us we showered the vicious giant pterodactyl with bullets.

Dropping onto its side, the red feathered beast wrapped leather spindly legs around its body, trying to hide behind its wings as it rolled and struggled to get away from the bullets on the ground.

Out of ammunition, I dropped the Colts back into their holsters, unslung the rifle and began butt stroking the beast's head with the stock of the gun. Blood splattered, and I felt bones crack and break beneath my battering.

I stopped when the giant bird stopped twitching and looked around. Skyla stared at me in shock, and I could feel pterodactyl blood running down my face. Winking, I pulled fat cartridges off my belt and began thumbing them into the *Eighty-Six* as I surveyed the fields around the village.

Those of us with guns had put up a hellacious fight, wounding several of the beasts and chasing the others off.

One of them, wings so pierced and cut through with bullet holes and sword slashes that they wouldn't support flight, bounced up and down along the neat rows of corn, smashing stalks into the ground and dribbling blood behind. Several Shayana chased after it with rifles, sheathed swords bouncing against their legs as they ran.

Another bird took flight, carrying a Shayana warrior in the clutches of its hind legs. As it bounced it smashed the body against the ground, over and over. After making it thirty feet off the air, a bullet hit the creature and the bird released the man. Flailing and screaming, the Shayana fell to the ground and hit like a rag doll amongst the potatoes.

The remaining heavily wounded bird was surrounded, snapping and turning after us. Circling the feathered creature, the soldiers and Shayana emptied their guns into it.

After such a great volley, it lay weakened and mortally wounded, gasping its final breaths.

Chief Thenory pushed between them and placed his ancient pistol against the feathered head and pulled the trigger. White smoke blasted from the muzzle as the lead slug burst through the giant pterodactyl's skull and buried itself into the dirt on the other side.

Cheers rose around us from the natives as Oscar and John carefully peeked out from our hut, then stepped outside. The former scientist walked over to the dead bird that almost killed my paleontologist, stood beside Charles, and stared in astonishment. "Incredible. How can such a giant beast lift off the ground?" he asked.

"Look at the size of the wings!" Skyla bent over and grabbed one. Grunting daintily, she lifted the flap of feathered skin up for a better look. "These must be over fifty feet wide! Far wider than the creature is tall."

I finished loading cartridges into the *Eighty-Six* as the two paleontologists walked around the dead giant pterodactyl. John joined them, walking over hesitantly as he looked at the surrounding carnage with a face showing shock. I was pleased to see he had a pistol in hand, but displeased at not having seen him helping out during the giant bird attack.

Charles slung his Winchester over a shoulder and reloaded his Schofield revolver. "This place is just bloody well full of surprises," he glared at me. "Not one of which isn't dangerous. Do you still think Skyla should be here?"

I racked the lever on my 1886 Winchester, driving a cartridge home into the chamber. Skyla was standing near the head of the bird with Chief Thenory and Lieutenant Daniels. Even after the fear of the attack, her eyes were wide eyed with excitement as she studied the new dinosaur.

Now we knew where Thenory's red feathers in his braids came from.

"Yes," I told him, "I think she should. But sometimes I really wish she wasn't."

***

Knives were quickly produced, and the dead prehistoric birds were quartered and butchered into large pieces and carried into the center of town as the wounded were taken care of and the unfortunate bodies and pieces of the slain Shayana and soldiers gathered for burial.

Today, it appeared, we'd feast and celebrate life. But the dead would not.

Several Shayana had been killed or carried off, along with at least one ape slave. As for our small group, we had lost two more soldiers from our escort. We all knew it was time to head back, while there was still any of us left to return.

But first, we ate the dead pterodactyls.

I sat beside Skyla and John, across from Thenory and Daniels, as we feasted on the giant birds inside their large meeting hall. The meat had a pleasing taste, much like turkey, and the herbs and spices used were simple, but effective.

The Lieutenant took a sip of water from a carved wooden cup, then turned to our host. "Chief, your men didn't seem surprised at the large breehas that attacked."

He shrugged and savagely ripped a piece of meat off the bone with his bare hands. "They are called merhah and they attack once or twice a season. Sometimes it is bad, like today. Usually, we lose a slave or two. This was a surprisingly large attack, but with thou help and the new weapons, we killed two and wounded the others severely. They may not be back for a long time after today's victory."

"Why do these merhah come here?" Charles asked.

The Chief glanced up from his meal. "They once preyed on the young breehas, now they prey on us."

"Pterosaur." Oscar put down the piece of wing he'd been gnawing on. "It's a type of Pterosaur. Of the same family as the breehas, or pterodactyl."

The Shayana near enough to hear him speak stopped eating and stared at him. One said, "I know not of what ye speak, but thou sayeth the breehas and merhahs are in a family?"

"No. It's a... sort of like... never mind." The paleontologist looked back down at his food, with a rejected look across his face.

With an indifferent shrug, the Shayana turned back to his food with his companions.

Daniels coughed loudly and caught Thenory's attention again. "Chief, we plan on leaving tomorrow morning, but we appreciate your hospitality and will certainly return the favor should you ever have need of us."

"We could use more weapons. With thou repeater rifles, we can protect our home better." The Shayana within earshot nodded eagerly.

"I'll have to ask my superiors. But I believe, with the common enemy that we have, we can help you out. But we would expect certain... help in return. Such as trade, shelter, guidance. Things of that nature to any of our troops who may come by."

The Chief nodded, his gold beaded and clawed necklace bouncing against his leather shirt. "That can be done, and we give thee thanks."

"And the 'axe men'," John spoke from beside me around a mouthful of pterodactyl. "When the time comes, you'll show us how to get where they are?"

"We will."

"Outstanding." The journalist grinned. "Another series of articles. I'll be famous around the globe by the time I write all these stories down!"

"If you survive," grumbled Sergeant Gibbons as he flexed his wounded arm.

John swallowed and looked down at his wooden plate as our group went silent. We'd lost a lot of men so far and the journey wasn't over yet.

"Cheer up," Daniels said in the midst of the quiet. "Tomorrow we head back to Fort Jipson. After that, civilization!"

Oscar and John gave half-hearted cheers, while the rest of us exchanged worried glances. Leaving would mean leaving the safety of the Shayana's mountaintop home. But then, as I thought that, I looked down at the pieces of cooked bird that'd attacked us earlier on my carved wooden plate and realized that really, nowhere over here was safe.

***

The next morning, we left as soon as it was bright enough to see. After weaving our way down the mountain, we rode into the dark and dangerous forest. Carbine was eager to go for a ride, he'd been cooped up for far too long. Typically, after more than a couple of days in a corral, he'd get antsy and his pranks would get more unbearable when I checked on him.

Chief Thenory was confident that we could make it to our canyon in two day's ride, but there were a good deal fewer of us than we'd started with.

Lieutenant Daniels led the way with Henon, followed by Skyla and Charles, then Oscar, John, and myself, plus three of the four remaining soldiers. Sergeant Gibbons volunteered to stay behind to keep working on the rough language of the apes, as well as serving as something of a goodwill ambassador from us to the Shayana. Oscar wanted to stay longer as well, but in the end decided to come back with a force of Pinkertons for protection. Personally, I hoped they were all eaten on the way. We also left behind the extra horses, but Reydan's personal paleontologist was insistent that we brought back his heavily laden mule. It'd been through a lot, and had numerous scratches, tufts of hair missing, and a wicked gash across its brown face from its time alone in the forest. It was a miracle the poor beast had survived at all.

Henon guided us on foot, and though we had tried to teach him how to ride over the past few days, the big Shayana never took to the horse. Like him, the natives didn't seem to have much use for the horses, and since they were all gelded and unable to reproduce anyways, I wondered how long it'd be before the ones we left behind were eaten.

The first day we managed to make the ride with only seeing a pair of Ankylosaurs and a herd of twenty or more crested dinosaurs eating and lounging around the edges of a large pond. That night we camped amongst a ring of rocks that made a natural fort of sorts. Henon said they'd used it often for patrols and scouting missions, and luckily, we had enough space in the center to bring in our horses and lone mule for protection. Daniels didn't like the fact that the Shayana had been using the naturally defendable place for some time; that meant the apes were most likely aware of it. But with no other options, we laid out our bedrolls in a tight circle, and slept with weapons close at hand.

The night was uneventful, and with a two-man watch posted at all hours, we were all exhausted and sleep deprived as we broke camp that morning with a flock of the giant brown flightless birds watched us from a hundred yards away. We were thankful for their presence, as it most likely meant that there weren't any predators or apes nearby.

By the second afternoon, we'd made it through the forest and onto the open plains that led to Fort Jipson. It was brutally hot, and we had to stop often to water the horses and take breaks in whatever shade we could find from small stands of trees. Our clothes were soaked through with sweat, and the horses were struggling. But we were making good time, and were all looking forward to returning to the fort and being able to relax to some degree.

Then, cresting a large hill, we came upon a Tyrannosaurus.

The massive dinosaur was sleeping with its tail wrapped around its giant head. It had a pale green skin, and long black stripes that ran down the sides of its body before disappearing amongst a light-yellow underbelly. Its sides flared as the beast breathed in and out in its sleep, and one of the large, clawed feet twitched like a dog dreaming.

"Oh no…" I quickly turned Carbine's head, praying we could walk our beasts away without waking the creature. The horses sidestepped fearfully at the sight of the giant dinosaur, and Henon, with a panicked look on his face, waved a hand at us to remain quiet as he backed away.

"It's a male," Skyla whispered and pointed. Oscar's jaw dropped.

"Great, sketch it later. We need to go," I whispered back forcefully as Smoke rolled her eyes and tugged at Skyla's reins to turn back.

At that moment, our lone mule whinnied fearfully and jerked back against the reins tied to Oscar's horse. Swearing, the former paleontologist struggled to control both his horse and the frightened beast.

A pebbled eyelid opened.

The terrifying beast's pupil enlarged as he took us in, and waving his small arms, the creature lumbered to his feet. Rear end rose first, then the heavy front balanced by the giant tail. The head swung toward us and the nostrils flared as it sniffed for our scent.

"Run!" Henon cried out in fright and took off on foot towards a small copse of trees nearby.

With my hat I slapped Smoke's rump and she bolted with Skyla barely hanging on to the saddle. "Ride!" I shouted and kicked my heels to Carbine's flanks. He bolted forward, fear giving him wings as the dinosaur roared ferociously and gave chase.

Charles rode Sir Lancelot beside the running Shayana. "Henon!" he shouted. As the man turned to look, the Brit grasped his arm and practically threw him onto the back of Sir Lancelot. "Hold on!" The native wrapped his arms around Charles' waist and held on for dear life. Quickly overtaking him was Daniels, John, and the soldiers. They all looked terrified. One of the soldiers drew his rifle from its scabbard and slapped the barrel against the side of his black mount, urging it to run faster.

Skyla and her gray ringed horse led all of us, running at top speed towards the trees.

There was only a dozen of them, tall ones, towering high above us with thick trunks to provide shelter below. We might be able to hide amongst them, but it didn't look promising. There was too much space between them. At any rate, we'd be trapped until the tyrannosaur decided to find something to eat elsewhere. We needed a plan.

Oscar was last in the group, his rough looking mule struggling to keep up with his horse and the pair beginning to overtake Sir Lancelot riding double. Charles' face was one of determination as he pounded his heels against the sides of the big Arabian horse. But I doubted his fancy stud could outrun the dinosaur for long while carrying the added weight of the big native.

Behind us came the heavy thuds of the chasing Tyrannosaurus. It moved faster than I'd have thought possible for such a giant creature. With head low, small arms tucked against its chest, and moving with a long lope, the large claws on the ends of its feet tore up chunks of sod and grass as it pursued us.

Turning Carbine's head, I slowed him and angled my horse towards Oscar. Grasping the hilt of the Bowie knife strapped to the back of my gun belt, I jerked the blade free and raised it over my head as Carbine brushed up against Oscar's horse.

"Jed! What are you doing? JED!" the paleontologist screamed as I slashed my knife towards him.

The heavy blade hit the rope tied to the mule and snapped it like a taut cord.

I shoved the thick spine of the blade between my teeth and with my now free hand, drew a Colt Peacemaker.

"Noooo!" he screamed as I swung the pistol around.

I fired.

The bullet hit with a splash of blood, low and through the chest.

The sacrificial beast toppled over in a cloud of dust. Whinnying in pain and terror, the mule twisted and thrashed, trying to rise to its feet. The saddle bags filled with Oscar's precious specimens ripped apart, sending pieces of plants and vegetation scattering. And amongst them, large chunks of rock, veined with gold that sparkled in the sun.

"You asshole!" Oscar cried out as his valuables spilled across the prehistoric prairie.

The Tyrannosaurus slowed abruptly and approached the wounded mule with an almost puzzled look.

Twisting in the saddle, I watched as it first sniffed, then shoved the whimpering beast with its big head. The thick tail swung ponderously back and forth, as though the dinosaur was thinking of whether it was pleased with the potential meal or not.

Either way, we'd just gained some significant distance on the monster.

Looking after us, the Tyrannosaurus roared terribly as the mule thrashed in sheer terror beneath it. With a sudden lunge, the dinosaur snapped large jaws down on the poor beast of burden, silencing it.

We rode past the stand of trees for another couple of miles over the rolling hills until we were well out of sight of the monstrous dinosaur before stopping. Charles let Henon swing down to the ground. The native rubbed his backside gratefully as he thanked the Brit for saving him.

Oscar pounded his horse beside me, pulling back on the reins and glaring at me with a look that could kill. "Do you realize how many priceless samples you just lost?" he shouted angrily.

"Keep your voice down. We don't know what else is around," I told him as I pointed my trigger finger at him. "You wanted to see one of those Tyrannosaurus things, well now you got to. It was either the mule or one of us. I don't know about you, but the mule seemed like the best option at the time."

"We're lucky the Tyrannosaurus stopped chasing us. Poor mule... if you'd killed it, Jed, that giant dinosaur probably would have kept chasing us. But leaving it alive interested the beast." Skyla's face was pale from fright, and she looked up at the sky and took several deep breaths to calm herself.

"Thank goodness for that. But it was just a poor shot. I was trying to kill it."

'But did you see it? It was magnificent!" she squealed in glee. "Fredrick is going to be so jealous!"

"First attacked by apes, saved by Englishmen, and now chased by a Tyrannosaurus! My goodness what an adventure!" John Parsons whooped as he wiped beaded sweat from his brow.

The Lieutenant shoved his horse between Carbine and Oscar and glared at him. "What the hell was all that gold about?" Daniels asked. "Is that what you've been up to? Robbing the Shayana?"

"What? No! They gave it to me! They just use it for trinkets and stuff, it's too brittle and soft to be used for anything useful they said."

The Lieutenant bumped his horse into the paleontologist's. "Next time, you tell me. I don't care what you and Mr. White have planned, or plan on doing, you let me know. I don't like surprises."

Oscar harrumphed and turned away, his face a mottled shade of red.

Charles watched Oscar ride away. "You should have just shot that little man instead. No one would have missed him."

Skyla rolled her eyes. She was a softie for her old boss, even though he treated her like a hired hand when they worked together.

"Well done, Jed," Daniels said as he wiped sweat from his brow. "But I suggest we keep moving. That big monster may still be hungry."

"Yes, sir," I said and clucked my tongue at Carbine. Turning his head, we followed the Lieutenant and his three remaining soldiers. The others fell in beside us. Our small group headed west towards the fort.

***

An alarm bell began clanging as we rode within sight of the entrance to Fort Jipson.

The previous makeshift fort entrance had begun being built proper now. A crew of eight men worked on a thick palisade of sharpened tree trunks rising eight feet high and in addition to the Gatling guns, we could see the large muzzles of a pair of cannons resting on top of the dirt and rock berms behind the palisade. Anyone coming through the canyon entrance would face a withering barrage of fire and cannon shot. Even the wide, lazy Trike River that ran through the canyon had spiked Cheval de Frise set in place. The spiked logs overlapped, blocking off entrance through the knee-deep water.

We made it a dozen steps in view of the entrance when a squad of mounted soldiers rushed out through the opening in the palisade on horseback. Daniels rode in front of us and waited for the lead rider of the approaching party to stop.

The man did, his horse side stepping as he stared at our group in disbelief. The other soldiers circled around us with looks ranging from bewilderment to surprise crossing their tanned faces. "Well, I'll be... Lieutenant, we thought you were all dead!" the leader spoke.

"Not yet, Sergeant Mayhew. But we've had a long trek."

The Sergeant looked around at our small group. "Is this all, sir?" he asked quietly.

"Other than your friend, Gibbons, it is. Everyone else is dead."

Mayhew took his hat off and held it over his chest. "Lord, I'm sorry to hear that, but of course Gibbons would make it, he's too proud to die." He noticed our guide standing behind us and stared at Henon's odd style of dress compared to ours. "Who is this?"

"A friend. He helped save us."

"He's welcome then. Follow me, sir." The Sergeant turned his horse and the group of soldiers with him backed away enough to clear a path.

"Let's go," Daniels ordered us, and we rode the beaten path beside the river into Fort Jipson.

***

The entrance wasn't the only thing that had changed at the fort.

There was a partially completed wooden building a hundred yards inside the gate. A dozen men worked on the framed husk, swinging hammers and working saws back and forth as they hurried to assemble the building from the pile of timber stacked nearby. A horse-drawn wagon was stopped next to the pile, and I watched in amusement as the young men unloading the lumber jumped out of the way and swore as they dropped a thick rough-sawn board. An older man with a long gray beard and a toolbelt, the overseer I supposed, yelled at them to stop fooling about.

Beyond the building, damaged tents had either been patched or replaced with new ones. A neat and orderly section of tents was filled with dozens of soldiers going about their day while another, less neat section, had been placed some distance past the scientist tents for the workers and what looked like a gaggle of Pinkertons. The workers scurried around the fort, working to build defenses while the supposed detectives sat around smoking, chewing, and jawing as they looked on with a mixture of boredom and disgust towards everyone else. I took that to mean Reydan and Cato were here somewhere, as Captain Brandthorn had forewarned days ago.

And where the large obsidian altar had once been, there was only a mound of shattered rubble. In the middle of the granite pile stood a single man, pounding large pieces into smaller ones with a heavy sledgehammer while another man used a wheelbarrow to cart the gravel away. Both were red faced, shirtless, and looked exhausted from working in the high humidity and bright sun. I pointed at the toppled over stone pillars, cracked and broken by what could only have been dynamite. "Looks like someone had enough of that ape altar."

"Captain had us blow it up," Mayhew spat in the direction of the mound of broken rock. "No telling how many men were killed on that cursed thing." He gestured at the two men working amongst the rock debris. "Now we use it as a punishment detail. Those two fell asleep on watch. This'll teach them to not do it again."

"Where'd the big chunk of obsidian go?" I'd never seen one so big, and it was so large it would have been all but impossible to have been moved. As big and strong as the apes were, I don't know how they managed to move it into place on top of the altar in the first place.

"Blew it up too. Most of the soldiers and Pinkertons took pieces of it to sell back in Granite Falls."

I nodded. Shame for such a large beautiful glossy black rock to have been used for such evil purposes. But there was no point in keeping it in the center of our territory. I bet that any ape scouts that may be watching us would be pissed off though at the desecration of their altar.

We pulled back on our reins as a group of Pinkertons cut in front of us. Walking quickly, they never so much as gave us a cursory glance before getting in our way. I choked back a comment and looked at Sergeant Mayhew.

He shrugged in disgust as the badged men walked off. "They've been strutting around here like they own the place. Don't get me wrong, the more guns the merrier, but these Pinkertons... well, they're something else."

"Reydan here, or Cato?" I asked bitterly.

"Mr. White? Yeah, he's here. Is Cato that gun hand of his? The one they call the Black Plague?"

I rolled my eyes at his nickname. "That's him."

"He's here too. If you're looking for them, they're usually in his office." The Sergeant pointed at the almost completed building.

"The Black Plague? I'll certainly have to interview him," John chuckled.

"Good luck with that," Skyla told him. I smiled at the reporter's confused face as I thought of the talkative man attempting to interview the silent gunman. That wouldn't go well.

Oscar looked at the building that the Sergeant had pointed towards. "With that information, I'll be parting ways with you all to see Mr. White. Skyla, a pleasure as always." He glanced at Charles and lifted his nose in the air before turning to myself. "As for you, Jed, you will not be missed." The scientist nodded his head to the Lieutenant and John before touching his heels to the flanks of his horse. The portly man bounced away to scheme with the tycoon as to how to get more gold from the Shayana no doubt.

"And I'll be off as well. I've my memoirs to write now. It has been an exciting adventure. Thank you all for keeping me safe." John smiled and waved to us as he rode away towards the corral.

Sergeant Mayhew glanced down at my twin pistols then back to me. "If you're looking to challenge the Black Plague, I'd recommend against it."

I looked at him in surprise. "Challenge him? Why would I do that?"

"Now that the man has a fancy name, all sorts of folks been wanting to try him. To see if he's as fast as they say he is. One of the Pinkertons bumped into him, intentionally picking a fight. Then he tried to outdraw him, high noon style. He died before his gun cleared leather." Mayhew whistled. "I saw the shooting. Black Plague is quicker than anything I've ever seen."

Skyla's eyes met mine. I could see the concern in them.

"Fool," I muttered more to myself than anyone else, but the Sergeant heard me.

"Yes, sir. Foolish and dead. Ah, here we are." We stopped in front of the large command tent, still singed and burnt in places from the attack, and dismounted. "I'm sure the Captain will be pleased to see you."

"Captain? Not Captains?" Charles asked as he tied Sir Lancelot off to a hitching post.

"Captain Hawney has rotated back to Granite Falls with his men. He'll be back in a couple of weeks." Sergeant Mayhew raised a hand to stop Henon as he moved to follow us. "Best let them speak first, sir, if you don't mind."

Henon nodded and went back to staring at the bustle of activity around him. I was sure he found the place odd and mystifying. By technological standards, we were over a hundred years more advanced. The Shayana stood out like a sore thumb in his metal breastplate and sword with a Winchester rifle slung over a shoulder. Lots of men watched him with interest as he stood outside the tent with the Sergeant.

Leaving the pair of men behind, we entered the large tent. Lieutenant Daniels walked in first, followed by Skyla and myself. Charles followed me closely behind. The few remaining soldiers from our expedition took their horses to turn out in the corrals.

No sooner had we entered the tent then Captain Brandthorn rushed forward, shaking the young Lieutenant's hand first, then hugging Skyla tight. "By God! We thought you were all dead. Where have you been?"

"Most of my men are dead, sir," Daniels stated firmly as he looked his commanding officer in the eye. I could tell the weight was heavy on him, it seemed to have grown with every new loss. The burden of duty and leadership is never a light one, especially when it comes to losing men. "We're here to debrief."

Brandthorn nodded slowly. "Aye, we sent out a search party when you didn't show up on time. They found the site of the ambush and a row of graves but were attacked and chased off by the apes before they could get a good look around." He grabbed Skyla's hand and looked us over. "They did find strange wounds on the ape corpses though, looked like they'd all been stabbed with something, even those who'd been shot."

"Swords, sir. We were rescued by men from the Shayana tribe. They're going to take some explaining…They're unlike anyone you've ever met… In fact, one of them is outside the tent with Sergeant Mayhew right now."

"What?" Brandthorn half turned towards the tent flap, then seemed to think better of it and leaned back against the table in the center of the room. Crossing his arms, he sighed. "Let's have your side of the story first and leave nothing out."

***

By the time we were finished telling our tale, Fredrick had joined us, and the Captain looked wearier than before. "A mixture of old English and Shaynee culture, huh? Great. And dragons are real! Good heavens…" He rubbed his clean-shaven face. "What you've seen fits in with what one of our scouts reported. He swore he saw a man riding a Pterodactyl to the east. We've all been giving him grief ever since. Now it's time for us to eat crow… And 'axe men'? They sound fun. So, now we've another civilization to investigate later for potential allies." He sighed. "All of that aside… right now, our biggest concern are the damned apes. They're laying low, but they are out there. We've lost one patrol already to a similar ambush that you ran into." He ran his hands through his hair as he studied the large map on the table. On top of it lay the smaller sketched map filled with information that Daniels had procured through talking with Chief Thenory. "We know the apes have been scouting us. We've seen a lot of signs the past couple of days."

"You think they'll attack?" I asked, dreading the answer but already knowing it.

"Yes." He said it simply, as though utterly convinced we were in for a fight.

Frowning, I turned to Skyla. "We need to get you out of here."

"Jed, we just returned from contact with a new tribe of people. A new civilization, one that came through a Shimmer like ours but from a different time period altogether! I can't leave now."

"I agree, we could really use both of you," Brandthorn added. At my disgusted look he shrugged. "New civilization that the two of you have ties with... we could use an ally against the apes."

"The Shayana are no good to us if the apes wipe us out first," I told him flatly.

"And they will," Fredrick said in disgust as he ran his fingers along his bushy mustache.

"Not this again," Brandthorn grumbled and pointed a finger at the famed hunter. "We're in a better defensive position than we were during the night attack."

"It doesn't matter!" the famous hunter retorted. "We're in a damn bowl. They can swarm down the cliff sides and hit us from any direction."

"We've taken precautions against that," Brandthorn protested as he raised his hands defensively.

Fredrick paced across the beaten dirt floor, shaking his fist at the tent entrance. "Gatlings pointed in every direction only does so much. Apes can stand on the rim and rain arrows down on almost the entire canyon. You've seen the range they have with them!"

"I'm with Jed. Skyla, you need to leave," Charles spoke from behind me. He'd been quiet the entire time, just listening to the Lieutenant tell the tale of our ill-fated expedition.

"No. I will not," she said angrily.

"This is not a discussion we'll be having. Your parents ordered me to protect you. I'll not let you be caught in the middle of a war!" He grabbed her arm and tugged her toward the door.

She jerked away, and I felt my pistol spring into my hand. I cocked back the hammer with an audible click. Charles froze, then incrementally moved his hand towards his Schofield pistol.

Fredrick looked at me, then down at the gun in my hand. "Jed..." he warned, raising a hand cautiously.

I locked eyes with the Stratten family butler. His were cold and calculating, there was no fear in them. But I could see the anger building up in them to match my own.

"Jed!" Skyla shouted, and I blinked rapidly.

With my thumb, I uncocked the pistol and relaxed. "That's the first and last time, Charles. Don't ever grab her like that again," I growled.

Red faced, the Brit sniffed, then spun on his heels and walked out.

"Dammit, Jed. You can't go around shooting your way out of every situation," Fredrick admonished me.

"Yeah, I know," I grumbled as I holstered my gun. He was right; I'd been living on edge for months now and the gun was quickly turning into my natural way out of dealing with a problem. If I wasn't careful, I'd make a mistake. And mistakes get you killed, or worse, someone else that doesn't deserve it.

Skyla grabbed my arm and looked up at me. "Jed. We're in this together. I want to stay, but if you really want me to go, I will."

I pulled my hat off and twisted the brim in my fists. "Alright, we'll stay. For now. But this ain't Granite Falls; if things get iffy, I'm throwing you on the back of Smoke and we're riding out of here. They've more than enough guns without us. Speaking of which," I turned to Brandthorn, "how many Pinkertons are here?"

"Several dozen and more on the way."

"That many, huh?"

The Captain shrugged almost apologetically. "Mr. White also sent workers. They're helping build the palisade in addition to the building. He wants our little foothold to succeed for running the rail through the Shimmer."

"Figures," I grunted.

"We should be thankful. He's also sending skilled loggers to us from California. Men who have experience cutting down the great redwoods. They've a particular knack that will come in handy around here." He pointed a finger at me. "Jed, you've a good reason to hate Mr. White. But he's been a boon to us. If it weren't for him, we would still be trying to eke out a bare bones camp while Congress debates what kind of resources we'll be given. Without the railroad's support it'd be nigh impossible to succeed here."

"Just because the man has merit now doesn't mean his sins have been forgiven. He could save a burning wagon full of nuns for all I care. He still has a score to be settled and a maker to meet." The tent grew quiet as I glared at Brandthorn. The officer met my gaze defiantly.

Daniels decided this was the moment to change the subject. "Sir, if you're ready. I'd like to bring Henon in. He's one of the men who rescued us during our ambush and helped bring us back."

"Certainly. I'm excited to talk to this man."

"I'm going to feed Carbine," I told them, still annoyed.

Sighing, Skyla turned to follow me out of the tent as the Lieutenant motioned for Henon to be sent in.

***

We walked over to the picket fence with our horses with Sergeant Mayhew. Carbine muzzled my chest, and I stroked his big face in my hands while Skyla promised Smoke she'd brush her down this evening.

My favorite paleontologist turned to me with a frown upon her lips. "You know, Jed, you don't have to be so protective-"

"Jedidiah Smith!" The words were spoken as though by a man used to adherence to his commands.

Gritting my teeth, I turned, slowly, recognizing the voice. My fingers flexed as they resisted the urge to draw my gun again and start blasting.

Reydan White and Cato were walking towards us, backed by five Pinkertons all carrying rifles in their hands. They appeared ready for a shootout or a lynching. Only thing missing, that I could see, was a rope.

The railroad tycoon stopped in front of me. He smiled coldly as he rubbed the ivory head on his cane between big hands. "Jedidiah Huckleberry Smith," he repeated slowly. Behind him, the Black Plague studied me carefully from beneath the brim of his hat, his fingers near his guns in case I tried something.

Ignoring Cato, the Sergeant stepped between us and looked the former raider in the eye fearlessly. "Good afternoon, Mr. White. What can I do for you?" The black gunman tensed, no doubt uncomfortable at the closeness of the soldier to his charge. I didn't blame him. Last time I was that close, I busted the tycoon's nose with my fist.

Drawing a folded slip of paper from his breast pocket, Reydan slapped it against the Sergeant's chest. "The Pinkerton Detective Agency will be taking Mr. Smith here into custody."

"Under what charge?" Skyla shoved past me and I stumbled intentionally, making the most of the opportunity to shift my hands until they were touching the grips of the twin Colt Peacemakers. If there was shooting, I was a dead man against Cato and the others. But I'd take Reydan with me, and as many of the Pinkertons as possible. But first I would have to get Skyla out of the way.

It was then I realized I had no desire to shoot Cato. The man had threatened me several times now, but he was also once my closest boyhood friend. I reckon I still had hope for the man, although I had no reason to. He seemed like a real asshole these days.

"Murder." The tycoon grinned evilly.

At the word, the Pinkerton agents leveled their rifles towards me. I gently grabbed Skyla by the arm and pulled her out of the way of any possible gunfire. She looked at me, scared.

"Murder of who?" I asked, far more casually and unconcerned than I truly felt. The answer would dictate a lot of what they knew about me.

"Timothy Shinneys."

I looked around. The Pinkertons' faces were firm and set. Reydan was beaming now, thrilled to have finally found a way to get rid of me. Cato's black face was expressionless as usual. Skyla looked terrified and Sergeant Mayhew turned to peer curiously back at me from under bushy eyebrows.

I knew how my face looked.

Confused.

"Who?" I blurted.

***

"This says he went by the name Timmy and you murdered him during the Battle of the Apes," Mayhew said as he glanced back down at the warrant for my arrest.

"Oh," I shrugged. "Yeah, I shot him, but it wasn't murder."

Skyla looked up at me, shock spreading across her face. "What?" she shouted.

"He tried to kill me. Right in the middle of the battle."

She glared at me accusingly. "I didn't know you killed a man while the rest of us were fighting apes!"

I blinked as I recalled the moment.

He'd shot at me first, clipping the edge of a building above my head and I raced across the street, both pistols blazing fire to keep him pinned down.

All around us were the screams and roars of battle. The crackle of gunfire. The stench and billowing smoke of burning canvas, buildings, and corpses. Corpses everywhere. Human, ape, trike, raptor. It was a bloodbath of unbelievable carnage. Hell had come to Granite Falls.

Maneuvering along the boardwalk, I'd surprised the man from the side and knocked the rifle away. He raised his hands, surrendering to me. His mouth opened as he began to speak, no doubt a plea, begging for mercy. But I had none to give. The gun bucked in my hand as I pulled the trigger.

I hadn't told her, or anyone for that matter, about the incident.

"Honestly, I didn't figure anyone would ever know or care," I said.

Mayhew faced me. "Jed, this is a serious charge. You're to be brought in. If you refuse, you're to be shot."

One of the Pinkertons racked a round into his rifle as if to emphasize the point.

I smirked at him. "You probably should have made sure your gun was loaded before approaching me."

He glared back as a slight hint of red crept up along the sides of his neck.

"I'll need your guns, sir," the Sergeant said solemnly as he carefully folded the warrant. "You'll be coming into our custody until we can get this sorted out."

"No. The Pinkerton Detective Agency will be handling this," Reydan stated abruptly. "It says so on the warrant for his arrest."

"Detectives? You mean your hired thugs!" Skyla accused. Her lower lip was trembling and her face blushing a bright crimson in anger, fear, and embarrassment.

Reydan looked down his nose at her, his eyes cold and calculating. "I assure you, miss, whomever you believe Mr. Smith to be, you are mistaken. He is a murderer."

"Is he also a slanderer? Or was he correct when he accused you of burning his home and killing returning Confederate soldiers in peacetime? Why should I believe you didn't have something to do with this?"

"Enough, Skyla," I said firmly in a tone that made sure she knew the discussion was over. She didn't need to get on the tycoon's bad side as well. "I shot the man, I'll answer for it." Slowly, I unbuckled my belt as the agents tensed. One of the Pinkertons snatched it from my hand. Another grabbed the *Eighty-Six* off my back and slung it over his own.

"Careful," I warned with confidence I didn't quite feel. "I'll be wanting them back."

"You won't be getting them," Reydan said with a chilling smile.

A pair of heavy iron cuffs were placed around my hands and a detective grabbed each arm firmly, pinning me between them.

Skyla rushed forward, ignoring the men on either side of me and grabbed my shirt collar, kissing me hard as tears began to trickle down her face. I felt them smear against my stubbled cheek as she pressed her lips against mine.

"It's okay, I'll be fine. It was a fair fight against a man with a history of violence. Don't worry, the judge will understand," I told her with as much sincerity as I could muster. I didn't believe it completely, but I wasn't about to let her see me worrying. Sometimes confidence is a blanket we can share with others even when we don't have it.

"Okay... okay," she repeated as her tears wet my cheek.

"Stay close to Charles. I'll see you soon."

The Pinkertons tugged me away gently. Another untied Carbine and led my horse after us.

The last I saw of Skyla, she stood beside Sergeant Mayhew with shoulders slumped, tears streaming, and a scared look on her face.

***

Shackled, I rode Carbine back along the winding trail of Prehistoria, through the Shimmer, and to the end of the railroad with an escort of Reydan, Cato, and a dozen Pinkerton Detectives. For anyone watching, they'd have thought Jesse James had been caught again with all the attention I was given.

Personally, I expected to be shot on the way back to the tunnel for supposedly trying to escape. The thought crossed my mind to give it a try. I knew Carbine well enough that I figured we would have a chance at getting away, even bound. And they had not discovered the sawn-off shotgun that was still wrapped inside my bedroll. But there was nowhere for me to go except perhaps the Shayana, and they would probably give me up for a crate of Winchesters.

In the end, I rode my horse quietly and hoped for the best.

Once on the other side, I was dismounted and pushed towards a train as Carbine was released into one of the corrals near the makeshift train town. I knew that Skyla would track him down and care for him once she made it through the tunnel. And I fully expected her to come looking for me. But I wondered when that would be. She would certainly try to come immediately, but would she be able to? Would Brandthorn let her? Most likely he would let her travel when the soldiers swapped out, but there was no telling when that would be. I could be dead and in the ground before we saw each other again. Gritting my teeth, I tried to think of a way out of this situation, but all I could think of was her pretty face.

***

The fall air was cold.

Without a coat, I shivered in the cattle car I was shackled in. It was a big change from the other side where the heat blistered and soaked your clothing with sweat. Here the wind whistled between the cracks in the walls, and I tucked my arms in closer to my stomach to retain as much body warmth as possible. My guards looked comfy in their thick buffalo coats, and they relaxed on a pair of hay bales tossed into the far corner and passed the time with a worn deck of cards. Hanging from a peg near them was my gun belt and rifle.

"Two pair again?" the thin guard scoffed.

"You dealt," the other snickered as he wiped a runny nose with the back of his hand.

I sighed. It'd been a long hour or so listening to the two guards bicker.

"Can you just hang me now?" I interrupted as I lifted the iron shackles around my wrists. "If I have to listen to you two idiots playing cards the rest of the trip, I just might strangle myself with these."

The thin one stared. "I heard you killed the Blue Ridge Kid."

"I did."

"Yeah, but I also heard you shot him through a table. That's pretty gutless, if you ask me," the other said.

"Maybe. But I'm alive and he ain't." My words stuttered from between cold lips as I shivered uncontrollably.

"Sounds like the sort of thing a murderer would say, right. Henry?" the thin one said as he adjusted the badge and gun belt on his hips.

"Yeah," Henry said as he blew his nose into a handkerchief. "Be a shame if he tried to escape and got shot."

"Yes, it would. But we'd be heroes for stopping a dangerous gunman and such."

"Big damn heroes," Henry replied with an evil twinkle in his eyes.

I rolled my eyes. "Fair enough. Enjoy your game." I slumped back against the rough boards, disgusted. Of all the things to be arrested for, killing a drunk asshole. I'd done much more than that in my thirty odd years. So, I reckon I should be happy.

The two of them turned back to their bickering as the thin one shuffled the deck and began to deal.

I closed my eyes and tried to sleep. It didn't work, too many thoughts running through my mind. There was Skyla, in a fort that was likely soon to be under attack by apes. There was, of course, the possibility of me being hanged as well. And there was my ranch, watched over by Jim and Bo; if I got myself hanged, they'd have to help Skyla manage or sell the place. There were a lot of dark thoughts running through my mind, but after a while I was finally able to doze a bit.

A thumping sound woke me.

Reydan White stood in front of me, tapping the point of his cane against the hardwood boards of the rail car with a smirk. My two guards were nowhere to be seen; their cards lay scattered across the hay bale that'd sat between them. It looked like Henry had been playing with a full house. Aces and deuces.

I glared at the former Union raider in disgust.

"Jedidiah Huckleberry Smith." He dragged over one of the hay bales and sat across from me, just out of reach. The rail tycoon rubbed a hand over his graying red beard. "Surely that's a fake name. But it's just us in here now, so tell me... What do you truly know about me?"

The scar tissue on my back twinged, and I willed myself to keep from stretching my shoulders. With my hands cuffed before me to an iron chain attached to a heavy pin pounded into the floor, I didn't have much movement anyways.

This was the first time we'd ever been alone together without Cato, and for all I knew I'd already missed my chance to kill Reydan. I should have known better. Sometimes revenge is a dish that should be served hot, and bullet riddled. My eyes flicked towards where my guns were on the far side of the car; if only they were within reach. Damn these chains.

Grinding my teeth, I looked him in the eye. "I know you raided all through South Carolina, from Chesterfield to Aiken."

He nodded, thinking. After several moments, he stretched a leg out before him and adjusted his dark suit coat. "Yes. I did," he sucked his lower lip thoughtfully. "You know, I think I remember you. You were just a scrawny kid... But you bit off Swanson's nose when he tried to hang you." He chuckled. "You were a fighter. Snot nosed and crying, but you fought back. That's more than that Confederate scum we hanged with you did. So, tell me... what have you been up to since our paths crossed all those years ago?"

"Doesn't matter." I wasn't about to tell the evil man anything else about my past. If he got a thread on it, he could unravel a lot about me. And I still had a chance to beat this murder charge.

"I suppose you're right, it doesn't matter." He leaned forward and fixed me with a stare and a twisted smile. "Because you're going to hang. Any witnesses you find, I'll intimidate until they tell what I want them to tell. No one will stand against me or the railroad. I own Sheriff Beauford and that new pipsqueak of a Sheriff in Cheyenne is so afraid to push back against me that I practically own him as well." He smirked.

I jerked my chains upright suddenly with a loud and violent clank and he jumped back quickly, overturning the hay bale and almost tripping on it. Pulling his cane up, he kept it between us defensively.

"And yet you're still afraid of me," I sneered.

Grunting, he lowered his cane and rested on the polished ivory head. "And you're still going to die."

With a free hand he smoothed his suit and slid open the door to the cattle car. The wind howled outside. "Goodbye, Mr. Nobody. This will be the last time you see me. Because as of now, you are irrelevant. An ink blot on a page of a book that I've burned long ago. My story continues on from here without you."

He left the door open behind him, leaving me alone with my murderous thoughts. A warning blast whistled from the locomotive, signaling that we were about to move.

***

Sheriff Beauford was waiting on the train station boardwalk when we squealed to a stop in Granite Falls. Shivering uncontrollably, the Pinkertons shoved my trembling body off the ramp towards him. I was so near frozen that I staggered and would have fallen had the guards not gripped me so tightly between them.

I had overheard the guards discussing that I would be taken to Cheyenne for trial. This was just a stopping place as I switched trains before departing for the capital of Wyoming. I suspected it was because trying to hang the Hero of Granite Falls in the very town he saved would most likely prove difficult.

My guns were passed over and the mustached Sheriff glanced at them disdainfully before slinging them over his shoulders. Grabbing me by the irons, he tugged me forward and away from the two Pinkertons. "I knew there was something wrong about you from the moment I laid eyes on you. Now I know why."

"Says you. You're in Reydan's pocket. How's it feel to be his pet?" I spat. "Fetch Fido. Fetch the bad man for the hanging. Intimidate the witnesses. Good dog. Sit."

The Sheriff snarled and jerked me closer. I could smell the tobacco on his breath. "Think you're funny? Well guess what. You ain't the only one who can kill. Just yesterday, I killed your boy."

A knot formed in my stomach as I tried to figure out what he meant by that. "Who?" I demanded.

"That kid that worked for you. Caught him cheating at cards," he grinned maliciously. "So, I shot him. And that old man you got working for you, he'll be in the cell beside you."

The knot in my belly tightened sickeningly as I felt my face flush with rage "You're a damned liar. Jim didn't even play cards."

Snapping his fingers to get their attention, the Sheriff passed my guns back to the detectives then spun back towards me.

A clenched fist busted my lips and the sharp metallic taste of blood flooded my mouth. I took two steps backwards, eyes cinching shut in pain. Peeking through the slits, I saw the Sheriff smirk and rub his skinned knuckles. A small group of passengers stopped and ringed around us, watching to see what was happening between their Sheriff and the man in chains.

"Call me a liar again and see what happens. You'll end up like your boy and all the others who crossed me." The evil grin stretched across his face, taunting me.

Raising my shackled hands, I wiped blood from my chin then reached up and took my hat off.

Beauford had made a mistake. He assumed being cuffed meant I wasn't still dangerous.

I lunged forward and brought the crown of my forehead down on his nose. It crunched satisfyingly as it broke from the force of the impact.

He grunted and staggered backwards, grasping at his crooked nose as blood streamed through his hands.

The smirk was gone now, but all I saw was red. I took a step towards him, swinging my right boot back, preparing to kick him in the groin hard enough to neuter any future generations he might be thinking of.

Which of the Pinkertons butt stroked me from behind with their rifle I don't know, but the stars that lit up in my skull sent me straight to the ground in a heap.

Everything went dark.

* * *

I woke on a thin cot. Bo stared at me through the metal bars from the cell next to mine. The old man's face was etched with grief and he held his hat between his hands, working the frayed edge with his fingertips. A dark bruise had formed under one eye and a smear of dried blood ran along the collar of his shirt.

Pushing myself upright, I blinked from the pain that racked through my skull. The chains clanked as I felt the knot the size of an egg on the back of my head. I didn't know how long I'd been unconscious, but there was a fire burning in the fireplace that warmed the room. The painful tingling in my skin from the heat told me that I hadn't been in the cell for long. In the middle of the stained boarded floor was my hat, tossed in there as an afterthought it seemed.

Groaning in pain, I locked eyes with Bo.

"Tell me it ain't true," I said sadly, knowing full well it was. Beauford was too smug to have been lying.

The old ranch hand nodded that it was and blinked back tears. "We went in for the supplies and lumber, like you said. Then we figured we'd stop by the bar for a drink. Beauford was in there, playing poker. Kept egging us on to play cards, and finally Jim agreed to a few hands." Bo shook his head. "I warned him… dammit, I warned him not to. There's something wrong with that man, I told Jim. He's twisted up, evil inside. But Jim and I'd been practicing cards, and Jim thought he was getting pretty good at it." He wiped the back of his hand over wet eyes. "And he was."

"What happened then?" I asked quietly.

"Jim started winning. Hand after hand. He was on fire. The cards were just dealing themselves to him. And I kept telling Jim to stop and leave while he was ahead, but Jim had the entire bar on his side. They were all working him up to a frenzy, telling him he couldn't lose." Bo looked around the empty room as though to make sure we were truly alone. "Beauford just kept getting angrier and angrier. Finally, he called Jim a cheat. Of course, Jim denied it. He'd never cheat, he didn't know how. But he was armed, and Beauford started telling everyone how only a coward is called a cheat and doesn't defend himself. Jim couldn't stand it, so he drew." A tear rolled down the old man's cheek and dripped to the floor. "Beauford gunned him down," Bo raised his empty hands and looked at them, "and he died right here, in these hands, as I cradled him. He just... bled out, mumbling about his momma through all the blood bubblin' past his lips."

I swallowed hard and blinked as I felt my eyes moisten. "Why are you in here?" I asked, trying to keep from thinking of how much I liked Jim and what a good kid he was.

"Beauford just stood over us, that badge on his chest shining, and he laughed when the kid died." Bo looked up at me, rage in his eyes. "He laughed! I tackled him, and only reason I didn't kill him was because they pulled me off before I could choke him to death."

I felt my face grow hot and my pulse quicken. Beauford was a rotten one alright, and he'd lived his life long enough. If I didn't hang in the next few days, I was going to end him. I spoke low, my voice hard and firm to make sure Bo understood me. "They'll let you out in a day or two. Then I want you to go back to the ranch and take care of it and Sara for me."

"But-"

"No. No buts. I may be hanged soon, and Skyla will need you to care for the ranch. You understand me?"

"Hanged? Why?" Bo looked incredulous. "And the Sheriff needs to pay!"

"Damn right he does," I growled. "And if I don't hang, I'll make him. But not you, you keep your hands clean. You've got to listen to me. Bury Jim on that hill in the pasture he liked so much, make him a nice cross too. I want to see it when I get home. But there's too much riding on you staying out of trouble."

The door to the building bashed open suddenly and Sheriff Beauford walked in with a piece of cotton stuffed up his right nostril flanked by the two Pinkertons. "Get up," he commanded as he approached the iron bars.

I shot a stern look at Bo and stood as Beauford unlocked the cell.

Dark circles were forming around the Sheriff's eyes and his nose was a mottled shade of red and slightly crooked from where I'd broken it. I looked him in the eyes. He was a dead man walking and didn't even know it.

The Sheriff's fist slugged me in the stomach.

Pain jackknifed me in half. Gagging and gasping for air, I dropped to a knee and heard the two Pinkertons chuckle outside the cell.

"I always knew there was something about you, Jedidiah Huckleberry Smith," he spat my name. "I just didn't know what sort of pond sucking scum you were until now. You like your cheap shots, huh?"

"Leave him alone!" Bo shouted.

He was rewarded with one of the Pinkertons pointing his rifle at his face. "Shut yer mouth, old timer," the badged man said in warning before spitting tobacco juice at him.

I twisted upright, angered by the sucker punch. Grabbing for Beauford, I moved right into a clenched fist that cracked against my jaw. Spinning, I fell against the cot and grasped onto the thin metal rail to keep from striking the floor. "Uggghhh." This time I spat blood.

The toe of his boot kicked me in the side, and I dropped to my knees, gasping at the pain that lanced through my ribs.

"He's soft," an unfamiliar voice, one of the Pinkertons, said from outside my cage.

"Yup," agreed the other.

Gritting my teeth against the pain, I spun about to lunge at Beauford and stopped abruptly.

Through the pain and rage, I realized the muzzle of a pistol was pointed at my face.

"Stand up," the Sheriff said from behind the gun.

I took a deep breath and stood on shaky feet, hoping that nothing was broken from his kick.

Beauford stepped closer, keeping the pistol within inches of my nose. I glared daggers at him, refusing to give him the satisfaction of knowing how helpless I felt.

"I should kill you," he hissed. "But I won't, because I like a good hanging. Something about the way they drop… it's good wholesome family fun. And it'd be a shame to let my old town of Cheyenne miss out on that. Unfortunately, I won't be there to see it. My duties keep me here… but I'm going to enjoy hearing about your demise."

I stood silent as murderous thoughts crossed my mind.

Beauford turned to the Pinkertons. "He's all yours."

They grabbed me under the arm and shoved me out of the cell towards the door. I glanced at Bo and gave him a slight nod. The old man's face was one of worry and concern for me. Still, I hoped he took my word and didn't try anything stupid when they let him out.

***

This time I rode in a passenger car, with lots of stares given to me by other passengers at the battered and bloodied man sitting between two Pinkertons. It was humiliating. I could make out some of the whispering about me, but it was also warm compared to my previous ride.

Once we arrived in Cheyenne, I was shoved into another jail cell with a plate of two hardtack biscuits and a tin cup of dirty water for dinner. I ate, drank, then lay in the rack and tried to sleep. It was difficult, thoughts swirled around my mind. I kept thinking of Skyla at Fort Jipson and Brandthorn's warning that they'd seen lots of ape signs around the canyon. They were going to be attacked, I could feel it. And then there was Jim. He'd been a good kid. My fingers clenched into fists. I wanted Beauford dead for what he did.

But first I had to beat this murder charge and get back to Skyla.

It should be simple. Timmy was a well-known miner with a penchant for violence. My fist fight with him hadn't been seen by many, but there were plenty of people who witnessed the mob that Timmy tried to stir into stealing the train to flee the Battle of the Apes. Comparably speaking, I was a local hero... but only because no one knew the truth about me. The only problem was how good was Reydan and Sheriff Beauford's reach? Could they really silence any witnesses? I suspected so. That meant it was up to me alone to convince the judge and jury that I deserved to go free.

Giving up on the circling thoughts, I tried to get my tender bruised body comfortable on the thin mattress and sleep.

It was probably near midnight when I woke to my name whispered in the darkness.

Sitting upright, I rubbed sleep from my eyes. Being in a safe location, I tended to sleep like the dead instead of sleeping as if worried about being attacked by the numerous enemies that I'd made over the years on both sides of the law.

"Psssttt."

I looked around the one room building. The Sheriff and his deputies were long gone for the night and the other cells were empty. Only moonlight streaming through the windows gave any sort of light inside the room.

"Over here." The voice was familiar. I stood on my tip toes and peered out the small window with iron bars over it.

It was my father.

"What do you want?" I hissed.

His bearded face laughed quietly. "I'd like to get you out of here."

"No thanks, I'll take my chances with the law."

"You always were a stubborn child, Orville."

"That's not my name anymore. And you used to be a good man. What happened?"

He looked away as if embarrassed for a moment, before turning back to me, his face set as though made of stone. "Times change. There's no going back to who we were, the law won't let us."

"Then adapt. I did, I've led a good life for the past two years without you and the gang."

He scoffed. "You've been hiding out in the middle of nowhere, using a rope instead of a gun. And look where you are now, waiting on a rope around your neck."

"Better to live in hiding than run with you anymore. By the way, I don't appreciate you letting your men try to kill me."

He grimaced. "It wasn't by choice; I couldn't have stopped them. But they didn't stand a chance. You may not be the quickest draw, but you were never one for fair fights. After all, I'm the one that taught you," he grinned conspiringly. "That's how I knew you had a pistol drawn under that table. I'd heard you were carrying twin guns now, and your left hand was hidden."

I snorted. "Good guess, but if you'd have been wrong, I'd be dead. Now, get lost. I'm not going anywhere."

He glared at me for a moment, lips pressed together into a firm line as he thought. "Too bad. Get ready to be on the run again." I heard the strike of a match, followed by the flare of light and then the sizzle of a burning fuse. He looked me in the eyes. "Oh, you might want to take cover, boy."

Swearing, I raced to the other side of the room, jerking the thin mattress upright and ducked behind it, praying that it'd be enough to protect me from the explosion.

Long seconds passed.

The wall exploded inwards, chunks of brick and mortar slamming against the mattress. The explosion in the room painfully knocked the air out of my lungs, and choking, I drew in large gulps of dust and smoke.

"C'mon! Let's go!" I heard shouted vaguely through my ringing ears. Shoving the mattress away, I saw father and another rider sitting in front of the blasted opening holding the reins of a horse with an empty saddle. All the horses were spooked, and the riders fought to control the animals.

Coughing, I waved them away as shouts of alarm sounded from outside. There was a banging on the door as someone tried to enter the Sheriff's Office.

Shaking his head in disgust, father whipped his horse around and took off with the other rider, dropping the held reins and leaving the most likely stolen horse behind.

Shoving bits of debris off the metal cot, I put the mattress back in place and laid down as the thick door to the building was slammed open. Resting my hands across my stomach, I closed my eyes and tried to ignore the shouts and fits of coughing as men made their way through the thick dust to my cell. Sighing, I tried to not think about how close freedom had been.

One of the deputies fumbled with the lock and key outside my cell. "Hey, you! Why didn't you run off?"

I shrugged from my uncomfortable bed. "Too tired, I reckon."

"Who was it? Did you see them?" he demanded.

It wouldn't be wise to tell them who it was; if they caught them, it'd only bring more attention to me. I was in a precarious situation already without sharing a cell with my outlaw father. I shrugged again. "Nope."

The door slammed open against the bars with a clang. I opened my eyes and once again found myself staring down the barrel of a pistol.

"Well get up. We're moving you to the other cell."

"Fine."

***

"Mr. Smith. Who tried to break you free last night?" the heavy-set judge asked me pointedly. He seemed tired, and his thick jowls weighed his face down into the collar of his black robes. He reached over and flicked a speck of dust off a shoulder as he waited on my answer.

I stood in my cell, curious as to why he would come here to see me instead of having me brought to court. "Not sure, your honor. Seems to have been a case of mistaken identity. Once they saw me, they took off. Being innocent, I decided to go back to sleep."

He tilted his head as if to get a better look at me from between the rusted iron bars. "That makes you sound very confident of your case. Do you declare yourself innocent of the charge of murder?"

"I killed the man, yes sir. But it wasn't murder. The man tried to commit violence upon me twice before, and the third time he was shooting at me in the middle of a battle between outnumbered people and hundreds of attacking apes. I did what I had to do to survive, for the town to survive. I took out a threat and kept fighting. He was armed, and he was lethal. There was no time to take him prisoner and nowhere to take him that was safe if he'd surrendered."

"That matches what the witness says."

"The witness?" I asked, puzzled. I wasn't aware that anyone had seen me executing the violent, drunk miner. And whoever it was, it was someone that Reydan couldn't intimidate or hadn't found out about yet.

The Judge nodded. "Yes. There were two witnesses to your shooting of Mr. Timothy Shinney. One, a man of poor reputation who cannot be proven to have been at the battle that claims you murdered Timothy in cold blood, and the other, a man of irrefutable reputation and standing who was certainly at the battle and says it was self-defense. He is a man I'm heavily inclined to believe. But I wanted to get your side of the story as well to see which matched. Now that I've received that, the charge of murder will be dropped, and you will be free to go shortly."

Surprised, I could only stand there with my mouth open. I fully expected a trial with the threat of a rope at the end. "Sir, I appreciate that."

He looked me over again, taking in my battered face with a raised eyebrow. "You should also know that Sheriff Beauford Johnson, a man of whom I have little regard for, will most likely take the news of you avoiding the gallows hard. He always loved a hanging. It would behoove you to avoid him as much as possible in the future. Perhaps to the point of going any direction other than that which leads you to Granite Falls."

"Thank you for the warning, your honor. But I've no choice but to head in that direction." I rubbed my face, it still smarted from his punches. Granite Falls was on the way back to Skyla and Carbine. Besides, Beauford had my guns and there was still the matter of him goading Jim into a card game then killing him for winning.

"In that case, do take care, Mr. Smith. I'll let the Sheriff know to release you." Folding his black coat over his arm, he walked out of the building.

I sat down on the cot, still trying to wrap my head around my luck when the door opened again and in walked Wolverine Wade Mackin. The famous westerner grinned as he crossed the room. He was dressed in his usual Western attire; a heavily fringed tan leather jacket and leggings, with an up turned brimmed hat cocked at a fashionable angle on his head. Around his waist was a gun belt with a black powder Remington New Model Army in the holster. In his hands he carried the heavy Ballard single shot rifle that he was well known for.

Shaking his outstretched hand through the bars, I couldn't help but smile. "So, you're the witness. I should have known. It appears you saved me from a hanging."

"I told you to watch out for Beauford. Seems he wants your scalp," he admonished me as he leaned the long rifle against the wall. "Best I can tell, he figured out you killed Timmy during the battle and found someone else to pay to claim witness to it."

"Beauford is in Reydan's pocket," I muttered grimly.

"No doubt but watch your back. You may find yourself with a bullet in it." Wade glanced at the closed door he just entered through then back to me, the expression on his face turned serious. "I didn't lie to the judge. I saw that miner try to kill you during the battle."

I nodded slowly. "I didn't know anyone saw that until the Judge said our stories matched."

"I saw it alright. I saw him shooting at you, and I saw you shooting back…" he paused and leaned forward, looking me in the eyes. "And I saw you kill him as he stood there unarmed, with his hands raised."

I grimaced, but my anger flared as I tried to justify myself. "I didn't have time for his shit. There was a battle going on and he was going to try and kill me? The audacity. Yes, I killed him. I'd do it again."

Wade raised his hands defensively. "I understand. But you did it with an uncommon callousness of someone accustomed to killing folks." He stepped closer to the rusted iron cell bars. "I've suspected it for some time, but now I'm going to ask point blank. You haven't always been on the right side of the law, have you?"

I stared at him, unsure of how to answer.

"It's fine. You don't have to say anything. I've run into more than a few outlaws in my days. You're the only one I've met that was trying to make a solid try at being lawful. And you've risked your life repeatedly for others. You're different." He grabbed the bars between us and leaned in close. "But I want to make sure you stay on the right side. The way you killed Timmy, you could have hung for that had anyone else seen it. And if killing comes that easily to you then you need to keep a hold of yourself and make sure that you don't end up like Wesley."

Wesley was an outlaw who'd found himself jailed in our town during the battle. Out of desperation the former Sheriff let him out, knowing that we needed more guns and Wesley was good with his. He saved my life and many others with his twin Colt Lightnings. But once the battle was done, he rode into the sunset with a saddle bag full of cash he'd stolen from the saloon. His wanted poster was hanging in the very jail we were standing in.

"I won't."

"See to it. I know how bad you want to avenge yourself with Reydan. But I'm telling you, don't. He's an evil one, but fate will take care of him eventually."

Anger burned hot again, and I felt it drip from my voice like venom. "And until that happens, how many people does he hurt? How many lives will he ruin or destroy? Look what he tried to do with me. There's a reckoning coming for him. The sooner, the better. And it will be from the end of my muzzle or the tip of my blade."

Wade stepped back, removing his hat and rubbing a pair of fingers along the braided band. He sighed, "Then don't get caught. Because if you kill a railroad tycoon who also happens to be a Senator's son, my good name won't be enough to clear you."

"You've forgotten his private army of Pinkertons."

He growled. "Those sons of bitches, huh? I've had a few run ins with them. Some are good, most are bad. They're hired guns, good for killing protestors and striking workers. Bullies with guns. Loyal to the highest bidder. If they're protecting Reydan, along with your old friend Cato, you'd best tread real softly."

"I know."

He rubbed his mustache and goatee thoughtfully. "What about Skyla? Does she know about your past?"

"I told her."

"How'd that go?"

I shrugged. Only time would tell as she realized the implications of being with a man who may have to run at the drop of a hat to keep from hanging. "She still loves me, so I guess she took it well," I said.

"Then treat her good, because you don't deserve her." Wade pointed a finger at the hole blasted into the wall inside my old cell. The opening had been hastily boarded up but would need extensive brick repairs to fix. "I heard there was an attempted jail break last night. That have something to do with you?"

"Yup. My old gang tried to get me out of jail. They want me to join them again and I refused, so they tried to force my hand."

He whistled. "Whew, have you given thought to riding on for a bit before coming back, maybe let things cool off in your absence?"

"Can't. Skyla is on the other side and hell bent on being involved with the lost world. All those dinosaurs are living proof of her work and theories. And so long as she's in danger's way, I'll be with her."

"Can't blame you there. She's a keeper."

The door opened, and Ashley James stepped in with a rifle slung over her shoulder. She wore a light tan dress with white laced throat and a dirty blond braid thrown over a shoulder. For the best sharpshooter I'd ever seen, you wouldn't think so just looking at her.

She gave me a smile as she stepped beside Wade. "Hello, Jed. I see you've been up to no good."

"Ashley," I grinned conspiringly back at her. "It's not for a lack of trying."

Slipping an arm around Wade, she leaned against the famed Westerner. "Heard you tried to escape last night but fell asleep."

I laughed. "Is that what they're saying about me?"

"That's what I'm telling everyone."

Shaking my head, I changed subjects. "How's business?"

"Changing, that's for sure." Wade kicked the cell bars with the toe of his boot. "Interest in the Old West has faded, but interest in the 'New West' has gone through the roof. We still have the financial backing, actually we've much, much more than we need. But now, everyone wants to throw money at us to round up some dinosaurs and bring them to cities and towns across America. So, we mean to fetch whatever we can. It's certainly not what I wanted, but we're in a position to make a lot of money so we ought to go for it while we can."

"You'll have your work cut out for you. Any success yet?"

"Some. We've a couple of trikes we captured running loose after the battle, and a bunch of those little green scavengers. Skyla telegrammed us that they are called Compsognathus," the famed Westerner spat the word out awkwardly, "but we've taken to calling them Compys. They're the smartest little things, we've already got them trained for a half dozen commands. But they'll nip the daylights out of you if you aren't careful. We've got to keep them well fed or suffer the consequences. We learned that the hard way when they tried to eat one of our newest hires. We'd also like to buy a few of your Protos you've been keeping at your ranch."

"You're welcome to them, no charge. They're as much yours as mine. I take it you're heading to Fort Jipson then?"

"No, just Fort York. We're still trying to get permission to venture through the Shimmer. And it seems you and the military have killed off most of the critters on this side."

"Only the sort that would eat your audience. Brandthorn ought to be able to let you through. But it will be even harder on the other side to round up critters. Especially with Fredrick aiming on killing them to have mounted in the Smithsonian."

"Ha! That marksman?" Wade laughed. "I reckon we'll have to beat him to them then."

I chuckled. "Well there appears to be plenty of them on the other side, so good luck to you both. When are you leaving for Granite Falls?"

"Tonight," Ashley said as she played with her braid.

"Then it seems we'll be on the same train."

As Wade picked up his rifle, Ashley reached out and patted my arm goodbye through the bars. "Good to see you, Jedidiah. Glad my Wade could save you from hanging."

"Me too," I admitted with an awkward laugh.

Walking out, the famed Westerner lingered at the door. "Think about what I said, Jed."

"Yes, sir."

The door closed, and I paced back and forth in the cell, anxious to be freed and back on my way to get my girl, guns, and horse.

***

Once the Sheriff got around to setting me free, I walked across town to Liberty Arms. I was self-conscious about being without my guns. I didn't have so much as a pocket knife. That would need to be addressed.

Cheyenne was a central hub for the railroad, and as such, the largest town in all of Wyoming. The streets seemed to stretch for miles, and the people seemed more and more strange and ethnic. A vibrant mix of cultures and people, from Indians, to Mormons, to Chinese… most trying to get along and get by. And a few hating each other.

I caught Carson Skinner outside of his gun store.

The wooden sign carved above the building read 'Liberty Arms – Purveyors of Fine Arms and Ammunitions' in large white lettering over the thick slap board siding. It was an imposing two-story building with wrought iron bars over the windows. He stopped sweeping the boardwalk in front of his store as I approached and looked me over from head to toe with a frown.

"Unarmed, I see. Why?" he demanded. He was dressed similar to how I'd seen him last. A black suit with gray vest underneath and a holstered pistol, the butt turned forward for a cavalry draw. He was an imposing figure of a man, taller than my six feet with high cheekbones and a neatly trimmed graying mustache and goatee.

Considering he'd given me one of my matching Colt Peacemakers and my *Eighty-Six*, I could see why he might be ornery.

"Got arrested for killing a miner who tried to kill me during the big battle in Granite Falls. Sheriff took the guns."

He nodded. "Sounds like he got what he deserved. You said Sheriff. Which one? Beauford?"

"Yes. He's taken a severe disliking to me."

"He dislikes everyone with decent morals." Pulling a ring of keys from his vest pocket, he unlocked the door to his heavily secured store. "Come on in, we can't have Beauford shooting you in the back without you being armed."

I followed him into the darkened store as he opened the shutters and allowed bright light to fill the room. We walked past racks of leather, gear and clothing. At the far end was a long counter with guns lining the wall behind it and a moose skull with massive antlers stretching across the wall. It wasn't quite a trading store, more like a gun store that offered some odds and ends for added income. The walls along the side of the room were decorated with stuffed mounts of deer, elk, antelope, and a lone bighorn sheep. A large grizzly bear rose on hind feet next to the door, greeting visitors with paws raised and fangs bared in a silent roar.

"How did the '86 work for you?" he asked about my rifle as we made our way between the racks of jeans and shirts.

"Excellent. I did put a few dents and scratches in it though," I said apologetically at the displeased look that crossed his face. "It saw a fair bit of combat, I even butt stroked an ape with it."

"A work of art... only two of its kind in existence... and you butt stroked a big monkey with it," he shook his head in disgust. "Outstanding."

"I know, I know. But it performed admirably; the .45-70 cartridges did the trick on apes and dinosaurs alike. The Colt you set me up with has seen its share of use as well."

Carson pulled a pair of stools from beneath the counter and perched himself on one, adjusting the pistol on his belt as he did so, and turning so he was facing the entrance to the store. I hadn't heard much of his story, but I knew it included demons in his past from the War Between the States. Bad enough demons that he changed his name and came west for a fresh start running a gun store that was fortified like a bank.

"I've read about the Battle of the Apes in the papers, but tell me all about it," he demanded. "And then catch me up on everything else since."

***

"Are you sure I don't owe you anything?" I asked as I turned over the Colt pistol in my hand. Carson had set me up with another Peacemaker, knowing that it was the pistol I was the most familiar with. This one was nickel plated with ivory grips. A bit too shiny for me, but a nice gun just the same.

"Not a cent." He flipped a holster and belt onto the counter and shoved them towards me.

I gently set the gun back on the folded cloth and stared at him. "You've given me several guns now, and I feel like I owe you something in return."

"First off, the Governor paid handsomely for the previous two guns. Second off... I know your father," he admitted with a sly half smile.

"What?" I practically shouted.

"You and I have actually met before, although you were a good bit littler and I was using a different name. But so were you... Orville. Now who do you think helped get me to move from Tennessee and start fresh here?"

Recovering from the shock, I glared at him. "So, the only reason you helped me was because of my father," I said accusingly.

"Nonsense. I helped you because I knew the Governor was good for the bill. But... I did give you the 1886 Winchester because of who your old man was."

"I'd like to give it back then," I said regrettably but firmly. If I had the *Eighty-Six* because of my father, I didn't want the danged thing.

"No. It's damaged. You said so yourself and I've a no return policy," he thumbed towards the end of the counter where a sign said just that. No Returns.

"Dammit, Carson."

"No. Shut it, Jed. I owe your father. The least I could do was help his son out and make sure he didn't go into battle with an ancient Spencer repeater and get himself killed. I don't much care what you think of him, he's helped me out when I was in a few tight spots. He's not a perfect man, but he's a good man."

"He was a good man. He's not anymore."

"I'm not going to argue with you about him. You've got something to sort out between the two of you, then sort it out. I'll not get in the middle of it. But you're keeping the guns, and that's the end of it."

He said it with such conviction that I knew I had to relent and relent I did. "Thank you then, but I liked you more before I knew you knew my father."

For the first time, I saw Carson Skinner laugh.

"So, who are you? Really?" I asked, curious since I'd met him over ten years ago at some point.

His laugh disappeared, and I knew I'd broken one of the cardinal rules of living in the west; I'd asked about someone's past. He fixed me with a glare. "That's none of your damned business. Now you want some ammunition to go along with that pistol or not?"

"Yes, sir."

"Good." He rummaged beneath the counter, shuffling boxes of ammunition in search of .45s.

I leaned over the counter, curious. "You do realize they may have hanged me… right? I reckon you weren't going to do anything to try and stop that?"

"Who do you think your pa stole the horse from last night? Besides…" He reached across the counter and flipped a piece of canvas over. Beneath it lay a Sharps rifle with a long, thin brass telescope mounted over the barrel and action. An expensive piece of hardware. "We had a backup plan."

"To shoot the rope with?"

For the second time, Carson chuckled. "Or the hangman. He's owed me money for some time now."

***

Once suitably armed and with a borrowed coat, I felt like a human being again as I waited at the train station for Wade and Ashley. After a couple of hours of people watching, they showed up minutes before the train boarded. By then the train was packed. The number of passengers and supplies going into Granite Falls had gone through the roof. Granite Falls had become a boom town, and unless the Shimmer disappeared, it was a boom town with no end in sight.

While we rode the train across the prairie to my town, we talked about what we'd been up to since the battle. Namely, Ashley's engagement to Wade. As thrilled as I'd been to not hang, I'd missed the ring on Ashely's hand until we sat down in the train seats and she rested her hands in her lap.

"You two are getting married?" I blurted.

Ashley laughed and leaned against Wade's shoulder. "Yes. And we'd like you and Skyla to come."

I grinned. "Wouldn't miss it for the world. Got a date set?"

"We're trying to get ahold of some relatives, but we'll be married back there in a few weeks," Wade thumbed towards the back of the train and the tracks that led to Cheyenne, then turned to his fiancé. "Besides, I feel like I need to give Ashley a little more time in case she decides to reject me."

The sharpshooter chuckled and flashed the ring at him mischievously. "Do I get to keep this if I leave?"

"Absolutely not! That's my grandmother's and worth at least several rifles."

She leaned her back against him and smiled mischievously. "Winchesters or Ballards? Because everyone knows repeaters are better than single shots."

"Oh no. I'm not listening to that argument again," I moaned.

"Well, that's because-" Wade started.

I closed my eyes and tried to tune them out. They'd go on for hours about which was better. Ashley carried a Winchester *One of a Thousand* rifle, a rare, customized model 1873 that had been selected for its almost legendary accuracy if placed in shooting hands as good as hers. Meanwhile, Wolverine Wade, stuck in his old ways, cherished his heavy, octagonal barreled, single shot Ballard rifle.

"No, Wade! I've ten rounds of .44-40 in mine and you've a single round of .45-100 and..."

I pulled my hat over my eyes and slunk lower in my seat. It was going to be a long ride.

***

We had a brief stop in Granite Falls as people and supplies were unloaded for the town and loaded for the end of the rail.

I left my friends behind on the train and took the time to go to the Sheriff's Office. Stopping on the boardwalk, I checked the Colt to make sure it was loose in the holster then opened the door and stepped through.

Beauford looked up and glared. His nose was a little straighter from someone resetting it and dark circles had formed under both eyes now. I hoped it hurt every time he opened his big dumb mouth.

"Try knocking next time," he growled from behind what had been Dan's desk just a few months prior. The thought of a good Sheriff like Dan and his deputy nephews being replaced by this man was enraging.

"Try being a decent Sheriff sometime," I snarled back, resisting the urge to shoot him on sight for what he'd done to Jim.

The lawman jumped to his feet and I swept my hand down, grasping the pistol butt, yet stopping short of drawing. His face flushed red as his hand stopped several inches from his gun. I'd practiced enough that I was better than most, but I was still no gun slinger.

"I know who you are. Who you really are," he sneered. "I know what you've done. Ever since I heard what you accused Reydan of, I started digging. Now I know all about you and your band of renegade Confederate misfits murdering up and down the East Coast."

My blood went cold. I tried hard to not show shock. But he saw it and grinned evilly. I swallowed hard, thinking of how badly I needed to kill him. If only Skyla didn't need me now...

"Prove it, asshole," I growled. "In the meantime, arrest me or give me my weapons."

He hesitated for a moment, obviously wondering if he could take me into custody. And I wondered if I was making a mistake by not killing him now. But as far as I could tell he had no evidence and I'd just been released on an American hero's word. It would be hard to get a judge to charge or convict me of anything else right now without solid proof. Also, if he arrested me the same day I was released, it'd look vindictive and petty.

He made his decision and violently jerked open a desk drawer. From inside, he pulled out my pistols wrapped in their holsters and gun belt. I watched him carefully, my hand never leaving the butt of my gun, as he pulled the pistols out and dumped the cartridges onto the desk. They bounced and scattered, most rolling off the mess of papers and onto the dirty floor. I let them roll against my boots without moving or picking them up.

Finished with my pistols, he shoved them back into the holsters and picked up my *Eighty-Six* from where it leaned against the wall.

I bristled as I watched him handle my rifle. He jacked the large rounds from the gun one by one and tossed the weapon on top of the paired holsters with a clatter.

Gritting my teeth, I used my free hand to sling the empty rifle and gun belt over a shoulder. Without a word, I carefully backed out of the room.

"Hey," he called.

I stopped and tightened my grip on the pistol butt.

His eyes glared as he worked the large wad of tobacco between his jaws. "You'll hang one day."

"Maybe. But if I do, most likely, it'll be from killing you." I stepped out, leaving the door open behind me. Surrounded by others, I felt safer as I walked back to the train. The chances of him doing something now were much less likely when there were so many witnesses.

***

Almost to the train station, a man stepped in front of me with an off-white envelope held in his hand. "Orville," he said calmly. He was thin, wearing a suit coat over white buttoned shirt and black trousers. A dark brown bowler's hat was perched on his head, and he had a peculiar squint to his left eye. He was also wearing a single gun on his right hip with its holster tied down.

I stopped abruptly. I'd reloaded both Colts and wore my old gun belt around my waist now, the *Eighty-Six* and borrowed Peacemaker from Carson Skinner were slung over a shoulder. I was loaded for bear, but it'd slow my draw down if it came to that.

Around us the crowd of people flowed on the boardwalk. We were just two people talking, nothing unusual about that. But I still drew glances with all the hardware I was packing. I tried to keep my face innocent and carefree, even though the man had just used my real name.

"What?"

He held up the envelope. "This is for you. It's from your father."

"I don't want it."

He raised his free hand apologetically. "Sorry, I was told to make you take it."

My fingers twitched near my pistols. I'd had enough of people making me do things lately. Being jailed and threatened with hanging had made me more ornery than normal. "I don't care."

He took his brown bowler hat off with his right hand. "Look, Orv-" At the look on my face he paused and started again. "Jed. I'm just delivering a message from your pa. I don't care if you read it or not, I'm just doing as I was asked. If you want to have a gun fight over a piece of paper, fine. Kill me and let one of these witnesses read this," he waved the envelope in the air. "See what happens then."

The man had me there. I wasn't going to shoot him over a piece of paper, nor fight him. I held my hand out and he handed the envelope over.

Folding it in half with one hand, I tucked it into my shirt pocket. "I'm not promising I'll do anything but start a fire with it."

"That's fine. Personally, I don't care, and I don't know what he sees in you anyway. You killed several of us. To me, that means there ought to be a bounty on your head. And not the 'locate but don't harm' sort. More of the 'kill on sight' type." He shrugged with one shoulder. "Nothing personal. But it makes us look bad if we don't kill you. But it's your old man's call. He's still our leader.... For now."

Turning, he walked away, quickly disappearing amongst the crowd.

***

Sighing, I started walking down the street then jumped in surprise when I realized Reverend was matching me step for step.

He smiled crookedly. "How are things on the other side, this... Prehistoria as they are calling it?"

"Wild, dangerous... prehistoric." His long legs easily kept pace with me as we dodged around a pair of stopped wagons whose drivers were arguing with each other about who was in whose way. "I bet you've had a lot of questions about it?"

"Yes. But there have been many strange discoveries that have shaken the belief in God. At one point people thought the world was flat, at another time, that the sun rotated around us. It makes no sense to us now, but at the time many believed it as a fundamental truth. We don't understand or know much, but humanity's pride makes us think we know everything."

"That is true. Luckily for me, I just assume there's a lot I don't know."

Reverend laughed. "How about your father? Has he sent more men to kill you?"

"Not yet. But he did try to break me out of jail."

"Well, that's love I suppose. Doing extraordinary things for those you care dearly for."

I skirted a rather large mound of horse manure and tried to keep pace with the preacher's long legs. "Yes, but he almost let me die first in the Bucket O' Blood."

"Did you ask him why?"

"He said he knew I had the drop on them and that I'd fight unfair."

The man of the cloth shook his Bible at me. "Fair fights are for suckers. Even God often used overwhelming force to defeat His enemies and show His might as much as He used an underdog. But it sounds like your father raised you to survive."

"That he did."

Abruptly, the Reverend grabbed my arm and pulled me to a stop. "I would tell you to forgive him, and you should. But I think you should try to understand him as well. He wouldn't let you die at one moment only to save you at another. By the way, that nice dressed gunman from the bar in the fancy boots... Someone shot him in the back right before Left Arm drilled him from the front."

I looked around the crowded street, puzzled at the news. "You're saying my old man shot him?"

"Looks that way. Like I said, give forgiveness and seek understanding."

Clasping him on the shoulder, I nodded. "Thanks, Reverend. Take care."

"Keep your powder dry, Jedidiah."

***

When I got back on the train, I was surprised to see Reydan's fancy car attached at the back end.

The big steel plated car gleamed in the sun, but there was something new about it. The top was covered with a large sheet of canvas over something sticking up from the roof of the carriage. I assumed it was a work in progress if it was still covered, but it made me wonder if it had something to do with the foreign made gun that'd been delivered before the expedition.

Shaking my head, I walked on past. I'd find out soon enough. But I wish I could have seen the look on his face when Reydan White learned I'd gotten away with murder. Almost literally.

The railroad tycoon's private car was attached after ours, and stepping into our passenger car, I was surprised to see Cato sitting at the back of it by himself. His dark eyes followed me as I walked down the aisle, passing where my friends sat. Wade shot me a warning look that I ignored while Ashley shook her head at me. This was the first time I'd seen Cato outside of his boss' shadow and I wanted to have a private word, assuming the man had the capacity to speak.

I sat on the bench on the opposite side of the aisle from him. Tucking my boots under the seat in front of me, I leaned back, turning my head to look at the expressionless gunman.

He was staring towards the front of the car, his dark eyes as unreadable as the plain expression on his face. He was clean shaven, as always, and wearing the same dark outfit as before. I wondered if he chose it, or Reydan, to make him more intimidating looking. His twin guns were tied down, the leather thong at the base of the holsters wrapped around his thighs to keep them in place for a fast draw. I idly wondered how many people he had killed with them.

Wade glanced back at me, concern on his face. It was obvious he didn't think this was a good idea.

The steam engine's whistle blew, and the huff of the engine increased as the cars jerked and began to roll. I waited to speak until we pulled away from the station and the noise of the locomotive began to even out.

"Cato," I said softly.

The gunman turned his head slightly, his eyes roving over my rough appearance. After a couple of days in captivity plus a beating, I knew I could use a bath and a change of clothes. The dark stubble on my cheeks was nothing new, I'd always been something of an occasional shaver. But the bruising under my eye and split lips showed I'd been put through the wringer recently.

Unsure of what to say, I blurted out the first thing I could think of. "What the hell happened to you?"

He blinked, but didn't answer. The silence was aggravating.

"You know who I am. You know what Reydan did to our home," I accused.

"Your home," he said simply. His voice was low and gravelly, a far change from the high pitch it'd been when he was a kid.

"No, it was our home."

He shook his head slightly. "I was a slave."

"Is that what you think? You were freed before father even brought you home. And if it hadn't been for him, you'd have been thrown into the sea because you didn't sell on the auction block."

"Not my father."

"Yes, he was. And you were his son. I reckon you don't care about what happened to our mother or sister either?"

"Yours, not mine."

"Dammit, man." I could feel the frustration growing inside me. "Do you only speak in three-word sentences? Mother's dead."

He was silent, but his jaw flexed. He'd been close with our mother. If we couldn't find him, he could usually be found sitting in the kitchen, his dark skin covered in flour, helping her prepare meals. She'd taken his disappearance hard.

I noticed the slight movement. "Yeah, you remember," I laughed sarcastically. "Whatever Reydan did to twist you around to becoming his lap dog, he didn't wipe out all the old memories, did he?"

"Stop talking."

"Your master hanged our neighbor that used to give us candy, burned our home, almost whipped me to death, then went pillaging and raiding all throughout the South with you in tow. Pa and I tracked them, searching all over the South for you. You didn't know that, did you? We hunted the raiders down, one by one. And we killed them. There's only one left now, your boss. And if I have to go through you to get to him, I will."

"Try it," he grunted and shifted his hands to rest on his pistol butts.

Sighing, I stood as the train jostled over rough tracks down a grade. "Better cinch your gun belt tight then. There'll be a reckoning eventually."

"How about now?" he asked quietly without looking up.

I glanced down at him, then back to Ashley and Wade who were watching our interaction intently. They were too far away to hear our words, but they were reading our body language and I'm sure things weren't looking good.

"I've some things to take care of still." Turning my back on him, I walked down the aisle to my friends and sat down angrily.

"How'd that go?" Wade uncocked his heavy, outdated Remington revolver that rested in his lap. Ashley had hers in hand as well. It was comforting to know they had my back, and if things got Western, they'd back my play.

"Well, he can speak after all."

"That's a pleasant surprise," Ashley quipped.

"I suppose. But he didn't have anything worth saying though." I gingerly rubbed my face in exasperation. "But I'm pretty sure when I go after Reydan, I'll have to kill him as well."

"You're on your own then." Wade shifted and holstered his pistol, apparently uncaring if Cato could see him doing so, and took Ashley's hand. "We've too much going for us right now to get killed over your past."

"Don't blame you there one bit."

"Nonsense. We're with you, Jed," the sharpshooter admonished her beau.

He grunted and shrugged. "Yeah, I suppose so."

"Thanks, but this is personal. When I go after him, I'll be doing it on my own."

***

By the time we rolled into the makeshift train town at the end of the rail line, I'd filled Wade and Ashley in on the expedition and everything we'd been up to since we'd seen them last. Which was a lot. The entire time Cato sat at the back of the car, unmoving as far as I could tell. I gave him a sour look as I stood and picked up the *Eighty-Six*.

And as I stretched my legs and walked off the passenger car behind Ashley, I realized it'd been one heckuva trip. I'd threatened a Sheriff and a gunman they called the 'Black Plague'. So that was nice. But I also hadn't been hanged and had my guns back. And soon I'd see Skyla and Carbine again.

We disembarked and went looking for horses.

I found Carbine turned loose in a corral with a bunch of US branded soldier horses, well brushed and happy. The stable boy came over and leaned against the rail, reaching out to gently pet my horse. I glanced down at the kid. "Thanks for taking care of him," I told him sincerely. Most stables wouldn't waste time on another man's horse unless paid for in advance.

"You're welcome. But I was just pleased to see the horse that the hero of Granite Falls rode into battle."

I laughed. "Actually, I sent him away before the fight. I figured if we lost, he might get eaten. And he's too good of a horse for a fate like that. As for me, I pretty much just stood on top of a roof and shot my guns a bunch. Nothing real heroic to that."

The kid stopped petting Carbine and looked up at me skeptically. "But isn't it true you ate the ape leader's heart?"

"You know…" I started and stopped myself before taking out my frustration on the kid. "Look, I just bit a chunk out of it. I would say it was poetic justice, but really it was just blind rage. The ape leader had been sacrificing men by cutting their hearts out and eating them. So, I did the same to him."

Carbine thrust his head against the boy's chest and pushed, eager for more attention.

"What'd it taste like?" the kid asked.

"Chewy and bloody."

The boy shuddered.

"Yeah, I don't recommend it." I pulled a coin from my pocket and dropped it into the kid's hand. "Thanks for taking such good care of Carbine. Now how about giving me a hand getting him saddled?"

By the time we got Carbine ready, Wade had managed to use his celebrity status to get Ashley and himself a pair of horses. But he still had to pay a steep price to borrow them. Apparently, word of his borrowing of a wagon the first time he came to the tunnel had circulated. It'd been returned full of arrows, busted boards from trike horns, and large smears of blood. Human, ape, and dinosaur alike.

"It'd have been cheaper to have bought horses outright in Cheyenne and brought them on the train," he grumbled to Ashley.

"Next time, I'll do the haggling. I don't have the reputation you do," she chided him.

"You're more than welcome to try, my dear." Wade dropped the saddle over the horse's blanket, shifted it into place, and began working the cinch. "I'm pretty excited to get permission to cross the Shimmer and see the other side again. You know I haven't been since we went together, Jed?"

I stepped aside as Carbine intentionally splashed water from the trough onto my pants with his muzzle. I swatted him on the rump with my hat for that. "Not much has changed, except for the buildup around the tunnel. But once I get to Fort Jipson, I'll talk to Brandthorn. You shouldn't have to wait long to come meet us, unless the apes attack that is."

"Count me out of that; fighting them at Granite Falls was enough for a while. But it'll be a big operation to grab some of these dinosaurs, so this will just be a scouting expedition for now. We're going to need plenty of men and such to capture them. But we'll start off small. Maybe try to snare a few of those little pterodactyls... could you imagine a crowd's reaction if we landed one of those big ones the Shayana ride? You need to talk some of them into coming over to our side and touring with us."

I shook my head. "I don't know about that, Wade. They're a couple hundred years removed from us. Kind of like the Indians when the Whites arrived on this continent."

"They'll come around. The Indians did, it just took some time and a lot of fire water."

"And a lot of shooting," I added.

"That too," Ashley clucked her tongue and turned her horse's head. "Let's ride."

I tapped my heels to Carbine's sides, and we rode towards the mountain that held the tunnel to the other side.

***

The last time the soldiers stationed at the Fort York saw me, I was in chains and guarded by Pinkertons. Understandably, they were a bit skeptical when I showed up and told them I'd been freed and needed to get back to Fort Jipson. Luckily, having Wolverine Wade with me proved to be a boon as the commanding officer of the small fort let me go on his word that I wasn't an escaped prisoner.

Blue uniformed soldiers put their shoulders against the heavy gates as I waved goodbye to Wade and Ashley. They'd be waiting for word from Captain Brandthorn before crossing with an escort. When the thick log doors swung open, I left my friends behind and rode Carbine through the Shimmer and into Prehistoria once again.

As I exited the tunnel, I drew in a breath of the hot, humid air and shrugged out of Carson's borrowed coat. The temperature was vastly different between the two sides, with fall on ours and what felt like an eternal summer on this side. I rolled the coat up and tied it to my bedroll.

This was the first time I'd traveled alone on this side since I'd first discovered it months ago. It was an eerie feeling to be riding along the same wagon tracked trail through the same forest that I'd so recently ridden cuffed in the saddle to be hanged by the neck until dead. But it was also dangerous. Less so in some ways, more so in others. I decided to ride off the side of the trail. It was much slower going, but lessened the chance of me being ambushed by a bunch of apes or a hungry dinosaur.

After an hour of a nerve-wracking ride through ferns and trees, Carbine stopped suddenly, his nostrils flaring and ears flicking forwards and back.

I tensed in the saddle and shifted my grip on the *Eighty-Six* where it lay across the pommel of my saddle.

The tall, overgrown forest had gone quiet. Even the strange giant bugs on this side weren't making their usual noises. That could only mean one thing: there was a predator nearby.

Then I heard it.

Faint breathing. Like a huffing sound.

Coming from my left.

I slowly pulled the stock of the rifle into my shoulder. Carbine heard the noise as well, and turned his head to look. A trickle of sweat rolled down my face, dripping onto the warm metal of the rifle.

A branch snapped as something heavy shifted its weight.

Carbine tensed beneath me.

He snorted, blowing air through his nose to get a better scent of whatever was in the forest with us.

That did it.

A beastly roar sounded, and Carbine jumped. Grabbing for the reins I barely managed to hang on as he spun to the right, burst through the trees and onto the wagon trail and took off with me fighting to stay in the saddle.

From behind us came the heavy stomps and crackling of undergrowth as something charged after us.

Regaining control of Carbine, I let him have the lead, instead turning in the saddle to see a long snouted beast burst free of a set of green and purple ferns and step onto the trail. Green and black striped, the dinosaur had a large fin that crested its back and stood at least ten feet tall. I got the impression it was a juvenile, but couldn't put my finger on what made me think that. Something about it seemed awkward and gangly.

The beast roared after us, opening its fanged mouth wide and showing off a long pink tongue.

We rode around a bend, losing sight of the creature. I kicked my heels against my horse's side, urging Carbine onwards towards the fort. The beast didn't appear to be following us, but I wasn't about to take any chances.

After a couple of miles, I slowed Carbine down, and stopped to give him some water. We were both on edge, and I quickly poured water into my hat and let the horse drink while keeping my eyes roving on the forest around us. We were about to break free of the trees and hit the open plains, which held its own threats and dangers and I wanted Carbine ready to run again if need be.

Saddling up, I took one last careful look around us, and we stepped out from the shelter of the trees.

***

The palisade at Fort Jipson had been completed, and the sharpened logs jutted outwards at an angle. Any trike charges against that would be met with disaster as the logs would wound, kill, and keep the enemy at bay as gunfire was poured into them from the Gatlings and cannon on top of the berm.

I just hoped that the apes didn't know that. I love a foolish enemy, but I doubted they'd ride straight into gunfire again. After the last attack, and the targeting of our Gatlings, I suspected enough ape survivors had made it back to this side for them to learn and adjust their tactics. But our soldiers were better armed this time with repeaters, and we had a solid defensive entrance. Hopefully, if they attacked, we'd be able to repel them with ease.

When I appeared in front of the canyon entrance, Sergeant Mayhew once again rode out with a squad of soldiers.

"Good heavens, Jed. What are you doing here?" He squinted in the sun at me. "Are you on the run? Because if so, you know we've got to take you in." His hand slid towards the flapped holster at his side.

I shook my head. "No, not on the run. The charges were dropped."

"Good." Removing his hat, he wiped sweat from his brow than put the blue hat back on. "Because Skyla has been raising hell. I thought at one point we were going to have to confine her to the command tent to keep her from riding off through Prehistoria by herself. She was scared to death you were going to hang."

I grinned and touched my heels to my flanks, heading towards the opening in the palisade. "Where's she at?" I called over my shoulder as I left the group behind.

"No idea!" he cried back as he twirled his horse around and rode after me with the rest of the soldiers close behind.

I rode through the palisade with Carbine's mane and tail blowing in the warm humid breeze, then directly to Skyla's tent. It was the first place I figured I'd look.

***

The flaps on both ends were tied open to let the air through.

Skyla sat just inside of them, with one of her leather-bound journals lying across her lap. At the thunder of Carbine's hoof beats she looked up. Her face turned from shock to overwhelming joy as she dropped the journal and jumped upright.

"Jed!" she shouted as I swung down from the saddle and swept her into my arms. Kissing me passionately, she knocked my hat back and grabbed my face.

"What... why... how?" Her hands ran over the bruising on my face then her fingers gently touched the cut on my lips. "You survived a hanging but took a beating?"

Laughing, I pulled her tighter to me. "Charges were dropped..." My enthusiasm faded as I thought of why I'd received my beating. "Skyla... Jim's dead."

"Oh no, what happened?" Her eyes, already reddening at seeing me alive, began sprouting tears that rolled down her cheeks.

"Sheriff Beauford killed him."

"What? Why?" she cried. "He was a good kid!"

"Cheating at cards, or so Beauford says. But from what Bo said, he was winning fair and square. I disagreed with the Sheriff as well, and," I pointed to my face, "you can see how that went."

Her lips pressed together into a thin line. "I hope that wicked man gets what he deserves soon."

"I'm sure he will," I agreed. Especially if I had anything to do with it. I planned on killing that man as soon as the opportunity arose.

"Where's Charles?"

"Exercising Sir Lancelot." She reached over and scratched Carbine behind me. He whinnied and shuffled closer to her.

"I'm so glad you're alive, Jed. I tried to come after you, honest. The Pinkertons wouldn't let me, and Brandthorn said I had to wait until he had a return group together before he'd risk me traveling to the Shimmer."

"I knew you'd try. It's okay, everything worked out just fine. I'm back here, and we've got this." I looked around the fort. "What about the apes? Any more signs of an attack coming?"

"Brandthorn has pulled his troops in, but the Pinkertons are still patrolling. They say they have their orders from Reydan and signed by the Governor to basically do whatever they want."

"Damn." I looked around the encampment. It looked like half the forces here were Pinkertons now. I'd heard they had thousands of them scattered across the United States, almost an army really. And Reydan must have called for as many of them as possible to help tame Prehistoria as fast as he could.

"What about preparations for a dragon?" I asked. I still couldn't believe this was a real discussion we were continually having.

"Brandthorn said if one appears, we'll just have to shoot it down. There's not much we can do otherwise. But he opened the cave paintings up for everyone to see; that's where most of the scientists are now, studying them."

I rubbed the stubble on my jaw. "I hope they aren't too angry about it being locked up for so long... but shooting them down is the best I could figure up also. Just shoot away and hope to get lucky. Well, let's hope if they attack, the ape leader won't have one."

"Yeah... I hope not... Oh, you haven't heard!" Her tear-streaked face lit up with excitement. "The Pinkertons caught a raptor."

***

I hadn't gotten a good look at the changes to the fort before I'd been arrested. But after putting Carbine into the pasture with the other horses, I walked the perimeter with Skyla.

In addition to the Gatlings and twin cannons facing the canyon entrance, wagons had been parked at intervals around the tent city to provide sudden cover should we be attacked again. In addition to the wagons, there was a Gatling gun placed at both internal corners of the camp. In effect, this created a large triangle of sorts with the heavily guarded canyon entrance being the northernmost tip. The south east and west corners were guarded with the crew served weapons and small palisades about waist high in case anything decided to climb down the cliff faces to come after us.

The corral was placed between the two corners, the fencing making a large obstacle for any attacking apes to either climb over, risk moving through dozens of horses, or to go around, thus placing them in a better area to be shot.

It was probably as defended as this fort could be. Unless we added another dozen Gatling guns. Which would be welcomed, in my opinion. Over here, you could use all the guns you could get it seemed. Especially when there was the possibility of a freaking dragon attacking us.

Holding hands, we walked past Charles riding Sir Lancelot whose only reaction to seeing me alive again was to tip his hat.

We found Fredrick sitting on a log, watching the caged dinosaur. After passing pleasantries and congratulations about my not being hung until dead, I squatted down on my haunches to look at the terrible little monster.

The cage was ten feet long and ten feet wide, built with thick, rough sawn boards reinforced with steel bands. There were fresh claw and tooth grooves on the wood, and I wondered how long the contraption would hold the raptor.

The feathered beast snarled at me. It was a light tan, furry in the body but colorfully feathered along the arms and tail that balanced the long creature. Bright red feathers on the back of the beast's head shook as it snarled and grabbed the caging with black claws. Screeching, it shook the cage hard, and I took an involuntary step back as it hurled itself towards me.

"Nasty little critters, aren't they?" Fredrick said.

"Pure lethality. It's amazing the apes managed to tame them."

"I guess it's like domesticating wolves. At some point, a lot of people probably got eaten before they turned them into dogs," he mused.

The dinosaur slammed into the cage again, its black talons screeching as they slid across a steel strap.

I shuddered. "How did they capture it?"

"Pinkertons found it on one of their patrols. Apparently, the apes had dug pits around the perimeter of the canyon when they still occupied this place, with the obligatory spikes at the bottom to kill whatever fell in." Skyla pointed at the creature. "This one managed to miss the spikes, but became trapped, and was so starved it was weak and barely alive. The Pinkertons managed to loop some ropes around it and haul it up. After we fed it some leftover cow parts, it perked right up."

I hadn't heard anything about the traps, but I felt very out of the loop between my time with the Shayana and then almost being hanged. "Pit falls, huh? Sneaky apes. I'm glad I didn't ride Carbine into one when I first found the place."

"We're lucky no one has ridden into one yet," Skyla corrected me.

"I don't like the idea of the Pinkertons riding patrols, most of them aren't trained for spit," Fredrick said as he poked the raptor with a long stick. With a quick snap of its jaws, the stick was jerked from his hands by the feathered dinosaur. "Hey!" He picked up a small pebble and flung it at the creature. It bounced off the beast's back harmlessly.

The raptor hissed.

"Anyways. Pinkertons aren't military. Well, some are formerly. But their leadership doesn't know what they are doing. And they're a bunch of trigger happy thugs anyways," Fredrick shrugged. "But if someone must get eaten while patrolling, I'm glad it's them and not some of Brandthorn's men."

I nodded my agreement.

A soldier ran over to us and placed his hands on his knees. Bent over and breathing heavily, he gasped for air before trying to speak. "Skyla... ugh..." he turned and retched. "Captain needs you. The Shayana... the Pinkertons shot some."

"Sonuva bitch," I swore and kicked the cage angrily. The raptor attacked the caging in a fury of snarls and scratching in response. "You called it Fredrick."

Skyla grabbed my arm. "Let's go."

Leaving the soldier, Fredrick, and the raptor behind, we took off at a quick walk across the encampment.

***

Several Pinkertons stood inside Brandthorn's command tent as we entered. The Captain stood before them, his face a bright red. Lieutenant Daniels flanked him from behind, glaring at the badged men.

"Damn you all! What have you done? They are our allies. The only allies we've got on this side!" Brandthorn shouted.

"They shot first!" one of the Pinkertons with a handle bar mustache said, stepping forward to challenge the Captain.

Brandthorn's face darkened and he stepped close to the man. "Listen here. I don't believe you, Thompson. And if you want to challenge my belief, I'm more than willing to stand back to back, then walk a dozen paces away from each other with a pistol in my hand. Do you understand me?"

Thompson looked at his two companions then stepped back. "Dueling is illegal, sir."

"This is Prehistoria and I'm in charge. If I want to duel you, I damn well will." Brandthorn turned to us and noticed me for the first time. "Jed, I'm glad you're alive and back. Now I need you and Skyla to help sort this out with the Shayana. We can't have a misunderstanding with them."

"What happened?" I asked.

The Captain glared at the Pinkertons as if daring them to tell the tale. After a quiet moment, Daniels coughed to clear his throat and spoke. "A patrol went badly." He pointed to the east. "Mr. Thompson here and several of his men killed some Shayana who were watching the fort from the cliff face."

"They were spying on us!" protested the mustached Pinkerton.

"Shut your mouth before I beat it closed, Thompson," Brandthorn warned. "As of now, they are our friends. They saved an ambushed expedition and you were briefed! Damn you!" The Captain crossed the room and kicked over a log chair. "Do you know what you may have done? This is how wars are started! A war we can't afford with the only friendlies we have this side of the Shimmer!"

Thompson's faced flushed crimson in anger and he glared daggers at the officer.

"Sir..." Skyla said quietly.

Captain Brandthorn turned, breathing heavily from the shouting and exertion. "Yes, sorry for the language, Skyla. What is it?"

"We can fix this. Let's talk with Chief Thenory. Surely they'll understand," she said calmly, her hands raised.

"What about Henon? Is he still around?" I asked as I looked at the map lying unrolled on the table. The Shayana home was a good way off. Having traveled the route, I suspected we could make it in most of a day if we rode hard and didn't run into any carnivores or apes.

Daniels shook his head. "He left yesterday. And let's not forget Sergeant Gibbons. He's still with them."

Brandthorn shoved a finger towards Thompson. "If something happens to my man because of your ineptitude, we'll be dueling whether you want to or not."

The Pinkerton had apparently had enough of this and stepped forward in challenge. "You just say when. You aren't my boss. I don't report to you. I report to Mr. White and Mr. White alone. Anything that interferes with his business on this side has our jurisdiction, and right now that means protecting this canyon, fort, and railroad employees."

"Do you see him in this canyon, Mr. Thompson?" Brandthorn's voice went cold, and I worried the Pinkerton had pushed him too far.

"That'll be all, Mr. Thompson," Daniels said abruptly as he shifted around to face the two of them. His face showed the same concern that I felt. "We'll figure out where to go from here. Please let your men know, no more shooting anything human. Period."

Thompson shoved past Brandthorn, "We'll defend ourselves as we see fit." The other two followed him as he stepped outside.

I sighed. "Alright. What's done is done. Skyla's right, we've got to fix this. With Sergeant Gibbons still there, we've got some goodwill hopefully. I'll go and-"

"No. Daniels will take a dozen men and go," Brandthorn said abruptly as he made eye contact with his subordinate.

"Yes, sir," the Lieutenant snapped to attention.

Skyla shoved me. "Stop volunteering."

"Well, I just know this side, and know Chief Thenory, so it seemed like a good idea…"

Brandthorn tossed his cap on the table and flipped over one of the logs to sit down. "For a moment, I was going to send you, Jed. And you, Skyla. But now that I'm of a calmer mind, I'd rather keep both of you close for now. I've asked enough of the two of you, and the army can handle this situation."

Skyla grabbed my arm and held it tight. "Let the Captain handle this for once without you getting involved."

The Captain nodded at her. "Thank you, Skyla. Lieutenant Daniels, do you feel confident you can fulfill my orders?"

The young Lieutenant stood a little straighter. "Yes, sir." He glanced at the map. "We'll leave first thing in the morning."

"Might want to take some peace offerings with you. Any spare knives, tools, things like that. That'd go a long way in tempering their anger," I suggested. "Anything they can't make, or we can make better."

"What about weapons?" Daniels turned to Brandthorn.

"Ask the armorer what he can scrounge up, from what you all tell me it sounds even a few would be a big deal to them."

"Yes, sir." Turning on his heel, Daniels walked from the tent.

"Captain?" I spoke up again.

"Yes, Jed."

"Wolverine Wade and Ashley are at Fort York; they'd like to cross over to see about capturing some of the smaller dinosaurs on this side."

"Absolutely not," Brandthorn growled. "I'd love to see them again, but there's too much going on right now to have them wandering about the woods as well. But next return trip, I'll send that damned raptor they caught. That should please Wade for a bit."

Skyla nodded. "That would make him very happy."

***

The next few days passed slowly, with Skyla splitting most of her time between observing the trikes and the caged raptor as we waited for the Lieutenant's return. Until one morning, Fredrick stopped by our small campfire as we prepared breakfast with a rifle in hand and a small bag slung around his waist. "I'm off to explore the cave."

"The one that's been sealed off since the night attack?" Skyla asked.

"Yes, ma'am. I'm going with Oscar and a squad of soldiers to investigate."

"Thank goodness. That man has been insufferable since our return." I waved at the finished building near Brandthorn's command tent. "He's been holed up in there with Thompson and Parsons and every time he steps out, he is complaining about the reporter's constant questioning and not getting to return to the Shayana with Daniels."

Fredrick adjusted the glasses on his nose and rested a boot on one of the rocks ringing the fire. "Sounds like he just wanted to fetch another mule load full of gold from them," he scoffed.

"I can believe it," Charles said as he pushed about the sizzling pieces of bacon in the pan sitting amongst the coals with a stick. "Are you sure the caves are safe?"

"It's been a couple of weeks now; if there was anything alive in there it should have starved to death by now or be too weak to fight back. But we've been tasked with finding out if it's a cave or tunnel."

I gave the hunter a grin. I was certain he was getting as stir crazy in this valley as I was. "Good luck. If you find anything exciting, shoot first and investigate second."

He grinned broadly and slapped me on the back. "See you this evening." He waved at Skyla and Charles and walked away, whistling happily and looking forward to his new adventure.

***

By midday, I was bored and practicing drawing my emptied pistols against an overturned log.

Skyla was back in the caves with another paleontologist sketching more of the paintings, and Charles was with her. I was all alone. Just me and my weapons. Just like the good old days of when I was alone on my ranch, just me, Carbine, and the big open sky.

Sighing, I picked up a small stone from a stack at my feet and hurled it into the air above me.

When I heard the rock thunk on the packed dirt between me and my target, I drew my left-side pistol, cocked the hammer, and lined the sights up on the log, but stopped short of pulling the trigger.

Staring down the sights at the darkened center heartwood of the log, I thought about how much had changed in the last few months. Dinosaurs, apes, my father and his gang, Cato, Reydan... all bad things. Skyla was the silver lining in it all. She was the only reason I hadn't lit out for new territories.

I holstered the pistol, picked up another stone, and repeated the actions. This time with my right-side gun. Then the left again. Then both guns at the same time.

Over and over and over.

Really, it was rather hard to practice drawing both guns at the same time and pretending to shoot. When I drew both guns, I was basically down to point shooting and not even using the sights. My entire intention then was to put as many bullets downrange as possible, and against a large dinosaur, most would hopefully hit.

Ideally, I'd be firing live cartridges during this little training session. But that was a big no-no inside the fort unless necessary.

I flexed my fingers painfully; they were beginning to cramp from the repetition of drawing.

Suddenly, the alarm bell rang once then twice, signaling returning riders.

Reaching into my pocket, I dug out the cartridges I'd emptied from my revolvers and began to reload as I watched Daniels ride through the palisade and into our encampment with Sergeant Gibbons behind him and a dozen other soldiers.

Figuring I'd go see what the news was, I finished the first pistol and began loading the second as I walked to the command tent.

Reaching it, I was waved inside by the soldier standing post outside. The Pinkerton's leader Thompson followed me inside.

Sergeant Gibbons stood in front of the Captain at attention. His uniform was dusty from travel and streaked with sweat stains. The bandage on the wound on his arm was missing, and the cut appeared mostly healed except for a long scab. Apparently, the Shayana knew something about healing that we didn't. I wondered what sort of plants they used in their poultices.

"Sir, they're pissed, sir," the black Sergeant said. "When the Shayana survivors and wounded returned, they locked me in one of those stone huts. They treated me well enough, fed me every meal, and occasionally one would speak to me. But they went from hot to cold pretty quick."

"Lieutenant?" Brandthorn asked.

Daniels shifted from foot to foot from where he stood by the table. "I don't know, Captain. They were pleasant, and they seemed appreciative of our apology. But there was something there, an underlying current of distrust now. We're not in the clear on this yet. It's going to take more to make them happy." He pointed at Pinkerton Detective Thompson. "They want him and his men."

"No!" Thompson shouted. "I'm not going to go visit those savages."

"I doubt they want you to 'visit'. Most likely, they want to put you in the ground for shooting their men," I told him.

"You don't understand," he growled. "They were spying on us! We've seen the tracks. They're keeping an eye on us. We shouldn't trust them."

"And we'd keep an eye on them as well if we could," Captain Brandthorn told him. He stood by the map, his back turned to us. "In fact, we were with Sergeant Gibbons. But don't worry, Mr. Thompson, I'm not giving you over to the Shayana. Tempting as that may be."

"Good to hear. Because I've a hundred men in this valley under my command who would disagree with that notion." Turning on his heel he stormed out, knocking the flap open on his way out.

Brandthorn swore under his breath. "Pinkertons... I can't wait until they're gone."

"Captain!" The shout came from outside the tent. Two soldiers stumbled their way inside. They were filthy, and one had blood smeared down the front of his shirt.

"What now?" Brandthorn growled.

"Oh hell, did the raptor get out?" I asked as I threw my hand down onto the grip of a Colt. I should have heard gun shots by now if it had, but if that little beast got amongst us, there'd be chaos to pay.

"No." Brandthorn narrowed his eyes at the men in recognition. "They're from the squad I sent to investigate the cave. Where's everyone else?"

"Dead, sir!" one panted.

**

After giving them some water and allowing them to catch their breath, they sat and told their story. "Captain, it's a tunnel all right. A big one, not big enough to ride a horse through, but you could lead one. And the tunnel wanders all over the damn place. At one point it splits, with one side going to an underground lake that you wouldn't believe could exist, and the other exits about a half mile past the edge of the canyon." The bloodied soldier reached over and tapped an area of the map to the south west of us. "Right about here, I reckon. There's a crack, well, more of a crevasse, that comes between a mound of great big boulders. You can't see it from outside unless you know where to look, but it's about five feet wide and hidden behind a bunch of vines and plants."

"Then what? Where were you ambushed?"

"Yes, sir… On the other side of the rocks is a road of sorts, about large enough for those ape carts to roll along. We followed the old roadbed a couple miles and it led to a ritual stone. Like the one we blew up, but much larger." He swallowed hard. "We were about to leave when they attacked. They came at us, screaming from every side. We shot them. It came down to hand to hand and they killed almost everyone. Only Rogers and I managed to get away."

Rogers put his head in his hands. "They wiped us out, sir. We didn't stand a chance. We just weren't ready."

"Where's Fredrick?" I asked.

The first soldier frowned. "Dead."

I felt like I'd just been punched in the gut.

Rogers looked back up, his eyes sorrowful. "Everyone's dead. There's no way anyone could have survived. We were closest to the tunnel and took off running. We waited at the entrance. Swear we did. But no one else came. Even the apes didn't chase us."

"Are you sure?" I growled. The soldier balked, unsure of what to say. I stepped forward menacingly. "Was anyone still alive when you ran away?"

Both of them looked at their feet, abashed at the thought that they may have left friends to die.

"Jed!" Brandthorn shut me up with a commanding voice. "There's nothing wrong with what they did." He looked at the two soldiers. "Go get some chow and rest. You did well." They rose dutifully and walked out, their heads held low.

I ran a hand through my hair angrily. Fredrick dead. It wasn't possible. The famous hunter had survived so much.

"Captain, we have to check," I pleaded.

"No," he answered firmly.

"Dammit, that's Fredrick out there!" I snapped angrily. "And your men! And even Oscar doesn't deserve to have his guts ripped out if that fat little weasel is still alive."

Brandthorn flipped the table over. It crashed onto its side, sending the map of the area and papers scattering across the floor. "I know!" he shouted. "I know! Do you know how many men I've lost now, Jed? Because I don't. All I know is every time I blink more of them are dead. If it's not the damn apes, it's the damn dinosaurs. This entire lost world is trying to kill us!"

"We don't know that they're dead, Captain," I told him quietly, as I reigned in my own anger and watched him.

"Yes! Yes, they are, Jed! Did you not hear them? The only two survivors of over a dozen men? Everyone's dead!"

"Let me go check," I offered, feeling the déjà vu of the moment.

"No. You did this shit once before the Battle of the Apes and you got lucky making it back. You're not doing it again."

"I'm still a civilian, I can do what I damn well please."

"Don't make me throw you in the brig." Brandthorn rubbed his face and calmed himself down. "Not that we have one. Besides, Skyla would kill me if I let you go anyways."

"You know what happens to anyone caught alive! They get their heart ripped out! I'm not going to stand here and let that happen!" I turned to leave.

Skyla barged into the tent followed by Charles. Breathless, she turned from Brandthorn to me. "I heard Fredrick's missing!"

I nodded and glared at Brandthorn, daring the man to try and stop me. "Yes, and Oscar. And I'm going to go find them."

"No, Jed!" Skyla shouted as she grabbed a fistful of my shirt.

"I'll go too," Charles said quietly.

"What?" The paleontologist spun around to face him. "Why?"

"He's my friend as well. And I won't sit here while an ape rips his heart out on a rock slab."

"Good. Let's go." Stepping around Skyla, I crossed the room, passing by the Captain on the way out.

"Jed!" Brandthorn caught my arm. He sighed and pointed a finger at me in warning. "No noble shit. If anyone's alive, you get back here, and we'll send the cavalry. You understand me?"

"Yes, sir," I said firmly as I avoided Skyla's eyes. "Charles, let's go."

The Brit grabbed Skyla's hand. "Stay close to the Captain. I'll be back before you know it."

"Then go. Both of you." Pulling her hand from his grasp, she turned away and crossed her arms.

Charles hesitated for a moment, lingering as though unsure of leaving Skyla. But my mind was made up. I pushed through the flap and jogged towards the corrals. I didn't care about Oscar, but I needed to know if Fredrick was dead for certain. Because if he was alive, I'd never forgive myself for letting him be killed when I had the ability to do something, and I knew he'd have done the same for me.

***

Saddling our horses, we raced across the valley floor, skirting around the large trikes' corral. The dark brown and yellow streaked beasts watched us from beneath their long black horns. Soldiers and scientists looked up as we rode past, startled at our speed and intensity at which we rode to the back of the canyon.

Reaching the waterfall, we stopped beside a pair of soldiers standing by the cave. A door had been built from thick slabs of wood, banded in straps of steel with a chain to reinforce it. If attacked, it would take some time for an ape to break it down, and by then an alarm could be sounded and reinforcements brought into the area. For that purpose, nearby lay an unlit bonfire, complete with stacks of green fern leaves to be added to create a thick plume of smoke needed to warn the rest of us that this corner of the canyon was under attack. A small crate of dynamite rested under a ledge in the rock nearby, just in case the tunnel needed to be destroyed to prevent our fort from being attacked from the rear.

"Open the door!" I commanded as we dismounted.

A Private stood, rifle cradled in his arms as he took me in. "Captain said no one is to open it without his express permission."

Pulling Carbine forward by his reins, I stepped into the soldier's personal space. "We have his permission. Open it and seal it behind us."

"Sir, I don't even know who you are," the Private stood his ground.

"I do," the other soldier spoke up, a Corporal by his insignia. "Johnny, this man here," he pointed at me, "is the one who ate the ape heart. Go on and open the door. I'll vouch for him."

I glanced at Charles and he nodded back; for once my heart biting moment was beneficial.

"Thanks, gentlemen. I promise we'll be as quick as possible," I said as they passed us a pair of lanterns.

Johnny unlocked the door, snapping the lock from thick bands of steel and pulling the chains through the bars. Considering how strong the apes were, it wasn't overkill, it was just... precautionary.

The surviving soldiers were right; the tunnel was just large enough for me to lead Carbine through, side by side. If I'd tried riding on his back, I'd have been knocked off by the tunnel ceiling before long. And for apes, it was most likely somewhat cramped already. There were cutouts in the rock, places for holding torches, and smoke blackened rock showed where they'd lit the way many times before. The tunnel appeared to have been naturally formed, but widened and straightened in places. There were even spots in the floor where chunks of rock had been filled in to level it out. But the tunnel still dipped and rose, twisted and turned, along its mostly natural path.

With our lit lanterns outstretched before us, we walked for a while before reaching a fork. Stopping, I glanced back at Charles and he shrugged. One way led to an underground lake and the other towards the tunnel exit. I should have asked which was which. Guessing, I picked the left turn and led Carbine along as Charles followed.

After a hundred feet I realized I'd picked the wrong turn. The ground was beginning to slope downwards, and the humidity was rising in the cool tunnel. But there was no room to turn the horses around. Our only option was to keep going until we reached the lake.

We walked on some ways until I stopped abruptly.

A faint glow came from ahead of us around a bend.

Drawing my revolver, I cocked the hammer back with a click louder than I wanted.

Nothing moved. The glow remained the same. Curiously, the light ahead of us didn't even flicker.

Looking back, I watched Charles draw his pistol. With Carbine's reins still in hand, I moved quietly, praying he wouldn't make a noise and trying my best to tiptoe in boots. The light never changed. Reaching the edge of the rock, I peeked around the corner.

Nothing.

But there was a glowing vegetation covering the walls.

Using my pistol barrel, I scraped the growth warily. It peeled off the rock in a clump. On closer inspection, it looked like moss from our side, but the small fibers growing on it were giving off a small, but bright light. Gingerly touching my fingers to it, I pulled a piece off and held it up. It glowed like dozens of miniature candles. Dropping it, I looked at the residue on my fingers. They glowed faintly, and as I watched, the light faded away. Whatever the plant was, the light only worked on the mossy fibers still attached to it.

I waved back at Charles and he caught up to me. Letting him inspect the moss on his own, I kept walking and reached the shore of the lake.

The lake itself was huge, giant even, and fed by an underground river that bubbled as it ran over partially submerged rocks from cracks in the cave walls. Plants grew in the water. Tall ones like cat tails stood upright, while others, like giant lily pads, floated. The pads were the size of a barrel top, and the prehistoric frog that sat on one near me snapped up a huge bug and crunched it in its mouth. The entire cavernous ceiling and edge was covered with the glowing moss, illuminating the lake for as far as we could see.

Carbine hesitated, jerking back on his harness. I swore and tried to pull him forward. From the way he shifted his hooves, it was apparent he didn't like the feel of the shells crunching beneath them, and the entire shore was littered with the large white and brown speckled pieces. I watched the waves of the black water gently lap against the shore. There was no wind, but I caught a glimpse of a large fin followed by a splash that sent ripples against the bed of shells where I stood.

Sir Lancelot didn't seem to mind the shells, and raced straight to the water, happily drinking as Charles knelt beside the lake. With a cupped hand he scooped water and tasted it carefully. "It's fresh water. Not bad either." Standing, he removed the canteen from Lancelot's saddle and unscrewed the metal lid.

"This moss would be worth a fortune in the mines on our side. It's unheard of. A luminescent plant, bright enough to light this enormous cavern." He threw his free arm towards the vast lake as he held the opening of his canteen under the water. I could hear it gurgling as it filled. "Imagine the worth of this?"

"It'd be worth a good bit... if it would grow." Turning Carbine back towards the tunnel, I felt a large shell crack and break beneath my boot. Looking down, I picked up the two curved white pieces, both about the size of my hand. Staring, I held them up, so I could see them in the moss light and touched them together, noting the way they turned together.

Shocked, I rotated them.

They weren't just shells.

They were egg shells.

And the entire beach was covered with them.

"Charles..."

"What?" He sloshed the water in his canteen and took a sip.

"Get away from the water. Now!" I ordered, spinning around to face him.

At the same time, Sir Lancelot jerked away from the shore, sending shells skittering as he dug his hooves in and backed away frantically. The sudden movement caused Charles to fall aside, his canteen dropping.

A massive alligator burst from the water; its teeth snapping shut on the canteen. The metal can let out an ear-piercing screech as it was crushed beneath the force of the monster's jaws.

"Bloody hell!" the Brit cried as I drew my pistol and began firing at the beast.

It thrashed, side to side, gnashing large maws as it tried to grab the scrambling man. Shifting my aim, I fired into the pink inside of the beast's open mouth as Charles drew his Schofield and began firing at the long snouted monster.

Blood sprayed, and water splashed as the beast quickly turned aside and disappeared back into the water.

The black water now had a red froth to it as it splashed against the shore.

Charles fell onto his back, scrambling away from the water and breathing heavily. Once he felt safe, he broke the pistol and emptied shell casings from the cylinder. Turning my pistol up, I began to reload as well as I walked over to his crushed canteen. Carefully keeping an eye on the water, I kicked the ruined metal container towards him. There were puncture marks in the crushed container from the beast's teeth that were large enough to put both my thumbs through.

"I reckon we're even now."

He groaned, and I grinned at him.

I patted Sir Lancelot as the big Arabian horse trembled from fear. "Biggest gator I've ever seen."

"I'm going to come back one day and turn him into a pair of boots," Charles retorted as he snapped the handle shut on his Schofield revolver.

"He's big enough to turn into a duster. But let's go." I turned Carbine around, took one last look at the black water and headed back into the glowing tunnel.

Once we reached the split again, we took the proper turn and walked to the end. There'd been no fresh sign of apes anywhere in the tunnel. It seemed they hadn't bothered to chase after the survivors, or perhaps hadn't noticed there had been any. Either way, it was nice to not get in a battle in a tunnel small enough that we couldn't turn the horses around. If we'd encountered any of the big apes, our only option would have been to gun through them and hope for the best.

As described, the end of the cave was hidden amongst large boulders covered with thick foliage of vines as big around as my arm and heavy leaves three times the size of my hand. With *Eighty-Six* in hand, I pushed through slowly, leading Carbine out into the sunlight and Charles followed us with his horse.

We stood in a small clearing, surrounded by towering trees and ferns as tall as me. The soldiers' tracks were easy enough to see, they milled around the clearing a bit before moving onto the ancient remains of a moss and grass covered rock path. Kneeling, I looked at the seams between the rocks. They'd been fitted carefully, with a mind to stay useable for a very long time. But it seemed the roads outlived whoever'd laid them, and eventually they'd been overtaken by the forest.

Mounting, we rode to the side amongst the brush and ferns, taking care to keep off the road, lest our horses' steel shod hooves clopping against the tightly laid rocks gave us away to any lurking apes.

After a couple of miles carefully walking along, we reached the sight of the ambush. The altar was similar to the one that'd been blown up in Fort Jipson. Large chunks of carved granite standing vertically in a circle around a massive slab of rock. But this one wasn't made of obsidian; it was made of the same rock as the standing slabs. It was older though. Like the rock paved road, this was something ancient.

"Count the bodies. There should be ten soldiers... plus Fredrick and Oscar," I told Charles.

Dismounting, I tied Carbine off and walked in a large circle around the altar with my rifle in hands. Tracks showed the battle clearly. The squad had walked down the rock road, and inspected the altar when a shower of arrows came raining down on them from the forest. At least six soldiers died where they stood, and the rest scrambled for cover around the granite altar.

But the apes had them surrounded, and there was no safe place to return fire from. The scattered shell casings were few. At least one of the soldiers survived the fight, because he was stretched out across the altar, his chest a gaping wound of raw meat swarming with large buzzing flies.

Whoever did this hadn't cleaned up yet, which I assumed meant they'd be back.

"I count ten, no Fredrick or that little annoyance, Oscar," the Brit told me as he looked over the sacrificial murder site.

I sighed in relief. I hadn't seen their bodies either.

"Alright, let's go." Pulling myself into the saddle, I waited for him to mount Sir Lancelot. Then I pointed with the muzzle of the rifle. "Tracks go that way. Judging by the side to side waddle, Oscar is walking, and someone else, who must be Fredrick, is being dragged. Let's hope they're still alive."

***

We found Fredrick a couple of hours later.

He was tied to a large wooden stake near a rock wall that surrounded an ape village. The rocks were piled at least six feet tall and nearly as wide, with only two entrances giving way into the mud and stick framed huts inside. Bundles of ferns thatched the roofs of the circular buildings, and the ground was beaten to a packed dirt between them.

Outside the rock walls were large fields with neatly laid out rows of strange plants, and some that looked eerily similar to ours. And one plant that definitely looked like corn. A stream wove its way between the rows of plants and into the village, coming in one side under the rock wall and out under another. Smoke drifted from three large fires that were being tended by females with stacks of chopped wood beside them.

I counted almost two dozen apes wandering through the village. Most were working in the fields, while others, especially the female and young, were inside the rock walls, cooking, or tanning what I guessed was large pieces of dinosaur hide.

It looked peaceful enough in the small valley, but there was no sign of Oscar.

Tapping Charles on the shoulder, we crawled backwards out of sight and into the thick ferns that ringed the hill above the valley.

"At least Fredrick is still alive. Until they need another sacrifice." I scowled as we moved back towards the horses. "But no sign of Oscar."

"You think this village orchestrated the ambush?" Charles swept his sweat-plastered hair off his forehead and squinted an eye at me.

"No... I don't think so, you?" I admitted.

"No, even counting the females, there doesn't appear to be enough of them for all the tracks at the ambush site. They must have had help, or else other apes dropped off Fredrick with them."

"I agree."

"Then I suppose we need to call in the cavalry."

I hesitated and looked back in the direction of the village. I hated the idea of leaving empty handed with Fredrick just sitting down there at the mercy of the apes.

"Don't, Jed," Charles insisted, obviously guessing what I was thinking.

I grunted. "Alright. I don't see how it could be done anyways."

He took Sir Lancelot's reins. "You just can't help it, can you?"

"What's that?" I carefully untied Carbine's reins from the thick tree branch. He'd been known to have left me before and I wasn't about to end up on foot on this side.

"Trying to be a hero."

"Oh, shut it. I wear a brown hat because I'm morally ambiguous."

"Morally ambiguous? Pretty big words. Jedidiah, you continue to impress me."

I rolled my eyes. "Glad I can."

***

"We need to burn them out," Pinkerton Detective Leader Thompson spoke gruffly. "Kill them all and torch everything left. It's the only way to be sure the lesson sticks."

"That's escalating things a bit," Skyla said, her eyebrows furrowed in frustration.

"I couldn't care less. They killed my men." Brandthorn rubbed his face. The bags under his eyes seemed to have grown with every hour he lacked sleep.

"Sir, best I could tell from the tracks, there were far more tracks at the ambush site than there were apes in that little village," I said.

"Then we'll kill them, find where the rest came from, and kill them too," Thompson muttered.

"They aren't all warriors down there," I protested. "There's plenty of females and children."

The mustached Pinkerton stepped forward. "Females fought at the Battle of the Apes, didn't they?"

"They did, and they were ferocious," I admitted.

"Then they are a threat. As for the kids... Let the Shayana have them as a peace offering," he pressed.

I shook my head. "I'll have nothing to do with ape slavery."

"We will have nothing to do with any of this," Brandthorn interrupted. "You, or me."

"What? Why?" Skyla asked.

"I've orders that we are to stay within the canyon and let the Pinkertons handle operations outside of here, signed by Governor Hale himself. No doubt because of Reydan White's pull though." Brandthorn stared at Thompson who looked smugly back at him. "You're in charge of your men. I'll be holding you responsible for minimal casualties on both sides."

Thomson shrugged noncommittedly. "We aren't accountable to you and I don't care how many apes die. But if Oscar and your friend are alive, we'll bring them back."

"I'll still be sending another squad of soldiers with you, to bring back the bodies of my men," Brandthorn stated firmly.

"That's fine."

"I'll go with you too," I told the Pinkerton agent. "To the village."

He pursed his lips to tell me no and I pressed my offer before he had a chance to speak. "In return, I'll take your orders. I'll just be a bystander who's good with a gun. I can help. I'm also the only person other than Charles here who has seen the village and can help you plan the rescue." I stared at him. "And it is a rescue."

Thompson nodded slowly, giving in. "Okay. Let's go." He walked out of the tent.

I gave Skyla a quick hug in return for a worried frown then quickly followed the Pinkerton agent out of the tent. Passing Charles, I leaned over and whispered, "Keep her in your sight."

He nodded, and I was reassured that Skyla wouldn't follow me and that he'd protect her in case of an ape attack. The Stratten family butler had proven himself to be a suitable guard for her, even if he was a bit showy and... British. But I could tell that Skyla was still upset with me and I wasn't making things any better.

***

Twenty detectives armed with Winchester repeaters and pistols followed me as we made our way through the tunnels, down the ancient stone road, and past the altar. There we left behind Captain Brandthorn's men who quickly began to gather the bodies of the fallen soldiers.

We kept moving on and made it to the top of the hill above the village without being detected by ape nor dinosaur.

Luck appeared to be on our side. There was no sign that the apes expected an attack and Fredrick was still tied to the pole near the far corner of the village. Otherwise, everything appeared as when Charles and I had left.

Thompson looked over the buildings and ape inhabitants intently with an extended brass telescope and a scowl on his face.

I didn't know his background, but it didn't appear to be military. He and his men lacked discipline on the way here, talking loudly and making noises as though they weren't in constant fear of being killed or eaten. Of course, they hadn't seen the apes fight yet. They probably assumed that their weapons would make all the difference, but gunpowder and bravado will only take you so far. At some point, being an idiot factors into the equation.

Thompson waved at his men and lining up, they stalked forward down the valley. I started to move but the Pinkerton Detective grabbed me by the shoulder and pulled me back. "No," he said firmly. "My men will handle this."

Shrugging free of his grasp, I glared at him for a moment before turning to watch the attack commence. I hated people touching me unbidden.

An ape saw the advancing men and shouted an alarm. The village turned to action as apes began running into their huts and emerging with bows and clubs. Some females grabbed the young and dragged them away from their playing, pulling them into the huts, while others grabbed weapons and stood with the males as they watched the Pinkertons stalk through the fields toward them with rifles raised.

One of the apes notched an arrow and drew it back, pointing it at the closest Pinkerton.

I held my breath.

The Pinkerton shot the ape.

The gunshot blasted through the valley as the big monkey crumpled to the ground.

At the sound, the other detectives opened fire. Gunfire erupted along the line of men, and apes dropped in droves. Several apes tried to take cover, hiding behind the stone walls and attempting to fling spears overhead. The thick shafted obsidian pointed weapons fell far short of the men, but those with bows were able to fire out arrows that fell amongst the Pinkertons with unnerving aim. A couple of detectives fell, and another was wounded, from the long green and yellow fletched arrows.

In return, the Pinkertons increased their rate of fire, emptying their rifles into anything moving or that looked like cover for the apes.

"Dammit, Thompson," I muttered as I watched the slaughter unfold before me helplessly.

As the wounded detective was being helped, the others reached the edge of the village and began executing any wounded apes that lay sprawled amongst the rows of corn and strange vegetables. Several men stopped and started cutting off thumbs for bounty with their knives. I watched in horror as a small ape, about four feet tall at most, struggled with a Pinkerton for a moment before being butt stroked from behind, then shot to death by another detective.

I spun towards Thompson. "Stop your men. Tell them to grab Fredrick and get out."

"They've been told what to do," he replied grimly. Even though his lips were pressed into a thin line, there was an air of excitement to him, as though he enjoyed what he was seeing.

I watched in disbelief as the men approached the stone huts and began entering them with weapons at the ready.

A pair of gunshots rang out from inside the closest hut. A female ape charged out, wielding a stone club and bashed down an agent. The man screamed as the ape beat the large stone against his chest. Another agent fired, and she went down.

Gunfire and roars erupted again, this time from inside the huts, as the females and young apes fought back against their would-be murderers.

"Sonuva bitch!" Racking my rifle, I turned and found myself staring down the barrel of Thompson's pistol. It was unwavering, and the large dark bore of the muzzle was pointed directly between my eyes. My knuckles whitened on the rifle as I fought the impulse to try and shoot him anyways.

"Unlike my employer, I've nothing against you, Jedidiah. But I'll blow a hole through your skull and say it was an accident. I'll act real sorry too when that pretty paleontologist of yours starts crying."

"Stop this madness."

"No. We're going scorched earth on these apes. We will kill them all, until they learn to avoid us like the plague. Just like the damned Indians."

My fists clenched around the rifle stock and barrel. I could feel the throb of rage rising like bile in my throat.

As we stared at each other, the sound of shots tapered off until there was nothing but silence.

After a moment, Thompson raised his pistol barrel and gently lowered the hammer. "It's done, Jedidiah," he smiled, his teeth baring like fangs. "We win."

Turning, I looked across the field. Tendrils of smoke began wafting into the sky as the huts and fields were put to the torch. A pair of detectives were bringing Oscar and Fredrick towards us. The former paleontologist must have been in one of the huts. Oscar wobbled along as normal, but Fredrick leaned heavily against one of the detectives. Blood was smeared down the side of his face and across his leather buckskin shirt. His glasses were missing.

"Damn you," I whispered as the stench of burning ferns and flesh reached our nostrils.

Pinkerton Detective Thompson watched the flames rise higher from the thatched roofs and shrugged. "You'll thank me later... After all these filthy monkeys are dead and gone."

***

Brandthorn cupped his face in his hands and sighed. "Jed. You're blinded to our situation. Our hold is tenuous at best on Prehistoria. We need the Pinkertons. Without Reydan's support, the military is going to have a hard time holding on here. Washington is shifting resources to get us more men and equipment, but it will still be several weeks before we can establish a real outpost. Right now, we are here to learn what we can, survive the best we can, and hold on to this small fort."

"They slaughtered ape children!" I shouted.

"I know. I KNOW! And we've done worse by killing Indian children. And that village wasn't innocent. They helped the group that ambushed and killed ten of my men. One of them was sacrificed. Sacrificed! You think I give a damn about an ape village that would do something like that? No. Screw it. Let it go. There'll be no charges filed against Thompson and his men because apes aren't people and there aren't any laws against killing them. As far as the law is concerned, apes are just mindless creatures. It's no different than shooting a prairie dog family. Except prairie dogs won't cut your heart out and eat it if they catch you."

"I know what the apes are. I've fought them longer than anyone else. But I'm not going to kill any of them that aren't a threat!" I shouted back at him.

Brandthorn slammed his fists down. "Then don't, dammit!" He pointed at the tent flap. "You can leave at any time."

Skyla had been quiet, chewing her lip and playing with her braid as the Captain and I raged at each other. She spoke up now, quietly, but firmly. "Jed. I need you here."

"Skyla! They-" spinning, I snapped at her, incredulous that she wasn't on my side.

"I know," she said calmly, her voice soothing in the room of tension. "Soon the Pinkertons won't be here. And it's a terrible shame what they did, but what do we do next? We move on. The fight for Prehistoria is just starting and now that Brandthorn knows what those detectives are capable of, it won't happen again." She looked at the Captain who nodded glumly.

I looked at her, shocked that she was so calm. "You want me to just ignore what happened?"

"No," she said sadly. "We can't. But they will answer for what they did eventually. In the meantime, you've enough enemies for now, don't you think?"

I nodded and looked away. Reydan White. Sheriff Beauford Johnson. My old gang. Maybe Cato. I supposed there was no need to add Pinkerton Detective Thompson to that list, but it infuriated me that he'd ordered the massacre of the ape village. Plus, I was still sore at having a pistol being pointed at my face.

"How's Oscar and Fredrick?" she asked softly, reaching out to grasp my arm gently.

I shrugged. "Fredrick is banged up some. But okay. They found his rifle as well, but the stock was shattered. He's pretty unhappy about that. As for Oscar, eh, he's fine. Seems they captured him without a fight as he was hiding under some ferns." I laughed bitterly. "He was probably considered too wimpy to sacrifice."

Brandthorn looked at me with a frown. "Poor choice of humor, Jed. I've got to write a letter to almost a dozen soldiers' families about their deaths. One of whom was gutted on that damned altar."

I nodded. "You're right, sorry." I looked around the tent and suddenly didn't feel like being here anymore. "I'm going to go check on Fredrick."

"I'll come with you." Skyla grabbed my arm tighter and smiled at me slightly. I could tell she was put off by having to go against me. But she had her points to make, and they were right. I tended to be blinded by anger a lot. And that's when people tended to get very dead.

Sighing, I pushed the tent flap aside and held it open for her before following her out.

***

As we walked across the fort, Skyla leaned in close to me. "Are we a team, Jed?"

I stopped in my tracks, knowing what she was getting at. "Yes," I said cautiously.

"Then can you please act like it?" Turning, she grabbed my shirt in both her hands and pulled herself close. We were close enough that I could smell the wood smoke in her black hair. "Twice now you've charged off without a care as to what I think."

I looked in her brown eyes and saw the concern she had for me. "Skyla... I know. But sometimes there isn't time to stand around contemplating, sometimes you've just got to grab your horse and gun and get to work."

She shook her head, unable to meet my eyes any longer. "You just... left. Twice. And you could have been killed."

Gently cupping her face in my calloused hands, I turned it back towards me. "I'm a man. It's not in me to shirk a job, avoid a duty, or let others risk themselves in my place. If there's danger that threatens me, a loved one, or a friend, I'm not going to sit idly by while others take care of it or hope it works itself out. I'm going to charge out there, guns blazing, and riddle it full of holes. That's just who I am."

"I know, and I love you for who you are. But you've a temper... not as bad as Brandthorn, but bad. Actually, worse in some ways."

I kissed her forehead gently. "That's why I have you, to help cool me off."

"Then listen to me. Let me help. You aren't on your own anymore."

"Okay," I admitted with a slight grin, then raised my pinky in the air. "Pinky promise."

She wrapped hers in mine and squeezed our hands together. "Pinky promise."

***

Lieutenant Daniels was with Fredrick and John Parsons in a makeshift hospital tent. The tent stank of blood, whiskey, and infection, and several soldiers were resting inside with various wounds. I nodded at them but ignored the Pinkerton agent with the arrow wound in his chest from the assault on the village. He could die for all I cared.

"Fredrick, how are you doing?" Skyla asked as we found him in the far corner with a bandage wrapped across his chest. Beside him lay one of his spare custom Winchester rifles.

He shrugged and grimaced at the movement. "Not bad, all things considered."

"You don't look too poorly," I admitted. Once all the blood was cleaned off him, he looked a sight better than he had after his rescue.

"Just a spear wound along the ribs and a scratch across the scalp. Nothing to fret about."

"Good."

Lieutenant Daniels nodded towards Fredrick. "He was just telling me about the apes."

The famed hunter smiled slightly. "It was an interesting experience... one that'll make a grand chapter in my next book."

"Then I'll make sure to leave it out of my articles," John said with a grin as he closed his notebook.

"What'd you learn?" I asked, curious.

"Well, for one thing, those apes in the village didn't attack us. Best as I could tell, the group of painted apes that ambushed us brow beats the villagers and conscripts young apes big enough to fight."

I groaned. The Pinkertons had just wiped out an innocent village. "How did you figure that out?"

"I saw them drag a pair of young apes away. The villagers seemed pretty upset about it, but the painted apes that attacked us didn't care. They lined them up, grabbed the two biggest, then dumped me and Oscar with the villagers. The group that attacked us was traveling light it looked like. I don't know what their plans were for us, but I suspected they were saving us for a sacrifice at a later date." His eyes met mine. "Did you see what they did to Private Theaton? Dragged him up there and sacrificed him as soon as the fight was over. Almost like a victory sacrifice, all chanting and hooting, beating their chests and what not. Bunch of savages."

Nodding, I leaned forward. "What'd their leader look like? Was he a big one? Kind of like old scar face that I killed back in Granite Falls?"

He looked at me strangely. "Yes. Big monkey. A dark mottled brown color, with lots of battle scars, but he wasn't horribly disfigured. However, he did stand a head taller than the others."

"That ties in with what the Shayana told me. They've some sort of leadership caste that's bigger." I glanced at the Lieutenant.

"We need to kill as many of them as we can then," Daniels muttered. "Wipe out their leadership and command."

"Agreed," I said.

"Did they say anything you can recall? Sergeant Gibbons has learned some of their language from the Shayana apes and might be able to decipher it," John said thoughtfully.

Fredrick winced and looked at the reporter. "I didn't even think to pay attention to what they were saying. It was all just gibberish to me."

John patted him on the shoulder carefully. "Don't worry about it. Next time we'll just hope Gibbons gets grabbed."

Looking over Fredrick, I realized he had another pair of spectacles on. "How many spare glasses do you keep?"

"Three. Because I'm practically blind without them," he scoffed, then reached out and took Skyla's hand. "You need to get out of here. Things are heating up and I think they're going to attack. This canyon will be a death trap if the apes hit us in force."

Skyla looked at me, her face worried. I knew she didn't want to leave before, but it seemed seeing Fredrick lying before us wounded had given her a new way of seeing things.

I nodded. "I agree. Let's get out of here until this threat blows over." I glanced at Lieutenant Daniels. "I'm sure Captain Brandthorn has more than enough men, plus he's got all of Reydan's damned Pinkertons. They're a small army all by themselves."

Daniels scratched the stubble growing on his chin. "Hell, there are more Pinkertons in here than soldiers. But I agree, it'd be best if we could get you out of here. Day after tomorrow our men swap out. In the meantime I'll suggest to Brandthorn that we clear every remaining civilian out until things calm down. Luckily most of the workers have already left, it's mainly scientists now, but things are looking more and more like they're about to get very Western around here."

"I'd like to stay," John offered with a hopeful look.

"I doubt it. The last thing Fort Jipson needs is a New York Times reporter getting killed in it."

"Well, in that case, I guess I will leave with everyone else."

"Glad you see it our way," Daniels said wryly.

Charles entered the tent and made his way to us. "Fredrick," he tipped his hat.

The hunter let go of Skyla's hand and stuck it out towards the Brit. "Thanks, Charles, I heard you went with Jed to find me."

They shook hands.

"Well, you and Oscar," Charles admitted.

"I'll pretend you didn't say that," Fredrick chuckled. "He groveled for his life the entire way, snot nosed and tearful. He balled like a girl when they dragged him into that hut. It was rather embarrassing."

I suddenly recalled the forgotten letter in my pocket from my father. It felt like it was burning a hole through my shirt. Leaning over, I kissed Skyla on the cheek. "I'll catch up with you later."

"Where are you going?" she asked.

"To check on Carbine," I partially lied. "He probably needs some exercise."

"Give him my love," she said with a big grin.

"Sure," I chuckled and tipped my hat at the others before walking out of the tent.

**

I strode to the corrals and found my troublesome horse. He whinnied and trotted over; in return I gave him a scratch. There were several Pinkertons grooming their horses, so I saddled up mine and rode towards the end of the canyon to find some peace and quiet.

Reaching the waterfall, I waved at the soldiers guarding the tunnel door, and tied Carbine off to a low-lying branch. Then, finding a nice-sized boulder, I sprawled out against it and opened the envelope. Inside was a piece of folded paper with familiar writing. My old man always had nice script.

Leaning back, I started to read.

"Son,

I know we don't see eye to eye anymore. But I've been thinking since our last talk, and I was wrong to try and force you back into a life of crime with me.

Things have changed since we started so many years ago. It's no longer clear who the good and bad folks are. This country has moved on from the War Between the States while we've still tried to fight the good fight against the carpet baggers and Yankee thieves. But, I suppose it's time I stopped pretending and accepted who I am now.

We started off to make right of a lot of wrongs, but we made more wrongs ourselves along the way. It's time for me to accept what I truly am; a bandit, a robber, and a killer.

And a damn good one at that.

But you've broken free of all this, and I'm proud of who you've become. I pray you'll make it.

If you need me, send word to Carson Skinner, and I'll come running.

Until then, illegitmi non caborundum.

Father."

"Never let the bastards grind you down," I repeated his favorite Latin phrase and carefully folded the paper and tucked it back into my pocket. It was basically the man's motto. But it didn't ring true; life had worn him down from a good man with an axe to grind to a bad man with a hankering for taking other people's shit.

A rumble of thunder startled me, and I looked up.

Heavy rain clouds were moving over the edge of the canyon, their gray shapes blotting out the sun and casting a moving shadow that inched across the grassy canyon floor. The trikes bellowed from their corral and I wondered if they knew something we didn't. We'd never seen rain here before, and I wondered just how bad the storm would get. From where I sat, I could see soldiers lashing down tents extra tight in preparation. We were in something of a flood plain, and I prayed that we wouldn't be washed out of the canyon. There was no sign that it'd happened before, but should it happen, we were doomed.

Suddenly, I heard the faint ringing of the alarm bell from the canyon entrance echoing against the cliff walls around me.

Leaping to my feet, I rushed to Carbine. Jerking his reins free from the branch, I threw myself into the saddle and kicked my heels against his sides.

There'd been no gunfire yet, so that was a good thing.

A winged shadow swept over me.

Glancing up, I spied a breehas with rider winging down into the valley. Near one of the corner stationed Gatling guns, a soldier raised his rifle and I shouted at him to hold his fire. The look on his face was priceless as he realized the pterodactyl had a mounted rider on its back.

Reaching the center of the encampment, Carbine skidded to a stop as I tugged back on the reins. The breehas had landed, and surrounding it were dozens of soldiers and Pinkertons with looks ranging from disbelief to suspicion.

"Lower your weapons!" thundered Captain Brandthorn as he pushed through the circle with his Lieutenant in tow. "This is a friend."

Unbuckling himself, the rider disengaged from his mount and dropped lightly onto his feet. Turning to me, I realized it was Chief Thenory. He was wearing his metal armor and had a sword strapped to one side, a Colt pistol on the other, and his lineage's black powder pistol tucked into his waistband. The leader of the Shayana nodded in recognition to me, then scowled towards the Pinkertons in the crowd.

I stepped forward with Brandthorn and Daniels.

"Thenory," I said in greeting as we clasped hands. I pointed to Brandthorn, "This is Captain Brandthorn. He leads us."

He nodded and shook the officer's hand. "Well met! Tis dire news that I bring." He pointed at the gray rolling clouds that moved overhead. "Hairy men move with the rains to attack and will arrive soon."

"What? When?" Lieutenant Daniels demanded.

The alarm bell began ringing again, this time frantically. The sort you did when you had an enemy at your gates.

The Chief of the Shayana shrugged. "They are here."

"Oh, bloody hell," Charles said from behind me.

Spinning, I saw him standing with Skyla and Fredrick. The famous hunter had even managed to find a shirt to cover his bandage and chest. He leaned on his rifle and frowned. Skyla looked worried as well. There was no sign of Parsons.

"Stop gawking! Get to your positions!" Brandthorn shouted as the crowd of soldiers and detectives burst into action. He turned back to the Chief. "Are you going to stay and help?"

The blonde native nodded his head and the claw and jewelry on his neck danced. He pointed towards the back of the canyon, where two dozen more breehas were flying into view. "Yes. Until the storm worsens."

"I appreciate that," Captain said.

The Chief grabbed onto his pterodactyl and hurled himself onto the back of the beast. Strapping in quickly, he nodded at me then drew the Colt pistol from his waist. "Good luck to thee." Tugging on the reins he urged the great dinosaur to flap its wings and lift off from the ground. Quickly rising above us, it circled, joining the other riders overhead.

Amidst the rush of moving people, I grabbed Skyla by the hand and pulled her close and out of the way of the stampeding men. Our small group clustered together.

"Charles, come with me. We need to get the horses saddled and ready," Fredrick said.

Skyla pushed closer to me as a group of detectives shoved by us. "You think it will be that bad?"

Wincing, the famed hunter pushed his glasses up on his nose. "This canyon is a death trap, dear. Captain has done everything he can to prepare us, but we are at a severe tactical disadvantage. I'd prefer we were ready to flee at a moment's notice. Charles, do you agree?"

The Brit nodded.

I pointed at the palisade. "Alright. Skyla and myself will be up there. If things go to shit, we'll all grab the horses and go out the back tunnel." I left out the part of how difficult it might be for us getting to the tunnel if the fort was overrun. Things could get real hairy, real quick.

The bell continued ringing, even though it was evident by now that we were about to be attacked.

"Skyla, I'll come find you after I've saddled the horses. The berm will be one of the safest places right now, it's heavily fortified," Charles reassured her.

"Carbine's already saddled, just move him to be with the others." I pointed at where I'd left him.

Giving her a quick hug, the Brit turned and jogged towards the horse corrals with Fredrick walking painfully after him.

Still holding Skyla's hand, we raced towards the canyon entrance and climbed to the top of the berm behind the palisade. Soldiers and detectives were lining the wall, and we found an empty spot and filled in.

At the far end of the canyon entrance, where the sides of the cliffs gradually decreased until they blended in with the open plains, spreading out to cover the entire opening on both sides of the river, were rows and rows of mounted trikes moving into position. The dinosaurs shook their mighty horns as the apes on their back began chanting and beating their painted chests.

"Holy-" I started. "That's a lot. There must be a hundred or more of them. Wait... where's the infantry? Last time the infantry charged first."

Lieutenant Daniels pushed in beside us, his blue cap pulled down low and his face set in a grim mask. "Must have changed their tactics after the Granite Falls battle. That's fine." He glanced down the row at the cannons and Gatlings aiming overtop of the sharpened stake palisade. "We'll still churn them to meat."

Rain began to drop, pattering against our clothes and the ground around us.

Daniels looked up at the sky and a grin split his young face. "Oh, those poor dumb apes..."

"What?" asked Skyla as she slid the rifle off her shoulder and checked the action to see if a round was chambered. Satisfied, she shifted her pistol slightly to make sure that it was loose and readily available if needed. She'd come a long way since I'd first met her.

"The apes are attacking during the storm because the Shayana's muskets won't fire when their black powder is wet," he smirked. "They don't know jack about our metallic cartridges. Self-contained gun powder, by golly... shoots no matter what. They're in for a big surprise."

Across the opening in the palisade that granted entry to the fort, men charged out carrying heavy Cheval de Frises. The raised spike embedded logs would block off the entrance. Two rows of them were quickly carried into place, effectively blocking off the only opening into our encampment. Even if the mounted trikes tried to charge through the river, they'd have a hard time with the sharpened stakes there as well.

I looked behind us; the Shayana still circled on the backs of their breehas. I wonder what they saw that we didn't. It was a shame we didn't have any way to communicate.

The bell stopped ringing, and the only sound was a faint murmur of men as we watched the massive group of trikes and apes waiting to charge. The chanting and breast beating had turned into a rhythmic thumping that filled the canyon. It was terrifying to behold.

A pair of apes rode in front of the wall of trikes.

Daniels passed me his telescope. One of the apes was the dark brown mottled one that Fredrick had seen, the same one who'd ambushed the soldiers investigating the tunnels. The other was a light brown, almost cinnamon in color, a yellow handprint marked his face. Both were big, powerful looking monkeys.

From the clouds above the trike army came a burst of flame followed by an ear-piercing shriek of what could only be considered unbridled rage.

Someone screamed, and men ducked behind the palisade in sudden fear.

Swooping out of the gray cloud cover came a dragon.

Twisting about, I focused the telescope on it. The beast was dark green with large scaled wings, a short neck and long tail. Its head was reptilian, just like in the cave painting, full of jagged teeth and a pair of black long horns several feet long that swept back along its neck. At the tips of its wings were its feet, with black talons.

It landed with a heavy thud in front of the army. The solid black-haired ape sitting on its back jerked the reins, and the blunt dragon head tilted skyward and let loose another belch of flame that shot a dozen feet into the air. It was an awesome sight to behold.

"We're all going to die!" someone shouted as the row of men along the palisade began to mutter fearfully.

"Shut the hell up!" I heard Sergeant Gibbons roar from somewhere down the line. "Are you cowards or are you men? Run and die or fight to live!"

"Skyla," I whispered as I passed the telescope back to Lieutenant Daniels. He peered through it and whistled.

"Yes?" she said.

I sighed with a frown, "It's a dragon."

She looked back at me in wide eyed amazement. "No kidding."

The chanting of the ape army intensified with the arrival of their army leader and dragon. They beat their painted chests even harder. Boom-boom-boom. Boom-boom-boom.

Captain Brandthorn stood on the rock wall with sword raised over head. "Cannons! Fire at will!"

He swept the sword down.

The cannon to our right fired.

BOOM!

A cannonball landed amongst the wall of trikes, punching through the first one and knocking several others off their feet. Ape riders were crushed as the beasts thrashed and fought to rise. The chanting and beating stopped as pandemonium set into the ape ranks.

The men around us cheered.

"That's it, Captain! Take the battle to them!" Daniels shouted as he thrust his rifle towards the cloud filled sky.

BOOM. The second cannon fired as the dragon flapped its giant wings and rose off the ground.

The cannonball hit well short of the pair of leaders, spraying dirt and grass clods a dozen feet into the air.

Someone shouted, "Booo!" followed by several mocking cat calls of the cannon crew to learn to aim properly as they struggled to reload the bronze cast weapon.

The ape leaders both raised large obsidian battle axes and pointed them in our direction. Above them the dragon flapped its wings, and the ape on it roared.

I held my breath.

In unison, the pair of ape leaders on the ground bellowed and swung their weapons towards us.

The mounted trikes charged.

Like a tidal wave of horned beasts, they swarmed around the two leaders and their mounts, and the big apes were lost amidst a raging sea of horned dinosaurs and prehistoric apes.

***

Both cannons fired again, both hitting and sending more trikes sprawling with their riders. As packed as they were across the opening, it was hard to miss at this point. They were even charging through the river, at places belly deep on the trikes. And as they ran, they packed in closer and closer as the canyon mouth narrowed towards our spiked palisade.

The Gatlings opened up.

All four of them, firing dozens of rounds into the teaming mass as their gunners quickly rotated the handle on the guns.

Pop-pop-pop-pop.

The apes rode into a hailstorm of bullets.

Trikes soaked up most of the bullets, but many ape riders and some trikes fell, and the ones behind trampled over the maimed and dead.

In front of us the gun smoke lingered, staying low on the battlefield from the pressure of the storm above. The smoke mixed with the light rain, creating a mist that began turning our visibility to crap.

I worked the lever on the *Eighty-Six*, sending a heavy cartridge into the chamber.

"Times like this, I wish our old crew was together," I shouted at Skyla to be heard over the gunfire.

She looked as though she was terrified but trying to put a brave face on when she grinned back at me. "I do miss them."

Someone rested a hand on my shoulder, and pivoting, I saw Charles had found his way behind us. Leaning in close to be heard over the crew served weapon fire, he yelled, "Fredrick is with the horses!"

"Good! He can't hit anything anyways," I shouted before raising my rifle and sighting down the barrel at the closest ape rider.

Along the line, soldiers and detectives began firing.

I steadied my breathing, watched the sights bounce over a moving target, and when the front bladed sight crossed his chest, I squeezed the trigger gently. The rifle boomed, and the ape slid off its mount to be trampled by the next horned dinosaur.

Racking the lever, I picked another target and fired again.

We mowed down the attackers. Apes and trikes fell alike before our withering fire.

Amidst the noise of battle, I thought I heard shooting coming from behind us.

I looked over a shoulder at our protected fort.

My blood ran cold.

From the far sides of the encampment, where the wagons and Gatling guns covered the twin rear portions of the defensive triangle, I saw the guns firing upwards at the cliff walls on either side.

Apes climbed down them, having approached hidden amongst the forested areas.

There were hundreds of them.

***

"To the rear! To the REAR!" I screamed as I grabbed the closest man to me and shoved him away from the palisade. The Pinkerton jerked free of me, his face twisted in fury and I jabbed a finger towards the encampment behind us. In an instant, his face reflected mine. Panic.

"Behind us!" he shouted as he began grabbing other men and pushing them towards our rear. He grabbed Daniels by the shoulder and leaned in close to shout over the gunfire.

The Lieutenant twirled about, then raced down the line towards where Brandthorn could be seen directing one of the cannons.

The fort behind us was coming alive with movement as Pinkertons and soldiers raced towards the wagons and Gatlings to shoot the attacking apes off the cliff faces. They spun and fired in multiple directions as arrows began to fall amongst them and the rain.

In front of us, the mounted trikes hit the palisade.

They crashed into it like a wave of dinosaur and ape flesh. The palisade shook and the ground beneath us rolled from the impact. Bellowing and painful roars filled the canyon as beast and ape alike embedded themselves on the sharpened spikes.

Gatlings fired at point blank range into the teeming masses. Cannons fired grape shot, peppering dozens of trikes and riders with round lead balls. And we shot into them as fast as we could work the levers on our rifles. A mound of dead began to form against the sharp spikes of the palisade.

The dragon swooped low, coming out of the cloud cover, its giant wings flapping as it steadied itself and breathed fire.

One of the Gatlings, and the men manning it, were consumed in the yellow and orange flames. Men screamed and ran, their bodies on fire. The ground around the crew served weapon burned, and the canvas tent that'd given the men shade collapsed in a burst of flames on top of the unlucky.

The Shayana attacked.

Diving from the cloud filled sky on the backs of their giant pterodactyls, they grabbed apes, pulled them off their mounts and flung them dozens of feet into the teeming mass of the trike army. One went for the dragon and struck its talons at the fire breathing beast's head.

The dragon swooped lower, turning and grabbing the breehas by the neck. The solid black ape leader roared and twisted in the saddle, ducking a swing of the sword by the brave Shayana rider as their mounts collided.

With an audible snap of its spine that could be heard over the battle, the breehas plummeted to the ground while the native rider fell and impaled himself on a pair of trike horns below. Screaming in mortal agony, the Shayana was quickly silenced by a swing of an ape club.

Skyla's rifle went empty, and dropping to a knee, she flipped her weapon onto its side and began thumbing cartridges from her belt into the tubular magazine under the barrel one a time.

Towering above her, I blasted an ape as he hurled a spear through the chest of a Pinkerton beside me, and the big monkey fell backwards, legs still pinned between sandwiched trikes. The detective gurgled, blood pouring from his mouth as he fell and twitched in death throes.

Working the lever, I took aim again and received only a click as the hammer dropped on an empty chamber. Ducking down beside Skyla, I pulled a handful of fat cartridges from my pocket and started loading them into the *Eighty-Six*.

She looked at me, fear etched across her pretty face.

"We're alright!" I lied. Even though we were only a couple of feet apart, I shouted to be heard over the roar of the battle. A hot brass shell, ejected from some rifle, fell between my bandana and neck. Swearing, I frantically shook it out before it burned my neck.

Taking a chance, I peeked over the berm.

Painted apes were climbing off their mounts and scrambling forward over the dead and dying with clubs and spears in hand. They were pulling themselves up between the palisade spikes and the fighting between man and ape was going hand to hand in some places.

We needed to shoot the dragon, but it was all but impossible with the apes so close to us.

"Look out!" I cried to Skyla while dropping the cartridges in my hand. Standing, I flipped the rifle around in my hands and swung it like a bat at an ape pulling herself between the sharpened logs. She saw it coming but barely had time to snarl before the stock thumped her across the yellow and green painted face and sent her sprawling backwards.

"Gotcha, bitch!" I screamed in defiance then ducked as an arrow zipped past me close enough to ruffle my shirt and embedded itself in the ground behind me.

"Language!" Charles shouted from behind me. I grimaced apologetically at Skyla as she finished loading her rifle. She rolled her eyes and began shooting over the berm between the spikes.

I looked behind us at the fort.

The men in the camp were putting up a valiant effort, but they lacked shelter and arrows rained down upon them. As I watched, another detective was pierced through the thigh with an ape arrow and fell shrieking to the ground.

Our forces were split by the ape army, and things were starting to look grim.

Shayana on their breehas were swooping along the cliff sides now, grabbing apes and dropping them from high up. One fell and bounced from the top of the cliff to the bottom, landing in a crumpled heap. The breehas' riders were helping, but they weren't enough to even put a dent in the apes climbing down the canyon walls to attack us from behind.

The cannons had gone silent, and I realized the line was thinning under the ape and dragon assault. More and more men were beginning to fall back towards the encampment. A Pinkerton was grabbed by an ape and flung backwards amongst the dead and dying trike mounts where he was quickly speared to death.

Charles noticed the line faltering as well and grabbed Skyla by the arm while gesturing towards the camp behind us.

"We can't!" I shouted angrily. If the palisade fell, we'd be defenseless on this side of the fort.

He leaned forward, and for the first time I noticed his usual calm demeanor was gone. His carefully brushed hair was hanging askew over his brow and his eyes were wild with excitement. "If we stay here, we die!" he screamed back.

As if to prove his point, an ape leapt between us, landing on the balls of his hairy feet and twirling a stone club. His chest was painted with red and yellow swirls and patterns, and there was blood running from a gash on his shoulder. His hair was plastered flat from the rain, and he stunk like a wet dog.

Charles lifted his rifle overhead as the club swung down and deflected the hit. But the forearm on his rifle cracked and splintered into pieces and the barrel bent.

Dropping it, the Brit lunged forward and tackled the painted ape around the waist. Together they fell off the back of the berm as Skyla screamed.

***

"Fall back! Fall back!"

The call came down the line from Brandthorn's position as apes swarmed between the angled sharpened logs and the fighting turned hand to hand across the line.

At point blank range, I fired my rifle in the face of one and its green and red painted face disappeared as the bullet punched through the front and back of its skull.

Charles was right; we had to get out of here, and fast.

The fort was falling.

"Skyla, jump!" I cried as I grabbed her hand and leapt down the berm. Skidding on our backsides down the slick mud and rock, we reached the bottom in a tangled heap. Swearing at my rifle sling, I fought to untangle myself and stand.

A hand reached down for me and grasping it I stood to find myself face to face with Charles. Blood marred his face, and he had a wicked gash across his cheek from ear to chin.

"You're hurt!" Skyla said as she reached out to touch his face.

"It's nothing." He drew his Schofield pistol from its holster and cocked the hammer.

"But you're bleeding!" she cried out.

"He can bleed later, let's go," I told him as I pushed her ahead of me.

"Get going!" Charles shouted as he fired upwards at the top of the berm. An ape tumbled down the mud, landing at his feet and grasping weakly for him. He shot her through the chest with a coupe de grace, his pistol barrel blossoming fire.

Another ape roared and leapt off the top of the berm.

Immediately, the big monkey was caught up in a pair of breehas' claws and carried aloft only to be dropped from high up.

I hoped he impaled on the wooden spikes.

Chief Thenory rode this pterodactyl and nodded to me as he fired his Colt pistol into the swarm of apes before swinging his leathered bird around and grabbing another monkey with a stone club off the berm to be flung back into the battleground on the other side of the palisade.

An ape paused her charge over the berm to loosen an arrow after them, and I fired from the hip, knocking the monkey spinning out of sight.

The dragon swooped over the berm where we'd just been, breathing fire and consuming a half dozen detectives and soldiers. Others fired their rifles after the terrifying beast as it turned and flew back out across the battlefield. I hoped every single round hit that thing.

I pointed at the closest Gatling emplacement that was also located near the corrals and where Fredrick waited with the horses. The wagons and minor palisade would provide some measure of safety and cover. "Get there!"

We ran as the ape assault behind us was momentarily stopped by the waist high flames from their leader's dragon.

Charles led the way, and we scrambled between tents and scattered equipment. Around us men rushed, this way and that, seeking shelter from the arrows that fell from the sky and firing wildly at the apes climbing down the cliffs.

Reaching the wagons, I slid to a knee and pulled Skyla down behind the wheeled spokes as arrows thumped against the wooden boards providing us shelter. Mud coated my legs and boots. I didn't know how much longer the Shayana could help us, the wind was picking up and lightning was beginning to split the sky.

Oscar was already here, cowering underneath the wagon as Pinkerton Thompson fired his rifle over the top. The mustached detective had blood smeared all over him from hand to elbow. Beside us, the Gatling gun fired with incredible accuracy at the apes that were just beginning to reach the bottom of the cliffs. They fell in droves as the bullets stitched across the fields in front of the rock face. The men loading the crew served gun worked frantically to keep the gun topped off with cartridges, even while one of their own lay sprawled out beside them pierced through with an arrow.

"We're going to die! We're going to die!" Oscar muttered over and over.

I resisted the urge to slap him across the face. It might make me feel better, but it wouldn't make him any braver.

Resting my rifle on the wagon, I pulled the trigger. An ape fell screaming from the cliff side as my bullet punched through his shoulder blade. Another ape took his place, and I chanced a look back at the palisade we'd just left. The last of the surviving humans were sliding down the berm and shooting upwards as apes crossed over the top in places where the dragon's flames had died down.

Captain Brandthorn stood gallantly atop the palisade. Alone.

The man's cover was gone, and his brown hair plastered from the rain. An obsidian tipped spear was thrust at the barrel-chested Irishman and he deflected the weapon with a swipe of his sword before twisting around and slicing the ape open from shoulder to thigh. Twirling, he decapitated the next ape approaching him with a vicious swing of his sword.

"Run, dammit," I muttered to myself as I flipped the peep sight on my rifle up and sighted through the small circular hole at the front blade to try and provide him with some help. It was a long way off. I'd have to aim high. An ape approached Brandthorn from behind, a stone axe held in hand. I fired, aiming at the monkey's head, and the ape folded in half from a bullet striking low, then fell out of sight.

Brandthorn took one last look down the palisade, ran for the edge, and jumped.

A spear pierced his back, puncturing through the center of his chest, and sending him tumbling down the berm.

"No!" I cried out as the Captain fell like a rag doll to the muddy ground at the bottom. He didn't rise.

From the top of the berm, rose a monster of an ape. Painted swirls covered his cinnamon-colored hair and black chest and a yellow handprint marked his face. One of the leaders. He raised his obsidian axe and roared with satisfaction.

I fired, missed, and swore as the ape leader leapt off the berm and out of sight behind the rows of tents between us.

The dragon flew over the berm breathing fire onto the roof of the only wood building in the fort, and as quickly as I could fire and acquire the sights, I worked the *Eighty-Six*, firing bullet after bullet into the terrifying fire breathing monster. It didn't even react as it breathed flames again and lit a row of tents on fire. Scientists ran screaming from the flames, and several of the tents thrashed and twisted about under the flaming canvas as the men hiding inside were burnt to death.

Our best defensive position that we had was gone along with our leader. The cannons and Gatlings on top were gone, burning in dragon flame. None of our other defenses were set up to protect us if the palisade fell. The apes were already beginning to flank us from the canyon entrance.

We were all going to die if we didn't get out of here, and quick.

A breehas plummeted from the sky, pierced with several long-shafted arrows through its wings and chest. The pterodactyl landed clumsily by the Cheval de Frises blocking the fort entrance, and the Shayana quickly unstrapped himself and drew his sword and plunged it through the chest of the closest ape. He and his bird were swarmed over by the apes, stabbing with spears and bashing with their clubs.

"Get to the horses!" I shouted at Skyla and Charles.

"What? You can't leave! The fort is still standing," Oscar shouted from beneath the wagon.

"No, it's not. Brandthorn's dead, the apes own the berm, and there's no cover for our flanks. If we stay here, we'll be surrounded or burnt."

Without waiting for a response, I grabbed Skyla's hand and we ran. We raced between the tents, narrowly being missed by falling arrows as the apes fired them from the forests that lined the tops of the cliffs.

The Gatlings and small defenses towards the rear were still putting up a good fight. But with the front of the fort gone, apes were beginning to move through the tented encampment and circle the small pockets of defenders. More and more soldiers and detectives began to fall back towards the corral.

An arrow zipped by, slicing through the air between myself and Skyla. I pushed her ahead as she fired her pistol at anything that got close to us.

Charles caught up, breathing heavily from sprinting after us and firing his pistol carefully one shot at a time, opening a path before us as we ran towards the corrals.

Fredrick was already mounted and shooting his rifle at everything that moved as we slid through the split rail fences to where our horses were tied off. His glasses were fogging up, so I hoped he was aiming for the biggest things he saw. The mounts tugged at their bits, uncomfortable with the sounds of battle so close by.

Another breehas fell from the sky, this one landing on several tents and crushing them under its weight. A pair of detectives quickly moved behind the corpse, using it as cover as they opened fire at the dragon fighting a pair of breehas riders above us. The Shayana were putting up a good fight, but it was obvious the pterodactyls and their riders were no match for the beastly dragon.

Grabbing the loose ends of reins, I began tugging them free. Sir Lancelot was first in line, and Charles was mounting him as I let him loose. Skyla was already on Smoke, reloading her guns, and watching the battle unfolding a scant fifty yards away from us.

Carbine was last, and as I slipped his rope out of its knot I leapt onto his back. He twisted, nearly dismounting me as he thrust his rear end up and lashed out with his hind feet. A meaty thud sounded, and an ape was sent flailing away with his chest caved in from the steel shod hoofs of my horse.

"Thatta boy!" I told him and twisted the reins to turn him around.

Pinkertons and soldiers alike were beginning to fall back to the corrals as the rear defensive positions with Gatlings were becoming overrun. Men grabbed horses and flung themselves onto them, riding bareback in their desperation to get away. But they had nowhere to go.

Lightning split the sky, bursting against the canyon edge and dropping several apes who were firing arrows at us.

Now the remaining Shayana were flying out of the canyon.

Chief Thenory was last. Taking one final swoop, he jerked an ape off the berm and flung it against the cliff wall on his way out of the canyon.

And then our allies were gone.

I locked eyes with Lieutenant Daniels as he fired at the approaching apes from behind a wagon, and he pointed at the rear of the canyon. "The tunnels! Go, go, go!" he cried.

Nodding at Skyla, I raced Carbine past the trike corral. The dinosaurs were agitated as well, bellowing and shaking their large horns. Within moments both Skyla and Charles' horses were outracing mine and leading the way while Fredrick and I struggled to keep up. Smoke was a dappled white blur, passing other fleeing men on horseback and some on foot as they fled to the back of the canyon away from the battle.

"Told you she was fast," I muttered to myself under my breath.

***

By the time we caught up, the soldiers guarding the tunnel entrance had already pulled the chains off the door and were unlocking it. The moment of truth would come when it opened. Either there would be apes on the other side to pour into the canyon and we would die, or we'd have a way out.

The door was jerked open, and we all kept our weapons trained on the darkened entrance.

Nothing moved.

I looked behind us. A stream of horses and riders were heading our way. And as I watched, apes moved the Cheval de Frise blocking the fort entrance and mounted trikes broke through. Among them bounded a handful of small vicious raptors. The small red feathered dinosaurs quickly outran their giant lumbering horned brethren and leapt over burning tents and attacked the men defending our remaining two Gatling guns.

As I watched, one of the little raptors leapt onto the back of a horse and took it and an unarmed scientist down in a splashing tumble into the river.

"Get going!" I shouted at Fredrick and Skyla.

Charles had already dismounted and was leading his horse with pistol in other hand into the tunnel. I assumed the Brit was going first to make sure the path was clear. Fredrick grabbed several lanterns as I passed Carbine's reins off to Skyla. Thompson and Oscar rode up next on the same horse, the obese paleontologist clinging to the Pinkerton like his life depended upon it. Dismounting, they left the horse behind and ran up the trail and into the tunnel on foot with Oscar taking one of the lanterns.

"Jed! Come on!" Skyla shouted to be overheard above the waterfall.

I hesitated. "I can't! There's more men coming!"

"Dammit, Jed!" That was the first time I'd ever heard her swear. She was becoming more western by the day.

"You're not a white hat!" She insisted. "You said so yourself. C'mon!" She clasped her arms around my neck, pulling me in close. I could smell her. The scent of burnt gunpowder clung to her wet hair and neck. I kissed her gently.

"I'll be fine. Don't worry, I promise I won't be last!" I winked at her with a grin.

Behind us came a belch of fire from the dragon again and the horrible screams of men burning to death among the roars of battle and gunfire.

"You'd better not be." She pounded my chest with her small fist before spinning on her heel and following Charles into the tunnel with Smoke and Carbine in tow.

Jerking the *Eighty-Six* into my shoulder, I held a lead on the nearest raptor and fired. The feathered little bastard was hit and went sprawling.

I looked behind me at the flung open banded metal tunnel door.

There was no way to secure it shut from the other side. We could hold them off for quite a while from inside, but eventually they'd circle around and come at us from both ends. The chances of them not knowing about this tunnel was all but impossible. It was their fort before ours.

My eyes fell on the small crate beside the door. The soldiers had been tasked with blowing the entrance if they couldn't hold it, and that was just what I was going to do. Jerking the crate open, I grabbed several sticks, twisted the fuses together, and tucked them under my belt.

***

Taking a knee, I braced my custom Winchester and began picking off apes as they chased after the survivors of the encampment. Most of the fleeing men were on foot, and the apes, faster by a long shot, were quickly overtaking them and killing them. Those on horses stood a better chance, as the apes and raptors focused on the stragglers. But all were vulnerable to the arrows being fired from the bows of apes that either stood along the edge of the canyon or were in it with us. The feather shafts fell amongst man and beast alike. And as I watched, a scientist took an arrow through the leg. Falling, he tried to get up only to be tackled from behind by a leaping raptor. Ripping and tearing, the small beast tore the man apart as he struggled to defend himself with only his bare hands.

Men raced to the waterfall beside me, dismounted and led their horses inside. It was a chaotic affair, with man and beast pushing and jostling to get out of the death trap we were all in. I saw John the reporter rush in, helping carry a wounded soldier. His eyes were wild, and he breathed in short, rapid gasps as he helped.

The dragon swooped from the raining dark grey clouds, and I jerked the rifle back into my shoulder and began firing as fast as I could at it.

I must have hit something vital, because the fire breathing beast suddenly veered to the side then dropped out of view above the cliff face. I shouted a roar of victory.

Several soldiers took a position along the narrow trail with me and began firing at the advancing apes, trying to give the remaining men some protection as they ran or rode for their lives. The corrals holding the horses were gone, they were in ape territory now, and over a dozen horses ran wild through the canyon, trying to flee the battle and flames that surrounded them. The captive trikes were free now as well, having broken down their corral and they trampled burning tents and bodies into the mud as they moved through the fort.

Daniels arrived, his cap missing, and horse covered in foamy lather from the short ride at full speed. Jumping off his mount, he began reloading his rifle.

"This is it, Jed." He glanced down at the crate of dynamite resting beside me. "Good thinking, but it's my job to do that."

"Yes, sir," I didn't argue as I kept firing. The rifle was hot, sizzling as raindrops pelted it, and brass shell casings were scattered all around me and the remaining soldiers. A small group of Pinkertons, their faces a bright crimson, hacking and coughing for air, reached us. Without so much as a glance at us, they charged up the trail and into the tunnel.

There were only a couple of men on horseback left in the canyon headed our way. Everyone on foot had either reached us by now or been overtaken by the apes.

I shot at a mounted trike, missing the rider and most likely hitting the large bone shield that jutted from behind the dinosaur's head. The apes were closing in on us, and the final men were killed by volleys of arrows fired after them.

And now arrows began to rain down among our position. I ducked involuntarily as several bounced and shattered off the rock ledge around me.

"Jed, go!"

I didn't argue. Spinning, I rushed down the tunnel. Someone had set out several lit lanterns along the way and I fumbled my way through the partially lit opening in the cliff face.

Behind me, I could hear Daniels and his remaining men's gunfire echoing down the passage after me.

Reaching the split that led towards the lake, I stopped. Several Pinkertons and a scientist I recognized from the night assault on our encampment were leaning against the wall, breathing heavily and looking terribly frightened.

I pointed them in the right direction. "That way!"

Pushing themselves off the wall and rising from the floor, they took off at a stumbled run. Their equipment and weapons clanging and banging as they left me alone.

The firing outside suddenly stopped, and several long moments later, a pair of soldiers helping another wounded one stumbled their way past.

"Who's left?" I asked.

"Just the Lieutenant!" the wounded man gasped as they dragged him by.

I waited, rifle at the ready, my body hidden behind the curvature of the tunnel. There came a hoarse breathing and a thudding sound of a man running in boots.

Daniels appeared before me. He was soaking wet, and a broken arrow shaft jutted from his shoulder, dark blood trickling down his arm. His eyes were wild and fierce.

"Run!" he screamed as he rushed past.

I started to race after him when an explosion came from behind me.

The force of it threw me forward onto the ground and I slammed into the rock floor and bit my tongue. Dirt and bits of rock fell from the ceiling, coating me. The lantern fell to the floor, bursting and sending flaming oil along the ground.

It gave off an eerie glow amongst the thick cloud of dust in the air.

Rolling over, I shook my head and coughed. My mouth tasted of blood and dirt. I spat a coagulated glob onto the ground and felt around for the

Eighty-Six. Feeling the stock, I dragged it close to me and leaned back against the tunnel wall.

Amidst the ringing in my ears, I heard a sound.

Turning towards the entrance to the tunnel, I was shocked to see shapes making their way through the murky cloud of dust and smoke.

Jacking the lever on the rifle, I rested it across my lap and peered into the darkness, trying to figure out what I was seeing.

A pair of painted apes loomed before the flames.

I fired from where I lay, blasting the first through the neck and dropping it with a gurgle. The other lunged forward, grabbing me as I tried to work the action on the *Eighty-Six.* Twisting the barrel about, I jabbed it into the ape's groin.

The big monkey doubled over, and I frantically fought to get free of its iron grip. Kicking and thrashing, I managed to draw my Bowie and stab repeatedly at the dark hairy shape in the tunnel.

Blood splattered my face and clothing. But finally, the beast dropped to the ground and I prized myself free of his grasp.

Gasping for more dirty air, I lay beside the ape's corpse.

The first monkey had fallen into the lantern flames, and the stench of burning hair was filling the tunnel.

It was as if I'd fallen into a lair of hell itself.

Another ape rushed through the tunnel, leaping over the smoking corpse and jabbing a spear towards me.

I flung myself to the side and drew both Colts. Firing quickly, I put the ape down with a pair of shots to the torso.

That was it for me. The opening hadn't closed. The apes would rush through and overwhelm the survivors. I couldn't let that happen.

Pulling the sticks of dynamite from my belt, I struck a match against the rough rock walls. A tiny flame flared on the end and I touched it to the fuses. Sparks fell to the floor and the gunpowder-filled cord sizzled.

With all remaining strength, I hurled it down the tunnel into the darkness. The bundle of dynamite twisted and turned, trailing its lit fuse in a sparking circle before disappearing into the darkness.

I crawled to all fours and grabbed my rifle from where it'd fallen. The tunnel was already weakened, and I needed to get as much distance as possible.

From behind me, the sizzling bundle of dynamite flew forward, thrown back in my direction and bounced against my foot.

"Ahhhh!" I screamed.

Kicking it swiftly, the lit bundle spun against the burning ape corpse, and I took off. I made it a dozen strides before the dynamite blew.

The explosion flung me forward again and I fell, then crawled, in a blind panic. Reaching out with my free hand I pulled myself forward and clawed my way along the floor of the tunnel. Rocks rumbled around me, and before I knew it, I was swallowed under the crushing weight of stone and darkness.

***

Three days later, I had two bullets left in my rifle, a full cylinder in the Colt on my right hip, and one bullet in the other.

My belt loops were empty.

I was bruised, slashed, cut, scraped, and generally beat to hell when I staggered into the valley below the cliff face that contained the Shimmer. High on the rising valley floor, hundreds of men toiled in the valley, cutting a path out as they began running rail this side of the tunnel. As I watched, an explosion blew a gout of rock and dirt high into the air.

A shout came up as I was noticed, and I dropped to my knees then rolled over onto my back, thrilled to have reached a faint resemblance of civilization. Lying there, I looked at the blue sky. A pair of small pterodactyls soared in lazy circles. It was a nice day.

Soldiers came pounding down on horseback, circling me with weapons drawn. Luckily, I still had most of my dirty and torn clothing on and I looked human.

"Jedidiah, that you?"

Turning my head, I squinted painfully. Lieutenant Daniels grinned at me from the back of his horse, his arm in a sling.

"Skyla, did she…" I stopped, afraid to ask the question that I'd been dreading for days as I worked my way through the forest on foot.

"Yes, she's fine. Fredrick and Charles too." He tossed me a canteen. I twisted the lid off before taking a deep drink.

It'd been hours since I'd found a stream big enough to sip from, and I had a powerful thirst. I took a long swig then splashed a bit over my face. Dirt and bloody grime trickled off me in rivets. I knew I looked terrible because I felt terrible.

The Lieutenant dismounted and helped me stand. "Mount my horse and tell me how it is you came to survive that explosion."

I pulled myself up in the saddle and he led the horse up the sloping valley floor. "That was just luck. But surviving the forest, that's a story on its own," I told him with a small grin that quickly disappeared as I recalled the battle. "How many made it?"

Daniels frowned. "About ten soldiers, fifteen Pinkertons, and a couple of scientists. Plus your friends… John, and Oscar."

I rubbed my face. "That means we lost almost two hundred men."

"Yes," he said quietly. "And if it hadn't been for that tunnel, we'd have all died."

My stomach rumbled. "Got any chow?" I hadn't eaten since the morning of the attack.

The Lieutenant stopped, opened a saddle bag, and pulled out some hardtack biscuits and jerky. "Eat up."

Gnawing on the biscuits, I looked around the valley floor as we moved. For once there wasn't a dinosaur in sight except for those flying high above us.

When we reached the tunnel, I saw Gatlings mounted on tripods in the backs of wagons with resting soldiers and boxes of ammunition. There were also cannons in weapons emplacements, set to have a field of fire towards anything attacking up the valley towards the tunnel. Pinkertons were everywhere, none of them doing a lick of work, just standing around with rifles and stern looks towards anyone getting near them.

"Ya'll appear well armed."

"For the apes of course... but also for the Chinese," he said almost apologetically. "There was a worker's strike in Granite Falls the other day. It turned into a real bloodbath. The Pinkertons killed over a dozen of them."

"Figures." I spat on the ground. "What a bunch of assholes."

Daniels shot a sympathetic look toward them, then dipped his head. "They're just doing their job."

"Is their job killing folks who want to be treated like people instead of animals?" I stopped the horse and dismounted, no longer interested in catching up the events of the past few days with the Lieutenant. "Where's my horse, and Skyla?"

"Last I heard she was heading to your ranch to mourn your death. Carbine is with her."

I grimaced at the thought of her needless suffering. "I reckon she won't need to mourn anymore now. Where can I find a horse?"

He shrugged and handed me back the reins. "Take mine, just be sure to return him." He gave the gelding a pat. "He's a good horse. There's also a coat behind the saddle. You're going to need it. It's cold on the other side."

I looked Daniels in the eye. "I appreciate it. I'll bring him back in a couple of days."

He grabbed his rifle from the scabbard and pulled it out before I slid the battered *Eighty-Six* into its place. "Take your time, Jed, I've got a spare."

Mounting back in the saddle, I clucked my tongue and rode past the freshly laid rails through the Shimmer and to my side of the world.

***

I didn't go home.

Instead, I rode out of sight then cut across the plains, sticking to gulleys and draws to avoid being seen by anyone until I reached the little house on the outskirts of Granite Falls. It rested in a scenic portion of the valley, not far from the river on the western side with a nice view of the waterfall the town got its name from. A real pretty place with a white picket fence and a small barn and corral beside it.

By the time I got there, it was well past sundown. Shivering in the cold beneath Daniels' heavy coat, I tied the gelding off and slipped down on foot.

I entered the house silently. Long years of doing things just like this came flooding back into memory. It was the sort of thing I'd prefer to forget. But not tonight. I gently shook the man awake, and his eyes went wide at the muzzle of my pistol pointed between his eyes. Raising a single finger to my lips, I threatened him into keeping silent.

"Get up," I commanded, and he obliged.

Indignation settled in as I marched him out the door in his bare feet and underwear. Turning back to me, he opened his mouth to protest, and I thumped him over the head with my pistol barrel. Hard.

Down he went into the frozen ground. Out cold.

With strips of rawhide taken from Daniels' saddlebags, I tied his hands together, then muffled him with his own bandana tied tightly through clenched teeth. He woke and struggled again. A big man, I had to wrestle him for a moment before laying him out again with another hard thump of the gun barrel. Now he had two goose eggs on his noggin for his troubles and I was getting annoyed.

Tying him to the borrowed saddle pommel, I led him away from the town and to the top of the valley.

As he walked behind the horse, he cursed and swore through the muffling rag, but I made sure he didn't get a moments rest as I kept the horse at a pace that threatened to drop and drag the man. At one point he grabbed the rope, stuck his feet, and jerked back with all his might, startling my horse.

For that I jumped the gelding, dropping the man into the dirt and dragged him for fifteen yards before allowing him the decency of standing back up. Now his bed clothes were ripped and torn open.

Good.

After a couple of miles, we stood in the open prairie, bathed in moonlight beneath the bright stars.

Without dismounting, I reached down and untied the bandana.

"Water," he croaked.

I shook my head. He'd receive no such kindness from me.

Just as he'd given Jim none.

Sheriff Beauford Johnson looked around.

Realization of what was happening had long settled into him. Dirt and smears of blood covered his face from where I'd laid his scalp open with the pistol barrel. His underwear was torn and shredded from being dragged across the grass and rock. His feet left splotches of blood in the grass from where they'd been cut and torn on the rough prairie rocks. He was an evil man, a murderer, and a liar. The man deserved no dignity in his final moments.

He spat and glared. "You'll hang for this."

Drawing my pistol, I leaned forward in the saddle and locked eyes with him. "Maybe. But you'll be dead."

The Peacemaker bucked in my hand and the bullet punched through his chest. He dropped and thrashed. Dismounting, I walked over to him as he lay gasping his final breath. I stared down at him as his fingers clawed at the ground as he struggled to breathe. Finally, he twitched, once, twice, then lay still.

I left his body for the wolves, vultures, and the little green, whip tailed Compy dinosaurs.

They had to eat too.

I didn't care if anyone found the corpse or not. Word around town would be that I was still dead, so I wouldn't be suspected. And the man had enough enemies that there would be no shortage of speculation as to his executioner.

But now the world was a little better off.

Holstering my gun, I clucked my tongue and turned the horse north.

***

Snow was falling when I reached my ranch, just enough to cover the ground with a thin layer but enough to tease a hard winter to come.

I was pleased to see the barn had been completed except for most of the trim and some windows, and from the looks of things the Protos were being kept inside. Hopefully laying lots of eggs for my little herd of dinosaurs to grow with.

Thin tendrils of smoke rose from the bunkhouse, where I suspected Bo was staying warm inside. Carbine was standing with his front half sticking outside of his pole shed, pawing at the ground. Seeing me, he stopped, ears flicking, then he bounced forward. Sprinting out of the corral, he jumped the fence, narrowly clearing the top rail.

I laughed as he reached me and leaned over in the saddle to give his ears a scratch while he gave Daniels' horse the stink eye. He didn't seem to appreciate me riding another horse. Dismounting, I grabbed the reins in one hand and patted the neck of my horse as he shoved his head against me.

"Good boy." I rested my forehead against his shoulder. "Thanks for taking care of Skyla. I owe you a bushel of apples."

Carbine neighed and stamped his feet in agreement.

Giving him a final pat, I crossed the yard and turned Daniels' horse loose inside the corral. With some coaching and a few muttered threats, I managed to get Carbine to go back in as well.

Turning towards the house, I saw Skyla standing on the porch, her trim outline framed in lantern light. Sara peeked her horned head around my favorite paleontologist and bellowed lightly.

Skyla rushed across the yard and threw herself at me. In my weakened state, I could only catch her and fall. The sound we made landing awkwardly was one of laughter and a grunt of pain. She kissed my dirty, stubbled face passionately.

Kissing her back, I pushed myself upright only to be knocked down again as Sara butted her bone shield into me. I laughed and gave her a hug around her leathery neck as well.

"You're alive," Skyla said softly, tears trickling down her pretty face and wetting the snow on her shirt. As happy as she was to see me, I got the sense that something was wrong.

"Sorry I was last," I apologized as I looked behind her at the shadows stretching towards us in the light of the house.

Charles stood just outside of the doorway, a slight smile playing across his lips and stitches ran along the gash in his face from the battle. Beside him was Elizabeth Stratten. Skyla's mother stalked across the moonlit snow-covered yard, her face twisted in fury.

Dusting myself off, I stood, helped Skyla up and grimaced. "Good evening, Mrs. Stra-"

The unexpected force of her open palm against my face made me stumble.

She held up an old, faded piece of paper with her other hand. On it, a terrible likeness of myself stared back. My wanted poster.

"Explain this, Orville!"

***

To be continued...

CHECK OUT OTHER GREAT DINOSAUR BOOKS

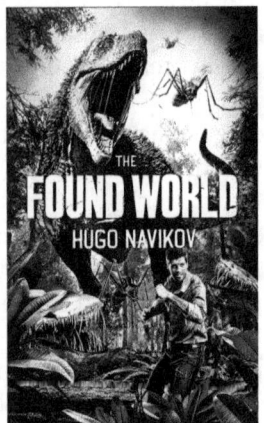

THE FOUND WORLD
by Hugo Navikov

A powerful global cabal wants adventurer Brett Russell to retrieve a superweapon stolen by the scientist who built it. To entice him to travel underneath one of the most dangerous volcanoes on Earth to find the scientist, this shadowy organization will pay him the only thing he cares about: information that will allow him to avenge his family's murder.

But before he can get paid, he and his team must enter an underground hellscape of killer plants, giant insects, terrifying dinosaurs, and an army of other predators never previously seen by man.

At the end of this journey awaits a revelation that could alter the fate of mankind ... if they can make it back from this horrifying found world.

HOUSE OF THE GODS
by Davide Mana

High above the steamy jungle of the Amazon basin, rise the flat plateaus known as the Tepui, the House of the Gods. Lost worlds of unknown beauty, a naturalistic wonder, each an ecology onto itself, shunned by the local tribes for centuries. The House of the Gods was not made for men.

But now, the crew and passengers of a small charter plane are about to find what was hidden for sixty million years.

Lost on an island in the clouds 10.000 feet above the jungle, surrounded by dinosaurs, hunted by mysterious mercenaries, the survivors of Sligo Air flight 001 will quickly learn the only rule of life on Earth: Extinction.

CHECK OUT OTHER GREAT DINOSAUR BOOKS

PRIMORDIA
by **Greig Beck**

Ben Cartwright, former soldier, home to mourn the loss of his father stumbles upon cryptic letters from the past between the author, Arthur Conan Doyle and his great, great grandfather who vanished while exploring the Amazon jungle in 1908.

Amazingly, these letters lead Ben to believe that his ancestor's expedition was the basis for Doyle's fantastical tale of a lost world inhabited by long extinct creatures. As Ben digs some more he finds clues to the whereabouts of a lost notebook that might contain a map to a place that is home to creatures that would rewrite everything known about history, biology and evolution.

But other parties now know about the notebook, and will do anything to obtain it. For Ben and his friends, it becomes a race against time and against ruthless rivals.

In the remotest corners of Venezuela, along winding river trails known only to lost tribes, and through near impenetrable jungle, Ben and his novice team find a forbidden place more terrifying and dangerous than anything they could ever have imagined.

PANGAEA EXILES
by **Jeff Brackett**

Tried and convicted for his crimes, Sean Barrow is sent into temporal exile—banished to a time so far before recorded history that there is no chance that he, or any other criminal sent back, has any chance of altering history.

Now Sean must find a way to survive more than 200 million years in the past, in a world populated by monstrous creatures that would rend him limb from limb if they got the chance. And that's just his fellow prisoners.

The dinosaurs are almost as bad.

CHECK OUT OTHER GREAT DINOSAUR BOOKS

FLIPSIDE
by JAKE BIBLE

The year is 2046 and dinosaurs are real.

Time bubbles across the world, many as large as one hundred square miles, turn like clockwork, revealing prehistoric landscapes from the Cretaceous Period.

They reveal the Flipside.

Now, thirty years after the first Turn, the clockwork is breaking down as one of the world's powers has decided to exploit the phenomenon for their own gain, possibly destroying everything then and now in the process.

A MAN OUT OF TIME
by Christopher Laflan

Five years after the Chinese Axis detonated an unknown weapon of mass destruction off the southern coast of the United States, Special Ops Sergeant John Crider and the members of Shadow Company have finally captured what they all hope will lead to the end of the war. Unfortunately, the population within the United States is no longer sustainable. In an effort to stabilize the economy, the government enacts the Cryonics Act. One hundred years in suspended animation, all debt forgiven, and a chance at a less crowded future are too good to pass up for John and his young daughter.

Except not everything always goes as planned as Sergeant John Crider finds himself pitted against a land of prehistoric monsters genetically resurrected from the fossil record, murderous inhabitants, and a future he never wanted.